WHY THE ROCK FALLS

The Falls Mysteries

When the Flood Falls
Where the Ice Falls
Why the Rock Falls

WHY THE ROCK FALLS

THE FALLS MYSTERIES

J.E. BARNARD

DUNDURN

TORONTO

Publisher: Scott Fraser | Editor: Allister Thompson
Cover designer: Laura Boyle
Cover image: istock.com/GROGL
Printer: Marquis Book Printing Inc.

Library and Archives Canada Cataloguing in Publication

Title: Why the rock falls / J.E. Barnard.
Names: Barnard, J. E., author.
Description: Series statement: The falls mysteries ; 3
Identifiers: Canadiana (print) 20200210734 | Canadiana (ebook) 20200210742 | ISBN 9781459741478 (softcover) | ISBN 9781459741485 (PDF) | ISBN 9781459741492 (EPUB)
Classification: LCC PS8603.A754 W59 2020 | DDC C813/.6—dc23

We acknowledge the support of the Canada Council for the Arts and the Ontario Arts Council for our publishing program. We also acknowledge the financial support of the Government of Ontario, through the Ontario Book Publishing Tax Credit and Ontario Creates, and the Government of Canada.

VISIT US AT

dundurn.com | @dundurnpress | dundurnpress | dundurnpress

Dundurn
3 Church Street, Suite 500
Toronto, Ontario, Canada
M5E 1M2

This novel is dedicated to

Ilonka
Anne
Gemma
and
Rosemary

who've had my back through many struggles in writing, in life, in ME/CFS.

PROLOGUE

The first, faint cry came from above and might have been a bird call. Lacey lowered her screwdriver and listened. The second cry was unmistakable. "Help!"

She hustled down the ladder, her workboots ringing the metal rungs, and charged up the terrace stairs three at a time. At the outdoor pool, she scanned the sun-dazzled water.

One floating chaise, empty.

One decorative waterfall, tumbling off a rocky ledge into the pool.

Two women being churned by the waters, their long, dark hair twining like eels.

As she dropped her tool belt, preparing to rescue them, Lacey realized only one of them was struggling ...

CHAPTER ONE

Four Days Earlier ...

The helicopter's blades shredded the hot August afternoon, their every thwap vibrating up through Lacey McCrae's workboots. Fed up with gazing down on the barren dust of clear-cuts and oil wells, she looked the other way, into the green cirque of Black Rock Bowl, at deserted ski chalets half hidden amid fluttering aspens. The ski slopes lay golden in the sun, their late-summer grasses split by peninsulas of pine and spruce. The chopper swung away, around the mountain. Immense limestone walls closed in, their jagged grey faces ripped by white granite veins. Ominously close, it seemed to her.

Jake Wyman, in the co-pilot seat, sat calmly as the rocky valley narrowed. He'd have been this way lots of times, visiting his well sites out in the Ghost Wilderness. Today was Lacey's first ride-along. After a day baking in the boulder-strewn wilds, she longed for nothing more than cool water and dust-free clothing. At each site, she'd tested cameras and motion-sensor lights, replaced one solar panel — and hadn't mentioned aloud the irony that oil companies used renewable energy to power their equipment. There'd been no sign of the vandalism her boss told her to watch for; only normal wear and tear from exposure to harsh mountain winters and the scouring winds of summer. She opened her phone and added *no sabotage* to the report. The sooner she emailed the document to Wayne, along with her time sheet, the sooner she could stop the clock and jump into a shower.

The chopper flew straight at a vast, sheer cliff, like a hummingbird about to splat on a picture window. She'd almost compared it to a mosquito, but that label belonged to the neon splash that was surely a mountain climber clinging to bare rock a hundred metres from anywhere. Soon she made out tanned limbs splayed against the grey cliff and traced the rope that anchored the climber from above. The helicopter hovered at a distance as the climber edged across the rock face. The pilot's voice came through her headphones.

"Up or down, sir?"

Jake's thumb went up. The machine followed. Soon the cliff-top lay below them. Two more brightly clad climbers sat in the sun while another guided the rope that dangled over the edge. As the helicopter settled on a flat spot well back from the valley, one of the sitters pulled off a helmet, revealing short auburn hair.

Jake said, "That's her."

The woman jogged to the chopper and scrambled in. Clearly an experienced passenger, she clipped herself into her seat and put on her headphones before speaking.

"Thank you, darling. You have my luggage, too?"

Jake nodded. The helicopter lifted off. The new passenger turned dark glasses on Lacey's workboots and sweat-stained T-shirt and as promptly looked away, chatting to Jake about her last climb, a 5.11b — whatever that meant — and her son Earl, the one still climbing. "He's head of our Denver office now," she said. "A far stronger leader than any of his brothers, although they won't admit it. Bart fills his desk chair when he remembers, and Ben is still rebelling against his father by protesting the company in ridiculous ways. He's been arrested more times than I can remember."

Nobody Lacey knew. She tuned out and watched the scenery unroll below: the Bow River, braided turquoise and blue; the navy depths of Ghost Lake, where boats darted around like water bugs; a dusty sage pasture dotted with black Angus cattle; the Trans-Canada Highway slicing the rolling prairie from Calgary to the mountains. The chopper picked up the greeny-grey Elbow River and followed it to Jake's estate overlooking Bragg Creek. After a gentle landing on the gravel helicopter pad, everyone except the pilot piled out. A young man in a green staff polo shirt brought a golf cart for the baggage and passengers.

Jake offered a hand to the red-haired woman. "I'll have a car for you in five minutes, Giselle."

"Make it twenty and give me a drink first," said the redhead. She linked her arm through his and told the driver to take them to the house.

Left behind, Lacey strolled toward the main swimming pool at the west end of the sprawling ranch house. The breeze cut off when she stepped inside the high walls. The pool was an oasis of luxury, with a waterfall tumbling down a fieldstone chute, a huge hot tub, a swim-up bar, and floating devices that ranged from inflatable alligators to lounge chairs complete with drink holders and waterproof phone docks. After her dusty afternoon a swim would be heaven, but today she was technically staff — well, Wayne's staff, but he worked for Jake — and her privileges did not extend to this area. Reluctantly, she opened one of the glass doors beyond the bar and followed the dim corridor to the airless, windowless security office.

The good news for Wayne would be the lack of vandalism. Drunken off-roaders sometimes broke stuff for fun, and hunters occasionally shot up equipment, but there'd been no sign of those today. No radical environmentalists, either. She wasn't sure how real that last problem was, but every oilman she knew was convinced eco-sabotage was a real threat. They told each other stories of the lunatic up north who'd waged a years-long campaign of pipeline damage before being caught. There hadn't been wide-scale sabotage elsewhere, but the oilmen's concern ran deep. An undetected pipeline blowout could poison a wilderness watershed and hand antipipeline activists a potent public relations weapon. Still, if oilmen weren't worried about eco-saboteurs, Wayne wouldn't have half his clients, and she wouldn't have the job of maintaining his on-site security equipment.

She finished the report, hit Send, and stretched. Day's work done and still time to do a few laps in the swim machine on the lowest level before Dee arrived for her workout. One small perk of her grey-zone existence between staffer and neighbour was Jake's willingness for her and Dee to use the workout space he'd built for his frequent hockey guests. He'd only offered because he still felt guilty about last summer's mess. Even though he'd played no intentional role in Dee's near-fatal attack, he had deviated from his own code and inadvertently exposed her to it. Access to his fully equipped workout area up the road from Dee's made him feel better and her rehab a lot more convenient.

Returning to the sunny pool, Lacey strolled past chaises with their striped cushions and headed down the cliff stairs to the terraces below. Halfway to the lowest one, she realized its glass wall was drawn back, opening the workout area to the lovely afternoon. The swim machine's hum warned her someone was there already. Dee wasn't supposed to swim without supervision, in case her weakened leg gave out. Lacey hurried.

The swimmer was a stranger. Pinned against the back wall by the current, her thin arms scrabbling at the small pool's rim, she dipped beneath the surface. Lacey dashed across the paving and knelt to grab one bony forearm. She pulled up until the woman's face cleared the water.

"I've got you. Take a few breaths." The woman was skeletally thin, light enough to hold like this indefinitely, but already too exhausted to help herself. Lacey adjusted her grip. "If I get you to the ladder and give you a hand, can you climb out?"

"I—" The woman coughed. "I think so."

After a few minutes' crawl to the ladder, and a few more while the woman rested up, Lacey finally got her out of the pool. The dark blue one-piece huddled on the tiles as water drained from the thin brown hair. The spidery limbs seemed uninjured, and the woman was breathing, although heavily. She coughed again.

"How are you feeling?"

"I'm fine, really. Had the current set too high." After a moment the woman added, "Can you help me up?" Lacey led her to a chaise and wrapped her in the terrycloth bathrobe spread across it. She lay there, wan and trembling, but when Lacey moved toward the house phone, one shaking hand came up. "Please. Don't tell. They'll worry."

"You should get checked out by a doctor. You're very weak."

"I'll be okay." The woman lay there, eyes closed, until the elevator chimed. Then, surprising Lacey, she scrambled up and pushed into the elevator as Dee exited. In a moment, she was gone.

"Who was that?" Dee asked, slinging her gym bag onto a chair. "And why are you wet?"

"Some guest was swimming with the current on and was too weak to get out on her own. This is what I worry about for you. Why I don't want you swimming without the harness. And supervision."

Dee looked back at the elevator as she stripped off her shorts and tee. "Scary. Tell you what, I'll wait right here while you change into your suit and drape your clothes in the sun. They'll be dry by the time we're done."

Ninety minutes later, Lacey pulled up before the neighbour's stucco bungalow. Dee slid from the passenger seat and hobbled toward the deck overlooking the Elbow River while Lacey released the dogs from the vehicle's rear compartment. Boney and Beau, their rusty tails aflutter, skirled around her legs until she snapped her fingers. Except for tilting his head toward Dee's departing back, Beau sat like a china fireplace dog, his red coat gleaming in the late afternoon sun. Boney's tail plume swept the brickwork. His ears twitched. His nose lifted, assessing the breeze. When she flicked her hand, he shot off after Dee with Beau lolloping along behind. It struck her then how thin Dee's legs still were, more than a year after the hit and run. Tanned, finally, but stringy like the dogs'. Was Dee overdoing the exercise, like that woman in the pool?

Lacey hurried after them all and stooped to hug Jan Brenner, who lounged as usual in a shady chaise. Picking a chair at Jan's side, she ignored the view over the Elbow River and the year-old Bragg Creek Museum, instead watching Dee step carefully over the doorsill into the kitchen. Not that skinny, surely?

"Jan," she said in a low voice, "do you think Dee's taking it too far? This fitness craze, I mean? It's barely been six months since she could walk at all, and now she's on the treadmill an hour a day plus the swimming. There's toning up and then there's obsession."

Jan's dark curls fluttered in the breeze. "Trust me; she's been leaner than this. Actually, I was thinking you and Dee both have lightened up a lot recently, like you're coming out from under a dark cloud. It's good to see, after the year you've both had."

Lacey nodded. It had been some year. Well, more like eighteen months, starting from leaving her marriage to Dan, and her RCMP career, behind in B.C. Then she'd hunted Dee's stalker, followed by all the upheaval of Dee's long convalescence. Just as they had both begun to get their feet under them again — in Dee's case, literally — Dee's mother announced her terminal cancer. That sad Christmas had been punctuated by murder. Lacey had broken three ribs, been concussed, burned both hands saving a witness. And those were only the big events. Jan didn't know about Lacey's nightmares or her frequent flashbacks to Dan's violence, or about the possibility that, as her divorce wound its way through the legal system, he would make his way to Bragg Creek, intent on finishing her. She would know if he left B.C., though. In her first private investigator course last spring, she'd learned enough about cellphones to put a tracker on his number. Every six hours, it alerted her to the phone's location. It worked because Dan, being a middle-class white male, an RCMP constable, and a chauvinist from hell, didn't consider a mere woman enough of a threat to bother turning off his GPS. She reached for her phone out of habit, even though the next update was two hours away.

"Earth to Lacey!" Jan waved a hand at her. "Why are you worrying about Dee being skinny? Is she eating okay?"

"Huh? Oh, yeah. No worries there." Lacey let the phone drop back into its holster. "There was a woman in the swim machine up at Jake's and —"

"Lacey saved her from drowning," Dee called through the open window.

Shit. Had she overheard Lacey gossiping about her? "It's nowhere as exciting as all that. I just helped her out of the pool."

Jan looked up the hill, where a corner of Jake's lowest terrace peeked through the trees. "Jake didn't mention any guests when I saw him last week."

Her husband, Terry, came through the sliding door with two frosted beer bottles. He handed one to Lacey. "Hungry? We can eat as soon as Rob gets here. He's walking up from the museum."

"You forgot my club soda, babe." Jan uncurled from her chaise and headed into the house.

Lacey watched her go. "She's walking really well. Unlike Dee, who's overdoing the workouts."

Terry nodded. "Jan would, too, if she could. But now there's finally some hope. That new med she started last month — which she only found out about because someone in her online support group took part in research at Harvard last spring — changes how her muscles respond. She won't be running a marathon anytime soon, but she might be strong enough to try that definitive two-day exercise test for mitochondrial dysfunction. The only lab in Canada that does it has opened in Calgary." He glanced at the kitchen window. "Dee's doing better, too, looks like. Less weight on the good leg."

Trust Terry to notice those physical details. It came from years of watching his wife's every movement in case she keeled over. Lacey rolled the damp bottle across her forehead, enjoying the cool. If Dee's old friends thought she was doing fine, there was nothing to worry about. Dee wasn't frail like that woman in the pool.

"Dee's 'better' is partly circumstantial, too," she said. "Her mom's death was hard, but she's more at peace with it than I expected. The grieving was mostly done up front." And Dee was freed from fear of losing her own house, now that her inheritance income topped up her disability pay. "Emptying Loreena's house was a catharsis, too. Hardest part was figuring out what to do with all those cancer medications. There was enough morphine around to overdose a dozen junkies: sublingual drops, pills, stuff for injecting into the IV line."

Terry looked out over the river valley, with its spruces wavering in the westerly breeze. "My worst Search and Rescue call-out was for morphine: a teen who stole his grandmother's leftover meds, hoping to get high."

"Did you find him in time?"

"Nope. OD'd in his childhood treehouse. What did you do with Loreena's drugs?"

"Returned them to the pharmacy. She wanted us to find a program that would redistribute them to the needy, but there didn't seem to be one in Ontario. The pharmacist thanked us."

Terry clinked his bottle neck against hers. "So do Search and Rescue, EMT, and the cops. Drugs like that should never be left loose in people's houses."

As Jan came back, carrying a glass, the dogs sat up, staring toward the driveway. "Rob's coming," she said.

"Hello, darlings!" The museum curator strolled around the side of the house, hands in the pockets of his khakis. "You'll never believe who's in town."

Dee returned, carrying two glasses of wine. She handed one to Rob. "Who?"

Rob raised his glass in a dramatic gesture. "Kitzu, that's who."

Terry groaned. "Oh, hell."

Jan sat bolt upright. "You're joking."

"Not." Rob dropped into a chair. "She came into the museum this morning with the Lord High Husband himself. And his entourage. They'll be using our Old West Post Office as a set for some cattle-drive picture he's making next month and screening each day's films in our theatre. I'm surprised Dee didn't tell you. The museum board had to okay the deal."

Dee shrugged. "A film crew is renting space in September. I didn't think it was newsworthy, but if you know the people involved ..."

"Not newsworthy?" said Rob. "When Mylo Matheson, three-time Oscar-winning director, will be swarming our little hamlet with half-a-bazillion movie actors, stunt people, and all the other Hollywood paraphernalia?"

Jan sank back into her chaise. "And Kitzu. Did she see you, Rob? Does she know I'm here?"

Lacey looked between their two faces. "Who is this woman you don't want to see?"

Terry glowered. "Their old university roommate, Kitrin Devine. Acting major, not Visual Arts. Her real name is Katrina Davenport, but she always used her actress name. I forget who first called her Kitzu."

"Kitzu?" said Dee. "Like kudzu? The vine that ate the American South?"

"Exactly," said Rob. "She was so clingy that the nickname couldn't help but stick. And look where it got her: married to a big Hollywood director, with a minor film career."

"Anything we'd recognize?" Lacey asked.

Jan shook her head. "Small parts only. Kitrin's kind of a heroin-chic version of that woman in the pearl-earring movie. Unless you're a stunt person, looking like a more famous actor is the kiss of death." She squeezed a lime wedge into her glass. "In our second year at SFU, she got work-experience credit for being an extra on a movie, although she only got the gig because she was seeing a guy who worked security on the film."

Lacey picked at her beer label. "Security on movie and TV locations is a full-time job in Vancouver. Some guys made good money doing close personal security for movie stars during a shoot. Of course, they had to call us whenever an incident occurred. Violent takedowns by bodyguards only happen in the movies."

"Kitrin's boyfriend wasn't a bodyguard," said Terry. "Just a beefy guy who stood at gates repelling rabid fans."

"He was working his way up to personal security," said Jan. "And he was a nice guy, not that it mattered to Kitrin. Once she came to Mylo's attention, that was the end of the boyfriend. Then she came up pregnant, and Mylo divorced his third wife for her. We figured she'd be home in a year with the baby, but it's closer to twelve now. How's she look, Rob? Still as waiflike as ever?"

Rob grimaced. "Honestly? Worse. Like those twig dolls they sell over at the Trading Post. Her hair's straw, and her skin is dry as scraped parchment. She moves slower than you do, honey, and that's saying something. Lord High ignores her existence, like he always did."

Terry trailed Beau's silky ear through his fingers. "She'd been in an eating disorder clinic for the summer before second year. Could be relapsing."

Jan sighed. "God, I hope not. I'll feel terrible if I've been snarking about her and she's really in trouble."

"You should visit," said Rob. "She and the Lord High are staying up at Jake's while he scouts outdoor locations. He won't drag her along in the chopper every day, I'm sure. She could blow out the window and drift away."

Lacey peeled back the corner of her beer label. "I might have met her this afternoon, and yeah, eating disorder is my guess."

"Lacey had to drag her bodily from the lap pool," Dee said. "She'd been swimming with the current turned too high and went under." She massaged the pale scar down her thigh. "That would have been me back in March, too weak to kick against the current."

"She's very frail." Lacey picked at the next strip of label. "When I was a lifeguard in high school, one of my squad mates was anorexic. She pushed herself hard, too, swimming extra laps and not eating enough to keep a cat alive. Died in her twenties from heart failure, I heard."

"Poor Kitzu." Jan shook her head. "It's got to be rough, with Mylo surrounded by young actresses who'll happily sleep with him for a speaking part."

Terry got to his feet. "I can see where this is going. You'll waste your energy visiting because you feel sorry for her. If you must go up there, take your scooter. You're not that strong yet, and I won't have you making yourself sicker again for a woman who never did you any favours."

Jan frowned up at him. "Yeah, all right. She might not even want to see me." Her phone trilled. She pulled it from a pocket. "It's Jake," she told them. "Hi, we were just talking about your movie guests … Oh, really?" Putting her hand over the receiver, she said, "Jake wants us all to come for dinner on Thursday. He's having people in to meet Mylo and says most of them will be our age."

"I'm busy that night," said Rob.

Dee shrugged. "I'm in."

Lacey nodded and surreptitiously texted her boss: *Wayne, Jake Wyman has a famous movie director and his wife visiting. Do we need security patrollers in case of paparazzi?* Extra hours would mean extra income to put toward her divorce.

Rob's phone rang as Jan closed hers. He glanced at the number, flushed, and hurried into the house. Jan frowned at his back.

"What's wrong?" Lacey asked.

"I think he's involved with someone."

"That's good, isn't it?"

"I'm afraid it might be someone, er, not single. He's been cagey about it."

"Involved with a married man?" Lacey frowned, too. "Seems sketchy for Rob."

"Depends, I guess, if the marriage is open or not." Jan bit her lip. "There was an older guy in university — his first serious affair — who strung him along for ages, always promising to tell the wife. But he didn't. Rob was heartbroken."

"He's a decade older now," Terry said. "He knows what he's doing."

Jan shook her head. "Just as well he isn't coming to supper on Thursday. Jake said one of the guests is a major homophobe. Well, he called Orrin Caine 'an old gay-basher from way back.' He wanted me to warn Rob so there wouldn't be any unpleasantness. Jake's so mellow that I forget men of his generation can be macho assholes."

"Not just his generation," said Lacey. "There are still plenty in the RCMP, even though they're more careful nowadays not to get caught using homophobic slurs in front of civilians." Fourteen months away from the Force, yet its toxic culture remained in her bones. She looked around at her friends and thanked her lucky stars she'd washed up on Dee's doorstep last year. Leaving Dan and the RCMP had turned out much better than she'd ever dared hope. "Cheers," she said, and lifted her beer.

CHAPTER TWO

Jan locked her seat belt as Terry backed out of the garage. "I just hope Kitrin isn't as badly off as Rob and Lacey said. I really don't want to get sucked into rescuing her again."

Terry wheeled the truck uphill from the driveway. "Keep telling yourself you can't spare the energy. I can do it for you, if I see you weakening."

"No, don't. Mylo will take offence, and then Jake will be annoyed. Let's just have a calm dinner and get home with no fallout. Do you know anything about these Caine people who are coming to meet Mylo?"

Terry slowed as the sunlight blasted fully onto the windshield. "Orrin's another oil man, bringing his wife and/or kids. I've met him, and I think the oldest son, too. Orrin's a stereotype of what everyone else in the country hates about Albertans: old white racist jerk who thinks he earned his own way, even though he went to private schools and the bank of Daddy set up his first oil play. Intolerant of anyone who didn't make their fortune in the oil patch, also of gay men, Indigenous people, anyone who speaks French, and women who dare to disagree with him. Politically connected."

"Of course he is," said Jan. "Our politicians love a deep-pocketed bigot with no respect for the environment. You make me glad Rob isn't coming, although it's too bad his own plans fell through." She waved at a Lexus SUV visible in the side mirror. "Dee and Lacey are right behind us."

A half minute later, both vehicles cruised through Jake's tall wrought-iron gates. As the Brenners pulled up to the main doors, the house steward steered Jan's power armchair onto the porch.

"Good evening, Mrs. Brenner. Drinks are being served in the great room."

"Thanks." Jan settled herself on the chair and wiggled the joystick back and forth. The chair swung, narrowly missing Dee as she mounted the steps. "Oops, sorry." She backed up the chair and passed through the door held open for her. "It always takes me a bit of getting used to after I haven't driven it for a while."

She led the way through the vast foyer, ignoring the familiar artworks and potted shrubs, steering fairly straight down the middle of the varnished oak flooring that demarcated carpeted sitting areas from the main dining room, with its floor-to-ceiling view over the lawns. *Please let Kitrin be healthy and happy, and please let Orrin Caine turn out less of an asshole than he sounds.* Terry's opinion wasn't entirely unbiased, after all. The first of his family even to attempt postsecondary education, he really had come up under his own power, from a dirt-poor bush farmer's son to chief geologist at Jake's billion-dollar oil and gas company. Silver-spooners who claimed self-made status made him cranky. And he didn't care for Kitrin or her husband.

As she arrived at the archway to the great room, Jan added one more wish to the list: *Please let there be someone here tonight that he'll thoroughly enjoy.*

Although Lacey had kept watch on the road to Jake's all day while she worked around Dee's yard, there was no sign of paparazzi or even an unfamiliar vehicle. No easy escape from her financial double bind: she needed money from work to pay the lawyer in B.C. to attend hearings so she could eventually get Dan to buy her out of the house in Langley so she could afford to finish paying the lawyer and someday get her own place again. Maybe Mylo Matheson or Kitrin Devine would want more security, if she suggested the option? She followed Jan's wheeled armchair through the great room's archway and stopped, half blinded by the sunlit valley vista beyond the dim room.

Jake's voice said, "Welcome, everyone. Come on in and let me introduce you."

Her vision adjusting, Lacey stepped around Jan to take the first hand that was offered. The skeletal fingers belonged to the frail woman she'd pulled from the swim machine two days earlier.

"How nice to meet you." Kitrin Devine, her thin brown hair twisted up in a straggling chignon, showed no sign she remembered Lacey. After a brief, limp touch of the fingers, she offered the same hand to Dee. Jan got a cheek kiss.

The movie director stood with one elbow propped on the wide stone fireplace mantel, clearly expecting people to come to him. Jan and Terry went first, briefly recalling their previous meetings in Vancouver. Dee gave a perfunctory handshake and sat down near Kitrin. Jan wheeled her chair up to theirs. Terry turned to Jake and said something about a work matter.

Then Lacey was face to face — eyeball to eyeball, since they were very near the same height — with Mylo Matheson. He was a wiry man all in black, with a face so smooth she suspected plastic surgery. His artfully greyed temples were the only obvious concession to age. She marked him as late forties or early fifties, not quite twice his wife's age. Now to get him interested in having more security, without it being obvious to Jake that she was shilling for work hours.

"How are you enjoying your stay, Mr. Matheson?"

"Mylo, please." The great man scanned the room and, apparently finding nobody else worth his attention, finally looked at Lacey directly. "This hilltop is ideally placed for scouting mountain backdrops."

After ten minutes, she still hadn't slid another word into his monologue about what he'd seen and where he intended to set certain key scenes. Hinting about possible security concerns wasn't possible. This man had no interest in anything except his movie. He probably had people to do the worrying for him.

The steward came back and caught Jake's eye. He stood up. "The chopper's coming. Who'd like to greet the Caines with me?"

Mylo left Lacey without a backward glance, snapping

his fingers at his wife as he went. Kitrin jerked upright like a marionette and followed. Jan, caught midsentence, stared after them with her mouth open.

"I'll wait here with Jan," said Dee.

That left Terry and Lacey to follow the others along the dim corridor between the security office and the attached garage. Mylo and Jake stepped out the glass doors, with Kitrin breathing hard as she hurried through behind them. The door swung shut, almost catching her turquoise caftan.

Left inside, Lacey muttered to Terry, "He actually snapped his fingers at her? I didn't imagine that?"

Terry's lip curled. "He hasn't changed a bit. And Kitrin is in really bad shape. How can he drag her out there when she can barely stand up on her own steam?"

"What brought them together when he so clearly despises her weakness?"

He reached past her to the door handle. "Mylo wouldn't be the first man to get sucked into a relationship by a woman's frailty and end up resenting her for it."

She eyed him, suddenly alarmed. "Do you resent Jan for being so weak? I'd never have guessed. You look after her really well."

"Of course I don't resent her. For one thing, she wasn't frail when I met her. The opposite, in fact. I used to worry about keeping up with her. Now I just worry about her." He pulled the glass door inward, stepping sideways to let Lacey pass. "She's doing really well again, compared to the past few years. We're finally getting back to a more normal life, and if anything happens to change that, well ... somebody's going to pay."

"It isn't your job or Jan's to rescue Kitrin from her marriage." But as the words left Lacey's lips, her gut squirmed. She hadn't realized how psychologically abusive Dan was until she'd been away from him for months. Kitrin, living in a world completely bounded by what Mylo wanted, probably couldn't see how abusive he was, either. What, if anything, to do about that was a question for another day. For today, Lacey's task was to get Mylo or Jake to ask for extra security. It was a twofer, really: if she was around more, not only would she earn more, but she could assess Kitrin's psychological and physical situation; maybe create a safe zone for her to see things more clearly. God, not even two minutes' conversation with the woman all week, and already the urge to rescue her was strong. Old RCMP habit. She willed it away and stepped out onto the pool deck, blinking in the sunlight.

"If you think Mylo's an ass," Terry murmured, "wait till you meet tonight's other alpha guest. Orrin Caine's a foul-mouthed old bastard, tinpot god of his own oil and gas conglomerate. If Jake wasn't my boss as well as my neighbour, you wouldn't catch me sitting in the same room with either of them."

The heat hit with visceral pressure, rebounding off the sun-baked tiles and only marginally eased by a faint breeze over the long, cool pool. Jake, Mylo, and Kitrin had stopped farther along the rim, watching a boy on the diving board. Kitrin's caftan, the same turquoise shade as the water, fluttered in the breeze, exposing a red ring of bruise around one wrist. Had Lacey done that when pulling her from the pool downstairs, or was that evidence left by Mylo?

"Michael." Mylo's voice echoed from the surrounding walls. "Get your shoes on."

The boy backed off the board and raced along the far side of the pool, hurtling over the arched bridge that spanned the decorative waterfall's foot. He snatched a towel and hat held up by a curly-headed woman. Shoving his feet into water shoes, he ran past Lacey and Terry with a muttered, "'Scuse me." The family passed through the gate.

Lacey brushed a drop of water from her bare arm. "Mylo sure has him trained."

Terry made an unreproducible noise of disgust and was thereafter silent as they walked across the lawn to the screen of trees by the helicopter pad. They joined the others in the shade and stood listening to the distant thwap of helicopter blades. After a moment Lacey realized there was another vibration, localized at her left hip. She pulled her phone from her pants pocket and checked the six-hour update. Dan's phone was still in the Lower Mainland, right where it should be: five mountain ranges to the west. She cancelled the alert and tucked the phone away again.

The helicopter appeared over the trees and began to sink, its downdraft kicking up hot, dry dust. Young Michael, at his mother's side, tugged down his hat brim and yelled something toward her ear. She handed over a pair of sunglasses from her caftan pocket, stifling a cough with her other hand. Jake moved forward with Mylo half a step behind. Lacey waited a protective arm's length from Kitrin, whose cough wracked her whole thin body. The dust began to settle.

The helicopter side door opened from within. The first passenger scrambled out. He was about Lacey's height, sandy-haired, broad of shoulder, with sturdy arms extending from his red golf shirt. Built, in other words, exactly like Dan. Golden-red hairs on his arms caught the sunlight, like Dan's did. Her hand reached for her throat. She forced it down, breathed in through her nose, out through pursed lips. Repeated twice more, thankful that the helicopter noise would cover the faint hissing of her breath. Damn Dan for still causing that instinctive panic.

Not-Dan stepped away from the helicopter. A boy jumped down next, his face and hair hidden by dark glasses and a ball cap pulled well down. The first man helped a slender, dark-haired woman out. The next passenger was an older man, taller than Jake and equally craggy. His silver hair rivalled the helicopter's white cowling.

As the chopper noise gradually died, Jake made introductions. "Orrin Caine, Mylo Matheson. Of course, you've been in touch already, over the cattle drive stuff."

Up close, the sandy-haired man was easily twenty years older than Dan. His name was Earl, and he called Orrin "Dad." The woman beside him, her loose, dark hair artfully highlighted, was Sloane, Orrin's wife and definitely not Earl's mother, being at least a decade younger than him. She introduced her son, Tyrone, as Orrin's youngest child. The boy left his shades and hat on, hanging back until she prodded him to shake hands with Mylo and Kitrin.

Michael Matheson stared at Tyrone. After a moment, he tugged Kitrin's hand. "Mommy, can he come swimming with me?"

Kitrin smiled. "That's a great idea. Sloane, can Tyrone go play in the pool with Michael? Our nanny, Georgie, will get him a swimsuit and keep an eye on him."

Jake, Orrin, and Mylo strode across the lawn, with Earl at his father's heels. The two mothers with their young sons followed. A couple scrambled from the helicopter after they'd moved off. Terry, assuming the role of second-in-command, introduced himself and Lacey.

"Bart Caine," said the younger man. He was built like Earl, but with dark hair and an easy smile. "My wife, Andrea."

Terry fell into step with them. Lacey followed, tasting the helicopter's dust and oil on the hot summer air. Something was crawling over her neck. She put up a hand, but no insect buzzed off, and she belatedly recognized the sensation: that creepy feeling triggered by memories of Dan or emails from him. Today's tipping point was likely the proximity of the phone alert to the arrival of a Dan-lookalike. Plus the two trophy wives. With their dark hair and bright jewellery and big smiles glinting in the sun, Sloane and Andrea looked like brunette versions of Camille Hardy and her posse from the Art Museum board and were probably equally devoid of conversation that didn't involve shoes, vacations, and gossip about people she'd never met. Suppers with those Camille types had been their own kind of purgatory, and this one also included Orrin Caine's legendary foul mouth and Mylo Matheson's arrogance. Jake's food would be excellent, but even if Lacey's taste buds could be coaxed into enjoying it, her stomach had already compressed like a coal seam under granite.

Up ahead, Terry laughed at something Bart said. Had he gotten past his ire, or was he putting on a good front for his boss's guests? As part friendly neighbour and part lowly part-time employee of Jake's contracted security company, Lacey must do the same. She caught up to Andrea, hoping her smile looked more casually friendly than completely insincere.

What an awful man! Predinner conversation over drinks had been bearable, even pleasant with Bart and Andrea, but being trapped across the table from Orrin Caine was horrid. Jan leaned back in her wheelie armchair as the "old gay-basher" jabbed his bloody knife at his daughter-in-law. He'd already waved it at both his adult sons, Earl and Bart. Jake hadn't been kidding when he'd said Rob wouldn't enjoy this meal. Or when he said most guests would be around her age. He and Orrin were the oldies, in their seventies, then Earl and Mylo, both pushing fifty. Bart and all the women were thirty-five or younger and as good-looking as they were healthy. Except for Kitrin. Sitting beside sturdy, tanned Earl, she resembled a consumptive from a Victorian illustration. Jake sat between her and Orrin's dark-haired, elegant wife, Sloane, who answered only when spoken to and matched Orrin's wine consumption to the mouthful. Mylo, Kitrin's egotistical husband, was tucked between

Dee and Lacey at the far end of the table, talking non-stop. Lacey's pursed mouth suggested she was stifling a yawn.

"Five years Bart's been married to Andrea," Orrin said, exposing teeth smeared red by the juices from his prime rib, "and not a kid in sight. When I was thirty I had two."

Bart muttered something that sounded suspiciously like, "That you know about."

Orrin's eyes narrowed. "I always heard people in those shithole South American countries popped out babies by the dozen. Bart picked a dud."

Earl said, "At least he's consistent."

Andrea, her face unnaturally calm, ignored the whole exchange and asked Jake about his ranch in the Milk River Valley. Jake was always happy to repeat the old outlaw tales of that region, but Orrin talked over him about his own ranch west of Sundre.

"I know every foot of my land," he boasted. "Been riding the bounds since before Earl was born. Had him in the saddle when he could barely walk. Bart here," he waved the knife again, "never took to horses. Scared little pussy. His ma babied him."

Earl gave Bart a smirk better suited to a sulky teenager than a grown man. No love lost between those brothers. Jan rubbed the dent between her eyebrows, trying to stave off a headache from the tension.

Eventually, all the wine Orrin poured down his throat had the inevitable result. He kicked back his chair and marched off along the corridor. As he vanished, Sloane put down her wineglass and picked up her fork.

Andrea put down her fork and squeezed her husband's hand. He smiled in return. Kitrin asked Earl about his life down in Denver. Soon she had him chatting about his wife and daughters, who'd recently finished their annual month at Orrin's ranch.

Bart said to Jan, "Did I hear right that you're a retired art historian?"

"Not exactly retired." Jan pointed at her armchair on its wheeled base. "I haven't figured out yet how to make my career fit around my limitations."

"That's quite the contraption," he said. "A custom job, obviously."

"Jake had it made to match the rest of the furnishings."

Jake overheard. "My company sponsors Beakerhead every year. You know about Beakerhead, right?"

Bart nodded. "The arts and sciences fair that used to run the catapult contest at Olympic Park."

"That's them. We paid to bring in the giant mechanical elephant from France one year, and another time a desert hut that keeps itself cool and collects drinking water from the air. Some young fellows in the parade had mounted armchairs onto power wheelchair bases and were letting people drive them around. I asked them to convert one of mine."

When the attention to the chair faded, Jan said to Bart, "So what do you do when you're not at work?"

"Enjoy rock climbing, mostly, and I can sometimes be convinced to go rowing with my wife. Andy's a regular at the Glenmore Canoe Club near our place. Anyway, about this art history thing. Maybe this movie could use your help with finding art from the turn of the century. Previous century, that is."

Andrea laughed. "Since when has Hollywood been concerned with historical accuracy? If it was a BBC production, maybe. A docudrama involving families living entirely like the early settlers?"

Jan grinned back at her. "One winter in a mud-chinked log cabin would be more than enough for the actors and the viewers. They could make an art film, though. Lots of famous artists used to come to the Rockies every summer. There's a great book detailing their hiking routes, with photos from the places they set up their easels, and then a picture of the painting the artist did of that spot. Back in the plate-glass negatives era, one painter took a full camera set-up on a six-week horseback trek. Boxes of fragile glass squares and all the fixing chemicals bounced along on a pack horse through the mountains near Banff. At summer's end, he carried all his plates back east by train and spent the winter painting from the photos."

The word *camera* had attracted Mylo. "Name of the book?"

"*Hiker's Guide to Art of the Canadian Rockies*. It's recently been reprinted."

"Get me one for my art director."

"Please," Kitrin added quickly. "I'd like to see it, too, Jan. You were always good at dating paintings from the clothing and scenery and things. But I guess you haven't gone hiking to find the vantage points yourself."

Terry joined the conversation at last. "We did a few before she got sick."

"Our Jannie," said Jake, "knows pretty much every painting ever made in these parts. She can tell you the history of every piece I own and which related one hangs in which neighbour's collection."

"Great," said Mylo. "You can work with my art director, make sure we get the right subjects and styles for my indoor sets. If you find me all original paintings, I might even win an Oscar for art direction."

While Jake beamed like a benevolent king and Mylo detailed which of his films had won which awards against what other films, Terry frowned at Jan. He wouldn't want her sacrificing her scarce energy for money they didn't need. But a job like that could safely test her new medication on a part-time, flexible work schedule, local enough to go home for rests. She wouldn't be working directly for Mylo, either, which was a real point in its favour. Still, no need to tackle Terry here and now. Time enough to fight that battle if Mylo formally offered.

She turned to Andrea and said, "Bart told me earlier that you used to be a vlogger?"

"Call me Andy, please," said Andrea. "And yes, I was a daily smash on YouTube before I got married."

Lacey, who had been in the silence camp with Terry, said, "Vlogger: that's a video blogger? I don't quite understand how you make money doing that."

Andy shrugged. "If you're talking about things your demographic is interested in, or demonstrating some skill they want, you get lots of hits and subscribers. Advertisers pay to place their products either right in your videos or in ads on the home page. Every ad seen gives you a small credit. Once enough eyeballs are seeing enough ads, you can earn a decent living. Or could." She fiddled with her fork. "It got to be too big a time-sink to keep up daily. I shut it down after we got married."

Bart took over. "Viewers want to think they're in your living room, and that you're just a normal person like them, only with ten times more drama. Basically you have to strip your soul naked every day to keep them coming back. It was bad enough before the wedding: strangers dissecting every aspect of our engagement, gift registry, home decor. They'd have been even worse after it, speculating about a celebrity smash-up or pregnancy whenever Andy had baggy eyes."

Mylo stared at Andy. "What was your topic?"

"Eating disorders," she said and looked at Kitrin.

Mylo's face hardened. He turned his shoulder to her and began telling Dee about an old-school stunt director who thought safety harnesses were for wusses. "Eight takes it took before he admitted the stunt double couldn't cling to the car's hood in a tight turn without one."

Kitrin didn't seem to notice any of it. Her prime rib lay on the plate with her abandoned cutlery, diced into a million pieces, of which Jan estimated she had eaten fewer than five.

Andy raised her voice a fraction. "I was very open about my eating disorder, and that resonated with a lot of young women. It began in college, with all the stress there."

Kitrin didn't look at Andy, but she picked up her fork and put another tiny shred of beef into her mouth.

Lacey said, "How did you get into vlogging?"

Andy smiled along the table. "Totally by accident. In my third semester of school I got so weak, I couldn't sit at a keyboard to write term papers. When I went into treatment, my therapist encouraged me to keep a video journal instead, talking through my feelings from my bed. After a year and a lot of hours digitized, we went through the recordings together. It was incredibly helpful to see myself as sick as I had been, and to hear my own thoughts from the depths of my disorder.

"Mainly I started to put it out there for my own benefit, kind of claiming my real self in a world where appearances are everything. Soon the comments showed me I could speak to other women caught in the same mess. I learned to edit older clips in with new stuff, sharing my reflections on the journey back to health. My subscribers soared. I had a list of resources right on my home page, helping desperate people find support in their region. So I kept going. Now I'll talk to anyone about it, any time."

She left the last statement floating and picked up her wineglass. "I might start up again when I get pregnant and am learning about babies. That's an area where I have absolutely no clue, but now that I'm healthy enough to take on a child, I could interview pediatricians, child psychologists, other mothers ..."

Orrin marched into the room. "That's what I need: grandkids. Sons are expensive. Ain't that right, Sloane? A million bucks a son, I promise them, and I get what I want. 'Bout now I'd pay that much for a grandson."

Dee's voice was cold. "Don't you have daughters? What did you pay for those?"

Earl glared at her. Bart sucked in his breath. Andy dropped her eyes to her plate. God, they were all terrified of this hideous old man.

Orrin guffawed, and the three relaxed visibly. "Good money for a girl? Naw. Earl's big sister, now, I invested in a feller's golf course over in New Jersey, and he married her to his son. Not a great money-maker, that course, but Debbie's husband is a lousy golfer and I clean up on side bets."

Dee set down her fork and left the table, probably too furious to keep her mouth shut if she stayed. To distract everyone, Jan leaned forward to make eye contact with Mylo. "What's your movie about? All I know is that it'll be shot around here."

"Cattle drive," said Orrin. "That's my part. We'll run a hundred head or so up and down the valley, fly over them with choppers, shoot from every angle. Isn't that right, Mylo?"

"I remember cattle drives," said Kitrin out of the blue. "Down around the Cypress Hills, where I'm from."

Mylo started to talk, but Orrin turned his full attention onto Kitrin. "Cypress Hills? Saskatchewan or Alberta side?"

"Saskatchewan," she said. "My mother's from Maple Creek. She lives in Regina now."

Orrin watched her with narrowed eyes. She dropped her gaze to her plate and stirred the slivers of meat around with her fork. Jan shivered in sympathy. Orrin's stare was really unnerving. When would this horrid meal be over?

She asked again, "Mylo, what's your movie about?"

"Think *Bridges of Madison County* meets *Brokeback Mountain*," he said, "with a side of Canadian art history. That's where your knowledge will come in, Jan. Real artists and art as background."

"There are a few to choose from," said Jan. "A.Y. Jackson came to paint here, for one. He taught at the Banff School of Fine Arts in the 1940s. But I doubt I can line you up a loaner Jackson painting."

"Too late, anyway. I'm going for the early 1900s. A lonely rancher's wife rents out a room each summer to a pair of visiting artists, both men. Of course she falls in love with one of them, a clean, erudite man who brings the life and culture she craves to her isolated mountain valley." Mylo elaborated on the palette of her life: grey clothing, beige curtains, cloudy skies. The artist would wear bright clothing and be shot in sunshine or lantern's glow, meeting her eyes, in strong contrast to the dour, dusty rancher she'd married, who would always be looking past her. Mylo's smile spread across the table toward Sloane. She lifted her wineglass to hide an answering smile.

Orrin, oblivious, bragged about his Rocky Mountain art collection and invited Mylo — who nodded at Jan — to come see it any time at his Mount Royal home. Now there, he said, was a house that deserved to be in a movie.

When he shoved another slab of beef into his mouth, Terry seized on the lull to say to Mylo, "Where does *Brokeback Mountain* come in? Just the scenery?"

Mylo's fickle attention left Sloane. "Oh, in their third summer the woman will discover the artists in a flagrantly sexual situation. That precipitates her crisis and drives the last, tragic act."

Earl's fork hit the table. Bart's knuckles whitened on his knife. Sloane emptied her wineglass and signalled for a refill. Orrin choked on his meat.

"You're talking about fucking faggots? You're not gonna film a faggot movie on my land."

As Jan's temper boiled up, Bart gave a small shake of his head. She let out a breath that felt like lava in her throat. Don't insult your husband's boss's friend. Especially not after you were warned about Orrin's foul mouth and gay-bashing. She dropped her hands to her lap and flexed the fingers, trying to shake out the urge to throw something — even words — across the table. Too bad she couldn't slip out unremarked like Dee. Curse this wheelchair.

Terry, she saw, was looking at Jake as if willing him to say something. It wouldn't happen. Jake wouldn't disrupt his business dealings with Orrin over a comment no worse than many he'd heard and maybe said himself in his younger years.

Mylo, apparently impervious to Orrin's outrage, said simply, "All that will be shot in the studio, unless we can find a suitable interior around this quaint hamlet."

"It better be." Orrin sprayed beef juices onto his plate. "Fucking faggot movie."

Jake stepped in at last. "Shovel in that final bite, Orrin. We'll have dessert on the terrace if everyone's finished here."

As everyone else left the dining room, Lacey waited for Dee to reappear. "Smart of you to skip out," she said. "That Orrin's a real piece of work. Think Jake would notice if we slipped away?"

"'Fraid so," said Dee. "But someone else can sit beside — what does Rob call him? — the Lord High Director? Tell you what. You spill something on Earl if he gets after Bart, and I'll accidentally drop my dessert plate if Orrin shoots off his mouth about gays or women again. That ought to break things up."

"Can't I be the one to smash something?" Lacey asked and held the terrace door open.

Outside, the westerly sun fell like honey across the flagstones, faintly stirred by an evening breeze that gently fragmented conversations. The group had spread out as they acquired drinks and dessert. Mylo latched on to Sloane, drawing her toward the railing, pointing toward distant mountains. Waiting her turn at the dessert buffet, Lacey saw him put a hand on Sloane's back, steering her into an intimate circle of two. Sloane's eyes cut sideways toward her oblivious husband, and then she leaned closer. Making a date or just flirting? Well, Orrin was twice her age and ugly in mind as well as body. Mylo was younger, handsome, and clearly willing. Lacey looked around to see if Kitrin was upset and caught irritation on Jan's face instead.

She bent over the wheelie armchair. "Lighten up. It's not your husband making a play for another woman."

J.E. BARNARD

Jan huffed. "He's always been like that. I don't know what she ever saw in him."

"Love or stardust, same diff." Lacey handed Jan a plate off the stack. "What can I load up for you?"

When she, Dee, and Jan had their desserts organized, Lacey carried all three plates to a small table and went back for the drinks. Earl was in conversation with Jake, out of stabbing distance of his brother. Now was a good time to get to know Bart and Andrea, the only members of the family who seemed to enjoy each other's company. She gathered up her plate and approached them.

"Mind if I join you?"

"Please do," said Andrea as Bart hooked a chair over with his foot. "You and Dee are housemates?"

Lacey had seen that speculating look enough in the past year and had her answer ready. "Yes, we were university roommates years ago. When our marriages ended, we moved in together for mutual support." Not that it was any of their business whether she and Dee were a couple or not.

"Nice to have a good friend like that." Andrea sighed. "I'm not in touch with any of my friends from school. They kind of abandoned me when I went into treatment." She glanced along the terrace. At the far end, Orrin was sitting with Kitrin, leaning forward intently. "I hope he's not terrifying that poor woman. She seems really vulnerable. Maybe we should invite her over here."

"I'll go in a few," said Bart, "if he hasn't let up on her. Or Earl will interrupt. He's got his eye on them, too." He grinned at Lacey. "You probably think we're all terrible. Orrin's a domestic tyrant, but we try not to let him bully non-relatives."

There was no polite response to that statement, so Lacey asked instead, "Did I hear you say you like rock climbing? We flew back through the Ghost Wilderness a couple of days ago and picked up a climber from a cliff-top. At first I thought it was a rescue, but everyone was fine."

His face brightened. "That was a rescue, from Earl's mother. She's hated us since before we were born."

Not enough to skip going climbing, obviously. "Were you up top or on the cliff?"

"Up top, I'm sure," said Andrea with a curl of her lip. "They always make Earl climb last. He thinks it's funny to flick rocks down at them, which is not only mean but dangerous."

Bart shrugged. "He spent his first fifteen years being told he was Orrin's precious, only heir. Then Ben and I — that's my twin — were born when Earl was at that awkward teenage stage. Our mom says Orrin constantly told him we'd be less of a disappointment, and we'd inherit everything. Not that we understood all that subtext as kids. We just knew our big brother hated us. We're nicer to our little brother, even though he's a pain occasionally."

"And he probably will inherit everything," Andrea said. "We don't need it."

"That's the boy who went off with Kitrin and Mylo's son?"

"Tyrone." Andrea nodded. "I love having him for weekends. We play games and eat junk and watch movies. Orrin would have insisted on him sitting with us all night if Kitrin hadn't sent them to the pool. He's probably making her pay for that right now." She nudged her husband with an elbow. "Bart."

Lacey followed her gaze. Orrin was leaning closer, and Kitrin was flattened against her chair cushions.

Bart set down his dessert plate. "I'll distract him and let her get away." He ambled over. The breeze blew away whatever he said, but Orrin looked around, frowning. Kitrin pulled out her phone.

Andrea said in a low voice, "Orrin's a born predator, and Kitrin smells like prey to him."

Bart came back. "She's calling the boys to join us for dessert."

A few minutes later, the two youngsters charged around the terrace from the outdoor pool. They stopped suddenly, dripping water, and Lacey, who had only seen Tyrone's face beneath a ball cap and dark glasses, blinked. Which boy was which? One was slightly taller, but both had wavy dark hair plastered to their heads and loose, preadolescent musculature. More than that, they had similar chins, noses, even eyebrows. They could be twins.

"Holy shit," Andrea said, very softly indeed.

CHAPTER THREE

"Shh ..." Bart, his mouth almost in his wife's hair, whispered, "Do you think Orrin knew her while Sloane was pregnant?"

Only a trick of the fickle breeze let Lacey make out his words. She started to nod and caught herself. Not her business.

"She hasn't acted like she knew him," Andrea whispered back.

"Shh ..." he said again.

Kitrin rushed to the youngsters. "Oh, Tyrone, what happened to your arm?"

The taller boy tried to cover a bandage with his free hand. The shorter one stepped in front of his new friend. "Nothing, Mommy. It's fine, really."

"Ty!" Sloane hurried over. "Are you hurt?"

Orrin looked up. "Let the kid alone. Tough as old boots, he is. Chip off the old block. He'll make a great CEO one day." He stared at the two boys together, and at Kitrin, her hand on Michael's shoulder. His bourbon glass tipped, dripping amber liquid down his leg.

Sloane pulled her son onto a chaise and sat beside him to examine his bandage.

He pulled away. "I told you it's fine. A rock fell off the waterfall. That's all. Michael's nanny fixed it."

"A rock fell off my waterfall?" Jake snapped his fingers for the steward and muttered an order. Then he called to Lacey, "Check the cameras. I want to know exactly what happened."

Michael spoke up. "I'm sorry, sir. That rock didn't fall. I picked it off. We were taking turns trying to sink each other's floaty, and I hit Ty's arm."

Tyrone stood up and faced Jake. "I apologize, too. It was my idea."

Kitrin frowned. "Where was Georgie while all this was going on? She's supposed to watch you."

Michael leaned on her. "It's not her fault, Mommy. She was bringing our supper from the kitchen. We had hamburgers. Really juicy ones. And potato chips like we have back home." As she paused uncertainly, he pressed on, "And you should see how big the pickles were. We ate like five each."

Ty picked up his cue as if they'd been tag-teaming all their lives. "We ate everything, even the vegetables. Can I have dessert?"

Orrin waved his glass. "Lotta fuss about nothing. My boy is tough."

Jake was still frowning. Lacey slipped indoors to the stuffy security office and cued up the cameras for the pool area. Scrolling backward through the most recent images, she soon realized those that should have shown the waterfall was dark. She went out the double doors and had a look, disturbing the nanny, who was lounging on a chaise with her phone. The camera on the wall above her was tipped lens downward, leaving a vent at the back exposed to the elements. From the dark smudges around the opening, where water and dust had collected, it had been like this for a week or more. It would have to be replaced.

Lacey turned away and then back. "Excuse me, Georgie?"

The nanny looked up. "Yeah?"

"What happened with Tyrone's arm?"

Georgie flushed. "I was only away for a couple of minutes, and I never dreamed they'd start prying rocks off the water feature. Two boys together make four times the trouble."

Well, that story checked out. "The injury doesn't seem serious, anyway. Did they get all the rocks out of the pool?"

"I made sure of that."

"Thanks."

After checking around the waterfall and easily prying two more rocks loose with her fingers, Lacey headed around the outside terrace. Back at the party, she crouched beside Jake. "The camera's down, but the nanny confirms their story. And lots of the rocks up the wall are loose."

"Thanks. I'll get that fixed."

Lacey went back to her neglected dessert and watched Orrin circle around Michael and Kitrin like a vulture over dying animals. After a while, Sloane said, "Leave them to eat in peace, Orrin."

Orrin turned straight back to Kitrin, like a hawk on a mouse. "Your mother, she's from Maple Creek, you said. Lots of oil and gas around there. I got a few gas leases myself in southern Saskatchewan. What's her name?"

Kitrin hunched down as if dodging the question, or his almost accusatory tone.

Jan turned her chair in a half circle and smiled insincerely at Orrin. "I remember your mother, Kitrin, although it's been a long time since I saw her. Not since we were roommates in university."

Kitrin smiled weakly. "That's right, I was in Theatre and Jan was in Visual Arts."

Orrin ignored Jan. "Where else did you live? I visited Estevan and Regina a lot. Oil leases. Of course that was thirty-odd years ago. I wouldn't have met you, but I'm sure you were a real cute little girl."

His drawl crawled over Lacey's last nerve. Forget waiting around to convince Jake or Mylo they needed more security. She'd try again tomorrow. She stood up. "Thanks for a lovely evening, Jake. It's been great to meet everyone, but we've had a long day."

Andrea was right behind her. "Yes, it must be time for us to leave, too. I love looking at the mountains from the helicopter as the sun is setting." She suggested Tyrone invite Michael to visit the ranch soon.

Earl scurried to the far end of the terrace to make a phone call. Orrin watched him go. "Can't be calling his wife already," he remarked. "Just got the old ball-and-chain on the plane three days ago with her kids. Four girls, if you can believe it. Don't know what's the matter with his little swimmers. He didn't inherit those from me. I've got four boys." He slung an arm over Ty's shoulder. "And here's the only one with real leadership potential. He's gonna inherit all my companies one day."

Lacey barely suppressed a curl of her lip. The way Orrin played favourites, it was no wonder Earl hated his younger brothers. The bigger surprise was that Bart didn't. Or so he said. Maybe he didn't care about inheriting his father's oil company. But was that the truth or just a charming veneer over deep-rooted greed?

As everyone else moved away along the terrace, Jan lingered. "Can we chat for a bit, Kitrin? We haven't had a chance to catch up."

Kitrin turned with a sad smile. "Sure. Come downstairs?" Once settled in Kitrin's private sitting room overlooking the middle terrace, she said, "Thanks for hanging around. I've ... missed you."

"You don't look well," said Jan. "Is everything okay?"

"You don't look well, either." Kitrin pushed her loose sleeves back on her bony wrists, absently rubbing a ring of reddened skin. "Everyone takes it for granted, you in that chair, but I never knew. What happened?"

"A neurological illness. It's been five years now, almost six. It's called myalgic encephalomyelitis, ME/ CFS for short. Relapsing and remitting neurological and immune symptoms with a mitochondrial impairment component and a whole bunch of related issues. Probably starts with a genetic susceptibility and is triggered by environmental stressors or virus exposure." That was the potted version of the very much more complicated illness process. Jan couldn't remotely recall how many times she'd given that explanation since she'd begun to rejoin the world last year.

"Can't anything be done for it?" Kitrin asked. "I can't believe you, who were so energetic, have to live in a wheelchair. And the way they all talk, you're doing really well right now, so I can't imagine how bad you must feel other times. I'd just die if I couldn't walk."

That was hardly tactful, but Jan decided against calling Kitrin out. "I've definitely been worse. I'm on a couple of new medications that help some symptoms, but mainly it's daily management. I have to measure my heart rate whenever I'm standing up, to keep it under my aerobic threshold. It's the exact opposite of what they say normal people should do to keep healthy. In my case, because of the mitochondrial dysfunction, aerobic exercise makes me sicker." And that was enough about that. Jan looked around the sitting room, done in cool greys and blues offset by pale purples in the upholstery. "Jake's had this place decorated since the last time I was down here. I don't remember that big crystal statue on the coffee table, either."

Kitrin stroked a hand over the figure of a woman and child. "Amethyst. Isn't it lovely? I saw it in Jake's study, and he said if I like it I can have it down here for now. He's such a good host, and we're really enjoying our stay. Michael loves the games room and the swimming pool, horses and golf carts to drive around. I'm glad he got to meet someone his own age, though. That doesn't always happen." She shivered, although the room was warm, and pulled a sweater over her bony shoulders. "It was an interesting group at supper. Except that old man. He was horrible. I used to hear old ranchers talk about gays like that, but I thought it would have died out by now. And he's obviously a total pig about women."

"Obviously. Jake warned us, but that was the most uncomfortable meal I've ever had here." Jan tried to shrug it off. "Anyway, he's gone now. How is your mom doing these days?"

"She's okay. Drinking too much, as usual."

Jan remembered the slim blond with the stretched face and surgically attached wineglass. She'd made no secret of being miserable in her marriage and yet remained despite her husband's unending put-downs. Like mother, like daughter, although there was no sign Kitrin drank too much. Eating was another matter.

"But are you okay? You're really thin again, like you were in second year."

Kitrin hugged her sweater closer. "I'm pretty stable now, but I had to go to a treatment place for months last year. It was really hard on Michael. Mylo's gone so much, I'm all he has."

"You two seem really close. And he's a very bright boy."

"Talented, too. I'll ask him to show you some of his drawings when he gets back. You'll like that, being all about the visual arts. I expected you to be teaching or running a museum or something."

Jan wasn't being sucked back into talking about her health issues. "How's your dad doing?" Half a second too late, she remembered the man had become an increasingly sensitive subject during their roommate years. "You probably don't see much of him, if they still live in Regina and you travel a lot with your husband."

Ignoring the slip, Kitrin talked about places she'd gone, usually for movie shoots. It didn't take a genius to figure out that she spent a lot of time sitting alone in hotels or sightseeing with Michael. She probably went along in hopes of keeping Mylo from cheating on her the same way he'd cheated with her. Not that it was any of Jan's business except that, as usual, Kitrin had a knack for making a person want to protect her.

After a bit, Kitrin brought up Michael again. "I think it's time he had a manny instead of a nanny, but Mylo won't budge. He thinks Georgie has established a good rapport, and Michael needs stability." She bit her lip. "He thinks I'm not enough. Not strong or smart enough to be what Michael needs."

"I'm sure that's not true. Anyone can see Michael adores you. There must be endless things you could do with him, even here. The art museum down the hill, for example. You saw that already. It's got local history stuff that a lot of kids like, and art classes for all ages. Maybe one of the art teachers could do you and Michael a special session in the clay room or something. Give Rob a call. I'm sure he'd be delighted to arrange it."

Kitrin gave a tremulous smile. "I'd like to see Rob again. Will he be down there tomorrow?"

"I think so. That's Friday, isn't it? Yes, from about nine a.m. to four-thirty." Jan scribbled the museum switchboard number on a notepad.

Michael burst in and threw his arms around his mother's neck. "Mommy, Mommy! Ty wants me to visit him at the ranch. We can ride horses and ATVs and go climbing on his very own climbing wall. Please say I can go."

Kitrin smoothed his ruffled hair. "We'll see. Daddy has to go there soon to look at some scenery, and maybe you can visit Tyrone then."

Michael's young face drained of animation. Clearly he had no confidence that Mylo would take him along.

To lift his spirits, Jan said, "I hear you like drawings. Would you like to see some I did of your mom when we were in university?"

Michael looked at his mother. "Do we have to ask Daddy if we can visit her?"

The house phone chimed. Kitrin answered. "Your husband is ready to go. Do you have to leave with him?"

"Unless I want to risk crashing this lovely chair on the road. I live partway down the hill. From Jake's gate, you could walk it in five minutes or drive it in two. Please do come when you have free time."

"I'll give you a call in the morning. Maybe we can do something this weekend." Kitrin wrapped her scrawny arms around Jan's shoulders. "I'm thrilled to see you again." Her voice cracked. "So-o happy."

While Terry steered his old truck down the hill, Jan said, "Tyrone and Michael sure do look like brothers.

Orrin thought so, too, but it was obvious he and Kitrin had never met. You don't suppose Orrin was adopted, do you?"

"No clue. If he was, that generation wouldn't have talked about it." Terry stopped beside the front door. "Especially if there was a chance his rich new daddy was infertile."

"He'd blame his wife for that. Orrin had to learn his chauvinism somewhere." Jan swung her legs to the ground. "I'll contact that art director guy and find out what he wants from me. It might be that he doesn't need my help at all, and Mylo just said that because Jake put him on the spot."

With that thought firmly fixed in her mind, she sent off a brief email to the address on the card, introducing herself and mentioning Mylo's suggestion, and then stretched out on the couch with the TV remote in hand. Even in the armchair with its high back for head support, sitting upright for five hours straight had exhausted her neck muscles.

The next morning, an answering email awaited. *Delighted to have you aboard. Please send a phone number where you can be reached early today.*

Phone call. Ugh. Still, she was awake and relatively well rested, considering the long evening out. She sent off the phone number, hoping this Davey wouldn't call right away. Her tray loaded with breakfast, pills, juice, tea, and her phone, she headed for the sunroom chaise. This time last year, walking this far without holding on to the walls had been as good a day as she could expect. Now she could do the walk carrying a tray, spilling nothing, her hands hardly trembling. What a difference a few new management skills and some research advances made! Not a cure, but a real sense of her body slowly coming under her control. Pillows arranged for maximum head and neck support, she donned her dark glasses and settled in, just in time to watch Lacey stride out of Dee's driveway. She went uphill. Jake's place again? Fixing that pool camera, no doubt.

As the sun warmed the glass room, easing the overnight stiffness from her muscles, Jan ate and drank, watching the daylight dance on the river below and an eagle float along the valley level with her windows. She'd barely finished breakfast when the phone rang. Job interview?

Twenty minutes later, vibrating with excitement, she began to plan. First to the museum, to scour the collection for likely pieces. Then she'd go through its database for people who had loaned or donated paintings and might have others at home. She could send Davey a list and photos of the prospects, and then she could approach owners individually as needed. That would spread the workload out nicely. Next week she could go take photos of paintings for Davey's final inspection. She set up her snacks and meds in her go-bag and then lay down for a good rest to prepare for the museum jaunt. But no way could she settle when the chance to do something useful again, to reclaim her own career in this small way, was right on her doorstep. She forced herself to do meditative breathing. Excitement wasted energy, and if she crashed from this, she'd have to fight Terry before she could ever accept another job.

Cut off from the sunny morning in Jake's dull-brown security office, Lacey unhooked her tool belt and hung it over the coat rack. She didn't need the equipment jabbing her in the back the whole time she was sitting there testing cameras. She tilted her chair and scanned the monitors, identifying each set of four images: front gates, front of house, hilltop terrace both angles, check; second terrace, upper stair, lower stair, lower terrace — aha! The one that should show the swim machine, and the sauna/change room doors beyond it, was dark. She made a note and carried on. Upper pool, including the west gate out to the grounds: pool presently occupied by Kitrin Devine on a floating chaise. Most of her was concealed by dark glasses, giant hat, and long-sleeved shirt. Upper pool camera that should show bar and waterfall: black screen of death, as expected. Garage frontage both ways: nicely shaded at this hour and showing an upper edge of the half-open pool gate.

On to the outbuildings: front and paddock side of the stables, then a panning camera inside for checking on the horses. That one was frozen, showing the ceiling and not much else. Another note. Staff quarters, exterior only. One for the helipad, one inside and one outside the back gate to the riding trail.

All in all, it wasn't as bad as she'd feared. Every access to the house or grounds was under surveillance, and only the cameras covering the pools or stables — recreational areas — were affected. Wayne had warned her those areas were popular hook-up sites at Jake's house parties. She let herself briefly picture some hot cowboy action on the hay bales and then shook her head. No sexual partners for her until she was totally past the nausea of Dan's last assault. And never on a paying client's property.

Movement on the second terrace caught her eye. She toggled that camera up to full screen and then wished she hadn't. Mylo Matheson's shoulder was turned to the stair camera, but his hand was quite clearly inside a woman's T-shirt. Kitrin was still, according to the other monitor, floating in the upper pool. It was Georgie's thick mop of dark curls that leaned on Mylo's shoulder. This creep, who'd been making passes at Sloane Caine last night, was fooling around with his son's nanny. Men. *Gah.*

Lacey jotted her final note about replacement parts and forwarded the tally to Wayne. Her watch beeped. Time to go meet the temporary security staff. She shut the security office and headed outside through the upper pool area. Kitrin was floating near the waterfall with an earphone cord running from under her hat to the waterproof phone dock in the chair's arm. If she noticed Lacey, she made no sign.

Once past the garage, Lacey had a clear view across the wide lawn. Two men stood outside the main gate.

One was tall and lean, the other shorter and stocky. Both wore the dark blue ball caps and T-shirts Wayne put on every casual employee. This was it: her first time in a supervisory role since leaving the RCMP eighteen months ago. She'd barely had time to get used to the idea since receiving Wayne's message that morning. *Jake decided he wants live-in guards for the duration of Mylo's stay.*

At first she'd been furious that she wasn't the first choice, that someone else would be paid to patrol the grounds she knew best. The follow-up email clarified things: Wayne wanted her to get them oriented, schedule their shifts, and take their reports. He was making her head of the team, with control over her own hours, and he'd raised her pay appropriately. She was in charge again. How much trouble could two trained guards be after she'd shift-bossed eight constables — mostly male, and half of them with more years on the Force than she had? She strode over.

"Hi, I'm Lacey, Wayne's on-site rep."

The taller man stepped forward. "Hi, I'm Travis, and this is my brother Chad." Chad. Why did that name ring a bell? Lacey looked closer at the short man. "Shake hands, dude," said his brother. Chad held out a hand. Lacey shook it, leaning forward to get another look at his face.

"Chad." The final, nightmarish straw of her RCMP career came flooding back. She shut her eyes briefly behind her dark glasses, took a slow breath, and refocused. "I haven't seen you since Vancouver. After the Capilano Gorge incident, where you were guarding that little boy. I came to visit you in the hospital, but you might not remember. You were pretty out of it."

He raised his head at that. "Corporal McCrae?"

"I'm a civilian now." She looked over his face again with the sun on it, showing faint scarring where his cheekbone and eye socket had been repaired. "You took quite a beating that day. How are you doing? Fully recovered?"

Travis stepped forward. "He's fit for duty, but it's been a long road back. Will you show us around?"

Lacey let the subject of Chad's injuries drop. Why hadn't she considered this possibility when choosing to work in private security? Not only did gangs from the Lower Mainland have tentacles in Calgary's thriving vice economy, but so did the people who investigated them. Lots of PIs and bodyguards had policing backgrounds, too. She might trip over more people she'd worked with back in Surrey. Even some who'd worked with Dan, who maybe believed his lies about why she had left. None of which was getting today's job done. She wiggled the tension out of her jaw.

"I'll give you a tour of the property, starting at the stables. This way."

The men stroked horses' noses over the loose-box doors while Lacey looked at the stable camera atop a glass-fronted cabinet. The lens was pointed straight across the ceiling, well above a square of straw bales stacked with folded stable blankets. She could too easily imagine couples getting off there and gave her head a shake. Whatever the hockey players and puck bunnies got up to during Jake's postseason parties wasn't her business. Instead, she pointed up at the camera.

"Can one of you climb up and adjust the camera angle downward by a quarter?" It wasn't a perfect fix, since the panning servo was likely damaged beyond repair, but at least they'd have a view down the aisle. Chad hurried to obey. He moved well, with no obvious stiffness from all his injuries.

Travis said, "Good horses here. We grew up on a ranch up in the Peace River country. Spent all our lives in the saddle. Do you ride?"

"It's been a long while."

"Happy to take you sometime, when work permits."

Was he hitting on her? She shook off the thought and led the brothers through to the paddock. Beyond was the wall that circled the estate.

"All this is Jake Wyman's," she said. "The guests are a Hollywood movie director and his family, who may attract paparazzi. You're both up to speed on Alberta laws about removing trespassers?"

"Yes," said Travis. "Chad's taking his Alberta PI course right now, and they covered it."

Lacey smiled at Chad. "I'm doing the same course. Up to module four in the online version. How far along are you?" They chatted about that while they walked the perimeter wall. She took them out the back gate, teaching them the alarm code as she did so, and described the trails that wound out of sight. "When you have a chance, you should each take a walk out here to familiarize yourselves. Anyone could find a satellite image of these trails and skulk around this gate with their camera ready."

She pointed out the staff housing, tucked away in the trees beyond the helicopter pad, and took them along the west wall in a loop back toward the house. "The hill drops off steeply on the other side of the wall along here. The gate we're coming up to accesses the outdoor pool, and you'll see how high above the valley we are. The director's wife might still be in the pool, but don't acknowledge her unless she addresses you."

Kitrin, however, had left the pool. Her abandoned chaise floated near the steps. Lacey pointed out the other gate by the garage wall, then the double doors into the house. "That's the closest outside access to the security office, which I'll show you later. You'll normally use the door through the garage if there are guests in the pool area. You're to keep a distance from guests everywhere unless they're in need of immediate protection."

They headed down the terrace stairs, with a glance at the open French doors to the guest suite, where Michael could be heard reciting Spanish verbs with his nanny's coaching. On the lowest level, Lacey showed the brothers the drop-off from the house to the highway below. Travis leaned out and down, assessing the rocky slope below the terraces, but Chad kept a good arm's length back from the railing. Had the Capilano Gorge incident given him a fear of heights? Was he really fit for this job? She backed up level with him.

"You okay?"

"Yeah." He licked his lips. "Just, well …"

"Bad memories." Lacey breathed out slowly as the shared memory squeezed her. Chad had been a bloody pulp on the platform at Capilano, but she'd been on the bridge with a front-row view when the old woman was thrown down the cliff. Both of them had been powerless to prevent a senseless death. Yet heights didn't affect her.

"How did you ..." Chad shoved shaking hands into his jeans pockets. "I mean, that was a rough go for both of us. I haven't worked steady since. You seem to be doing okay, though."

"It killed my RCMP career," she said. "I was lucky to land among friends out here."

"My brother's my luck," said Chad. "I'm physically okay now, but the thought of someone else depending on me to save them ..." He shrugged. "This gig is a warm-up, right? Nobody's really out to get these principals?"

"Not that I know of."

Travis pulled his head up. "Looks secure enough against anyone but Spider-Man. What's next?"

After a quick tour of the bottom-floor workout area and games room, then the second-floor guest rooms and lounge — avoiding the suite where Michael's lessons were under way — Lacey brought them up through the kitchen and introduced them to the house steward.

"This man will assign you beds in the staff quarters for the week. Meals are served there, too."

The steward nodded. "Put your uniform shirts in the staff hampers at night, and I'll get them back to you the next morning. If you need a change sooner, you can take any green polo shirt in your size. They're kept in the upper staff hallway, the stables, and the main garage."

Lacey walked Travis and Chad around the main rooms on the top floor — breakfast room, formal dining room, great room, and the various alcoves — and pointed out Jake's study, the one door nobody opened without an invitation. She showed them the access to the attached fleet garage, where Jake's SUV and his three guest convertibles lived. Finally, in the security office, they went through the cameras and monitoring schedule.

By then it was nearly lunchtime. There was no excuse for her to stay longer, clocking higher-wage hours. It was up to Travis and Chad now to keep intruders at bay, and up to her to face the emotions bubbling under her businesslike surface. If only there'd been time and money enough for the trauma therapy she'd promised Dee's mom she would find. Maybe after she got her PI certification, she could get on staff somewhere. Wages plus benefits … who knew she would miss them so much after bailing on both Dan and the RCMP?

CHAPTER FOUR

By lunchtime, Jan's work in the museum library had yielded eleven possible paintings from the collection, all done between 1903 and 1914. When Rob texted to say Michael was hoping to see her before he left, she packed up her notes, filed the collection folders, and drove her loaner scooter to the museum kitchen. Michael and Rob were drinking juice while Georgie played on her phone over in the corner. Michael gave her a grin a hectare wide.

"Mrs. Brenner, hi. Isn't this place cool?" He set aside his glass and told her, accompanied by hand gestures, about the taxidermied animals, the replica settlers' cabin, the old post office, and some historical differences between the Kainai, or Blood Tribe, who lived along the mountain front, and the Plains Cree who lived — he waved a hand to the south and east — out in the plains. "There are Siksika people, too," he said with careful pronunciation, "on the other side of Bragg Creek. You can see their land from Mr. Wyman's house, Rob says. He'll come up to show me later. It used to be all their land around here. They're part of the Blackfoot Confederacy with the Kainai and another tribe I can't remember. 'Confederacy' means like a bigger group of allies, Rob says. And up north is another tribe called the Nakoda. They speak a different language from the Blackfoot or Cree. I can show you on the map in the gallery." *Rob says. Rob says.* A tiny bit of hero worship going on there.

"You've learned a lot in a short time. Well done."

Michael grinned wider.

Rob said, "When you visit Jan's house, Michael, check out the game system. If you're around this weekend, maybe you could play with Terry and me."

Jan raised her eyebrows. Rob had never shown interest in children before. She firmly seconded the invitation for a visit and said she had better get home for lunch.

Georgie lifted her head at last. "If you're going up the hill, can you give us a ride? It's a freaking steep road."

Michael thanked Rob and followed Jan out to the lobby. As they passed a corral with three other scooters, he said, "Isn't this where you park?"

"I'll drive outside to my van. Rob will come out and drive the scooter back in. Unless you think you can do it?"

"I drove your armchair around last night after you left. It's kind of wobbly on the corners."

Jan laughed. "I don't think they'll catch on for street use. When you park this scooter, give the key back at the information desk." As she climbed into the van and opened the windows, Michael drove off with Georgie trotting alongside. They were soon back. She delivered them to Jake's gate with a promise to call his mom about a visit. As she pulled away, she saw a stocky man in a navy T-shirt peering around the corner of the house. Navy tee like Lacey wore on the job. She made a mental note to ask Lacey about new security and drove home.

When she phoned Kitrin, the cell didn't answer. The house steward wouldn't put her through on the landline. Mrs. Matheson, he said, was resting and not to be disturbed. He couldn't say when she would be available, but Jan might try closer to the dinner hour.

Leaving herself a voice memo to call again later, Jan went to her disused studio to dig up her drawing portfolios from university. Half an hour later, her arms and sundress streaked with decade-old charcoal, she stared at Kitrin's haunted face in a sketch dated Halloween of their final year together. She texted Rob. *In all my drawings of Kitrin from my portraits semester, she's looking totally devastated. Do you remember what was going on with her then? The fall before she met Mylo?*

Sketchbook in hand, she wandered out to the couch and settled down with her feet up. The new drugs were keeping her orthostatic intolerance symptoms at bay, but she still needed rest after being out two days in a row. To convince Terry she could handle this small contract for the movie and pave the way for future jobs, she couldn't risk getting overextended and having a crash.

The phone chirped. Rob replied, *Long story, tell you later.* A photo came, too: him and Michael in front of the gallery on the top floor of the museum. Probably some of the paintings on her list were hanging there right now. She enlarged the image, trying to see what hung on the wall beyond the glass doors, and stopped with her finger beneath the matching chins of Rob and

Michael. How had she not noticed the similarity before? As a mental art exercise, she tried to place Tyrone in the frame, too. He had Michael's nose but not Rob's. All three had similar chins and infectious smiles, like that British musician, Duncan James, but with a Canadian summer tan. As she settled down for her rest, her mental movie screen added more actors with similar chins and then spun off to similar haircuts and eventually facial hair. Somewhere around Skeet Ulrich's moustache, she slid away into blissful sleep.

Lacey crossed the bridge over the lazy late-summer Elbow River and cruised up the hill with the parts for Jake's vandalized cameras. Wayne had offered to show her his rogue's gallery of hockey players behaving badly around the pool and stables — from before they got wise to the cameras — but she refused. If she knew which trophy wife had been getting off on the weight bench with which defenceman, her lousy poker face wouldn't suppress an eye roll the next time the same sleek wife walked into one of Jake's parties on the arm of her aging oil-baron husband.

Passing Dee out walking with Boney and Beau, she waved. Dee hadn't been up yet when Lacey had left for Calgary at seven. Lacey shouldn't have been up that early, either, considering how much sleep she'd lost over all the memories stirred up by Chad. She and Dee had sat around the firepit on the back terrace until late, discussing the day, but it hadn't cleared her mind completely. She'd had nightmares.

"I felt guilty about him for a long time," she'd told Dee. "If I'd left my phone on when I went to bed after my night shift, I would've picked up that distress call and sent the North Van RCMP ahead to the gorge. Looking at Chad today, with his scars and his twitchy eyes and the way his big brother hovers, ready to step in when he can't cope ... that one incident destroyed his life."

Dee frowned. "And it and Dan together nearly destroyed yours. Don't go borrowing other people's trauma when you have plenty of your own."

Lost in the memory of that dank Vancouver afternoon, with the rain drizzling down and mist winding through the cedars along the rocky gorge, Lacey felt in her gut the moment she'd recognized Chad in that bloody mess on the wet planks. She snapped herself out of it with an effort. "He's lucky they weren't closer to the bridge, or he'd have gone over, too."

"It was his risk to take," said Dee. "Just like when you were on the Force and ran toward a brawl or a shooting, how many times a week? It's not your fault he took a beating on the job."

Lacey poked a log deeper into the flames. "I guess you're right. It's just ... and I guess I feel even more guilty for thinking this ..."

"What?"

"I wish he wasn't on my job," Lacey said at last. "I feel really bad that he's carrying this, but his mental state is a liability, and on my first supervisory job since I left the Force. If anything goes wrong up at Jake's because he's screwed up, I'll be wearing that. I need good current references to show to PI agencies when I get my course finished. I need a job with benefits so I can get my teeth cleaned and stuff."

Stuff including finding a therapist who could treat her for the lingering effects of that last year with Dan, and all those shitty child abuse cases, and the lack of support from her sergeant. She was at least as scarred in her way as Chad was in his.

"Wayne'll be your reference, and he won't blame you for Chad. You've got a year of solid job performance with him now." Dee tipped her head back. "I love the night sky out here, far from Calgary's lights, when you can see the stars tangled in the spruce."

Far overhead, a single star winked at Lacey. She wished on it that Chad would prove fit for work and that she'd get lots of hours at the higher rate to pay her lawyer. After the divorce, she'd be able to pay for a therapist. *Please, no nightmares tonight.*

But they had come, anyway: faces of the dead and the traumatized, and Dan laughing as he choked her until she woke up gasping.

Today, with the bright sunshine reflecting every-where and heat already radiating off the dusty road, Lacey had a plan: watch Chad today, and if she still doubted him tonight, she'd ask Wayne to replace him. At least then her ass was covered if he did screw up. She'd feel guilty, sure. But Dee was right; she had her own trauma to deal with, and Chad had to handle his.

She pulled up to Jake's gate, now kept closed as it should have been all week, and clicked her radio.

"Travis, Chad, can one of you buzz me in the front gate, please?" Nothing happened. She radioed again and then saw Travis trotting from the helicopter pad. He hit the gate control and stepped aside as she drove through.

"Sorry about that," he said. "I was doing a perimeter check."

"Where's Chad?"

Travis frowned. "He should be watching the monitors. Must have gone to the can."

One strike, Chad. "I'll be at the stables, fixing that camera mounting."

"I'll give you a hand. All quiet today, anyway. The boy and his dad went off in the helicopter a while ago."

"Thanks. Can you bring me a folding stepladder? The equipment shed is —"

"I found it already." He jogged off and arrived back at the stables in time to hold the door as she carried in the box of gear. He was good for handing stuff up while she swapped out the damaged mounting, and she tried not to wonder if he was watching her ass, which was pretty much at his eye level the whole time she was on the ladder.

As she was coming down, her boot slipped. His hands were there right away, one each side of her waist, not clutching but supporting until she found her footing. Even that workaday touch from a man made her skin crawl. Apart from the odd hug from Rob, and cheek pecks from Terry on special occasions, no man had touched her since her arrival in Bragg Creek fourteen months ago. None had been inside her personal space at all since last Christmas, when she'd finally faced up to the memory of Dan's assault. She suppressed a shudder and put the damaged mounting into the box with her screwdriver.

"Chad," she said into her radio. "Can you please test the range of movement for the interior stable camera?" In a moment, the camera began moving. It rotated through its full lateral and vertical range.

The radio crackled. "Where do you want it centred?"

"Travis," she said over her shoulder, anxious to put some distance between them, "can you go stand between the paddock door and the hay bales, please? Chad? Focus on Travis and widen the angle so it covers the door and the hay. From the waist up is fine." The camera moved.

The steward came in and placed a stack of green polo shirts neatly in the glass-fronted cupboard. "Putting a damper on the hanky-panky, are we?"

Travis's eyebrows flew up.

"Jake's hockey guests," Lacey explained, "like to angle the cameras away from potential hook-up spots. Wayne has to repair and replace some equipment every summer. Mind carrying that ladder to the pool?"

She picked up her tools. The steward followed along, regaling Travis with tales of wild guest exploits the staff had witnessed or heard about. As they reached the garage, he veered inside the first open bay with his remaining shirts for the mechanic. Out of habit, Lacey counted vehicles. Jake's SUV and one of the guest convertibles were out. She paused at the pool gate. Kitrin was once more floating near the waterfall. Lacey would have to come back later to replace the rain-damaged camera. Meanwhile, Travis could leave the ladder and go patrol. She'd make a second trip up the terrace stairs to fetch it quietly. If Kitrin woke up, well, at least Lacey was a familiar, friendly, and female face rather than a strange man.

The honk of a car horn turned them both around. The third of Jake's orange convertibles sat outside the gate, with an unfamiliar SUV pulled over behind it. The horn sounded again.

"Leave the ladder and check that vehicle in," she told Travis. "Thanks for your help."

As she was making her second trip down the terrace stairs, angling the ladder carefully around the bend, she saw Chad. Or rather, Chad's foot ... coming out the French door from the guest suite.

"Chad?"

The foot vanished.

She hurried down. "What are you doing in there? That's a private area."

"Fetching sunscreen." He came out into the sunshine and held out one hand. In it was a plain white tube with small black lettering. "She asked me to."

Squinting against the glare off the white plastic, Lacey made out a couple of *Ms* and a smaller line that read *SPF 30.* "The woman in the pool sent you for it?"

He nodded. So he'd been out by the pool when he should have been monitoring the cameras to buzz her in the gate? A second mental check mark against Chad. It wasn't even noon, and he was already on his last throw.

"All right, get on with it. And in future stay away from any area where there's a house resident or guest. Okay?"

"Uh-huh." He hurried up the stairs, leaving her to wrangle the ladder down to the third terrace while she mentally wrestled with the wording of her replacement request. Travis wouldn't be happy about that, but he'd just have to deal.

CHAPTER FIVE

A little after ten on Saturday morning, Jan stopped at Jake's gate. Closed, for the second day in a row? Usually it was left open during daytimes because of all the social comings and goings. A green SUV was parked nearby. She stared at its heavily tinted windows. Was anyone in there? A security guard, perhaps, who could let her in? Or maybe not. A man came out through the people-gate in the wall, wearing the kind of blue T-shirt Lacey sometimes wore for work. He stooped a bit to look in her van window.

"Good morning, ma'am. Your name and business, please?"

"Jan Brenner. I'm here to see Mrs. Matheson."

"You brought the boy home yesterday?" He pushed a remote, and the gate opened wide.

Jan kept her foot on the brake. "When I leave, how do I signal you to come open the gate?"

He handed her a business card. "I'm Travis. That's my cell number. If you'd care to text me just before you're ready to leave, I'll come, or send Chad."

"Chad?" Jan reviewed her glimpse of the man who'd watched Michael and Georgie yesterday. Something clicked in her visual memory. She stared at Travis. "Is Chad from Vancouver?"

Travis slanted a look at her. "Yes, ma'am, he was. Did you know him there?"

Jan gave her head a smack. "Oh my God. That's Chad, Kitrin's ex-boyfriend. That's why he's been watching Michael." Travis gaped. She said, "I was roommates with Mrs. Matheson in university, in Vancouver, while she was seeing him."

The surprise faded from his face. "Thanks for telling me." His lips tight, he waved her through the gate.

Her nerves twitching from the implications, Jan drove up to the house. Chad had kept silent about guarding Kitrin. After she dumped him for Mylo without warning, he'd spent a month moping around their parking lot with flowers, gifts, pleadings ... until Kitrin left for California and never came back. Did she know he was here?

The wheeled armchair waited on the front steps. Jan drove it inside, determined to find Kitrin and make sure she knew about Chad. She steered through the main floor, didn't see Kitrin anywhere, took the elevator down to the second level, and knocked at the guest suite without result. Then she went to the kitchen to ask the staff if they knew. The steward said Kitrin had been wearing a swimsuit when he delivered her breakfast.

"I hope she's not in that swim machine again," said Jan. "She got in a lot of trouble down there the other day."

"I'll go right down and check." The steward hurried out.

"I'll check the outdoor pool," said Jan and sped toward the west end of the house. As she reached the dim corridor toward the pool doors, she swung wide around the security office's open door, only to clip the half-open garage-access door in the other wall. It bounced off the trailing leg of a staffer in a green polo shirt. "Sorry," she yelled as she stopped at the automatic door-opener button the staff used when they were serving out by the pool.

Outside, blinking in the bright sunlight, she groped for her sunglasses as she surveyed the area. The first thing she saw was an empty floating chaise. The second was a body in the pool, floating face down near the waterfall.

"Kitrin!" she yelled.

The woman in the pool didn't stir. Dark hair eddied around her head like weeds in a stream.

Jan raced around the pool's edge, the chair wobbling madly as she cornered, and climbed off where the bridge beneath the waterfall began. Kneeling, she reached out as far as she could. Kitrin floated just beyond her fingertips, motionless except where the current tugged at her slack limbs. A faint trace of red coiled up around her head and thinned to vanishing point in the turquoise water.

"Kitrin!" Jan screamed again and jumped into the pool.

She surfaced and found her footing, floundering toward the drifting body. She grabbed Kitrin and turned her over, clearing the strands of wet hair away from her mouth and nose, trying to remember how to do CPR on a person still in the water. Pinch, breathe, release, listen. Repeat. After five rounds with no result, she raised her head and screamed as loud as she could toward the house.

"Help, help, Kitrin needs help!"

She started the breathing routine again.

CHAPTER SIX

The first, faint cry came from above, and might have been a bird call. Lacey lowered her screwdriver and listened. The second cry was unmistakable. "Help!"

She hustled down the ladder, her workboots ringing the metal rungs, and ran for the terrace stairs. Taking them three at a time, she reached the outdoor pool and scanned the sun-dazzled water.

One floating chaise, empty.

One decorative waterfall, tumbling off a rocky ledge into the pool.

Two women being churned by the waters, their dark hair twining like eels over their limbs.

As she dropped her tool belt, preparing to rescue them, Lacey realized only one of them was struggling: Jan Brenner, her dark curls plastered over her face. She clung to Kitrin Devine, trying in vain to drag them both away from the cascade.

Lacey scanned for options. The pole hanging on the wall was too short by far. There was nothing handy to throw and no guarantee Jan would be strong enough to grab it. She pressed the Call All button on her radio and yelled, "SOS, outdoor pool, SOS." Then, dropping the delicate device heedlessly onto the paving, she went off the edge in a racing dive.

Surfacing halfway across the pool, she slid smoothly into the speedy crawl she'd perfected as a teenage lifeguard. She snagged the floating chaise as she passed. Reaching into the waterfall, she grabbed an arm and pulled. Jan floated toward her, pulling Kitrin.

"I tried," Jan sobbed. "I tried to give her CPR, but I don't know how long she was down. The current sucked us under the waterfall."

"I'll take care of her. Can you get onto the chaise by yourself?"

"No. But I can hold on. Please, help her!"

As Lacey pulled Kitrin's unresisting body closer, a huge splash sounded. Waves churned across the pool as Chad floundered toward them. She pointed him at Jan and flipped Kitrin into a tow position. Although it was almost certainly pointless, she said, from old lifeguard habit, "I've got you, Kitrin. Just float and I'll get you out."

She walked backward until the bottom step touched her heels. Chad was waiting there to gather up Kitrin. Her lank hair trailed over his arm as he carried her up the steps. Lacey hurried around him to lay a chaise flat, issuing orders: "Put her here. Call 911. Bring the defibrillator from the security office."

As she bent over the inert body, she was conscious of Travis wrapping Jan in towels. Then all her concentration narrowed to Kitrin, blue lipped and motionless on the brightly striped cushion. She began to check for vital signs.

CHAPTER SEVEN

Trembling to her bones, Jan huddled on a deck chair while the horrific scene unfurled, soundless to her like a movie on mute. Lacey was doing chest compressions on Kitrin. Wasn't she supposed to breathe into Kitrin's mouth sometimes?

Travis returned with a yellow first aid box and took over chest compressions while Lacey slumped into the puddle of water seeping from her jeans. Jan yearned to bring her a towel, but standing up was too much effort. The steward brought one instead, temporarily blocking Kitrin's limp body. Staff gathered, shocked and silent, on the far edge of the pool.

Chad returned with paramedics, his face ghostly in the morning sun. Their thudding feet shook Jan's chair. The waterfall's noise roared into her ears, ten times louder than before. She clapped her hands to her head as RCMP boots pounded the tiles. Full sensory overload, and she'd lost her dark glasses somewhere. As the running stopped, someone brought her a mug of hot tea. She took it in both hands, watching Kitrin's pale face beyond the paramedic's shoulder, willing her to cough, to twitch. Anything to show she wasn't … wasn't …

Lacey slouched into the next chair. She'd acquired a second towel to drape across her thighs and bent to laboriously unknot her soaked workboots. How had she swum in those?

Jan dragged her stunned mind toward Lacey's voice. "What?"

"I said, are you okay? The paramedics can look you over before they go."

"They have to stay with Kitrin." Jan's tea sloshed onto her hands. "She needs them."

Lacey took the mug away and blotted the hot liquid. "I'm sorry. There's nothing more they can do."

The words hit Jan in the ribs. "She can't be." Then, as she forced in a breath, she wheezed, "Where's Michael? He can't see this."

"He went off with his father today."

"But he'll come back and want his mother." Jan's eyes overflowed. She mopped them on the towel. "Somebody has to phone Mylo. He can't bring Michael home without telling him."

Lacey put the tea back into her hands. "Drink this. The police will need to ask you some questions."

"Police? Why? She drowned. You said yourself she was too weak to be in the water unsupervised."

"Deep breaths. Drink your tea. The police will take you through it, and I'll be right here with you. Do you want me to call Terry to take you home after?"

"He's out at SAR training." Maintaining his Search and Rescue certification took just two hours a week and one weekend a month, covering everything from why lost people behave like they do, to how to strap one into a basket for a helicopter lift. So why did it seem like, whenever disaster struck near home, he was either in training or out on Search? Jan swallowed a mouthful of tea. It seared her throat, but the warmth was a balm spreading in her chest. "God, I'll have to tell him, too. And Rob. We've never lost a friend before. And she was a friend, you know. Even if I wasn't glad to see her at first, we talked after supper, and she loved her son so much, and …" She mopped her eyes again.

The paramedics were packing up their gear. One of them knelt before her. "You were in the water, too, miss?"

Jan nodded.

"I'd like to take your pulse and check you over, just to make sure you're okay."

What could possibly be okay in this situation? She sniffed. "Yeah, I guess." She sat while he listened to her heart and cuffed her arm for blood pressure, and then a policewoman took his place. She said dully, "Yes, I can answer questions," to the woman and rubbed her forehead. The shade over her scoured eyes was a relief. "I arrived at the gate about ten o'clock and went looking for Kitrin. I couldn't find her at first…. How long? Maybe ten minutes. The steward thought she was swimming, so I came out here." She looked over her shoulder. "Through those doors. She was floating face down, and when I got near, I saw blood in her hair. I thought she'd tipped her chaise and hit her head on the side. I jumped in and tried to give her rescue breathing, but I stepped on a rock from the waterfall, so I was off balance and the current in the pool pulled us under the waterfall. Lacey came and pulled us out."

The officer looked at Lacey. "Did you notice any loose rocks?"

Lacey said, "There was an incident recently with boys loosening rocks and throwing them into the pool. It might be one of theirs." She pressed Jan's hand. "Do you remember approximately where you stepped on the rock? I can go look for it."

Jan pointed toward her armchair, abandoned at the near end of the little bridge. "About a stride off the side there." She watched them walk away and then forced herself to her feet to look down at Kitrin.

"Step back, please, ma'am," said an officer.

"I just want to say goodbye. She was my friend."

"I'm sorry for your loss. Please sit over there."

Defeated, Jan returned to her chair.

CHAPTER EIGHT

A flush creeping up the back of her neck, Lacey tugged her towel tighter and toggled through all the cameras again. Constable Markov said nothing out loud, merely watched past her shoulder. But in her mind, he was thinking everything she'd be thinking — and possibly saying — about a slacker who let a camera go to hell on a security system for weeks without noticing. Worse, she'd left Chad unsupervised, and he had, accidentally or on purpose, turned off more cameras, thereby missing vital footage of the pool area at the time Kitrin died. She flipped back to the camera covering the garage frontage and scrolled backward, pausing on one that showed half a person's head and one green-clad shoulder near the pool gate.

"See, the only person who passed there is a staffer. You can tell by the polo shirt. One of the outside staff, because of the ball cap." The wisps of visible neck hair looked brown or reddish, although it was hard to be sure with the shade of the garage over the staffer and everything beyond in bright sunlight.

Markov peered closer. "So this person could confirm whether Mrs. Matheson was in her chaise when they passed the pool gate, letting us narrow down time of death almost to the minute. Can you figure out where they went after this shot?"

Lacey skimmed through the other working cameras over the terraces, but none showed the staffer. She backed over to the garage camera and time-stamped a still of the head to print out for Markov. "They could have gone either into the house through the pool doors — no cameras indoors — or around outside the pool walls."

Markov scratched his head. "I don't like that the only working camera there was off-line while Chad must have been talking to her. Is there any connection between them, that you know of?"

Lacey shook her head. Chad had absolutely no excuse for turning off cameras or for chatting up a house guest. She'd have to report him to Wayne now. "I'll stay here and log every person who was caught on other cameras in this area for half an hour either side of the approximate time of death."

Markov shook his head. "Do nothing until the homicide squad comes to supervise. Chain of evidence, you know. I should lock you out of here."

"Except then I won't be able to watch for your people arriving at the gate and instruct Travis who to let in. You know some sharp reporter will have monitored their police scanner, and there are only a half-dozen houses on this road. They just have to drive straight up to find out the incident is at this one."

"Yeah, I guess." He looked at the photo in his hand. "I'd better get on with the staff interviews."

Lacey glanced at the console clock. "You'll find most of them eating lunch in the staff dining room." She pointed it out on the estate map. "Ask Sergeant Drummond if he wants me here as a Victim Services volunteer for when the husband and son get back. I've met them both."

"Will do."

When Markov left, Lacey picked up the house phone and asked the cook to send sandwiches to the security room and the gate. It could be a long afternoon. Then she started a past-twenty-four-hours backup running to the remote server Wayne kept in his city office. The air conditioning kicked in, reminding her she was still wet and now chilled. What a day to be without her gym bag. She clutched her phone in wrinkled white fingers, thankful it had been in her tool belt on the tiles instead of in her pocket in the pool, and texted Dee. *Can you run a change of clothes up to Jake's? Undies and all. You'll have to leave them at the gate. I'll tell you everything when I get home.*

In the end, Lacey combined the roles of witness and Victim Services volunteer for Jan. Once the homicide team from Calgary released them, she drove Jan's van home. As they pulled up outside the Brenners' front door, she flashed back to the first day they'd met, over a year ago at the art museum. She'd driven Jan home that day, too, in a similar state of collapse. This time she knew a lot more about Jan's illness and had a better idea how badly the stress and shock could affect that flaky brain wiring.

"Stay in your seat," she told Jan. "I'll unlock the door and get you inside." Jan sat limp, eyes closed, while Lacey set up the portable wheelchair from the back of the van. "Sunroom or straight into bed?"

Jan frowned, as if even that small decision was painful. "Living room couch."

Lacey put her there, lifted her feet to slide a cushion under them, and draped an afghan over the whole. "I'll make you some tea, unless you want a cool drink."

"Rehydration drink in the fridge. Yellow pitcher."

The yellow pitcher was labelled in permanent marker, *Jan's goop*. Lacey poured out a large glass and carried it, already condensing around her fingers, into the next room. "You get that into you. I'll call Terry."

"No, don't. It's whitewater rescue training today. They need everyone." Jan tipped her head up and sipped the cold drink.

"Then I'd better make you food before I leave. Soup?"

"Rob's coming up soon."

"You're sure?"

Jan shivered and set the glass aside. "Yeah, he invited himself for supper. Wanted me to invite Michael, too, but he was going with Mylo to Tyrone's ranch and didn't know when he'd be back."

"Rob's playing with kids? That's new."

"Uh-huh." Jan shut her eyes again. Tears seeped from the corners. "Poor Michael. I wish they'd come back while we were there. He'll be all alone except for Mylo, who is probably useless with emotional support."

"Where's his nanny? Georgie?"

"I thought she went with them. She always wants to be near Mylo." Jan sniffed. "Poor Kitrin. If you could have seen her face when Michael said his nanny had gone off to a meeting with Daddy.... I'm pretty sure she thought they were having an affair. It would be on form for Mylo."

Well, that was interesting, especially when added to Lacey's glimpse of Mylo and Georgie on camera yesterday. The nanny had better have been somewhere with witnesses. The police hadn't yet ruled out homicide, and they'd look really hard at Mylo's lover's whereabouts while his wife had a fatal accident. Probably more so since Mylo was in a helicopter with the pilot and his own son at the time, and thus cleared of personal involvement in a potential domestic killing. "I'll head out. Call if you need anything, and I'll come right back up."

"Thanks so much. You've gotten really good at taking care of me."

Lacey smiled. "Spinoff benefit from a year of Dee's recovery. Get some rest."

It wasn't quite a three-minute walk down the road and up Dee's driveway. When Lacey opened the mud room door, Dee called out from her office. "What the actual was going on up there? I saw half a dozen police vehicles from the gate, but the guy I gave your clothes to wouldn't say a word."

Lacey slumped into the spare armchair and propped her feet on a tapestried footstool. There was no sense keeping it quiet. Someone had died on her second day as a security team supervisor, and there was no record because she had stupidly left unreliable Chad to his brother's supervision. "Kitrin Devine was found dead in the swimming pool."

Dee gasped. "By you?"

"Worse. By Jan." Lacey rubbed at an incipient headache above her eyes. "She saw Kitrin floating face down and jumped in to rescue her. I heard her yelling and pulled them both out. Too late for Kitrin." She summarized the past few hours and dissuaded Dee from going up to comfort Jan immediately. Then she sat down with a glass of iced tea on the shady back terrace. Time to bring Wayne up to speed.

"We can't keep Chad after this," she said once she'd described the drowning and the camera situation. "It's beyond incompetent to have shut down three security cameras so he could chat up the celebrity house guest. For all we know he was hitting on her and dumped her in the pool when she turned him down."

"You think he's an incel?" Wayne asked. "He didn't strike me that way."

Lacey considered. "No, maybe not. He was strictly professional when I briefly worked with him in Vancouver. But that beating and its long recovery could have left nasty psychological trauma. If he did hurt her, it would be an impulse attack. I saw him coming out of Kitrin's suite minutes earlier, and he wasn't more than ordinarily nervous then at being caught where he shouldn't be."

Wayne made that growling noise she associated with his most annoyed mood. "Turning off cameras, invading guest quarters, making contact with Jake's guests … none of it looks good. I'll come out tonight and deal with him after I reassure Jake that there's no murderer on his estate, lurking to kill someone else. There'll be reporters once the news breaks. Can you spell off gate shifts over supper until reinforcements arrive?"

"Glad to. I'll eat now and be back there in an hour." Wayne hung up, presumably to start calling his contacts for more temporary security people, and Lacey sat a while longer, soothed by the wind shushing through the spruces. Wayne didn't blame her for Chad. Her job seemed safe. She could leave Kitrin's death for the active-duty RCMP to handle. It was probably exactly what it seemed: accidental drowning of a woman too frail to be left unsupervised. But she would mention to investigators that she'd spotted Mylo and Georgie in a heavy make-out session, just in case it wasn't.

The sun fell behind the western peaks before Lacey got home again. She was hot, tired, and cranky, as well as stuck with Chad for now. Wayne simply couldn't find a replacement he trusted more on short notice. She was self-aware enough to know her foul mood was partly from that and from being surrounded by male RCMP officers all evening. Men who walked and talked like Dan, who wore the same uniform. And here she'd thought Earl Caine was triggering. Constable Markov had been released when the Major Crimes squad took over, leaving all unfamiliar officers rather than those she knew from the Cochrane detachment. The squad had photographed every inch of the waterfall area, grilled everyone possible about the boys' rock-throwing incident, and taken over the security office to make their own copy of all the camera footage. They'd interviewed every staff member on the grounds that morning, too, but none would admit to being nearby at the critical moment. Were they afraid of being charged with negligence — or merely fired by Jake — for not keeping an eye on Kitrin in the pool? Would Mylo, being a litigious American, try to sue Jake or someone else who might have saved his wife? She made the rounds of the house, doing her usual nighttime check, and wondered what news the morning would bring.

She woke in the dawn to buzzing and grabbed her phone before it shook itself right off the nightstand. "McCrae."

It was Wayne. "Can you be ready to head up to Jake's with me in half an hour? We're cleared to repair those cameras. And I need to talk to you about something that might become quite urgent."

"Now you've got my attention," said Lacey as she steered her tired body toward the bathroom. "About Kitrin's death?"

"No. Do you still keep a bug-out bag packed?"

That was new. "No, but I can have one ready by the time you get here."

"Do it," said Wayne.

With five minutes to spare, she waited for Wayne on the deck between the garage and the house with her steel coffee mug filled and her backpack at her feet. Above her, the pale morning sky was streaked with high, thin clouds. Another hot day ahead. Watched by the two sleepy dogs flopped over in their shady pen, she pulled the hose from its reel and watered all the flower baskets hanging from the pergola. For good measure, she rinsed and refilled the dogs' water trough and their splash pool. Wayne's truck turned into the drive as she stowed the hose. She climbed into the truck with her gear.

"All right. My bag's packed. What's up?"

Wayne headed down the drive. "Might be nothing. We'll know more by the time we're done with those cameras. You may have to take my truck up to Orrin Caine's ranch. But you can't say anything to anyone about this." At the road he swung hard right toward Jake's hilltop.

"I'll go, but what can't I tell anyone?"

"After Mylo Matheson and his son left the ranch yesterday afternoon, Orrin took his youngest boy, Tyrone, for a drive. They didn't say where they were going and didn't return last night. No answer from their cellphones. Could be as simple as a flat tire stranding them outside cell range, but the ranch hands went out on horseback and ATVs to check all the usual places and didn't find them. Search and Rescue is staging this morning, and the RCMP is going house to house looking for anyone who might have seen Orrin's old Rover on the surrounding roads."

"What do they need a security person on site for?"

"Ostensibly, you'll brief their staff on repelling reporters without getting charged for assault, and hang around to monitor cameras, etc. The news isn't out yet, but it will be if he's not found today."

"That's bigger news than the death of a Hollywood director's wife?"

Wayne rolled an eye in her direction. "A drowned stranger against the disappearance of a king of the oil patch? Do you have any idea how many individuals and businesses will be in turmoil if there's a sudden power shift at the top of Caine International?"

"I'll have to take your word for that. Less ostensibly, what am I going there for?"

Wayne pulled up at Jake's gate and tapped his horn. Travis climbed out of a truck parked just inside and opened up for him. As Wayne drove through, he said, "This is the part you keep under your hat. Orrin asked me on Friday to start a rush investigation that could have nasty implications for his family. You've met most of them. There's a lot of resentment, and it's possible one of them wanted him unavailable, or even dead, this weekend. You need to quietly find out whether that's likely, and if so, which of them is behind it."

The truck stopped at the stables, and Lacey unbuckled her seat belt. Another chance to prove herself competent. She wouldn't blow this one. "I'll give it my best shot."

CHAPTER NINE

Jan's bedroom door opened, flooding the room with light that spilled around the edges of her sleep mask. She crooked her arm over her eyes and groaned. "What?"

Terry said softly, "Sorry, but Mylo's phoned three times already. This time he says it's urgent. It's about Michael."

She pushed her mask up, blinking in the light, and reached for the phone. "Hi, Mylo? What's wrong?"

"Jan," said the voice on the other end in a caressing tone she'd last heard him use on Sloane Caine. "I'm so sorry to disturb you. Yesterday was awful for you as well as us. I wouldn't do it if this weren't an emergency. For my son."

"Michael? Is he hurt?"

"Physically, he's fine. But as you can imagine, it's been a pretty awful time since we got back yesterday." Mylo heaved a sigh that stopped just short of theatrical. "He told me you invited him to play video games this weekend. Could you still manage that?"

"Today?" Jan struggled upright. "You want him and Georgie to spend the day here?"

"Just him." Mylo paused. "Georgie is being questioned by the police about her movements yesterday."

Jan sat stone still. "Do they think Kitrin's death was suspicious?"

"If you could manage ..." Mylo said, evading her question.

Part of her wanted to toss the phone and put her head under the pillow, but it wouldn't help. The inside of her forehead was showing the same old video: Kitrin lying drenched on the chaise, water pooling around her head, faintly tinged with pink. If the police were still all over the house and pool, poor Michael would be even more traumatized.

"Of course he can come here for the day. Should I send someone up to get him?"

"I'll bring him down myself. I have some things I need to tell you."

Jan was in the kitchen, sorting out her pills for the morning, when one of Jake's orange convertibles spun into the turnaround. "Terry, they're here. Let them in, please." In a moment he was back with Mylo and Michael. She crouched beside the boy and put out her arms. "Honey, I'm so sorry about your mother."

Michael let him hug her, but he didn't return the pressure, just leaned against her. After a moment she let him go. "Terry will show you our video games, and Rob from the museum will be here soon. You know he's determined to beat you at that alligator game." Michael nodded listlessly and went off with Terry. Jan got back on her chair. "Do you want coffee or anything, Mylo?"

He shook his head and wandered around the island, looking out each window in turn. "Nice little place you have here. Panoramic."

"You should see the view from the sunroom. You had something to tell me?"

Mylo pulled out a chair across from hers. He leaned his elbows on the table and stared at his hands. After a bit he said, "I didn't answer you on the phone because Michael came in then. But yes, the police think my wife was killed." He lifted his fingers and let them drop helplessly. "She has bruises on her arms, and they think someone held her under the water. This should be a movie script. This doesn't happen in real life." He looked so broken that Jan almost believed he loved his wife. Almost. With the image of Georgie in mind, she resisted the urge to reach out a comforting hand.

"The police should talk to Lacey McCrae. She hauled Kitrin out of the swim machine the other day. That would leave bruises, too."

"That wouldn't crack her skull." Mylo didn't take his eyes off his hands. "They seem to think someone hit her with a rock from the waterfall. Who but us knew they were loose?"

Jan shivered. "I turned my foot on a rock when I was trying to pull her out. I thought the boys missed one the other night."

"We all thought of the boys. Jake even asked me if Michael might have thrown one, playing, you know, and then was scared to tell us because of … what happened. But we were already gone, halfway to the Caine ranch.

When I finally heard, I didn't know how to tell Michael why we had to come back early."

"He was playing with Tyrone?"

"Yes. I was way out in Orrin's back forty or whatever they call it up here, out of cellphone range. They had to send someone out to find us. Then we had to drive back along this perfectly straight line cut through the forest."

"A seismic line," said Jan, "where the oil companies surveyed the ground underneath, looking for reservoirs."

"We'd never want to film on those lines. Too manmade." The first sign of animation lit Mylo's face. "The scenery is as spectacular as Orrin promised. My film came to life before my eyes. I'll have crews up here doing background by next week."

"You're going to keep working? What about Kitrin's funeral or memorial service?"

"The police won't release her body for several days yet. I don't know what all they have to do, but it's going to be really grim for Michael. You're one of Kitrin's oldest friends. Can you please get him away from that place as much as possible during the days? He's used to behaving on film sets, so he won't be a bother if you take him along while you're hunting art for me."

"You think Georgie will be arrested? Or you don't trust her with Michael anymore?" Jan hardly bothered suppressing her irritation. If Georgie had killed Kitrin, she'd almost certainly done it because of this selfish man who thought of nothing but his movies and his own gratification.

Mylo only shrugged.

"Fine," said Jan. "I can have him here today, and tomorrow, too, if need be. Surely Kitrin's mother and father will be here soon?"

"Unlikely. If they do dare show up, you can't let them be alone with Michael." Mylo pushed back his chair and stood up. "Promise me."

"If you say so. But why?"

"Kitrin probably didn't tell you, but her mother tried to get custody of Michael last year. When Kitrin was hospitalized last time, I sent him up to Regina while I was on location in Spain. That bitch didn't want to give him back afterward. I had to threaten her with arrest for cross-border kidnapping."

"Wow. Kitrin didn't tell me. We only had a few minutes together the other night. She was going to come down with Michael today." Tears stung Jan's sleep-weary eyes. She blinked. "Okay, I'll keep Michael with me, and if Kitrin's mother shows up, I'll get hold of you right away. I don't have the authority to keep her from seeing him, though. She's a relative and I'm not."

The sound of a car pulled her gaze to the kitchen window. Reinforcements, in the shape of Rob, had arrived. She got to her feet. "Is it all right if I tell Rob about Kitrin's mom? He'll want to look out for Michael, too. I'm sure he'll take him down to the museum for an afternoon again."

"If you must." Mylo flicked a business card onto the island and stalked from the room. A moment later, Rob walked in. He glared out the window, where Mylo could be seen climbing back into the orange Beamer. "I take it Michael is here already. What's with that ass, dumping off the boy the day after his mother died?"

Jan went to him. "Hug me, please. I'm so afraid for that child. The police think someone killed Kitrin. And Michael's grandmother might be coming to kidnap him. It's all so horrible."

CHAPTER TEN

The call Wayne was waiting for came before noon. They'd finished camera repairs and made a full circuit, testing locks and keypads at every entrance to the grounds. He listened for a few minutes and said, "I'm sending a rep up to brief your staff about keeping the media out. Can you give her a bed while the search continues?"

Lacey was going to the ranch.

Twenty minutes later, she left Jake's place in Wayne's bulky truck, lifting a hand at Travis in passing. She wasn't altogether sorry to be assigned elsewhere for a few days. Eventually, he'd invite her for lunch or coffee, and she'd have to make it plain she wasn't interested. Who knew how he'd take that? Who knew how any man took rejection until it was done? That brought her back to Chad. Had he turned off the cameras to hide a pass at Kitrin? Hey, what if he'd snatched a green polo shirt from the garage? It might be him visible on the edge of the garage camera. Or not. She'd have noticed if he wasn't wearing his Wayne-blue T-shirt when she caught him at Kitrin's suite. And his shoulders were too wide. The one shoulder in that tagged image was sloping and nowhere near as muscular. Which left one of Jake's staff lying to the RCMP, for reasons that might have everything or nothing to do with Kitrin's death. She'd suggest that Wayne recheck the summer staff's references in case one of them had a reason for avoiding police interviews.

"Not your investigation, McCrae," she muttered out loud as she crossed the bridge into Bragg Creek. Lunch would be a takeout burger from the bistro, eaten while she headed north. Hopefully Wayne's air conditioner was fully charged. Late summer in the Ghost Wilderness would be baking hot and dry, a far cry from the bone-chilling cold and snow she'd experienced up there last Christmas.

An hour later, she was deep in the woods, well past the Black Rock Bowl turnoff, when she rounded a bend and saw a rusty brown half-ton truck angled across her lane. She braked hard. The dust from her tires swirled past as she opened her door to investigate. When it drifted away, she saw the truck's right front wheel had dropped into a narrow drainage ditch. A scrawny individual in a shabby jean jacket and weathered cowboy hat was prodding at the front fender with a length of wooden fence post.

Lacey hurried over. "Can I help?"

The person turned a lined, tanned face to hers and demanded, in the voice of a cantankerous old woman, "Who're you, missy? Another of them Search and Rescue bunch? Orrin's a damned fool, causing all this fuss."

So the word about the missing Caines had spread. Well, it wasn't Lacey's job to add to the rumour mill. "I'm just passing through. If you stand on your back bumper, at the highest point, that might shift the weight enough for me to get this log under the axle."

The old woman muttered something that sounded like "bossy," but she went. Once she was on the bumper, holding on to the tailgate, Lacey pushed the post as far under the frame as she could. Using the ditch's rocky rim for leverage, she hung her weight off the other end of the pole. The truck rocked before settling its high rear wheel back onto the gravel. Another shove put the fence post securely under the wheel. She grabbed another post from the truck's bed and added it beside the first, making a ramp.

"Step off," she called. The truck settled slightly, but the posts held. "You should be able to back out now."

The woman got behind the wheel. It took a good shove from Lacey at the front fender, but the truck got its dropped wheel back onto the road. She hauled up the muddy fence posts, returned them to the half-ton's box, and walked around to the driver's window.

"Thanks," muttered the old woman. "I don't like folks, but you're kinda handy."

Amused by the faint praise, Lacey replied, "I don't like many people, either, but you seem pretty tough."

As the old woman put her truck into gear, she said, "Searchers could use you. Ghost airstrip is their base camp, five miles up on your left."

While she sat waiting for the old woman's dust to die down, Lacey took a minute to check her phone. There was a message from Jan. *Having a bad day. Any chance you could come visit? Need to talk to you about Kitrin. Terry is gone on an SAR call. Again.*

Poor Jan. She'd seemed so healthy lately that it was easy to forget how trapped she still was by her malfunctioning body, unable to leave home or do much to distract herself just when she most needed distraction. She sent back: *On business for Wayne today, not sure when I'll be free. Dee is home & would come. What about Kitrin?*

While waiting for a reply, she drove on. The short road leading into the airstrip was clogged with vehicles. Others were parked on both sides of the road. Amid the constant mosquito buzz of small planes, a helicopter rose above the trees. She found a parking spot behind the last roadside vehicle and walked the rest, passing Terry's red truck along the way. She spotted Constable Markov first, on his phone and unavailable to give her a search update. Beyond him, Terry was bent over a box of radios. As she approached, he set down the last radio and yelled to a woman who was coiling a rope over her shoulder, "These are tested."

He saw Lacey. "Hey, are you joining the search?"

"Not right now. I'm on my way to the ranch. How's it going?"

"I'll show you." Terry led the way to the command unit, a big RV with a satellite dish on top. Outside it, under an awning, were tables with detailed maps of the area spread out and weighted down. "We have no information about where Orrin Caine was heading, which makes targeting the search difficult. Fortunately, his company promised fuel for any small plane that signed on for aerial survey. Some of the pilots are company men, too."

Lacey scanned the maps. They covered all the rocky, wooded, gully-slashed, and clear-cut terrain between the prairies and the mountain front, starting in the south at the white gravel banks of the Ghost River and running many kilometres north to the murky dark line of the Red Deer River.

She flapped her hand at the nearest chart. "That's gotta be fifty by a hundred square kilometres. Where do you even start?"

"At the ranch, of course. Security cameras showed his Range Rover turning north out the front gate at three twenty-five p.m. yesterday." His finger tapped on the stretch of Highway 40 north of the airstrip. "That's the last anyone knows. The family didn't worry about it until he wasn't home at his son's usual bedtime. By then it was dark. They searched some first, and called the RCMP in the wee hours."

Lacey looked closer at the map. Going north, Orrin would run into the Red River eventually. But he could've gone east or west at several points before then. "These clusters of lines on the map. Are they all roads?"

"Roads, four-wheel-drive tracks, off-road vehicle trails, seismic cutlines, hiking paths, everything down to animal tracks." Terry shook his head. "Needles and haystacks. Making it worse, his Range Rover is dark green, deliberately chosen to blend in with the bush when he went hunting. Before you ask, he didn't take any guns. At least we're not looking for a firearm accident."

No. Just a boy alone with an old man and plenty of wolves, cougars, and grizzlies. What a time to leave all the guns at home. Speaking of which …

"Did you leave Jan home alone? She's taking Kitrin's death hard."

"Rob's staying over. They have Michael, Kitrin's son, for the day. The nanny is being questioned, apparently, and Mylo doesn't want Michael to see that."

"I guess that's what Jan wanted to talk to me about. I hope she's okay."

"She takes shocks hard." Terry chewed his lip. "Just needs rest and quiet. Look, my team's heading out soon. I'll be out of cell range so I can't update you, but any news will be phoned through from here to the ranch right away. Earl's appointed himself liaison."

Lacey's neck tightened reflexively. Of course Earl would assume command. He was a control freak, like Dan, and would probably take over the whole company if Orrin didn't return. She pointed to the map. "I thought you said Orrin went north. Why are these teams marked in the southwest?"

"He turned north, sure, but there are lots of trails he could take that lead west and then back south. The family says he likes to circle his vast territory and gloat over it." He gave her a sideways glance. "'Gloat' being my word for it. You've met him."

"Yeah. Gloating he'd do." Lacey drew a wide circle with her finger around the dot that marked the ranch. "So he could be anywhere in this whole area, from Water Valley or Sundre all the way to the mountains? I flew over that territory last week. If the truck's not in a clearcut, it'll be invisible from the air."

"Pretty much," said Terry. "I'm not holding out much hope for a fast resolution unless the house-to-house survey turns up someone who saw him going in a particular direction. I just hope they have food and a water purifier kit."

"They won't freeze, that's one good thing." Lacey'd had enough of frozen bodies last winter.

Nodding goodbye, she headed back to Wayne's truck. Given that vast, wild search area, she'd be using every item of clean clothing in her knapsack before Orrin and his son came home. If they came home.

CHAPTER ELEVEN

At the rear of an SUV parked outside the ranch's main gate, a pair of women in reflective vests eyed maps spread on a fold-out table. SAR, Lacey deduced, rather than reporters. With luck, the news about the search wouldn't identify the two missing persons today, giving her time to organize Orrin's outdoor staff. A herd of cowboys couldn't be any worse to wrangle than the sometimes surly constables she'd supervised in Surrey. She turned in at the open gate, got out, and closed it behind her. Any others leading to public roads must be closed ASAP and guards posted to check visitor ID. She drove on.

The winding drive through the firs opened to a wide green lawn and looped in front of a huge house made of red logs. The roofline's many redwood peaks echoed the not-too-distant mountains, now cool and shadowy against the late afternoon sun. She pulled up between a wide portico and a massive wood carving of rearing bears. The driveway meandered toward a long building set with half-a-dozen garage doors. As she pondered whether to knock at the house or seek a staff person at the garage, a man in faded jeans and T-shirt came from a side door in the log mansion. She got out of the truck.

"Hi," she said. For an instant she thought he was Bart Caine, but he showed no sign of recognition. After lifting her sunglasses for a better look, she started over. "I'm Lacey McCrae, the security rep, here to train the outdoor staff to legally evict trespassing reporters."

"Ah." The man smiled, his resemblance to Bart growing. "I'm Ben, and by the way you're gaping, I guess you've met my twin, Bart."

"Oh." Lacey grinned back. "Yes, I had the pleasure, down at Jake Wyman's last week."

"Right then, security person. Park by the garage and I'll introduce you to Ike, our foreman."

"I'd better see the rest of the family first," said Lacey, "so they don't freak out at a stranger wandering around." And to evaluate whether any of them looked a little too relieved that their domineering patriarch hadn't come home.

"Whatever you want. Park over here." He loped toward the garage. She followed in the truck, wondering if he'd suggest somewhere she could go jogging out here in the wilderness. Along the dusty gravel roads? Or maybe there was a path through the forest. It wouldn't do to get slack now that she was finally close to fighting fit again.

Pulling up where he waited, she left her backpack behind and locked up. There was no sense hauling gear until she knew where she'd be sleeping. If she'd even be staying over. Orrin and his son might come stumbling out onto a logging road any minute now. She crossed her fingers for that happy outcome and strolled beside Ben back to the door he'd appeared from. He held it open for her to enter a dim mud room and tugged a wedge out of the hinge, letting the panel close behind him.

"To your left," he said and led her along a varnished wood corridor lined with oil portraits. She recognized, in passing, Orrin, Sloane, Earl, a twin, and Tyrone. A cluster of framed photos showed Earl with his blond wife and daughters, Bart and Andrea, and Tyrone with Orrin and Sloane. Ushered into a huge, hexagonal room, she counted heads. All the family members she had met at supper were spread around the space: Sloane sobbing in an armchair near one fireplace, with an unfamiliar woman hovering over her; Andy and Bart side by side on a leather sofa, their knees touching; Earl pacing and yelling into his phone. He hurried over. His fist, the one not clutching his phone, tightened like he wanted to punch someone. Her?

"Who let you in? Why wasn't I informed?"

Ben said, "I saw her truck from a window. It might have been someone bringing news, so I went out to meet her."

Earl gave his brother a glare that sent a chill up Lacey's spine. As he transferred the look to her, she saw the resemblance to his father. And to Dan. Holding her ground with an effort she hoped was invisible to him, she held out her hand.

"Lacey McCrae. We met at Jake Wyman's the other evening. Wayne sent me to brief your outdoor staff."

He unclenched his fingers and forced a smile. "Welcome, Lacey. Wayne said someone was coming. I've set you up with a security fob that will allow you access to the buildings, and I assume you have passwords for the cameras and related equipment." He handed her a black plastic fob on a stretchy band.

She slipped it over her wrist. "Thank you."

Andy waved. "Lacey, hi."

Lacey crouched in front of the sofa. "I'm so sorry about Tyrone and Orrin. You must all be very worried."

"Not as much as you might expect. Or not yet. Orrin's always taken his boys out hunting or hiking or riding on the land. This is far from the first time he's been gone overnight. Just — not without telling anyone when to expect him back. And Ty's mom, well …" Andy raised her voice. "Sloane, here's Lacey. She's going to coordinate security so you aren't bothered by reporters on top of everything else."

Sloane looked up with a wan smile. Her cheeks were streaked, her eyes puffy, and her nose red. She might not be upset at the absence of her arrogant old husband, but her only son was out there with him. No wonder she was freaking out.

Lacey said, "I just came from the SAR base down at the airstrip. They're very well organized, and every small plane available is flying grid searches. There's sure to be some news soon."

Sloane nodded and dabbed at her eyes. The woman with her, a bit older and sporting dark, short hair, put a hand on her shoulder.

Bart leaned toward Lacey. "That's Sloane's assistant, Cheryl. They were friends before Sloane married, and she came up here soon after to keep Sloane company while Orrin was away on business. Cheryl manages the houses, and she's almost a second mother to Ty. Although you wouldn't know it to look at her, she's about as worried as Sloane is."

"No idea where Orrin was taking Ty?"

Andy shook her head. "We thought they were going to Water Valley for ice cream to make up for cutting short Michael's visit. It's a hellacious road but only a half-hour drive the way Orrin tackles it. They weren't at supper, but everyone figured they'd decided to grab a burger, as well, maybe come home by a different route." She smiled. "Michael's a great kid. He fitted in like he was born here. We were teaching him to climb on the wall when his father came and said they had to leave immediately. Have you heard how Michael's holding up? I was so worried about his mother — she looked so fragile — but I had no idea she'd already damaged her heart to that extent. It can happen with eating disorders."

"You think she had a heart attack in the pool?" Maybe it really was that simple: Kitrin's heart, weakened by self-imposed starvation, had spasmed or whatever, causing her to tip her chair, hit her head, and drown.

"It could have happened to me." Andy looked at her hands.

Bart gave them a squeeze. "Is someone looking out for Michael?" he asked.

"He's at Jan's today. She and Rob, who was Kitrin's other university roommate, are keeping him away from the police investigation as much as possible. If someone could introduce me to Ike, the foreman, I'd better get to work."

Ben said, "I'll take you around. She's sleeping at your place, right, Andy?"

Andy nodded. "I'll find you later, Lacey, if you don't find me first."

Ben led Lacey to a set of French doors. As they stepped through, she got her first real view of the ranch. Behind the house was a vast, stone-paved terrace, beyond which the land dropped sharply away to a broad, grassy valley filled with dusty brown cattle. Another treed ridge rose in the middle distance, with a gravel road running diagonally up it. Was this the whole ranch? It wouldn't have taken long to search, even in the middle of the night.

Ben crossed the terrace to a low stone parapet. "This valley and the next two going west are ours: all cattle and forest, no wells or cutlines. We run south almost to the airstrip and north halfway to the Red Deer River. We've got a block on the east side of Highway 40, too." His voice hardened. "Orrin drilled it as soon as he bought it."

"You disapprove of him drilling, even though the family money comes from oil?"

He waved a hand. "Do you see a single clear-cut over here, or a well site? None of that visual pollution in Orrin's panorama. He did all that where other people had no choice but to see it. Across the highway he destroyed hundreds of hectares of irreplaceable watershed, and for what? A few trucks of logs and a few more barrels of oil." His words came faster, his gestures sharper. "And he lied to get that land. It was supposed to go into a nature conservancy, to come to me and Bart eventually for ongoing protection. That's what he promised the owner, and us. He had the seismic crews in there before his signature was dry." His clenched jaw added to the picture of deep anger at his father.

One suspect for the mental notebook, assuming this whole mess was not Orrin simply being too arrogant to phone home. Then there was whatever confidential matter Wayne was looking into for him. Was it infidelity? Could Orrin have taken Tyrone away to punish Sloane, or to ensure he kept custody when he divorced her? She made a note to see if Wayne had someone checking in Calgary for the missing pair.

Ben took a deep breath and seemed to shake off his anger. "Bart and I rode all this area at first light, in case tire tracks were missed during the night. Wherever Orrin went, it's not likely west of here. Now, the layout. If you look along this ridge to the south, you can sort of see the cabins. We each get one when we marry, for summers with our theoretically growing families. Earl's is first, a hand-me-down from Orrin when he built the new place for Sloane. Earl has bedrooms and bathrooms enough to satisfy his wife and four daughters, plus assorted guests. Past it is Bart's place, a shack in comparison: only four bedrooms and three baths."

Lacey made out roof peaks through the forest. Gravelled paths led toward them, and a wooden staircase descended the bluff to the working ranch below. "You don't have a cabin?"

"Not married. And if I was, Orrin wouldn't give me a two-by-four to build it with. Not as things stand now."

"What did you do to upset him?" She almost added, "Talk back?" but figured that was one personal question too far.

He gave her a wry grin. "I'm an environmentalist. Next to damned commies and faggots, there's no lower form of life."

She eyed him curiously. Sooner or later, she must discover whether Orrin despised his son only in a general sense, or if they'd had a particular quarrel. There was no immediate benefit in alienating her guide with probing questions, though.

"What's along this cliff in the other direction?"

"The garage, and where it slants down over the edge, that's our climbing centre. When we were kids, it was all natural rock and open to the sky. We went up it like lizards, not bothering with ropes or gear. After Ty broke his arm following Earl up — he was five at the time — Orrin had it roofed over, and someone came out from Calgary to build proper climbing walls. Guy named Matt, used to own the Stronghold, where Bart and I had climbing lessons. The natural rock's still in there, but now there's gear on it, too."

"Andrea said they'd been teaching Ty's friend Michael to climb?"

"Yeah, there's a good beginner wall. It was kind of overkill to connect the climbing gym up with both this upper garage and that big machine shed down below. But then overkill is Orrin's signature style. And the elevator comes in handy sometimes."

The aluminum-sided machine shed was the largest of several buildings along the valley floor. On its right stood a stable that could house a cavalry regiment, then an old wooden barn and a few open-sided sheds filled with hay. Beyond them all was a long, low building with tan siding, almost invisible against the dusty golden grasses. That was the bunkhouse, Ben told her, where the ranch hands lived. A dirt road followed the line of buildings, intersecting with wooden fences and metal chutes that were doubtless important for managing livestock. It crossed the valley floor and climbed the far ridge at a slant. Surely the ranch hands, and the twins, had checked in that direction for the missing pair.

"Was it unusual for your father to leave without telling anyone where he was going?"

"Absolutely not. He's a law unto himself."

"Could something have gone wrong with his vehicle?"

"Unlikely," Ben said. "It lives in the fleet garage with the rest and has a regular maintenance schedule. It's weird he took that one if he was headed for Water Valley, though. He's the only one who's ever driven it, but it's pretty beat up from bouncing along cutlines and river bottoms. For anything town-ish, where other people would see, he'd normally take his brand-new Rover Discovery, with the air conditioning and shit. It's so shiny, you'd see it through the deepest bush. But maybe he was going to teach Ty to drive and didn't want to risk his new one."

"At barely twelve years old?"

"In Orrin's book, twelve is the official start of manhood. Ty already runs around on quads and dirt bikes. We all did that, although I think we were fourteen before we got to drive the trucks." Ben shook his head. "The gullies off some of these back roads are sheer drops, like twenty metres or more into rocky creek beds. If Ty was driving, and they went into one ..." His jaw tensed. "Well, maybe they'll wash out again in the spring floods, because we won't spot them otherwise. Come on. Ike should have everyone gathered in the staff common room by now."

Following him toward the garage, Lacey added up the security issues she had to cover: nine buildings, an unknown number of gates, and several kilometres of split rail fencing. Every gate should have a guard, as well as camera coverage. And the number-one security issue on Wayne's mind: which of Orrin's family members wanted the foul old man dead enough to help him along? Was Ben's anger the kind to sabotage the vehicle only his father drove? If she had nothing concrete by tomorrow, would Wayne help her out by telling her what he was investigating for Orrin?

"Don't you believe they'll be found safe?" she asked.

"I don't know what to hope for." He trudged on, shoulders hunched, his hands in his jean pockets. "If Orrin's alive, nothing changes. Unless he got Ty hurt. Then Sloane will shoot him where he stands."

Lacey mentally added questions beside Sloane's name: *Did she sign a pre-nup, and what does she inherit if Orrin dies?* Not that a bad pre-nup would matter if her son, Orrin's clear favourite, survived to inherit the majority of assets. "You say Sloane is very attached to her son, yet she didn't raise the roof when he wasn't home by bedtime?" That might have sounded judgmental, but the words were out now.

Ben shrugged. "Ty's not a little kid anymore who has to be put to bed while it's still light outside. And

I'm not even sure if she was home. She goes places with Cheryl."

"You weren't here last night, either?"

He shook his head. "Andy's house in Calgary. We drove out together when Ike called to say Orrin hadn't come home."

Lacey watched him out of the corner of her eye. "Why do you call him 'Orrin' instead of 'Dad' or 'Father'?"

"Habit, I guess. Our mom always referred to him as 'Orrin.' Ty calls him 'Pops,' but we'd never have dared. To his face, we still call him 'sir.' Fob here, please." He opened the human-sized door into the two-storey garage. Across the corridor was the elevator he'd mentioned, and two other doors. One was a fire door with a staircase symbol, while the other had a slit window into the garage proper. He steered her along the corridor until glass panes on her left showed they were out past the bluff. "Look back at the cliff. You can see the cabins from here."

Lacey looked. Earl's house was about half the size of his father's, with two peaked wings bracketing a central core and a flagstone terrace looking over the valley. A glimpse of turquoise water suggested a swimming pool. Beyond it, the ridge sloped. On a lower ledge was a log house rather like Dee's. Cathedral windows reflected the sunlight angling nearer the mountaintops. Sunset would come, and another night with Orrin and Tyrone stranded — possibly — out in the wild.

"Where's this staff common room?"

"Down on the ranch hands' level, part of the machine shed. We'll take the elevator."

The common room had the impersonal atmosphere of a hotel lobby: comfy chairs, a couple of couches, a huge TV on one wall, a pair of tables and a kitchenette. A dozen or so men standing around the closest table all looked up at her, each wondering, no doubt, what a woman was doing here and how much she'd interfere in their manly efforts. She stiffened her spine and stared coolly back as if they were rookie constables and she their new corporal.

Ben stepped into the circle. "Ike," he said to a tall man at the end, "this is Wayne's representative. Lacey McCrae." Two men shuffled aside to let her join them at the table. Maps of the area were spread out, with the ranch's borders marked in thick brown marker. An eyeball estimate told her the area covered was several kilometres per side. Had they really searched it all?

"As Ben said, I'm Wayne's representative. I'm here partly as technical support for the security cameras, but also to run you through what you can and can't do to any reporters who come snooping out here once the news leaks that it's Orrin Caine who's missing." She looked around at all of them. About half met her eyes. "Which it will do by this evening if he's not found. Ike, I assume the land is properly posted: gates, fence corners, and in between? Those gates should all be shut immediately, and guarded. Wayne wants half-hourly patrols everywhere there's a road along the property. Do you have enough people for that? I can take a shift if needed."

"Yup," said the tall man. "Do you ride?"

"Yes." Honesty compelled Lacey to add, "I'm rusty."

"We'll leave it to folks familiar with the land. Now, you're supposed to teach us how to handle intruders? We can't just rough 'em up and toss 'em out?"

There was some general muttering. Lacey didn't need a translator. Ranchers preferred to punch first — or shoot — and ask questions later. Incidents appeared in the news often enough, and every RCMP officer who'd ever been posted to rural Alberta or Saskatchewan had a story in which a trespasser lay bleeding at the feet of an angry landowner.

She cleared her throat. "Regardless of what you might want to do, don't physically touch anyone you find inside the fencelines. If they're reporters, they'll start recording the instant they see you, and anything you do will not only be all over the internet an hour later, but also have to be answered for in court as to whether it seemed reasonable in the circumstances."

Ben interjected, "Reasonable to a city judge, not to our neighbours out here."

Lacey nodded. "You absolutely should not shoot, not even over their heads. That invites charges against you, and potential lawsuits against you and your employer both. Worse, you could end up with a human life on your conscience." About half the men were listening intently now. Good. "Patrol in pairs so you always have a witness, and if you do encounter someone inside the fencelines, your best bet is to get between them and their vehicle so they can't leave. Then call me right away, and I'll come out to deal with them."

Ike's lip curled. "And I suppose you let them off with a warning?"

Lacey shook her head. "I'm ex-RCMP, with years of experience handling trespassers. I'll offer them a choice: delete photos and other recorded data or be escorted to the nearest RCMP to face charges. Those would involve confiscating their equipment as evidence. This story isn't worth that much to them." Yet. If Orrin and his son weren't found soon, a media circus would be the least of the ranch's problems. "Seriously, if you don't want to spend a night in jail when you're most needed here, keep your hands off the reporters."

Ben added, "Listen to her, guys. Orrin might clap you on the back and put up your bail, but while he's gone, it's Earl who holds the chequebook."

Ike said, "Hear that, men? Hands off the reporters. Let this … Miz McCrae handle them. You radio me and I'll bring her right over."

She looked at the map again. "Are these distant gates covered by cameras?"

Ike shook his head. "No power that far out."

"I'll set up solar-powered camera rigs today."

Ike sent teams off to the various gates, then said to Lacey, "If I hire in some hands to spell off my men, can you give that speech again in the morning?" She nodded. He said, "Ben, you mind taking this lady out to the gates? Take a farm truck. Better clearance than her city half-ton."

"I'm on it," said Ben. "And put me on a gate for graveyard shift."

"Yes, sir," said Ike and began rolling up the maps.

When they were in the main machine shed, looking over a cupboard full of keys, Lacey's voice echoed around the big metal threshers and tractors. "Why did you remind them about Earl? It sure changed their attitude."

Ben selected a key ring. "The men all know what to expect if they cause Earl a problem he'll have to explain to Orrin."

"He'll fire them so blame won't fall on him?"

Ben laughed. "You've got us nailed, all right. We'll do anything to avoid Orrin's wrath. If it was up to us, we'd have waited another whole day to even consider calling the RCMP. But Sloane's more scared for Ty than of Orrin. Come on. We'll drive up and collect your camera gear from your truck."

She followed him to a jacked-up Jeep with immense knobbed tires. Its body was neon green, so bright it looked like a kid's toy on steroids. "We really need something this gnarly to reach a gate on a road?"

"No." He grinned. "But this is way more fun. Climb on up and strap yourself in."

Soon they were lurching at speed along a narrow downhill track. Lacey kept flinching as tree branches slapped her window. In the back, her equipment bounced and jostled. She spared a grateful thought for the padded cases all Wayne's new equipment travelled in and clutched her tool belt, with its fragile iPad, tighter in her arms. At last — although it was probably less than ten minutes — they burst out of the trees onto the open valley floor.

Ben gave a whoop. "Awesome, eh?"

Lacey's teeth were still rattling. She wiggled her jaw before saying, "Sure."

He wasn't fooled. "No fear, it's all road to the south gate now." The big Jeep ran remarkably smoothly once it was on the gravel. It stopped in a swirl of dust. "Okay, what do we need to unload from back here?"

He proved very helpful, following her with the gear and climbing the gate pole to secure the camera bracket around it. He balanced up there easily, leaning back against his harness like he had all the time in the world, while she checked the camera's angle on the iPad. He made a couple of adjustments at her request, and once she was satisfied with the camera's field of view and the strength of its Wi-Fi signal, he tightened the screws and easily backed down the pole. It wouldn't have surprised her to find that he could go up without bothering about the harness.

"Is it all road to the next gate, too?" she asked hopefully. He only grinned and climbed back into the Jeep.

They rigged the remaining cameras with no more difficulty than finding a good spot for the west gate's solar panel, where it would get sun most of the day. The shadow of the mountain would fall over it early in the evening, though. She should probably bring a second battery for this one to keep it working through the dark hours. Then it was another nerve-jangling race back to the machine shed.

Ben jumped down with a laugh. "See what I mean? Much more fun than driving a standard half-ton."

"Thanks for your help," she said. "I'd better get into the security room and check that all the other cameras are working."

"This way." He led her to a door at the back of the machine shop and waited with his hand on the knob while she flashed her fob at the keypad. Once again he held the door for her to step through. On the other side was another huge space, the air cool on her bare arms, with a roof that sloped upward. Skylights eased the gloom high above, and other lights came on with loud clicks as she took a few paces inside. The back wall was natural rock, with carabiners dangling from many cracks. The wooden walls to either side bulged irregularly and were dotted with brightly coloured handholds.

"Wow." She craned her neck to follow a taped climbing route all the way up.

"Yeah," he said. "It's every kid's dream. There's a workout room off to the left, with all the usual equipment, and this door leads back to the elevator." Again he held the door for her to pass through. The corridor beyond doubled as a cloakroom, with coats in various weights hanging from hooks, and bins full of work gloves, ball caps, toques, and other outdoor wear on shelves. A second door led back to the elevator lobby and the stairs. This time she noticed a door beyond those, leading to a path along the base of the bluff. It passed the bottom of the outside staircase and continued into a copse of scrawny aspens. "That's how you'd get to the cabins from here?"

"Uh-huh. But not today." He pointed to the elevator pad. "Get used to using your fob. You can't go anywhere without it."

She flashed her fob and the elevator doors opened. At the top he directed her to the main garage. The lights came up automatically as they entered, showing three cars, two SUVs, and an empty space at the far end.

"Security room is upstairs," he told her and turned to an open staircase up the near wall. "After you."

The heat rose as they climbed, turned at the corner, and went on up to an L-shaped hallway covered in utilitarian beige panelling and sturdy brown carpeting. The door on the short arm of the "L" read *Security*. Lacey looked around the corner to orient herself and saw a long passage with doors on both sides, ending in another fire door. "What are all these doors for?"

Ben pointed past her shoulder. "On the left, Cheryl's apartment, then the house staff's common room with their bedrooms and bath opening off it, then Ike's apartment. On the right is storage."

She checked her phone messages for Wayne's entry code and let herself into the security office. It was faintly dusty, as if used very little, and cooler than expected from the extra air conditioning needed to counter the computer equipment's heat.

"Thanks for showing me around," she told Ben.

He gave a quick glance over a trio of monitors that showed scenes around the house and grounds. "When you're done here, come back to the main house. Andy can take you to her place to unpack." He put his hand in his pocket and took it out again. "I didn't bring a fob. Can you let me into the house so I don't have to disturb anyone?"

She followed him across the baking lawn, flashing her fob at a pad as he reached for the door handle. Teamwork already. She'd once been in sync with Dan like that. As Ben entered the house, she turned away quickly, hiding a frown. He seemed decent enough, respected by the ranch hands, and undeniably eye candy, from the dark, wavy hair to the very firm ass in his faded jeans. Too bad he reminded her physically, if not psychologically, of Dan. And so far, he seemed the most likely son to have done his horrible father a mischief.

The garage's interior lights hadn't gone out by the time she collected her backpack and tool belt from Wayne's truck. While she refilled her water bottle at the garage sink, she spotted a staff contact list by the wall phone. She snapped a photo of it so she could call Ike or the kitchen as needed and climbed the stairs. Before settling into the security office, she scoped out the long hallway. It smelled stale, like any interior corridor that never got fully aired out. Doors on the left were all locked. At the far end was another staircase down to the garage and to the staff parking lot. On the right was an interconnected series of storerooms, half their doors open. Their shelves held everything from auto parts to Christmas decorations. She left them as she found them and retreated back to the office.

The security room seemed even dustier. Probably nobody came in here between Wayne's monthly maintenance checks. After opening the lone window, for all the good it would do with no cross-breeze, she started a scan of the old and new gate cameras. They were all closed and guarded by Ike's men. Good to know.

Her phone chimed. A text from Jan. *Sorry didn't get back to you. Michael was here. Rob just took him home. Any chance you can phone me when you get this?*

CHAPTER TWELVE

Jan had just gotten fully cocooned on the chaise when the phone rang. She stuck one hand out and slid the screen toward her. Lacey. She pushed the speaker button. "Hi."

"You sound exhausted."

"Yeah, I'd forgotten just how much noise video games can make when one player is an excitable kid. I don't think I'd cope with children of my own yet." She was sinking into lethargy when Lacey spoke again.

"So, you have things to tell me."

Jan struggled to remember what those things were. She had known five minutes ago. Now her overstimulated brain was just so tired. Her whole body felt like it had sprouted bruises in the rebound from Friday. Even with the new meds letting more nutrients into her cells, that postexertional flu-like reaction was a real kicker. Bruises. That was it.

"When Mylo dropped Michael off this morning, he said the police questioned Georgie because of bruises on Kitrin. I remembered you pulled her from the swim machine a few days ago and thought you better tell them that so they don't think she was attacked."

"Oh. Good call," said Lacey. "I can ask about her heart at the same time."

"What about her heart?"

"Andy said eating disorders can weaken it. When she first heard Kitrin died suddenly, that's what she assumed: heart failure."

Jan shuffled around to make her legs more comfortable. She should have brought hot rice bags in with her. "I guess I should tell the police about her eating disorder, too. Mylo pretends it doesn't exist."

"The coroner probably spotted it already." Lacey paused. "I'm sorry if Chad is a friend of yours, but he's caused a lot of extra work for the investigators, and annoyance for me. If he hadn't turned off those security cameras around the pool, there'd be no need to question everyone, hunting for that one person who might have seen her tip over without realizing she couldn't get back up by herself."

"Chad did what?" Jan listened in horror as Lacey filled her in.

Lacey finished, "I don't understand why he'd do that unless he was hiding that he approached Kitrin despite orders. Was she famous enough to attract stalkers?"

"No, but I can tell you what he was hiding. He's Kitrin's ex. She dumped him for Mylo when we lived in Vancouver."

Lacey swore. "If Wayne or I had known that, we'd never have left him on that job. You have to call the police and tell them that right away."

"Do I have to?" Even to herself Jan sounded whiny. "I'm so exhausted right now."

Lacey's voice sharpened. "He was dumped, and badly. Do you realize how many men kill their exes, even years later?"

"All right. I'll just lie here for fifteen minutes with my eyes closed to gather up some reserves."

Lacey softened. "You do need the rest. Tell you what, I'll explain to them about Chad, then you'll just have to confirm it later."

"Thanks so much." Jan yawned again. "Rob's coming back to make me supper. He'll stay until Terry gets home, maybe overnight if he doesn't have a date. Terry's out with Search and Rescue. I never know when he'll be back from those."

"I saw him at the SAR base on my way here."

"Where are you, anyway?"

"Orrin's ranch."

Jan rolled over to the other side. Her legs still hurt. "Are you coming back tonight?"

"Nope. Two, three nights at least."

"Sounds like a big job."

"Didn't Terry tell you what it was about? The search, I mean?"

"No. Is it someone we know?" When Lacey hesitated, Jan added, "Tell me. Wondering is going to drive me crazy now."

"All right. But I don't want you to lose sleep over this. Orrin and his son, Tyrone, went for a drive yesterday afternoon and haven't come back. That's the search Terry's on. The other Caine brothers say their father might have taken Tyrone off somewhere without telling anyone. He's got history that way."

Jan hung up the phone a few minutes later, feeling completely defeated. Kitrin dead, Michael as good as an orphan, and now Tyrone, Michael's new friend, was missing. She wasn't in shape to do anything about any of it. She dropped the phone and pulled the blackout mask over her eyes, ignoring the tears that crept down toward her ears.

Rob came back while Jan was still lying there like a mummy. She poked her hand out to show she was awake. The armchair by her head creaked.

"How'd Michael take going back?" she murmured. "Was Mylo there to meet him?"

"No," said Rob. "Fucking Lord High was off doing some film business. His wife is dead barely a day, and his son is completely in shock, and he goes off to work on his fucking movie. He doesn't deserve either of them." After a bit more language, he said, "Sorry. It just pisses me off. Kitrin's mom can't get here too soon for Michael's well-being."

"Mylo won't let her be with Michael, either. Remember, he threatened her with legal action to get him back last year." As Rob swore again, she added, "I wish I knew how Kitrin felt about it. So much I can't even guess about her life. You're supposed to tell me what happened that last year she lived with us. When she was looking so wrecked, I mean. All my drawings of her from October and November are just haunted."

"If she was alive, it would be her business to tell you or not." Rob got up. "I need a drink for this. Do you want anything?"

"My rice bags heated up, please."

When he came back and they were both settled, he began. "That fall, when she moved back to school, her parents started marriage counselling. Twenty-five years of nastiness all came out at once. On Thanksgiving, they had a big blowout over the third bottle of wine, which was when Kitrin found out her mom had been screwing her dad's business associates for years. Her dad said straight out he'd always believed she wasn't his daughter."

"Oh, that poor girl. Why didn't she tell me?" Thanksgiving was only a few months before Kitrin leaped into bed with Mylo, a man old enough to be her father. It made sense now, in a terrible way.

"She was afraid it might be true," Rob went on. "He wanted her to take a DNA test. She thought she'd be cast out of the family if it came out wrong. Lose her tuition and living allowance, be forced to get a loan, learn to survive on her own. She was paralyzed. And her parents sent her back to school without even thinking that she might need help dealing. Those fucking self-centred clowns. I tried to get her to talk to someone in Student Services about counselling, maybe ask for a deferment on the semester, but she wouldn't. Then she got that extra slot on Mylo's movie and the rest, well ..."

"She saw an escape route and dived into it." Jan hugged her warm rice bags. Poor Kitrin. No wonder she'd clung to that marriage, that man who barely spared a thought for her. "Did she ever get her DNA test?"

"Not that she told me about."

"I wonder if she told Chad."

"Who's Chad? Wait, you mean that guy she dumped that Christmas?"

"Yeah, and picked up again in January, and then dumped again when she took up with Mylo six weeks later."

"What's he got to do with anything?"

"You didn't recognize him up at Jake's, then."

Rob shook his head. "Haven't been up there lately."

"New security guard. I saw him when I went up the other morning." She shook her head. "God. What a disaster this weekend has been. Did you know this search Terry's on is for Orrin Caine and his son? The youngest one, Tyrone. We absolutely can't tell Michael his new best friend is missing."

As Lacey finished her camera survey, she added up the tally. The cameras covering the bluff staircase and staff parking area were dark. Two more, in the gym area, were misaligned, pointing at upper walls and ceilings instead of entrances or exits. She'd been surprised at how many other indoor spaces were being recorded: the machine shop, garage, stables, and the hallways in the main house. Maybe the gym cameras were someone's protest against the pervasive surveillance. Earl's daughters, for instance. They might not have been comfortable being spied on from up here.

The garage camera ... was Orrin's Range Rover kept in this building, or down in the machine shed? She called up the external disk drive where the backup images were stored and found the old green Range Rover parked in that empty slot at the far end of the garage. She zoomed in. Beat up it undeniably was, with dents and scrapes along the driver's side and a crack in the window over the back fender. Not that seeing it got her any further forward. What had she expected? A sign taped to the window that said, *Off to St. Louis for a ball game, back Tuesday*? Still, for completeness, it was worth a closer look at the last place the truck had been seen. She strapped on her tool belt and left the room, hearing the office lock click as she pulled the door shut.

The garage's overhead lights came on when her foot hit the landing, glaring down on the row of expensive vehicles. The spot where Orrin's Rover usually sat was a testimony to the vehicle's age, the only place where fluid leaks marred the concrete. There were two: a faint trace of something clear where the left front wheel would be and an oily yellow slick under the engine compartment. That wasn't old; rather, a fairly fresh leak that hadn't been cleaned up. She touched one finger to the puddle and raised it toward her face. Light amber oil that smelled sweetish, like marshmallows? Lacking an evidence kit with its assortment of bags and bottles, she dipped a bit of paper towel into the yellow stuff and folded that corner into the middle of several layers. Wayne might know what it was. The clear oil, which smelled very faintly of fish, got the same treatment. Where the sun hit the floor, she could make out faint gleams in a tread pattern; the Rover had tracked the clear fluid while backing out.

As she took phone photos of both substances from different angles, for the first time she seriously considered whether someone had sabotaged Orrin's vehicle.

On hands and knees, she played her phone flashlight beneath the other vehicles but found no stains or drips. Repairing the cameras could wait. First she had to check back on the garage recordings to see if someone had been working on Orrin's Rover. Back upstairs she went and left Wayne a message about her discovery. She forwarded the photos, too, switched the Dan-phone update on her phone to Silent lest it go off at an inconvenient time and noted with relief that he was still five mountain ranges to the west of her.

She was scrolling backward through archived garage footage two hours later, looking for anyone doing anything near Orrin's old green Rover, when there was a rap at the door. She leaned over and turned the knob. Andy stood there, fanning herself with a hand, small curls sweat-stuck around her forehead. She stepped inside.

"It's lovely in here. I didn't realize how much I'd overheated sitting on the terrace waiting for news. Had to get out of that house, but it would be impolitic to go far when we might hear something any minute. Not even down to the gym for a workout, although I could really use the stress-busting." She perched on the arm of the only other chair. "Any sign of reporters yet?"

Lacey pointed to the front-gate camera. "None. That truck is a Search and Rescue vehicle for people who are walking the cutlines across Highway 40."

"Thank the Crone for that mercy."

"You were expecting trouble?"

Andy watched the monitor flick past a few more images from various gates. "Just, um, cautious. I had some bad experiences with them during my fifteen minutes of celebrity. Let me know if you see any, okay? So I can avoid them." She stood up. "Anyway, I really came to ask if you're hungry yet? Supper's in the main house."

"I expected to eat with the staff."

"You're welcome at Jake's table, so you're welcome at Orrin's. Don't worry, we're all going casual tonight. Let's take your stuff to my place now, so you'll know your way. Then we'll eat. All guys except us. Sloane's hiding in her suite, and only Cheryl's allowed in. Try not to let the stink of testosterone spoil your appetite."

In the typical understatement of oil-baron families, Andy's so-called cabin was half again the size of Dee's estate home at Bragg Creek. In the clearing before it, a lone green Mercedes convertible occupied a brick parking pad big enough for four vehicles. Indoors was an open-plan main floor with bookshelves, computer table, and a huge TV screen tilted for viewing from a collection of soft sofas and big easy chairs. A wide oak staircase curved up to the top floor. Andy showed Lacey to a corner bedroom, pointed out the shared bathroom, and left her to unpack.

As she emptied her hastily packed bag, Lacey checked out the surroundings. One window overlooked the wide, golden valley, and from the other, a swimming pool was partially visible through the trees. "Earl's," Andy had said as they walked the breezeless forest path. "We don't use it unless specifically invited. And we won't be now that his wife and kids went back to Denver."

Lacey'd made a mental note to find out exactly when they left. She hadn't seen anyone near the Rover in the days she'd scanned so far, which suggested that tampering, if it occurred, hadn't coincided with Orrin's urgent assignment for Wayne. However, someone might have tampered with it while everyone was around for the annual vacation, knowing Orrin would drive off eventually. That type of motive would take more digging.

When her few clothes and toiletries were stowed, Lacey went downstairs.

Andy was sprawled on a sofa, scrolling through her phone. She looked up. "Unpacked already? I've barely opened Twitter. Main meals are usually at the big house, but that might not suit your schedule. Eat down here whenever it suits you. I'll show you where."

In a pantry off the white, cottage-style kitchen, Andy showed her an iPad attached to the wall. "Eat whatever you like that's around, but list your specific food and drink wishes on this program, and the housekeeping staff will stock them for you." She glanced sideways. "Any chance you go for vegetarian cuisine?"

"I don't mind some. Why?"

"Ben. The staff's been ordered not to take his requests. We have to sneak what he likes into the menu when he's staying with us."

Lacey's mind jumped back to Ben holding doors for her during their tour, then putting his hand into his pocket last thing and saying he'd forgotten to bring a fob. Did he even have one, or had Orrin ordered that privilege, too, removed?

"What's he done to deserve that?"

Andy tapped her short blue fingernails against the iPad. "Ben's a hardcore environmentalist, chains himself to trees or sabotages logging equipment to protect an old-growth stand. The family's fixers had lawyers on speed-dial from here to L.A. when he was in school. Then he led the opposition to the Black Rock Bowl resort expansion that Orrin was backing. They fought the whole time about how much habitat was being damaged by the new lift platform. Ben refuses to ski there or even visit. He says the sewage from that little shopping mall at the bottom gets into the Ghost River to damage the ecosystem."

Lacey nodded. "I wondered why they needed a shopping mall at all, but there's no doubt it's a lively place in ski season."

"Uh-huh. So much traffic, and for what? Shit they could buy in Calgary or Banff any freakin' day." Andy opened a cupboard door and showed her a jar. "Add Bart's granola, would you? Anyway, the final straw was this spring. Orrin found out Ben was working on the Ghost Wilderness's latest land-use survey, estimating the damage done by off-road vehicles and oil-and-gas exploration. Just where Orrin was expanding his leases, in other words."

"Leases? Oh, leased land where he wants to drill for oil?"

Andy nodded. "Yeah. Sloane's birthday supper was when it came crashing down. Orrin all but disowned Ben on the spot. I thought he was going to shove him off the bluff, but he heaved a deck chair over instead. He couldn't outright forbid Ben to come to our house, but he makes it as unpleasant as possible. Not having a fob forces Ben to park outside the main gate and walk in. And he can't get into buildings or take a dirt bike out or anything without one of us opening doors for him. Nor get food that he likes. Petty shit."

"Sounds grim."

"Yeah, and so unfair. But you may have gathered Orrin doesn't play fair." Andy opened another cupboard door.

Ben's motives for getting his father out of the way were mounting by the minute, but would he risk his little brother?

After a glance at the pantry's collection of tea and staples, Lacey checked off food items on the iPad's menu — eggs, flatbreads, orange juice, canned tuna, cold meat — and added items as Andy suggested them for Ben. After that, they headed back up to the big house. The forest path was still breathless; when they reached the terrace, the westerly sun hit them like molten lava.

As she opened the dining room's French doors, Earl leaped to his feet, yelling.

"If he hasn't disinherited you yet, I'll force you out the instant I'm in charge."

Ben, nose to nose with him, snarled back. "You can kiss my ass. Or better yet, kiss Sloane's. Because if Ty's alive, he'll get everything. And he loves his mom at least as much as you love yours."

Lacey stepped up to intervene before remembering she wasn't paid to break up brawls now. The boot was on the other foot, actually: as a civilian, she could face charges if either man got hurt during her intervention. Her impulsive movement had broken up the confrontation, anyway. Earl, very red in the face, glared around the room and stomped out. Ben's shoulders settled back slightly as the footsteps receded.

"Sorry about that," he said. "He gets up my nose on a good day, and today sure as hell isn't one."

Andy patted his forearm. "I know. You want to be out doing something, and they won't let you join a search team."

"I'm just as at home in the back country as any of them," he grumbled. "More familiar with this area, too."

Bart, who'd been standing by a buffet table with a half-filled plate in his hand, dug a serving spoon into a bowl. "We should have certified for SAR when we talked about it last spring. Then they'd have to let us help."

Ah. They'd been sent home by the search manager. Or by Constable Markov, in his capacity as official RCMP liaison. As Lacey served herself from the long table filled with cold cuts, salads, rolls, and drinks, the twins argued about whether to ride the whole ranch again or wait until morning. Andy eventually appealed to Lacey, who didn't hesitate to shut them down.

"Stay off the trails. Every disturbance you make muddies the signs for the trained searchers."

"But we're the ones who—" Ben began.

"No." It was harsh, but it had to be said. "You'll be far less help than you think. The certified searchers all know each other and drill together every week. They know to maintain their distance, sightlines, and so on. They can tell if a person has passed that way, but not who. The more you muck about, the worse the odds get for them to find signs of your little brother." After a moment, when neither twin offered any new arguments, she changed the subject. "Is it possible Orrin took Ty away to keep him from Sloane? Is that marriage on the rocks?"

Silence fell, punctuated by puzzled looks between the family members. Finally Ben said, "Um, probably not. If anything, Sloane would try to hide him from Orrin, as leverage for a settlement."

"Honestly," Andy added, "she hasn't got enough spirit to dump his ass, or she'd have done it long ago."

"Orrin might take off for some perfectly legit reason," said Bart, "and just not tell us. I'll get his secretary to check his credit cards online tonight. We might find out they've gone to a ball game in Texas, and Ty left his phone in the truck at the airport."

Andy put her head in her hands. "God, that would be just like Orrin. And here we've all been rushing around, short on sleep and brain cells, not asking that obvious question."

It wasn't likely to be that easy, but if it let them all sleep better tonight …

CHAPTER THIRTEEN

Quietly skeptical of the others' hopes for Orrin's credit cards, Lacey went back to the office after supper and examined every moment the Rover was visible on the garage camera during the previous week. Nobody had gone near it except in passing. Every half hour, she'd looked away from the archived images to check the real-time cameras, but nothing moved around the upper buildings except a server having a smoke near the kitchen and, later, Cheryl carrying a tray along an upstairs hallway. Down below the bluff, a couple of quads came back to the machine shed with the sunset, and at full dusk Andy, Bart, and Ben could be seen trudging along the lower footpath toward the climbing gym. Andy was getting her stress-busting workout at last. Lacey could stand a workout herself. Was staff permitted to use the gym equipment? She made a note to ask Andy later and went back to her garage footage while the skylights in the climbing gym glowed beneath her windows.

An hour later, her neck and shoulders stiff from staring at screens, she checked outside again. The lights were still lit, which could mean someone was there or simply that a timer hadn't cut off since the people left. If she could realign those cameras tonight, she'd start the morning a bit ahead of herself. She slung her tool belt around her hips, locked the office door behind her, and headed out. The garage lights clicked on as she reached the landing, gleaming on vehicles and accentuating the creepy silence. She might as well be at a deserted industrial park instead of a foothills ranch an hour from Calgary. She took the stairs down and paused in the propped-open door to the climbing room, checking for occupants. Spotlights in the rafters lit up the deserted climbing routes from various angles, sharpening the nuances of each handhold. The natural rock at the back sparkled subtly, calling out "come and climb me." It must have been irresistible to the small boys growing up on the ranch.

Someone laughed. She leaned farther in. There was no sign of Bart, but Ben was looking up. He let out slack in a rope harnessed to his waist as Andy's legs appeared past a built outcrop in the nearest climbing wall. When she reached bottom, he lifted her off the last hold by her hips. She leaned back, her hair against his cheek, looking surprisingly comfortable as his hands slid around her waist.

Lacey's tool belt scraped the door frame. "Sorry," she said, stepping into the echoing room as Andy separated herself from Ben. "I didn't realize anyone was still here."

"We were just finishing up," said Andy, walking coolly toward her. "Is there any news?"

"Nothing, sorry."

"Oh." For a moment the younger woman seemed at a loss. Then she pushed the dark tendrils of hair off her sweaty forehead. "I'm off to the treadmill, then. See you back at the house." As she pushed open the door to the workout room, Ben coiled up her belay rope and hung it neatly on a peg among several others. He hung up the harnesses on another hook and sorted a plastic tub of short gear pieces with carabiners at one or both ends.

"So," he said after a long moment, "I'm just going to work around here a bit, unless you need something?"

That was the end of Lacey's plan to fix cameras tonight. The one facing the machine-shed door was way up the wall, anyway. She'd need a stepladder.

"I was just wondering if the workout room is for family only, or if I could use it too? Tomorrow."

Ben shrugged. "Technically, if you're staying at Bart's you're a guest, anyway. So go for it. You're stuck here until Orrin's found?"

"Yup. Are you really not concerned about your father being missing more than twenty-four hours?"

He fiddled with a strap. "I guess I think the old guy is indestructible. He's always been a force of nature. Tyrone's just a kid. Even if they're eating hot dogs in some ballpark, he's stuck with Orrin, who is, well, 'unpredictable' is the nice way to say it. There's no buffer between him and Ty if he flies off the handle."

"Surely Tyrone is the star in Orrin's sky," said Lacey. "At least, that's the impression I got last week."

"He was an ass down at the Wyman place, right? And that's his company behaviour. Our mom only put up with it for a few years." He ran a length of rope through his hands. "The divorce was better for us, anyway. We weren't trapped in this macho environment continually, the way Earl was."

"You don't seem lacking in machismo yourself. All outdoorsy and muscular." Oops! That sounded like she'd noticed his muscles particularly. She had been kind of admiring them, but not in a personally interested way.

He blushed faintly. "I can't help being more muscular than Bart. He's an hour younger and a desk jockey. Although he's pretty tough in his own way."

"As twins, did you do everything together? Same school, same hobbies, same friends?"

"Not everything. He was more chess club and art class, I was soccer and tennis. We divided our school holidays between our mom's place out on Vancouver Island and wherever Orrin wanted us. Usually someplace that would toughen us up more. There's no room for pansies in Orrin's world. Direct quote."

"I've heard his thoughts on that." Lacey moved past him to peer through the workout room's skinny window. The camera in there was mounted high above the treadmill, where Andy was running hard, and pointed straight at the front wall. The exterior door in that corner was most likely completely out of its lower frame. She'd need a ladder for that fix, too. "Did none of your brothers ever stand up to him?"

"Not Earl, for sure. His mother wouldn't let him, in case Orrin demoted him from Heir-Apparent to Also-Ran. Giselle never got over feeling stiffed because our mom made way more money off us than she did having Earl."

Oh yeah, the million-bucks-a-son deal. And wasn't a girl mentioned, too, at Jake's horrible dinner party? "Earl's sister, Orrin's only daughter ... she's not coming to hold vigil with the rest of you?"

"Not her. As soon as she was appropriately married off, she became the property of her husband's family. Orrin has no use for daughters. Earl only having girls is a constant thorn in his side. That's the main reason he married our mom, and then Sloane: to have more sons, more male options to maintain his business empire. Earl was into some stupid teenage shit at school, and Orrin decided he wasn't worthy. So he dumped Giselle, who didn't want more kids by then, and took up with our mother. I'm not surprised Earl hates us. He's been told every day of our lives that we were born on purpose to supplant him."

Their anger at supper had been mutual. Nothing Ben said about Earl could be taken at face value, or vice versa, but about other relationships — things she could verify elsewhere — he was worth another question or two.

"So Giselle keeps Earl in line, but your mother doesn't?"

Ben clicked another couple of carabiners onto their spike. "Our mom doesn't give a shit about money or position. She left when we were eight, moved out to Cumberland to start her pottery studio. It's a hippie town on Vancouver Island, full of artists and musicians and fire dancers. We loved it there. No haircuts, no bedtimes, no routines. Orrin had us for vacations. When we were twelve, he sent us to the same uptight academy Earl had attended. We stuck it for a while, but it wasn't our bag at all. See me in a school uniform?" He frowned. "Bart was bullied constantly, and I punched out a few guys to stop it. Back then I figured Earl got his old school pals to turn their kid brothers against us, but maybe we were just too different. Free spirits instead of lockstep rich boys. When I got expelled for fighting, I told Mom Bart couldn't stay there without me. She moved us to a boarding school near her, and we got to go home on weekends, bum around the beach, learn to surf. Best thing for us. We're much more human than Earl is."

He seemed like he could go on dissing his brother all night, but it wasn't revealing possible motives for sabotaging Orrin.

Lacey retreated to the door she'd entered by. "I'd better make sure all the gates are covered for the night."

Back in the office, she made a last sweep of the real-time cameras. She couldn't see much now that night had fallen, except the movement of men around the gates, and then only if they were smoking or staring at glowing phone screens. Wait. Wasn't there a motion-sensor light on the main gate? She checked Wayne's equipment roster. Yes, there was. Every time someone crossed the gate, the light should go on. She called Ike.

"Oh, yeah," he said when she asked. "They bitched about the light messing with their night vision, so I killed it at the master switch box. It's in a closet off the upper elevator lobby."

"Thanks," she said and hung up. No point calling him out for leaving her out of the loop. If any motion-sensor light could be shut off at that closet, then someone could have shut off the garage's interior light the same way, right before they walked in. Any one of those dark digital images she'd skimmed through tonight might have included a shadow subtly moving around the Rover. She'd have to look again, but not until morning. Rubbing her gritty eyes, she started a backup of the whole hard drive to Wayne's office server. Hundreds of gigs worth of images would take ages to upload even over Orrin's fast data link. No point doing it in daylight when she needed the computers for other jobs. She secured the equipment, locked the room behind her, and left the garage.

The night was still and sultry, as if there was a thunderstorm in the offing, but the sky above was clear, with a half moon riding high above the peaks. Somewhere out there, young Tyrone might be settling in for his second night in a broken-down vehicle, wondering when and how he'd get back to his own bed.

As she crossed the wide terrace, heat radiated off the stones. The quiet was so intense that a calf bleating down in the valley startled her. Her footsteps crunched onto the gravel path. Branches creaked in a breeze so faint it barely stirred the shadows. It was only too easy to imagine a cougar's eyes evaluating her from the darkness. She hurried thankfully into the lit clearing before Andy and Bart's cabin and was just about to wave her fob at the door when it opened from the inside. She jumped back.

Ben stretched an arm inside for a backpack. "Sorry, did I scare you? I'm taking over at the south gate soon. Any news on the search?"

"None that came to me," she said truthfully. Her speculation about the Rover wasn't news. Yet. "The search'll start again at first light. Hopefully they'll have a clearer target area by then, from the RCMP's information-gathering sweep. Or Orrin will have checked in with someone."

Ben nodded and wordlessly disappeared into the shadows of the forest trail, leaving her standing in the slash of brighter light from the open door. His boots crunched in the silence until the trees swallowed the sound. No sign of his earlier anger now, which reminded her: he'd been yelling about Tyrone inheriting everything. As the boy's next-of-kin, Sloane would presumably get whatever was coming to him as long as he outlived Orrin by a single minute. She might have sabotaged the Rover, not expecting Orrin to take Tyrone driving with him. Possibly she'd hoped her son would be busy with his new friend when his father left. However it came about, if Tyrone inherited the "everything" Orrin had declared he would at Jake's dinner party, Sloane would be sitting pretty. Maybe that's why she was hiding in her suite: nobody but her faithful companion to witness her complete lack of concern for her husband.

She wasn't the only one with a strong motive, though. If neither Orrin nor Tyrone were found alive, with no clear way to distinguish which died first, the older brothers would inherit according to whatever default conditions were in force. Had Ben been officially disinherited after the Black Rock standoff, or was that only an angry threat made in the moment? On the whole, she thought the old man would have rubbed his son's nose in a *fait accompli*, leaving Ben nothing to gain by killing his father except satisfaction, while every day Orrin lived was another chance to get his inheritance back. For the other brothers, the reverse applied. As long as Ben was disinherited, there was a bigger pie for Earl and Bart to split. She'd have to ask Wayne in the morning if he knew what the dispositions were for Orrin's wealth, and if his secret investigation had anything to do with disinheriting a family member.

Inside the "cabin," Bart's voice said, "There's really no choice but to carry on for now as if Orrin will be back tomorrow. Can you stomach it?"

"Yeah, but it feels so sneaky, doing it here," Andy replied. Then she called, "Shut the door, Ben. You're letting in flies."

Lacey walked in, pondering those ambiguous comments. Carry on with what? Clearly Ben knew, or they wouldn't have talked about "it" while believing he still stood in the doorway. Could three people keep a conspiracy a secret if two of them were twins?

Andy was sprawled on the couch, her head on Bart's thigh, while the evening news flickered mutely on the big screen. She looked up. "Was that you? Sorry, I thought it was Ben communing with the night. Are you packing it in?"

"Yes. I need to be rested for whatever tomorrow brings. Will you be able to sleep?"

"I hope so." Andy yawned. "I'd barely dozed off last night when Sloane called us in a panic."

"I'm not sure I will," said Bart. "I'm still waiting for word from Orrin's secretary, but on thinking it over, I'm not buying the ball game theory after all. More likely the truck broke down on some forsaken cutline to nowhere when he was stranding Ty. That's one tough kid, but he's never been abandoned in the wild. Not like the rest of us."

"All of you?"

"Oh, yeah. Orrin made a point of dumping us individually in the forest to find our own way home."

"You're kidding, right?"

Andy sat up. "He's not. His father started when they were little, would take them for an afternoon drive and say he wanted to show them something special. Once they got out of the truck, he'd drive away without them and let them find their own way home."

"That's barbaric."

Bart nodded. "I thought so. It was terrifying trudging down a cutline or back road knowing there were cougars around as tall as me. My mother put a stop to that as soon as we told her, but Earl's mother never stood up for him. I think he was lost for something like thirty hours one time."

While Lacey was still wrapping her mind around the abusive parenting Bart had so casually revealed, Andy said, "Do you want a cup of tea or a snack before you go up?"

"No thanks. Good night." Lacey climbed the stairs, rinsed off the day in a shower, and fell into bed. She slid into sleep accompanied by a thousand images of a solitary boy plodding through a dark forest while animal eyes glittered from behind every second tree.

Early the next morning, before anyone in the house was moving, Lacey headed down to the workout room and ran for a solid half hour. The treadmill faced the north window, allowing her to watch the shadows creep away from the valley floor as the sun climbed. Someone in a cowboy hat went from the bunkhouse into the stables, but that was the only sign of life. She finished her run and walked the space to cool down, exploring it. The only surprise was behind the mirrored west wall: a washroom, spotlessly clean and clearly not intended for use by the ranch hands. It included a shower stocked with body washes, lotions, razors, and hair care products, plus drawers labelled with family members' names, which she assumed contained personal changes of clothing. Open shelves were stacked with towels and washcloths. Rather than shower only to put her sweaty workout clothes back on, she stripped off her T-shirt for a splash and then draped a towel around her neck while she stretched. She'd get properly cleaned up back at Andy's.

Before leaving, she took a better look at the mis-aimed camera. It seemed undamaged and only needed tilting down to cover the exterior door again. She had to stand on the treadmill's handlebar and surge upward to reach it, bracing herself with her left hand on the window frame. Her other hand connected twice, with barely enough combined force to nudge the back end up and around, pointing the lens end a bit farther down. She scrambled down and was about to head up to Andy's when the external door opened. Ben entered. She took in his lined eyes and tousled hair, the jeans and jacket he'd been wearing last night.

"You look bagged. Were you out on the gate until now?"

He rubbed the back of his neck. "I've just been relieved by the day shift, planned to knock out some kinks going up the walls. Any chance you know how to belay?"

Spending another half hour with him, now that his anger at Earl had faded some, might get more of her questions about the family answered and give her a better sense of whether he was truly a straight shooter who'd rather punch someone in the face or a devious creep who'd tamper with a vehicle. She'd stay.

"I've belayed once before. I can probably do it again if you run me through the basics."

"Great," he said. "Give me a minute to get out of these jeans."

She went into the climbing centre and looked up at the bare rock. With the spotlights augmented by the sky-lights, it looked less seductive, more forbidding. She'd never been afraid of heights, but the thought of Ben, Bart, and Tyrone as little kids following Earl up that nearly sheer cliff was enough to make anyone nervous. It was a wonder young Tyrone had only broken an arm.

Ben came in behind her, wearing spandex shorts and a T-shirt that clung to his impressive upper body. Despite the general physical resemblance to Dan, in a bench lift she'd back him over her ex any day. Maybe in a fight, too. Whether he was psychologically stronger, too — well, her gut wasn't committing either way on that.

He called her over to the gear shelves and handed her a harness. He climbed into another one, snugging it up his thighs and fastening the belly strap. She got her harness into position while he selected other gear. He threw a pair of climbing shoes onto the bench for her and held up one oddly shaped clamp.

"You've used a GriGri before?"

"I know enough to keep my fingers out of it and to keep one hand on the braking rope at all times, because even though it's supposed to auto-lock, you don't risk a life on it."

"Safety first. I like it." He grinned. "Okay, clip it on you. Now, I outweigh you by a good thirty kilos. I'm probably not going to fall, but if I do, I could drag you off your feet. Would you feel safer with a floor anchor?"

A full hour later, Lacey backed down the beginner wall, supported by the rope attached at her waist, with Ben's sure hand feeding out the slack as she needed it. Exhilaration flooded her body and mind. How long since she'd had a real physical challenge to master? Her hands were chalky, her fingers ached from crimping on the holds, and she really needed a shower now. As her feet flattened onto the floor, she blotted her forehead on her sleeve.

"That was awesome!" Even better, she hadn't felt the slightest twinge of terror when, at the top, she'd hung for a moment to look down at the floor, which had to be nearly four storeys below. The moment had quelled her wee, lurking worry that she, like Chad, harboured a fear of heights from the Capilano Gorge. She'd been up high, and she was okay. Better than okay. "Climbing is seriously extra."

Ben handed her a water bottle. "I won't say you're a natural, but I'd let you climb with me."

"Thanks." Lacey drank. "It was a better workout than I expected. All my large muscle groups are shaky."

"Come on up to the cabin and I'll scramble us some eggs."

When they'd both changed their shoes, he led her out past the elevator to the south door. At the sight of the footpath leading along the bluff, her endorphin-high brain kicked back to work mode. The camera at the top of these steps wasn't working; she'd fix that early today, and the higher one in the climbing centre, too. The camera over the door she'd just exited was recording her chalk-covered butt right now, and it wouldn't be the only one before she could change clothes. Orrin's camera fetish was almost Hitchcockian.

As she tackled the first of those five flights of stairs up the bluff, she checked out the surroundings. That aspen-grove path led not only through the copse but also veered out to the dusty road beyond it. Could a person entering through one of the distant gates — last week, before the new cameras were added — avoid the surveillance along these buildings and get into the garage without being seen? Maybe, except the fob system recorded every door access. If she nailed down a time for possible vehicle tampering, she could correlate that with the fob log and find out who had opened which doors at that time. It might even be possible to tell from the footage whether the person using a particular fob was the same one it was signed out to.

Trying not to stare at Ben's ass, shifting easily at eye level ahead of her, she climbed on with not quite enough breath for conversation. She hadn't learned much more about him this morning, except that he was patient with noobs. Their entire climbing hour had consisted of his clear, short instructions and her responses — on-belay?/belay on, climbing/climb-on, take/brake — all interspersed with simple suggestions and corrections from him on her climb, such as "try the green to your left hand" and "are you three-points stable?" His voice hadn't once slipped into impatience; nor had his words implied she was incompetent for not following instructions better or faster. So not like Dan, who had always claimed he was toughening her up by berating her like the drill sergeant at Depot. Either Ben wasn't the misogynist his father was, or it was buried deeper.

Ben talked as they climbed. "I've been racking my brains to think where Orrin might have gone. When we were little, he used to take us out over the ranch, but not much farther."

"Your brother said," Lacey gasped, "that he used to drop you off to make your own way home."

"I forgot about that." Ben paused on a landing, looking down at her with a frown. "Our mom made him stop early on, but Orrin got around it by not coming all the way home. If we caught up to where he was having a nap in the truck, he'd reward us to keep our mouths shut. I think he's been better with Ty, but maybe since Ty turned twelve, Orrin thought the time had come." He looked out over the valley, his frown deepening. "If he drove away and then realized Ty'd gone the wrong way and set out hunting for him, they could both be lost separately. But not on our land. It's impossible for Orrin to get lost here, even if Ty did."

More grateful than she liked to admit for the halt, Lacey leaned on the railing beside him. "Why wasn't your mom more, well, subservient to Orrin, the way Earl's mom was?"

Ben's laugh had a sour edge. "He was hoist on his own pre-nup. A million bucks for a son, he'd included, and she popped out the two of us first go. She threatened to sue him for the double payout." He started up the next flight too soon for Lacey's lungs. "When she got it, she put half in trust for us and invested the rest for herself. Once you're no longer dependent on Orrin's money, you don't have to kiss his ass quite as much."

"Is that how you financed your environmental studies?" Lacey barely got the long words out without gasping for breath in the middle.

"It's a trickle, but it lets me give back to the world to make up for Orrin plundering everything he touches." At the top, he looked over the valley with the hard expression she recognized from yesterday. "He should have been stopped long ago. As much as I can give back, it will never be enough."

After breakfast with Ben and a fruitless phone check with the SAR base, Lacey hurried to the office to get her tool belt. Today she'd repair those cameras, and then she'd get into the technicalities of lightening up dark garage images. Too bad Orrin hadn't sprung for infrared sensors. A warm-blood crossing that cool concrete would light up beautifully. But this wasn't the movies, and there wouldn't be a satisfactory conclusion after two hours. At least now she had an idea what might be tampered with. Wayne's text from an hour ago had specifically said to get the brands of transmission, brake, and power steering fluid used by the Rover.

The garage was not deserted, for a change. At barely 8:00 a.m. on a Monday, one man was checking oil and radiator levels on two SUVs while a second did tire pressures, topping up the valves with a compressor hose. When the compressor's racket stopped, Lacey introduced herself.

"I didn't meet you two yesterday down at the common room."

Oil guy shook his head. "We don't live here. Don't work weekends unless they're haying or hauling stock."

Not even when their employer went missing? "What's with these SUVs? Are you going out to help with the search?"

"No, ma'am," said tire guy. "We're loading up with food from the kitchen to take to the airstrip. Cheryl says we gotta keep those searchers fuelled up."

"Good idea," she said. "Which of you would've last checked the oil and stuff on that Range Rover of Orrin's?"

Oil guy wiped his hands on a shop rag and picked up a clipboard. He made a note with a pen hanging by a filthy string and then flipped back a page. "Me. Fifteenth of August."

Two weeks ago. That gave her a starting window. "And everything looked normal? No leaks or worn belts or anything that might cause a breakdown?"

He shook his head. "All tickety-boo."

"You didn't have to add any to the power steering, brake, or transmission fluid?"

He shook his head again. "Why?"

She pointed. "There's something like that on the floor where it was parked."

He crouched and touched the puddle on the concrete. After rubbing the stuff between finger and thumb, he smelled it. "Steering," he said. "Likely it dripped when the boss topped it up. If he was goin' for a hard run and we weren't around, he'd poke under the hood first."

"A hard run? Like off-roading? Fording a river? Going up a cutline?"

He shrugged. "Any or all of 'em. That truck's been everywhere. I'll get that cleaned up now you've mentioned it."

Lacey retreated upstairs. Another lovely late August morning, and she'd be spending it in this stuffy office, staring at computer screens. But first she'd fix those cameras. She cued up the workout room and found the camera above the treadmill now caught more of the open bathroom door than the exterior one. Another adjustment to make, and her legs were already stiffening up from the wall-climbing. Next trip she'd be taking the elevator.

When she hit the garage floor again, with the camera system's iPad tucked into her tool belt, oil guy said, "If that's your truck out front, best move it to the staff parking. The boss doesn't like our vehicles to be seen from the house."

Tire guy muttered, "Earl ain't our boss yet."

Oil guy frowned at him.

Lacey said, "I'll move it right now."

She drove along the garage to the staff lot and parked between an older Pathfinder and a crate-sided half-ton. Unlocking the chain on Wayne's aluminum stepladder, she pulled it clear and carried the ladder over to the building. It stood easily on the concrete sidewalk, and she went up without a wobble to replace the dusty, cracked camera with a spare from the truck. With another spare and some hardware in a carryall, she hauled the ladder to the terrace and set it up under the bluff-stairs camera. As she climbed again with her calves grumbling, the sun lifted above the surrounding trees to kiss her face. She paused to appreciate the view. Down in the valley, ranch hands were loading horses and saddles into a trailer. Were they SAR-certified themselves, or merely providing horses to searchers who were? No one else seemed to be working with the cattle or repairing fencing or whatever else cowboys usually did. All normal ranch work must be suspended while Orrin and Tyrone were missing, just as up here, all the usual routines of the family were out the window.

She, however, wasn't here to idle. She had to discover which of the family might want Orrin out of the way enough to sabotage his vehicle. What if it was something to do with his business? Orrin made enemies every time he opened his mouth. In half a century of oil drilling and other businesses, that could be a long list. Too bad he didn't have video surveillance on them all.

As she leaned to unscrew the camera bracket, the ladder shifted in the gravel. She looked down in alarm in time to see two sets of hands grab the legs.

"Need a hand?" asked Bart.

"That would be great," said Lacey. In a moment she had the old camera down and handed it off to Andy at the other side.

"You brought extra cameras along?" Andy asked as she handed up the spare. "Did you already know how many there are out here? It's like living in a psycho motel."

"Or Hearst Castle," Bart added. "Citizen Caine of the oil patch. Ever see that movie where Hearst's got guests on his yacht for the weekend, and he spies on them with cameras?"

"Nope. But I was surprised how many cameras are inside the main house. Usually they're only outside, against intruders." Lacey connected the new one, waited for its green light to come on, and climbed down. "Thanks."

"No prob," said Andy. "Earl's girls are death on the cameras. How many were out of action this time?"

"A few." Were Earl's daughters hooking up with the ranch hands, like Jake Wyman's hockey guests with the trophy wives, or was that sheer rebellion against their grandfather's overarching intrusiveness?

"We're going to work out," said Andy. "If today's anything like as tense as yesterday, at least we'll start out calm."

Lacey waved as they started down the wooden staircase. She'd adjust that workout camera later, when the gym was empty. She hauled her equipment back to the truck and returned to the stuffy security office. First, she scrolled back through the night's images. No disruptions at the gates, but with the dawn came a panel van sporting a TV news logo. It was still there on the real-time feed, parked directly across from the main gate on Highway 40. She ought to go out there and draw the line clearly for the reporters, before one of the ranch hands decided to. She glanced at her empty coffee mug. Soon.

All looked normal on the other cameras. Gates were all covered by two people, and pairs were patrolling the fences on quads. Were they the same as yesterday, or new hires?

She phoned Ike's cell and left a message. "Did you get more hands who need my speech about handling reporters?"

The gym camera over the treadmill showed a reflection of Andy working her upper body on a machine, and Bart's upper body at the outside door. Lacey toggled to the surrounding cameras and realized there was no external coverage of that door, either. Probably the stable one was supposed to cover the outside. More of Earl's girls' work? Wayne wouldn't have been so sloppy setting up. She'd fix that angle later, when she went down to true up that indoor camera.

She flipped back to a view of Bart still in the doorway. From the back, he and his twin were similar in general build and hair length, although his shoulders weren't as muscular. Full front, she'd spotted differences. Bart's face was softer and less tanned, even at the end of August. Ben's was bonier and weathered. Bart's hair was short and styled, while Ben's sun-bleached curls hung down his forehead, tossed around by the weather, the way he'd looked this morning when he strolled into the workout room. Truth to tell, he'd looked quite tasty, and if there'd been a few hay bales and stable blankets handy … She shook her head. Nope, no flings with hot strangers for her.

How had he gotten in there, anyway, if he didn't have a fob? Borrowed Bart's for the night? Earl, the temporary master of the house, surely wouldn't issue one to a brother banned by their tyrannical father. And this idle thinking wasn't helping her identify a saboteur in the garage.

She said goodbye to the bright morning outside her window and closed the blind. The darker the room, the better her night vision would be for the long slog through dim garage footage.

Her phone rang: a number with no name attached. Telemarketer or a search update? "McCrae speaking."

"I expected a status report by now," said a male voice.

"Who is this, please?"

"Earl Caine," he said, in a voice every bit as snidely demeaning as Dan's. "I'm in my father's study. First on your left as you come in from the garage."

"I'll be right there." Earl wasn't Wayne's employer — technically that was still Orrin, until proved otherwise — but he'd be signing off on invoices and thus must be treated with deference, if not actual respect. Grabbing her travel mug, she locked the security office and headed to the main house.

Earl sat at his father's desk, grappling with a sticky drawer. She tapped on the door frame. He waved her in with a frown. "Well, report. How are you earning your fee?"

If he expected her to be intimidated, he'd never met her old drill sergeant. And however much he might sound like Dan, she wouldn't be thrown by that, either. She walked straight up to the desk and listed her camera repairs, with no reference to his daughters.

"That's it?"

"I've briefed the staff on handling reporters and other trespassers and will do the same later today with any new hires. No reporters have attempted access yet, but there's a news van at the front gate now. Do you want to make a statement, or do you want me to send them away?"

He looked down at the drawer. "Tell them the family has no comment at this time. Refer them to the SAR manager at the airstrip."

"Yes, sir." She headed out the nearest exit and meandered up the shady drive to find two cowboys staring suspiciously at the news van. One of them opened the gate for her. As she approached the driver's window, it opened. A woman in the passenger seat leaned across the male driver and flicked on a hand-held recorder.

Every word and movement would be on the record, just in case a story broke.

"Good morning," Lacey said. "Can I help you with something?"

That woman asked, "Is it true Orrin Caine is missing? Which of his sons is with him?"

"The family has no comment. For more information on the search, the media centre is down at the airstrip."

The woman asked another question, but Lacey ignored it. She stepped back and snapped a couple of phone pictures of the driver and passenger to be circulated among ranch security at the other gates. She smiled at the reporters and walked away. Another hour, another camera recording her butt. It was that kind of day.

In the ranch kitchen, she got more coffee and a fresh muffin, listening to the three cooks natter as they prepared sandwiches for the searchers. There was no revealing gossip about the family; in fact, no mention at all except when one said, following a phone call, "Mrs. C and Cheryl will breakfast upstairs. Call Cheryl when it's ready." Passing Orrin's study on her way back to the garage, she saw Earl rattling the drawers of a file cabinet. So Orrin hadn't trusted his supposed second-in-command with keys? She could have told him how to break in, but that wasn't her business. What she needed was to find out who had a door fob for the garage.

She tapped on the door frame again.

"Excuse me, Earl. Can you tell me who all has key fobs for the various buildings? Do they all have access to everything? Or are some restricted?"

He looked at her blankly for a minute. Would he ask why she needed the information? But he only shoved a folder toward her. "Don't take it out of the room."

"It" was a printout dated last Monday and organized by fob number, the name of the family member or staffer who had one, and a series of letters after that, which she recognized as designating buildings on the ranch map. Her fob was one of five listed as *Guest* at the bottom, with her name printed beside the second "guest" number. The name beside the first one had been heavily scratched over in pen.

"Who had this one?" she asked, looking up, and saw that Earl had gone. She lifted the page to the window. The scribbling-over had been thorough. She photographed the list and a close-up of the scribbled area. Maybe Jan's artistic eye could sort out a name from that mess. Now, it was back to the security cameras and their very dark footage. At least nobody could be recording her butt while she was sitting on it. How did people live under this constant surveillance?

CHAPTER FOURTEEN

With Monday's breakfast sitting heavy on her stomach, Jan stared at the art director's email in dismay. He wanted her to phone this Harder woman and invite herself over to take pictures of a complete stranger's log house. At short notice, too. Maybe that was the Hollywood way. Did everybody there have daily housekeepers who kept their home camera ready? Here in Bragg Creek, people were lucky to have a weekly. Still, she had accepted the job and must therefore overcome her intense dislike of the phone.

How bad could it be, really? When she was sickest, trying to concentrate and hold up the phone with fingers that shook, struggling to get her words out before she forgot what she was trying to say, it would have been impossible. Now she was better. Not cured, but functioning more hours of each day. She could do this.

In the few seconds before the phone rang, she veered between *Pick up so I can get this over with* and *Please don't be home so I don't have to do anything except leave a message.*

A woman answered. Jan introduced herself and invoked Mylo Matheson.

"Oh, of course," Mrs. Harder cooed. "I'm delighted to have him consider my humble cabin. When can you come over? This afternoon?"

Already? Jan swallowed panic. It was only ten. Surely she could recover from a single phone call by after lunch. "How about two o'clock?"

"Wonderful. Do you need directions?"

"You're off West Bragg Road, right? That's not far from me."

"Wonderful," said Mrs. Harder again and hung up before Jan could ask about accessibility.

Jan disconnected, shaken. What had she let herself in for? The house might have huge stairs to its front porch or be down a steep riverbank from the parking area. She cued up Google Street View and found the address. Whew! No stairs out front. A gate, a level court-yard, and then a short, flat walk under a varnished-log porte cochère, leading to a middle-aged log house built long and low. It probably had picture windows on the river side that wouldn't work for an 1890s ranch house, but she had to try. Meanwhile, on to the next job: contacting owners of paintings. She shook off the jitters and settled on the couch with her list of paintings from the museum's loaner catalogue. The Harder name jumped out at her, marked beside several items. She phoned the museum.

"Rob, what do you know about a local collector named Harder?"

Rob said, "Harder?" Keys clicked. "Don and wife live in West Bragg Creek, donated two minor artworks to the Pioneers collection, and have ten other pieces they would loan if a suitable exhibit was being formed. Oh, it says he's deceased. So I guess it's just her. Why?"

"I have to go see her log cabin for the movie people this afternoon. I can take a look at her paintings while I'm there. Want to come along?"

"Nope. Michael is coming down with his nanny this afternoon. I've asked the clay club to let him attend their hand-building session this afternoon. Working with clay is really therapeutic for troubled emotions."

"I forgot you had that art therapy class among all your other courses. Are you seriously appointing yourself Michael's grief worker?"

Rob hesitated. "Well, we were around when he was conceived and knew his mother better than anyone here. We're the closest he has to an aunt and uncle."

"I guess. I might stop by on my way back if I have the spoons left."

Jan hung up after Rob's final caution against over-exertion. The risk was always there. If the house wasn't too big, and if she could sit down while photographing the paintings, she'd get through just fine. Driving along West Bragg from her place to the Harders' wouldn't require any particular concentration, either, given the low traffic usual on a late-summer weekday. She had to get through it, or Terry would put his foot down about the job, and she'd have to use up more energy fighting with him.

She was outside after lunch, loading her tripod and camera bag into the van under the blazing August sun, when Jake's oldest paint horse plodded up the road, its head low. Jake touched the brim of his faded cowboy hat, and when she waved back, he turned the horse into the driveway.

"Afternoon, Jannie. Where are you heading off to?"

"I'm going to photograph some artworks. Do you know any Harders?"

Jake's grin faded. "That woman's been married to two of my friends now, and only one of them outlived her. I think she has her eye on me for a third."

"Not interested?"

"I had enough of marriage with the last one. Although," he winked at her, "if you or Ms. Dee were available, I might just change my mind."

"You're shameless." Jan shook her finger at him and changed the subject. "I saw another RCMP van go up to your place this morning."

Jake tipped his hat back and frowned up the hill. "Yep. They're putting divers into my pool today, looking for that poor woman's cellphone."

"They haven't taken anyone else away for questioning?"

"Not so far as I can tell. Gotta say, Jannie, I'm mighty disturbed that this could happen at my place. It was bad enough thinking someone died accidentally in my pool. This other thing ... No stranger could walk in there and do that without standing out a mile. And me with extra guards, too."

Jan shivered. "We have to hope the RCMP know what they're doing."

"They're working hard enough, I'll give them that. You could keep thinking on it, though. It was you and young Lacey figured out the trouble last summer." He resettled his hat. "I'll be off and leave you to your picture taking. You don't know me, mind, if she asks."

Jan watched Jake turn his old paint back to the road. He was too accomplished a horseman to slump in the saddle, but his hat brim dipped in parallel to the horse's drooping neck. So much fallout. A chivalrous old man, shaken by the killing of a fragile house guest. A lonely boy, devastated by the loss of his mother. Rob was angry, confused, and protective of Michael. And herself? She was furious. Shaking so hard suddenly that she couldn't fit the key into the ignition. How dare someone wreak all this destruction on her friends?

Dropping the key ring on the passenger seat, she called Lacey. When it went to voice mail, she said, "Hi, it's Jan. You don't need to call me back. I just need to get this off my chest."

Two deep, calming breaths later, she continued, "How on earth do you deal with murderers? Not the investigating part, the emotions. It's very clear now that someone killed Kitrin, and I'm so freaking angry I'm vibrating. I want to find them and — I don't know — punch them and kick them and hurt them so badly for what they've done to my friends." She found her teeth clenched so hard they hurt and took a moment to waggle her lower jaw. "The cops are searching for Kitrin's phone now in the pool. It doesn't sound like they did anything about Chad. You did tell them, right? Talk to you later this evening, maybe?" When she hung up, her hands were less shaky. Now she had a job to do. She got the van started without difficulty, settled her dark glasses, strapped in, and started driving.

Ten minutes later, she pulled into the Harders' gate. The entrance was as flat as it had looked on Street View. She slung her camera bag over her shoulder, picked up the tripod, and headed for the varnished front door. A middle-aged woman with spiky auburn hair answered her ring. She was as tall as Lacey, and as lean, her exposed skin tanned and dry.

"Mrs. Harder? I'm Jan Brenner. We spoke on the phone."

"Right. Come on in." The woman stood aside.

Jan set her camera bag on a gnarled log bench. "You have a lovely home."

"It's not mine. My husband's children from his first marriage could sell it out from under me tomorrow." As Jan wondered silently if the movie would risk renting a house that might be sold before the shoot started, Mrs. Harder turned away. "I don't know what all you need to see, but this is the main area, and there are bedrooms back down this corridor. Kitchen and dining that way. There's an elevator to the lower level from when my husband's mother lived down there. It's quite modern, the basement. You probably don't need that part."

Jan smiled. "That depends where you keep your paintings. I found your name in the art museum's loaner catalogue, and I'd like permission to photograph some we're interested in for set dressing. You and Mr. Harder have quite a collection of late-nineteenth- and early-twentieth-century Rocky Mountain art."

"Not Don. He only liked the tax receipt when one was donated. Those paintings are mine, from my first marriage. We split up the collection when we divorced. What do you want to see first, paintings or rooms?"

Jan spent the next half hour taking photos, video, and measurements of rooms and hallways, with Mrs. Harder adjusting blinds and lamps to capture various states of light and shadow. One bedroom could work as it stood: walled in old pine, with knotty wood bedside tables and bedframes, beds covered in homey patchwork quilts. She praised its authentic feel.

The woman turned away with a shudder. "My husband liked it. He died in here."

"Oh, I'm so sorry. Was it recent?"

"A few years. I didn't have the money to get it redone, so I have to look at it every day and remember how much pain he was in. Do you mind if I leave you?"

"Not at all. I'll be finished soon." Jan got several shots from various angles, walked through slowly with her video camera, measured it with her laser ruler, and then found her hostess in the living room. Log walls and square ceiling beams supported wagon wheels; they'd fit the movie. The big windows overlooking the river were modern but could be disguised with drapes or other movie magic. "Now," she said, when she'd recorded all that the movie people might need, "may I look at your artworks?"

"Sure. Which paintings did you want, again?" Mrs. Harder showed Jan into the single-person elevator and took the half-log stairs down. They met up again in a large room, white walled and flooded with sunshine through patio doors and a picture window. Reflections off the river danced on the stucco ceiling. Around two walls were oil paintings, while the third held framed photographs and war memorabilia. "The war stuff is my husband's. I haven't had the heart to get rid of it."

Jan started at an end wall, identifying paintings from the thumbnail images that accompanied her catalogue listings. Two by Marmaduke Matthews and one John Fraser from the late 1880s, when the railroad was barely done; an early Banff sheep painting done by Carl Rungius; a Roland Gissing sketch from just before the First World War, when the artist was an adolescent cowboy; and two postwar oils by mountain climber and artist Belmore Browne. Although technically the last few wouldn't have been done yet by the fictional ranch wife's era, Tunnel Mountain painted in European landscape tradition looked pretty much the same from one decade to the next. The rest of the collection dated from the 1930s on, when Peter Whyte, Catherine Robb, and the Banff School of Fine Arts were drawing artists from all over the world. If this was only half the works, the other half might be even more spectacular. Would the ex-husband be willing to lend, too?

With light pouring in from the river windows, she set up the tripod and zoomed in on each of the paintings. When Mrs. Harder went off to answer a phone call, she packed up the camera and rested on a loveseat facing the war memorabilia wall. The black-and-white photos, mostly women whose hair and clothing recalled the 1930s and early 1940s, hung in clusters between cases containing soldiers' postcards, a prisoner-of-war map printed on silk, and assorted hand weapons. A face in the final cluster caught her eye. The subject wore a V-neck blouse and form-fitting jacket. Her face was a quarter profile showing smallish eyes, bumpy nose, and a pointed pixie chin. She could have been Kitrin Devine, if Kitrin had eaten more regularly and heavily pencilled her pale eyebrows.

"Who is this woman?" Jan said when her hostess returned. "She looks very much like a friend of mine."

Mrs. Harder gave the picture a glance. "My first mother-in-law. Pale thing, wasn't she? You'd never know she had a temper like a wild boar. Don liked this picture for the hairstyle, so I gave it to him for his display. His mother's hanging upstairs. She had jowls like a walrus but the temperament of an absolute pussycat." She looked at her watch. "If you have everything you need, I need to go."

"Thank you for being so patient." Jan took the little elevator back up and followed her hostess outside. As she stowed her equipment in the van, she said, "Your first mother-in-law, she wasn't from Saskatchewan, was she?"

"As far as I know she was Coaldale born and never went farther than Calgary."

Once the woman's elderly Jaguar had blasted past her, Jan drove sedately back along West Bragg Road and pulled into the art museum parking lot. Thanks to the little elevator and the level entrance, her afternoon hadn't been particularly exhausting so far. She texted Rob. *Is Michael still there? I'm out in the parking lot. Any chance you could wheel me inside to see how he's doing?*

In a moment she got a text back. *Five minutes?*

That was long enough to tip the seat back, tuck her feet up, and have a rest. Terry mustn't come back from his search to find her wiped out by this first day on the job.

She was sliding into a light doze when Rob tapped on her window. As she struggled upright, he said, "Sorry, I got held up by a phone call."

Jan swung her feet outside and sat waiting to be sure she wouldn't be overwhelmed by dizziness. "So, is Michael still here? Did he enjoy the clay?"

"Yeah, he's here." Rob ran his hands through his hair in a familiar gesture of frustration. "And so's Chad, of all people. He's sticking to Michael like white cat fur on black velvet. The nanny is around somewhere, too. Last I saw her, she was out by the river, playing on her phone."

Jan frowned. "Chad's been weird about both Kitrin and Michael. I saw him watching them around the corner of Jake's house the other day. I really hope he didn't do anything stupid. I mean, more stupid than turning off those cameras." Then she had to explain to Rob what Chad had been up to, according to Lacey, and how Jake said there was no doubt now that Kitrin had been deliberately killed.

Rob said, "I kinda wish you hadn't told me that. Now I have to go back in there and be cheerful in front of Michael, knowing his mother was murdered. Is it worse that I can readily believe Chad did it in a fit of rage, even though I'm sure he never raised a hand to her when they were a couple?"

Jan put a hand on his arm. "I'm sorry. The whole thing makes me so angry, I just had to share."

"Well, let's get you indoors before they leave." He unloaded her folding wheelchair. A whole year's intermittent practice had left him as handy with it as Terry was, and soon she was sitting comfortably on the moulded seat cushion, being wheeled along the shady log colonnade to the front entrance. Rob hit the wheelchair-access button and waited for the door to swing open. As he turned her to go through, the plate glass reflected an RCMP car at the stop sign across the road. Had they found Kitrin's phone already? It probably wouldn't help them after two days in a chlorinated pool. She shivered, less from the cool shadows than from the memory of her struggle in the water with Kitrin.

Michael ran over when they entered the atrium. "Jan! You should see what I made: a T. Rex in a space helmet. The clay lady says she'll bake it for me when she does her next firing, and Rob says he'll mail it to me if I'm gone already. Do you want to come downstairs and see it?"

"I'd love to," she said and looked past him. "Hi, Chad. What brings you here?"

"The nanny took off," he said, his eyes lowered.

"Really?" Rob looked out the big windows. "She was on the terrace a while back."

Michael drooped. "She told us she has a meeting with Daddy, and would Chad bring me home. She meets with Daddy every day now."

Jan bit her lip lest she blurt out her opinion of those "meetings." Behind her, Rob said "huh" and then, "Are you strong enough to push Jan to the elevator? I've got to check in with my office for a minute."

"Sure I am." Michael immediately took position behind the chair.

Rob moved to the elevator. As he pushed the button, the museum's front door whooshed open. The colour drained from Chad's face. Jan turned her head in time to see two uniformed Mounties stride in. *Oh, shit.* They had finally caught on to Chad's history with Kitrin and were coming to question him.

"Michael," she said quickly, "go hold the elevator door for Rob."

Instead of heading for Chad, though, the officers went directly to Rob. One said, "Rob Waters? Is there somewhere we can talk?"

CHAPTER FIFTEEN

Lacey rubbed her eyes and tried zooming in on the image one more time. But all she saw was the same dark blob in a halo of bluish light. She'd been stuck in this office since lunchtime with the August sun baking down on the sloped roof, and with only this one anomalous moment of video to suggest someone tampered with Orrin's Range Rover. She leaned back, stuck her feet up on the desk, and called Jan's number, crossing her fingers that her friend wasn't resting. The phone rang once, twice, three times. Just when she thought it was going to voice mail, Jan answered, sounding flustered.

"Lacey! Oh my God."

"What's the matter?"

"I think Rob was arrested."

Lacey sat upright in a hurry. "Rob, not Chad?"

"Yes, Rob. I thought they were coming for Chad, but they walked right up to Rob and asked him if he would go talk to them."

"Did you ask what it was about? Did he ask?"

"No. Michael was with us. So was Chad. I didn't want Michael to overhear if they asked Chad about

Kitrin's death, so I sent him over to Rob and then they went there and … Oh my God."

"Wow. Deep breaths. Come on, deep breaths." After breathing along in a calming way, Lacey asked, "When did this happen?"

"About half an hour ago. I just got home."

"Did they actually take him away or just talk to him?"

"They asked to talk to him. So we — Chad and I — took Michael down to the clay room right away to see his project. But when we came up a few minutes later, the officers were putting Rob into their car. Why would they arrest Rob? He hadn't even seen Kitrin since they arrived. Or wait, he did once, that time she came to the museum with Mylo. That's the first we knew she was in town. Can you find out more from Wayne or some RCMP pal?"

"I'll try."

Lacey hung up and dialled Wayne's voice mail. "Hi, boss. Two questions. What do you want me to do with this oil sample from the garage floor? The mechanic thinks it's power steering fluid. And can you find out through any buddies in Major Crimes why they want Rob Waters in connection with Kitrin Devine's death?"

The odds weren't good on getting an answer about Rob. Even if Wayne had the connections, he'd surely say, "Need to know, McCrae, and you don't need to."

She called Jan back. "I've left a message, and Wayne will get back to me. As soon as he does, I'll let you know. Now, you were pretty upset when you called me earlier. What was that about?"

"What? Oh, I was on my way to look at a house with some artworks, and Jake stopped by. He's so sad about her dying at his place. Rob's angry and Michael's upset. Chad's got this glazed look. And I am really pissed off that somebody killed my friend and caused pain to all these people I care about." Jan took a couple of audible breaths. "Well, not Chad. He's been creepy. But the ultimate straw was later, when Michael said he wished he could go hang out with Tyrone. Nobody's told him Tyrone's missing in the wilderness, and I sure wasn't going to be the one. Not when they might be found any minute."

"So what did you say?"

"I told him Tyrone's gone away with his father for a few days. I feel like such a shit for lying." Jan really did sound awful. Probably overtired from this job, plus taking so much responsibility for Michael. And with nobody home to make her look after herself.

"Are you at least lying down with your feet up?"

"Yes," said Jan with a sigh. "At least, now I am. I was pacing, and not the good kind."

"Well, stay down now. Is Terry still on search today, or is he coming home to make supper?"

"He might be home tonight, or he might not."

"Do you want to ask Dee to come up and make you supper? In case neither Rob nor Terry gets back?"

"I have leftovers, and I truly am more resilient with these new meds. I don't know what shape I'll be in tomorrow, though. I feel just helpless with Michael, and now Rob."

"I can understand that. There might be a way you can help me, if you're fit enough. Could you look at a video clip?"

"Maybe. What for?"

"I went through garage surveillance footage, watching the Rover Orrin drove off in. The garage lights are supposed to come up automatically when anyone opens a door, but one night last week they didn't. There's a person's silhouette, like they're crossing the garage in the dark, with a flashlight in front of them and the camera behind. If I sent you the clip, could you, I don't know, lighten it up or blow it up or something, and see if you can make out some identifying features?"

"That actually sounds useful. I can do that."

"Thanks so much. I'll email you. If you're really too exhausted, leave it. I'll send it to Wayne and let him find someone." Lacey hesitated before bringing up her other idea. Jan was just starting to sound hopeful. It wouldn't do to get her stewing about Kitrin's death again. On the other hand, this was a way she could help that investigation, too. "Would you mind looking at a photo from one of Jake's cameras, too? It's half a staffer going toward the pool on the morning Kitrin died. None of them will admit they were in the area. You've met or seen them all, and you have such a good eye for line and shape that you might be able to identify the person from the part of their head and neck that's visible. Then the police can shake them up and find out what they saw or did that day."

"I could help catch Kitrin's killer? Do you even have to ask?"

Lacey hung up feeling better about Jan. Having something useful to do that wasn't going to tax her scarce energy would likely keep her from brooding today while she waited for news from Rob.

The phone buzzed its quarter-day update on Dan. Still in the Lower Mainland. Was she being paranoid by continuing to monitor his location when he hadn't come after her once since she moved? A question for another day.

Uploading the relevant clip to a shared file, she sent the link to both Jan and Wayne. In a separate email to Jan, she enclosed the still from Jake's. Her phone chimed on her hip, a double repeat for Wayne. She picked up.

Wayne said, "Number one: can you run that fluid sample down to the Ghost airstrip? Markov from Cochrane detachment is there again today, and he can bring it to Calgary. I'll get it analyzed. Seal it up in a clean plastic bag. Oil won't go bad."

"I do remember that much about evidence collection techniques."

Wayne ignored that. "Per the Devine case, no charges yet, just interrogations. The husband's not a suspect; he was in a helicopter through the requisite time frame. The nanny he's been shagging managed to scrape up an alibi. She'd walked down to Bragg Creek that morning, hung out in a coffee shop hogging the Wi-Fi, and was remembered by a waitress she'd been rude to."

"Charming." Lacey ran her eyes over her monitors, counting heads. Cheryl carried a tray out of Sloane's suite on the second floor. Earl paced between the great room and his father's study, yelling into his phone. Bart and Andy were stretched out on the terrace under a big umbrella. Ben was presumably still asleep in their cabin. At the three gates on the back roads, ranch hands were settling in for another night sleeping in the bed of a pickup truck. Labour laws didn't seem to apply to those men, or they were getting good overtime. She hadn't had to give the speech again or chase off another reporter. If there were no more such tasks tomorrow, her presence here would be questioned.

"I can summarize for you who wants Orrin gone the most," she told Wayne. "Earl's already trying to take over the business, although he doesn't have keys to Orrin's desk or filing cabinet. I can't see him taking the initiative to tamper with the vehicle. He'd be too afraid of being caught and unable to blame it on someone else." Was that true, though? The cowboys believed Earl would throw them under the bus to evade Orrin's wrath. The mechanics might be his scapegoats for a vehicle malfunction. Hopefully Jan could enhance the garage intruder clearly enough to rule Earl in or out.

"Ben's the next best suspect." It cost her a pang to say that. She'd enjoyed learning to climb and was looking forward to a run around the home-quarter loop with him tomorrow morning. "He's been feuding with Orrin for years over some land that was supposed to be in a nature conservancy for him and his twin. Things recently got worse. Orrin all but banished him from the ranch, tried to humiliate him with petty restrictions when he did visit, and last night Earl said if Orrin hadn't fully cut Ben out of the family business, then Earl would finish the job. That thing you're investigating doesn't involve disinheriting Ben, does it? Or a possible infidelity by Sloane?"

Wayne ignored the questions. "Ben's capable of tapping a power steering line, you figure?"

"I don't see why not. However, there's the access problem." She explained about his lack of a fob. "How could he get into the garage without being seen when he can't even open a door without an accomplice?"

"Would his twin help him?"

"Maybe to the extent of lending him a fob. They banded together in self-defence all their lives, against Earl and Orrin. But Bart seems content with his life. He gets along well with his wife, has a job he doesn't mind, and some hobbies he enjoys. Like Ben, he has a trust fund from his mother that makes him somewhat independent from Orrin. And he has no apparent interest in acquiring more power in the business."

"Hmmm," said Wayne. "And Sloane Caine?"

So he still wouldn't answer. "I know nothing about her from direct observation except that she was flirting with Mylo Matheson last week. She hasn't left her suite since soon after I arrived here yesterday. Her maid-slash-companion, Cheryl, takes her food in and keeps her company. They were out together on the Friday night and didn't realize until midnight that Orrin and Tyrone hadn't returned. Not that it means much now that I suspect the tampering was done a week ago, except that she wouldn't have let Tyrone drive off with his father if she knew the vehicle wasn't safe."

"Now that you've gathered first impressions," said Wayne, "I'll send you my dossiers on the family members. It's only public stuff, what my internet snooper could come up with on short notice, but maybe it will suggest angles for further inquiry."

"I'll go over them right away and let you know if my friend can narrow down the garage intruder."

"Thanks." Wayne didn't hang up right away. "I'm putting my trust in you, McCrae. One suspicious death and two missing clients in the same week is the kind of crisis that can destroy a security firm. While I'm keeping Jake Wyman calm and covering my regular clients, you're my thin blue line up there. In blue jeans, get it?"

Wayne must be really rattled. Not only had he praised her — he'd cracked a small joke. "Uh, sure thing, boss. I've got your back."

She signed off and headed out to the truck. What would she learn at the SAR base? Did they have a firm direction for the search yet?

Over supper with Andy and Bart, Lacey passed along what she knew about the day's search. "No sightings yet, but more people out camping in the back country have been alerted to watch for the vehicle, and for Orrin and Tyrone, alone or separately."

Andy frowned. "Why would they separate?"

"It might be on purpose," said Lacey. "Ben thinks Orrin could have dropped Tyrone off somewhere and driven away, then waited for him to catch up."

"Ah," said Bart. "And if Ty went the wrong way, and Orrin went looking for him in another direction, they could be circling within a few miles of each other. Except I'm pretty sure Orrin would have come out to cell range and yelled for help ASAP if he hadn't found Ty by dark."

"Unless something went wrong with his truck, and he couldn't." Lacey took in Andy's worried face. "I'm sure it won't be long now before one or both of them stumble out to a road and get spotted. The weather's great, and there are plenty of creeks to drink from. At worst they'll have to be treated for waterborne infections, and maybe sunburn."

"Yeah, I guess." Andy didn't look convinced. "It sure isn't the same around here without Ty. He could be a pain, but we played a lot of board games and stuff, too."

"Ben and I spent some time with the map this morning, trying to figure out all the places Orrin dumped us." Bart rubbed a scrape on his cheek. "I rode out this morning to check all the locations we remembered on the ranch. I know you said not to, but horseback sign can't be confused with a missing person on foot. Beyond our borders we're hopeless. We were so young, we didn't grasp how much wilderness is around here. Isn't there more that could be done from the air?"

"Every volunteer pilot who knows how to do a grid search was up today. The cameras they're using are set up for crowd-sourcing analysis, too."

Andy's eyes came to life. "That's where they put all the photos up on a website and volunteers at home go over every inch, looking for traces of people."

"I know," said Bart wearily. "We watched that documentary together." It was the first sign of irritation he'd shown, and quite minor given the two days of strain. A basic nice man, Lacey decided.

"Also in new tech," she said to change the subject, "they've got drones that can look for phone signals. If the phones have any charge left and they're within whatever the radius is under the drone, there'll be a ping back to the operator. Then they'll send ground teams directly to that spot."

Bart leaned his elbows on the table. "Cool. Assuming they have an idea where to look, I guess. Drones don't have unlimited range."

"No, and there are only a couple of SAR-certified drone operators in the whole province so far."

"Why don't they have them everywhere?" asked Andy. "It seems like a no-brainer."

"The technology is pretty new. And for SAR work, it's not like any weekend hobbyist can show up, any more than they can for ground searches. The operators have to be SAR-certified plus have training in both drone operation and aerial search techniques. If we had a vehicle as a starting point, the odds would be exponentially better." She didn't say that if the Rover had gone into a deep ravine because of steering loss and/or brake failure, they'd be exponentially worse. Summer trees were a significant handicap; a green vehicle could stay hidden until the trees dropped their leaves in October.

Her companions' tired eyes and drooping faces looked like innocence and stress. She'd spend an hour with their dossiers tonight, but her gut said these two nice people had the least to gain or lose by Orrin's death.

Changing the subject a second time, she told them, "I think I might be addicted to climbing. Ben gave me a beginner lesson on the wall this morning, and I haven't done anything in years that was both physically and mentally challenging. Complete concentration, back and forth in sync with your climbing partner, knowing where your hands and feet are and where their hands and feet are, connected by the rope. It was pretty intense." She was going on like a giddy schoolgirl, but why not, when her whole body still buzzed with the thrill?

Bart said, "I don't mind showing you more tonight."

Andy shook her head. "Leave it to tomorrow. Did Ben tell you, Lacey, that you can strain your hand tendons through early overwork? Free-climbers train for months or years before a big expedition, to cling on to almost invisible cracks in the rock and hold their body weight for long enough to move some other hand or foot. It's a very demanding sport, and I'd hate to see you spoil it for yourself by overdoing it in the first flush of enthusiasm."

Bart was looking sideways at Andy, but he dropped the climbing and said instead, "I'm heading in to the office tomorrow morning. Got to show the family flag and reassure the staff that the place won't immediately collapse without Orrin's hand at the helm. It's going to be a challenge when I'm not feeling it myself. My hopes were pinned on Orrin's credit cards showing he's flown off to Texas for a long weekend or something, and now I know that's not a possibility. His secretary said none of his known accounts has been tapped. At least there are no big deals hanging on his word. Things will keep turning over until he's found."

Lacey schooled her face not to reveal anything but mild inquiry. She wasn't ready to spill that someone had apparently sabotaged Orrin's Rover, but what if it was someone from the company? Executives had probably been invited to the ranch a time or two and might have figured out the security holes.

"Would you be able to tell," she asked, "if anyone seemed particularly happy that Orrin's unavailable?" As Bart stared at her, she scrambled for a rationale. "When a strong boss unexpectedly goes away, any worker with something on their conscience might take advantage of the situation to cover their tracks."

"If you say so." He eyed her curiously.

Andy got up to clear the plates, and he silently gathered glasses. They brushed aside Lacey's offer of help.

Later, skimming the monitors from her office chair, she saw the couple on the new bluff-stairs camera, going down. They were probably getting in their last destressing workout. Once she'd gone through Wayne's dossiers, she would go down with the ladder to be ready for the morning's camera adjustments. If they were climbing, she could watch and get pointers without straining her finger tendons. She opened Wayne's email with the dossiers and clicked Download All.

CHAPTER SIXTEEN

In her dusty studio, Jan squinted at her biggest monitor, magnifying and brightening a still from Lacey's garage video. With each manipulation, the general outline became clearer. The individual wore a dark sweater or hoodie and probably gloves, given that the hands weren't showing up, either. They held a small flashlight and reached under the open hood of the Range Rover. At this camera angle, the body's shape and height were hidden by the next vehicle. She did what she could to enhance the image and then saved it as a new file. Back to the video, to advance it frame by frame and find another good shot to brighten and contrast, maybe when the person left the vehicle and came toward the camera. It wouldn't be a firm identification, but it might eliminate a few suspects.

A door clicked down the hall, and she looked up. "Terry, is that you?"

"No, it's me."

"Rob!" Rushing out, she threw her arms around him. "I was so afraid you'd been arrested. Have you been with the RCMP all this time?"

"I'll tell you," he promised, weariness in every line of his face. "But I really need booze and food."

She followed him to the kitchen. "There's pasta salad if you want. Or something hot? I can warm you up soup. Canned, not as good as yours."

Rob splashed whisky into his glass and drank half straight. He topped it up with water and slumped onto a stool.

She sat across from him. "I don't mean to nag, but I've been frantic. Didn't know if I should call you a lawyer or what. They can't seriously think you'd hurt Kitrin. You've hardly seen her in a dozen years."

He stared at his hands. "I'm a former roommate, and I didn't like her husband. To the police, that spells potential jealousy."

"But Chad's the jealous one, not you. Why haven't they called him in for questioning?"

Rob rubbed his forehead. "I don't know. They're fixated on me, and I can't tell them where I was on Saturday morning."

"Why the hell not?"

He swallowed more whisky and lowered the glass to stare into it. "I was with someone who can't confirm it."

"Shit, I knew it. You're involved with someone married again, aren't you? Damn, Rob. How can you put a cheating lover's marriage ahead of your own freedom? You have to make him back you. You have to tell the police where you were."

"I don't *have* to do anything," Rob snarled. Then he sighed. "Sorry. I know I can't let this stand. I'm going to talk it over with him tomorrow. If there's a way we can do it without fallout for him, I'll be clear. But I have to have his consent. There's more at stake than you can possibly understand."

"I'm your oldest friend. There's nothing I can't understand if you explain it to me."

He avoided her eyes. "Well, this time there is something I'm not explaining to you. You'll just have to trust me."

He would not be moved from that position. Jan warmed up his soup, anyway, simmering with discontent. After he'd gone for a shower, she texted Lacey the news that he was back and still under suspicion, and then texted Dee to ask about a criminal lawyer. If he were hauled in again, she'd send help.

Her head jostling with biographical details about the brothers, their wives, and Orrin's wives, Lacey looked out her office window at the skylights glowing on the climbing gym's sloping roof. She stretched, skimmed through the camera monitors again, and stood up. The ladder she'd left in the garage this morning was still there. She hitched it over her shoulder, opened the door, and flashed her fob at the elevator. Going down.

When she reached the climbing gym, Bart was nowhere to be seen. Music filled the space from unseen speakers — she recognized a Frank Turner tune — and once again it was Ben belaying Andy on the wall. She was coming down when Lacey pushed the door open. Ben didn't wait for her to touch bottom but again lifted her off the last bit of wall. She turned in his hands once her feet were on the ground, smiling up at him. When she saw Lacey she stepped back, looking down to unhook her harness. Her dark curls fell forward, hiding her expression.

"Oh, hi," she said in a tone not particularly welcoming. "What are you doing down here at this hour?"

Lacey leaned the ladder against the wall. "I have to adjust the camera in the workout room. It's not covering the back door properly."

"Bart's running on the treadmill, and he hates to be disturbed. Can't you do that in the morning?"

The window into the workout room was dark. Bart wasn't in there, or if he was, he was running in darkness. It seemed Andy wanted her to leave and was lying to make her go. Still, any request from the client's family was an order. Lacey leaned the ladder in the cloakroom area, climbed the stairs, and headed back to the security office. There she checked monitors and reread dossiers, looking for items she could turn into casual-seeming questions for the various family members, and tried unsuccessfully to ignore the sting of Andy's abrupt retreat from friendliness.

> **Giselle Burns Harder**. Born 1952 in Saskatoon, Saskatchewan, family moved to Calgary in 1965. Unfinished BA at UCalgary in Theatre. Married Orrin Caine in 1970. Two children, Earl and Debbie. Nasty divorce in 1988, initiated by Orrin.

She tried to gain a bigger settlement by citing his numerous infidelities but lost due to a pre-nup agreement that diverted her share of his company holdings to her children. Post-divorce, she worked as an activities coordinator at a seniors' centre, where she met Don Harder. She married him in 1995. His mother lived with them until her death in 2002. Giselle was widowed in 2015. Lives in West Bragg Creek. No criminal record.

Earl Caine. Born in 1972 to Giselle and Orrin. Attended public school in Calgary. In Grade 9 attended Craigeilen Academy in Ontario, where he had an undistinguished academic career, played sports, and was popular with his peers. Interviewed by police after a hazing incident resulted in a student being hospitalized; no charges but a week-long suspension. He took a B.Commerce at U of Toronto and an MBA in Chicago. Worked at his father's company summers in various departments; headed the Calgary HR department after graduation; named Canadian VP of HR in 2002. Six years ago he took over the company's American operations and moved to Denver. Widely expected to succeed Orrin as board chair when his father retires. Married Susie North of West Virginia in 1996, has four daughters aged 22, 19, 17, and 15.

Bart Caine, born 1990 to Orrin and his second wife, Cassandra Landry. Attended a private elementary school first in Calgary (1995 to 1998) then 5 years in a private day school on Vancouver Island. At age 12 went to Craigeilen Academy for 14 months, abruptly withdrawn in November of Grade 9 after a student incident left him with a cracked rib and black eye. Finished high school at Airth Academy on Vancouver Island, attended UC Berkeley, worked summers as a lifeguard down there, and graduated with a B.Admin. He returned to Orrin's business in the Land Management department and took over the Alberta Lands division at age 28. Married at age 25 to Andrea Constanza Juarez.

Ben Caine. Born 1990 to Orrin and Cassandra, same academic career as Bart, including Berkeley, where he took a BA in Environmental Science. While at Craigeilen was suspended 3 times and expelled once, all for fighting. He spent summers and university protesting at environmental hotspots, was arrested 14 times, charged 8 times of which 5 were dismissed, pled to 3 misdemeanours (2 in USA) and was named an honorary member of an Indigenous tribe in Brazil for helping them successfully fight a Canadian mining corporation in which his father's company held a minority ownership stake. Retains his right to travel in USA although is on the environmentalist watch-list. Never worked for Orrin's companies. No spouse, no long-term relationships on record.

Andrea Constanza Juarez. Born 1993 in Argentina to an oil magnate (deceased). Raised by mother and stepfather in Connecticut. Attended UC Berkeley, where she met Bart. Most notable for minor celebrity status as an early video blogger on YouTube, where her followers topped 2 million in her final year. Legal issues involve restraining orders against two paparazzi and one obsessed fan. Had a public meltdown in 2014 and became obsessed with her personal privacy. Shut down her vlog and all public appearances on marriage to Bart Caine in 2015.

Cassandra Landry Caine. Born 1968 in Baton Rouge, Louisiana, married Orrin Caine 1989, divorced in 1997. Mother of Bart and Ben. Lives in the Comox Valley on Vancouver Island, where she owns a pottery studio and has two convictions for possession of illegal substances. Applied for a pardon after federal marijuana laws changed; outcome pending.

Sloane Carter Caine. Born 1985 in Toronto, had a brief career as a preteen catalogue model, high school cheerleader, attended Ryerson but left with an finished BA (no major declared). Worked as a hostess at the National Club in Toronto, where she met Orrin. Roomed with best friend Cheryl Marr until married to Orrin in 2007. Mother of Tyrone Caine, born in 2008. No criminal record or legal proceedings.

Lacey closed the final dossier page and looked up from her keyboard for the usual monitor survey. The lights in the workout room had gone up. Two figures, male and female, were half visible on the still-misaligned camera as they hugged inside the open bathroom door. Aw ... Bart and Andy being affectionate. He'd been there after all.

When he pulled Andy's T-shirt off over her head, Lacey shut down the monitors for the night. She made her final phone check with Ike and headed out into the balmy summer night. Passing the lighted great room, she wished she could sit and stargaze over the sleeping valley. But barely an hour after being politely put in her place by Andy, she didn't feel comfortable resting on a chaise in a family area.

Surely she could lean on the railing atop the bluff stairs without causing offence?

She'd hardly settled there when she heard footsteps crossing the stones. Bart, fully dressed in the clothes he'd worn at supper, leaned on the rail beside her.

"Evening, Lacey. Are you heading back to our place now?"

She nodded, unwilling to open her mouth while the implication of his presence upended what she thought she'd seen heating up in the workout room.

"I'll walk with you, if you don't mind," he said. "Keep the cougars at bay."

They paced through the trees together, Bart discussing the reactions at their Calgary office and Lacey silent under the knowledge that Bart's wife was indulging in a sexual workout with his twin brother. So much for the happy couple who supported each other amid the constant tensions of the Caine homestead.

After breakfast, clutching her phone to her ear with one hand, Lacey used the other to zoom in the camera covering the front gate. "I see three vehicles parked by the highway gate, one unmarked and two with media logos. Do you want me to send them away?"

"No," said Earl. "One of my people will go."

"Yes, sir." She'd seen several men in suits conferring with him in the great room earlier. Presumably they were lawyers, executives, or media spokespeople from Orrin's business empire. She disconnected and messaged Ike. *Please alert everyone that three groups of reporters are being turned away at the main gate and may try other accesses.*

A ping signalled an incoming text. She looked

down, expecting Ike's acknowledgement. Jan had sent *I'm up. Please call me if you have a minute.*

Lacey checked on the workout room and climbing centre. Andrea was still doing her morning round of the weight machines. Phoning it would be.

After the usual greetings, Jan said, "So you got my message last night that they released Rob? He won't tell me who he was with last Saturday morning. Says it would cause problems for the guy to provide his alibi. I can't believe in this century, gay men are still hiding behind marriage. I wonder if his wife knows, or if she's beating herself up, thinking she's not sexy enough to keep her husband interested."

"You're jumping to conclusions," said Lacey. "Lots of people nowadays have open marriages. Lots of relationships are polyamorous, too. Maybe Rob's lover is bi."

Jan sniffed. "Possibilities, sure, but none of them are good for Rob's long-term happiness. Or his short-term happiness, either, if this guy won't come out and tell the police that Rob was with him when Kitrin was killed."

"Rob needs a lawyer the next time he talks to them."

"I emailed him Dee's top suggestion already. How are things going out there?"

"Not well." Lacey chewed her lip. "The people I thought least likely to gain anything by Orrin going missing have shaken my faith in them." She told Jan about seeing Andy and Ben. "And then I walked back with Bart to the cabin, and he was chatting away like normal, obviously not thinking anything of the fact that his brother and his wife were together." She toggled through the camera images again and caught a ranch hand taking a leak against a fence post. If not for Andy's early offer of a bed — which she might be regretting now — Lacey might have been sharing the bunkhouse bathrooms with all those men. Ugh. "Almost as weird was getting up this morning to find Ben waiting to go for a run with me. When we planned it yesterday, I thought he was a pretty straight-up guy, and now I know he's a horndog with no morals. I didn't have a decent excuse for refusing — or none I was prepared to spell out for him — so I went. It's a good five-k route, along the bluff, down into the valley, and back up the other end. I backed off another climbing lesson, though. Claimed my fingers were sore from yesterday."

"Did you think he was going to hit on you?"

"Nothing like that. I'm just mentally adapting to the idea that an environmentalist is untrustworthy. In my book, serious greenies should be more ethical than us normies. I didn't expect Andy to go behind her husband's back, and worse, in a place where anyone with a key fob might walk in at any moment. I must have interrupted their foreplay last night, too, when I took down the ladder."

"What did you just say to me about not jumping to conclusions? Tell her you know and see what she says."

"If we were actually friends, I'd do that. But technically she's part of the family business that contracts Wayne, who subcontracts me. And if this in-house affair is in any way connected to Orrin going missing, letting her know I know could impair the investigation." She thought. "Could it have been a woman on that video clip from the garage? Andy's my height, only a bit shorter than Bart and Ben."

"I didn't get a clear enough image to estimate height," said Jan. "I'd have to compare her height to whatever make of SUV was parked beside the Range Rover."

Lacey groaned. "I'll sort out which vehicle was parked where that day. Orrin's was usually in the end spot because it rarely moved."

"Let me know when you've got something for me to measure against, and I'll tell you how tall your shadowy intruder is. I can guesstimate, once I have the vehicle data, how wide the shoulders are and whatever."

"It'll all help narrow down the suspects." But would it? The women here were tallish, even Cheryl, and it was easy to disguise a shape beneath baggy clothing. Men could slouch, too, and round their shoulders. Every one of them knew where the cameras were, even in the dark.

She said goodbye and checked the gate cameras again. Someone in a cowboy hat was talking to the guys on the south gate. As she watched, he got into a dusty F-150 and drove off. Just a neighbour checking in? Probably several had done so without her eyes on them. Neither guard was picking up his radio, anyway. Out front, another news van was pulling up. She held the feed there while someone climbed out and joined the cluster of reporters chatting in the shade. Whatever Earl's "people" had told them, it hadn't discouraged them one iota. She checked the ranch's phone directory and texted Andy.

Lacey here. Several reporters around front gate. You might want to stay out of sight.

A half minute later, Andy messaged back. *Thx. Can you smuggle me out to Calgary this aft?*

Lacey pondered the message. Should she leave the ranch? Wayne had sent her here to keep an eye on all of them. On the other hand, alone in a vehicle with Andy for two hours or more, she might learn quite a lot about the family that wasn't available on the internet. Things Andy wouldn't normally say but might tell a friendly female driver to fill in the time. Covering her bases, Lacey texted Wayne. *Permission to drive Bart's wife into Calgary this afternoon? She wants protection from reporters.* His *yes* freed her to reply to Andy with *Sure. What time, and how long do you expect to be gone?*

When that was settled, she loaded up a video still to her phone, with the clearest view she could manage of the SUV that was parked beside the Range Rover last Monday night. The logo was in deep shadow, but she could faintly make out the shape of its windows and a few other features. Then she went down to the garage floor. The two mechanics were elsewhere and two slots were empty, but she compared the photo to vehicles until she was sure the SUV she wanted was the Porsche Macan Sloane drove. Today it occupied the second-to-last slot. She didn't recall seeing it move. She lined herself up with the garage camera, estimating by the faded blotch on the floor approximately where the saboteur had stood to open the Rover's hood. Hoping nobody would come in and catch her, she posed upright, bent over as if to reach into the engine compartment, and then moved slowly along the Macan's side, holding each position for at least ten seconds to be sure of getting it onto the video feed. She took photos of the SUV from several angles, including the logo, for Jan's reference points, and checked the mechanics' clipboard for make, model, and year. Upstairs again, she looped back through the footage, captured the segment of her awkward acting job, and sent it with the vehicle photos to Jan.

With that taken care of, she watched the cameras flip through their cycle. In the hallway outside Orrin's study, Bart was shoving a map at Earl, jabbing it with his index finger. No fists flying yet, so she scrolled on. Andy was leaving the climbing centre. At last! Lacey strapped on her tool belt, collected the camera system's iPad, and headed down in the elevator to reclaim her abandoned ladder from the cloakroom. This job would be checked off ASAP.

She'd reckoned without the treadmill. It was too heavy and awkward to shift by herself, so she angled the stepladder in as best she could beside it and climbed up to perch unsteadily, alternately nudging the camera's lens another finger width and staring down at the iPad until the image updated. Note for Wayne: upgrade this iPad's programming so she could fix its feed to one camera at a time. When she was satisfied that the camera was covering the exit correctly, she climbed down and went to open the outside door, just to be sure it would fully reveal anyone coming in or out.

When she touched the handle, though, the door swung inward. Not locked? Something fell past her face. Startled, she stepped back and bent to pick up a wooden wedge that showed the tell-tale striations of being pushed into a gap many times over. She looked along the doorjamb and then down the door's edge. The lock's tongue was sawed off level with the plate. This door hadn't been secured except by this bit of wood since ... when, exactly?

She looked over her shoulder at the newly realigned camera. The door, she already knew, wasn't covered from the outside, either. Someone could have entered here, crossed the climbing gym, climbed the inside stairs, and reached the main control panel for the motion-sensor lights without being caught on a single camera or stopped by a single locked door. Right up to Orrin's Range Rover.

CHAPTER SEVENTEEN

They were several miles away down Highway 40 when Lacey slowed and let the dust clouds settle behind the SUV. "Nobody followed. You can come out now."

"Are you sure?" Andy peered from under a blanket in the back.

"Yes. Want me to pull over so you can get up front?"

"I'll climb over." Andy's effortless scramble over the two intervening seats gave Lacey a pang of envy. If she tried that, she'd end up scrunched between the seat back and the roof, unable to move. That they were the same height was an added slap in the self-esteem. Andy buckled her seat belt. "Thanks for this. I'm a bit freaked out by media attention. I just needed to know I could escape."

"Understandable," said Lacey. As Andy peered at her with a frown, she added, "I searched you online to see your vlogs and get a sense of your followers. After reading about that stalker, I can see why you'd be nervous around reporters."

Andy shuddered. "The guy was always outside my apartment, and even when I snuck out the back, some passerby hoping to make a buck from a celeb site would tweet where they'd seen me, making it easy for him to find me again. Reporters circled like vultures, waiting for me to crack or him to attack. It's horrible having them camped outside the gate."

Lacey nodded. "I can see why it would creep you out. One thing that wasn't clear online, though, was how it all started. Seems like one week you appeared on talk shows to great applause, and the next week there were skanky stories about you everywhere."

"Please tell me you didn't believe those."

"Absolutely not. They were way too outlandish. And now that I've met you, I believe them even less."

"Thanks for that." Andy rooted through the glove compartment. "I should've brought my backpack. It has a stash of sugar-free candies. It's what I do when I don't want to slip back into smoking or some other self-destructive behaviour."

"There's sugar-free gum in my pack if you want it." Lacey pointed. "In the back seat. Side zipper pocket."

Andy reached for it. As she popped out a piece, she said, "All I seem to be able to do today is say thank you. I feel totally lame."

"I don't mean to be pushy, but did you talk to anybody about that stalking when it was over? A counsellor or other professional?"

"Yeah." Andy sighed. "That's partly why I want to go into town. I have a therapist who takes phone appointments, but there's no way in hell I'd spill such personal shit under Orrin's roofs. Bart says I'm just being paranoid, but I wouldn't put it past the old buzzard to have bugged our cabin. We'll soon find out if — I mean when — he comes back and hears what was said about him in his absence." She shoved the gum into her mouth and spoke past it. "Mind if I hit some music?"

"You're the boss."

Andy flashed a grin. "You're Orrin's employee, not mine." She dropped her phone into the slot and leaned back in the seat as a pop beat filled the speakers. The chorus seemed to be about breathing in and breathing out. The next song suggested letting go and having a safety net. After a while, Andy opened her eyes and turned the music down. "That's better."

"Who's that singer?"

"Kate Alexa, an Australian pop star from my university days. She's most famous for songs on teen TV shows, but she helped me find some joy during my darkest times."

Lacey slowed to wind her way through the Waiparous Village curves. "Don't talk about that time if you don't want to. But I might protect you better by knowing more."

"Not sure I need protection anymore, except from reporters. It was lifetimes ago in internet years. Would you believe, the cops said because I'd gone for coffee with him first — just the one time, before he got weird — I'd encouraged him, and therefore it was up to me to discourage him? Like they couldn't grasp the awful vibe he gave off from me simply telling him I didn't want to hang with him a second time. Then following me for months, sending flowers and gifts because he's convinced I'm his one true love." She faked gagging.

"Plus selling his stalker photos to celebrity websites and shit-posting about me on my own fan sites under dozens of aliases. When I was being interviewed in any public venue, he'd start blasting that Lady Gaga song on his phone about following me anywhere? I couldn't listen to any LG after that." She chewed her gum and drummed her fingers on her thighs until a White Stripes song came on. Then she smiled. "This song reminds me of how Bart dropped everything to come and stay with me in New York City after the cops blew me off. He was my best friend from Berkeley. It was him who came up with the plan to kill the guy's delusions once and for all."

"By getting married?"

"Exactly. Plus his dad had so much money, I could be sure of protection. That creep was never going to get within fifty metres of me again." Andy examined her painted fingernails. "I think Orrin's fixers had a word with the guy. They can be kind of intimidating when they want."

"Those guys in the dark suits who are running around the ranch? They didn't intimidate the reporters at the gate."

"No, those are head office types. They're used to a deferential *Calgary Herald* reporter or someone from *Forbes* writing a puff piece on Orrin. Did you ever see the TV show *Angel*? The law firm on that show was kind of like Orrin's fixers. Nothing they wouldn't do for their rich clients. They supply Orrin's bodyguards when he goes to Niger and other places where the locals hate his corporate looting of their resources." She picked at a flake of polish on her thumbnail. "Which makes it even more weird that he would go missing from the ranch. It's always been his safe haven. You don't suppose he has dementia, do you, and we never noticed? Ty doesn't drive and wouldn't be able to navigate back if Orrin got them lost because he suddenly can't remember his way back."

She closed her eyes again, leaving Lacey to drive on with her thoughts for company while Frank Turner and Ed Sheeran sang songs suitable for country roads on sunny afternoons. So Andy had married Bart for protection from her stalker. They were good friends back then, and clearly still, but maybe they had no chemistry, and it had never blossomed into a truly passionate relationship. That didn't excuse her screwing his brother, but it helped explain it. Maybe Bart didn't know, and maybe he did but didn't mind.

The Husky station at Highway 1 was coming up, and Lacey had to interrupt her passenger's reverie. "Do I go into Calgary on the Trans-Canada or Highway 8?"

"Glenmore Trail and 8, please. I'll direct you from the Grey Eagle Casino exit. We can cruise the block first and make sure nobody from the *Herald* or *Sun* is lurking."

Lacey drove on south. She'd be passing within ten minutes of home. If she'd known the route sooner, she'd have asked to swing by to pick up clean underwear and fresh T-shirts. But Andy presumably had a timeline for her therapist phone call. Maybe on the way back.

Half an hour later, they were creeping along a quiet street in Lakeview, on the north side of Glenmore Reservoir. Large suburban homes lay amid shaved green lawns or lurked behind wrought-iron gates. Children rode bikes on the sidewalks.

Andy said suddenly, "Shit, that grey sedan," and ducked beneath the dashboard. "Keep going. Don't even slow down for a second. Take the next right."

Passing straight along the street, Lacey barely made the grey car with a camera pointing out the driver's window. She watched it in the rear-view mirror to make sure the driver didn't follow.

"Good catch," she said. "I'd have missed him. I was looking for a marked media vehicle."

Andy sat up and smoothed her hair back into place. "They play the stealth game, looking for embarrassing shots. When we get around the corner, you'll see the sign for the Calgary Canoe Club. Pull in there. I'm a member, and we can park all day."

Lacey signalled for the turn. "That guy in the car was a shock. I didn't think Calgary had paparazzi."

"They're not as vicious or as professional as the ones in New York, but they're there. Mostly it's wanna-be journalists, sometimes security guards or PIs who supplement their income by selling photos to the local news services. Orrin's an oil baron, and we've all been hiding out at the ranch since he vanished, so the first one who gets a current photo of a family member gets a big payday and bragging rights."

"I'm surprised you would risk coming out with just me to protect you."

"You don't look like personal security, which keeps attention off me, too." Andy pointed out the canoe club's parking lot. "Drive right down to the clubhouse."

Lacey parked near the building. The area had a weekday deserted feel to it. Even in the shade, the grass was browned by the baking sun. Just below them, the reservoir lay deep and blue. Rowers in a dragon boat left a sparkling wake. Birds chirped. A bumblebee blundered by. It was all very peaceful. There was nobody at hand to notice their arrival.

After a moment, Andy slid out of the SUV and let them into the building. She opened a locker and changed into a different T-shirt, tied a hoodie around her waist, pulled her hair through the back of a baseball cap, and switched to a different pair of sunglasses. Then she changed her sandals for running shoes. She looked at Lacey's feet.

"Can you run in those boots?"

"If I have to."

"Here, take this other hat and glasses. We can pretend we're suburban moms out for a walk. It's not perfect, but just in case that guy's connected to someone outside the ranch who's seen you …" Back at the front door, she filled a neon orange water bottle from a drinking fountain. "You go outside first and see if anyone's around with their cellphone raised."

Lacey strolled across the parking lot, checking out the other vehicles. None had occupants, and only one person was in sight, heading slowly away along a path with an elderly black Lab ambling along behind. She beckoned to Andy. "Looks clear."

"Good. Let's get across that road before someone does come along who'll recognize me." Andy led the way. "We'll take the field path, basically making for the fence behind those houses but farther along. There's a gate into my backyard. If it looks clear, we'll go in that way. If not, we'll just keep walking and circle back to the parking lot to drive away. Are you good with that?"

Lacey nodded, but her feet curled up at the thought of a long walk on hot ground in her workboots. Her jogging shoes would have been so much better for walking. Or running, if it came to that. She plodded across the road behind Andy. The tall, dry grass rustled. Somewhere a dog barked. A child's laugh echoed.

Andy waved her hand. "There's a playground over there." She made her way toward copses of poplar and aspen, pausing frequently to sip from her water bottle and check out the surroundings. As they got closer to the fenceline, she stopped more often.

Lacey asked, "Would you like me to go ahead now?"

"Please. Just keep going along the fence and watch out for anyone walking. If they have a dog they're probably okay, but that's no guarantee."

Lacey reached the first trees, slowed, and took a good look through the trunks and underbrush. Was a payday photo of Andy enough to make someone risk ticks and other creepy-crawlies for hours of on-spec waiting? She called on her old RCMP search training for wooded terrain and looked closer still. No flare off a camera lens or binoculars, no unusual movement of leaves or branches. She waved Andy forward. "I think you're good to go."

Andy unlocked the gate and stepped through.

Lacey followed her into a shady passage between a garden shed and a pool pavilion. Nobody would get a shot of the yard unless they were perfectly lined up, and that would show only a narrow strip of walkway leading to the house. The gate locked behind them, and she looked around. It was a nice yard by city standards, part lawn and part paved with interlocking bricks around an oval pool. Loungers, sunshade, tables, and a single air mattress surrounded it. The house had ells protruding at each end with a semi-enclosed patio between them, half shaded by a balcony above.

Andy let them into a cool, white kitchen. She dropped her hat and sunglasses, untied the hoodie, and flung it onto the grey granite island. "Thank God we're here, and in time for me to rinse off before my appointment. I'll be about an hour. Help yourself to a drink or something. Wi-Fi password is on the fridge, or books and TV in the room to the right. I don't need to tell you to stay away from the windows, right?"

She hadn't gone two steps from the kitchen when she looked back, waving frantically. She put a finger to her lips, and pointed up the curving staircase.

Lacey had barely untied her workboots. She kicked them off and hurried over, immediately identifying the sound from upstairs. Someone was walking across a floor.

She signalled Andy to lean against the wall, out of sight, and started up the steps. Technically, she should call this in as a break-in, but she'd bet the intruder was a sneak-thief who would run when confronted. Illegal but not dangerous. Still, she looked around for something heavy enough to serve as a weapon. The upper hall was empty except for small framed paintings. Hand to hand, then, if it came to a fight.

Ahead of her, someone coughed. A male voice answered. The sound brought Andy charging past her.

"Bart? Is that you? What the hell are you doing here?" She flung open a double door. Lacey almost ran into her when she stopped in the doorway, staring at a rumpled king-sized bed that took up half the hardwood floor.

Bart, over by the balcony door, was pulling on a shirt. Thankfully, he'd already got his pants on.

Andy said again, "What the hell? Do you know there's a paparazzi out front?"

Bart's eyes flickered toward a closed door. Lacey barely had time to think *Shit, he's got a lover in there* before Andy screamed, a primal sound of sheer rage that echoed off the glass doors. "You fucking asshole. You brought the paparazzi home in the midst of this mess just to get your fucking rocks off?"

Bart came toward her, hands raised in a pacifying gesture. "It's not like that. I didn't plan this."

"Fuck you!"

He stopped, rubbing one bare foot over the other. "Honest, babe. Something came up. We had to talk it over in private, so we came here, and one thing led to another. Look, it's not a reason to panic."

Andy hoisted a heavy crystal vase and drew it back like a shot put. "You in the bathroom. Get your fucking ass out here."

The bathroom door opened. Bart's mystery guest appeared around the door frame. As he saw Lacey, his eyes widened.

She stared back. "Rob?"

CHAPTER EIGHTEEN

Jan groaned. So much for perfection. As the video panned around Mrs. Harder's Old West bedroom, it captured one vividly out-of-era detail. On a shelf under a knotty wood bedside table was a wicker basket filled with bright yellow prescription containers, clearly marked in modern black fonts. How had she not noticed that in the eight times she'd viewed the clip before including it in the final video? She snipped the revealing frames and chose a replacement image from her still-photo file. In it, the oblique sunlight was highlighting those same white labels and yellow pill bottles, but she photoshopped balls of grey wool in their place. Inserted into the video, the image displayed small and then zoomed in on the pretty quilt to distract from the wool seams. She watched the whole video again. Was it perfect? No. This time she caught a reflection in the dresser mirror of Mrs. Harder leaving the room. Just the back of her head and torso, but the modern clothing and short auburn hair were enough to ruin the illusion. She replaced that shot with a still, too, and watched for what seemed like the hundredth time.

As the last frames of the log cabin video flickered by, she checked her watch and decided it was good enough. Maybe not up to Hollywood standards, but she was only an art director's assistant's contract helper. She started the video uploading to Davey's site and set aside the laptop. A good day's work. Once she'd rested up from this, she would call Jake's place and see how Michael was doing, maybe invite him to come along to her next art collection excursion and get some ice cream.

She'd barely closed her eyes before a vehicle pulled up outside. Not Terry's truck. It sounded like Rob's car, but what would he be doing here at quarter after four? He didn't usually leave the museum until five. The front door clicked. "Rob, is that you?"

"It's me. Are you awake?"

"Sort of. What's up?"

"Remember those things I wouldn't tell you yesterday?"

She sat up, wincing as the light struck her over-worked eyeballs. Rob stood in the doorway, looking as shattered as she had ever seen him. She rolled off the couch and went over, wrapped her arms around him, and held on.

After a while he pulled back. "I'd better tell you all this now. Lacey will be up in a few minutes."

"She's home? Did they find Orrin and Tyrone?"

"No. Nothing to do with the search. She happened to be handy when things exploded this afternoon, and we drove out from Calgary together. She'll be heading back to the ranch soon, and I'll need both of you up to speed before she goes." He dragged himself into the living room and slumped on one end of the couch.

She crawled back into her nest at the other end. "Okay, talk to me."

After that highly confusing beginning, he didn't seem to know quite how to go on. Eventually, she prodded him.

"Is this about your alibi for Saturday morning?"

He nodded. "You remember I said I couldn't out my friend without his consent? Well, I set up a lunch meet with him today. Figured if I explained the situation, we might come up with a workaround, so I could get my alibi without him being outed. Like, say we were doing something else together. It wouldn't pass a lie detector, but they'd have no reason to suspect him of collusion."

Going by his miserable expression, his lover wasn't willing. She waited, giving him space to get the words out in his own time.

Looking down at his hands, he said, "We were discussing activities we could both swear to that wouldn't be what we were actually doing, but not quite a lie, either. I hoped Lacey could feed the alibi to the investigators without him going on the record, where it might come out and get him into trouble. She did it before, for that student last winter. Remember?"

"Uh-huh. So this guy is willing for you to be cleared as long as he doesn't have to confess that you're involved with him?"

"Of course." He looked at her oddly. "It's not a casual relationship. We just have to minimize the fallout."

"But you said 'things exploded.' That's not a positive outcome."

"It would have been, except …" He flushed. "One thing led to another, and his wife arrived home unexpectedly. She kind of freaked out when she walked in on us."

"She didn't know he was sleeping with —" She changed from "a man" to "you" at the last moment.

"Oh, no, she's always known that. About him, and about me from early on. We haven't met before, though, and it wasn't a great way to meet today."

"Because you were in her house?"

"Because a photographer followed him home and was staking out the place." He scrubbed both hands through his hair. "You've met them, Jan. It's Bart Caine I've been seeing for the past, well, since the spring."

"Bart Caine is gay? Orrin Caine's son?" Jan sank back against her pillows. "No wonder he really doesn't want to come out. What a disaster for you both."

"No shit." Now that the news was out, Rob looked fractionally less tightly wound. "Lacey brought Andrea into town this afternoon. You probably don't know, but Andrea had paparazzi trouble before she married Bart. She can spot a camera lens a kilometre away, and there was one out front of their house while we were inside."

"Did he get photos of you going in, or anything compromising?"

"I don't think so. The most he'd have got was me walking up the street and being buzzed in at the gate, because I parked around the corner, like usual. But you can see how this would make a great side-scandal in the midst of the search for Orrin. Suspect in Hollywood murder involved with son of missing millionaire!" He shuddered. "Tabloid city, and Andrea would be caught in the middle of it. I can't blame her for screaming."

"So she freaked out because of the photographer, not because you were sleeping with her husband in her house?"

"Pretty much. She thought Bart was risking everything they've kept hidden just for sex. She calmed down a bit when we explained that Bart's my alibi for Kitrin's murder. Except she didn't know Kitrin had been murdered, and she got mad at Lacey for not telling her."

"Jackpot or what?" Jan hugged herself, chilled by the narrowly averted feeding frenzy. Orrin — assuming he came home alive — would probably disown Bart. Rob would still be a suspect if his only alibi was a lover. Reporters would hound Andrea, yelling questions about her marriage and sex life every time she set foot out her front door. Her marriage might not survive. "Will she forgive Bart?"

"I don't know. She was going to talk to her therapist and hopefully calm down. Then she and Bart will come this way to pick up Lacey. So I guess we'll find out when they get here." He stretched his legs and propped his feet on the coffee table. "She's good at misdirection, that's for sure. She sent Lacey and I out the front door with a wrapped painting, making it look like Lacey'd been there since before Bart got home. If we're identified, well, I was there collecting a loaner painting from the Caine collection, and she was its security escort. Bart and Andy will sneak out the back way and pick up the vehicle she and Lacey left at the canoe club. The photographer can keep staking out an empty house."

"Wow." Jan lay there with her head whirling. Bart Caine, son of possibly the most homophobic man in Alberta, had been hiding his true self from his father all his life, even marrying as a disguise. Yet Andy had married him, knowing that? She gave her forehead a smack. The most important matter for her was clearing Rob. "So does Lacey think she can pass along your alibi without forcing Bart to give a formal statement that might come out later?"

"God, I hope so, because it doesn't look like the police have lost interest in me. An officer was at the museum this morning asking for my phone logs and appointments calendar, even a handwriting sample. He asked me to come in and give my fingerprints voluntarily. I said I'd have to ask a lawyer about that. I'm pretty sure they'll be back to arrest me unless someone with more motive turns up."

"But you don't have any motive."

"That isn't strictly true." Rob bit his lip. "But I better wait to tell you that part until Lacey gets here. I didn't want to tell her before you knew."

Jan pushed back her afghan. "I need some iced tea to help me digest all this. Do you want anything?"

"No. I'm too spun right now to even drink to unwind. God, Jan. What if I don't get arrested, but Bart still throws me over because I've involved him in a murder investigation and forced him to come out before he was ready?"

There was nothing Jan could say to ease his fear. She brought him a glass of cold water, figuring dehydration wouldn't do him any good on this hot day, even if his life wasn't falling apart around him.

Jan was icing a fresh pitcher of tea when she saw Lacey striding up the drive. She set the pitcher and glasses on the island and settled on a stool as Rob brought Lacey in.

"Okay, Lacey's here. Now tell us why you're the chief suspect in Kitrin's death."

Rob flushed. "Fine. But please remember this was back in university, and I was still finding out who I was." He pulled up a picture on his phone and turned it to face them. It was the selfie he'd sent Jan, of him and Michael at the art museum, the day before Kitrin died.

It took a moment for her to realize she was looking at a text message to Kitrin: the photo followed by a single line that read *Is he MINE???*

"But …" she said, "how could he be?"

Lacey looked from the photo to his face. "There is a resemblance."

Rob turned the phone and looked at the picture. "Kitrin didn't answer me. I intended to visit Saturday afternoon after my date with Bart, to see if she'd tell the truth."

"But … you slept with her?" Jan asked. "While we were all living together?"

"Yeah, I did."

Jan sat in shocked silence while Lacey spelled out what it looked like from her perspective.

"So, Rob, you had more of a relationship with the dead woman than you previously admitted. You might have fathered her child, a fact that she kept from you for more than ten years. That would make some men very angry. Worse still, you put the possibility in writing, where Kitrin's husband might find it. That would make him very angry." She pointed a finger at him. "What did you think ego-driven Mylo Matheson would do if he saw this? If he thought his wife had tricked him into marriage while pregnant with another man's child?"

Rob looked stricken. "You're not saying he killed her over my message?"

"No. I doubt he's even seen it. He's in the clear for the time of death, so unless he hired someone ..." Lacey frowned. "But you acted without thinking, and it's going to make you look impulsive to the police. Like a man who'd lash out. You'd better tell me from the start, so I can assess how damaging this is. Especially since you told the RCMP you'd had no relationship with her beyond being roommates, a decade ago."

Rob looked at his phone again. "It was one time. Kitrin was so miserable. Her dad was being such an asshole, and Mylo had finished filming and gone away without a hint about wanting to see her again. Jan and Terry had gone away for reading week, but she and I stayed in Vancouver. You remember, Jan?"

"I guess." Jan twisted her empty glass between her hands.

"You were unsupervised," said Lacey. "Go on."

Rob cancelled the picture with the swipe of his thumb and put the phone face down. "Kitrin was a mess. She couldn't handle Mylo's abandonment on top of her dad's rejection — I guess you don't know this part, Lacey: her father wanted her to take a DNA test because her mother had been screwing around throughout the marriage. Kitrin was already fragile because of that, and after Mylo left she was pretty much suicidal. I didn't dare leave her alone for an instant, so I offered to hold her until she fell asleep." His neck reddened. "She pretty much begged me to show her she was still desirable, that somebody would love her again someday. Honestly, she was only the third woman I'd ever slept with. I'd only been with one guy by that point." He raised his eyes briefly to Jan's. "And you know how badly that went. So I guess I needed some comfort, too. It never dawned on me that she might have gotten pregnant until Michael walked into the museum looking like my Grade Five picture. When he told me when his birthday is, I realized it fit. I sent that text like two minutes later. I've wished ever since that I had held off, spoken to her in person."

Lacey frowned. "Do you know if the RCMP investigators now have this text?"

"They didn't mention it the first time they took me in, just kept hammering at me about what exactly my relationship had been with her, and if we'd been in contact before she arrived here. How much I'd seen her in the intervening years. Over and over and over."

Jan groaned. "They had divers in Jake's pool, looking for that phone, but surely they could access her cloud backups or whatever?"

"Probably. Go on, Rob."

"I kept telling them I hadn't seen her. We hadn't spoken or emailed or anything since that first year she went south with Mylo. I don't even remember if we sent her a baby present."

"I sent one," Jan said, "and put your name on the card, too." She let out a breath. "Why didn't you tell me any of this sooner? I'm your best friend in the world." Was he ashamed of sleeping with a woman? Would he kill to avoid being reminded? That was not the Rob she knew. That Rob wouldn't raise a hand to anyone to ease his own path. But the RCMP didn't know that Rob.

He turned his phone over again. His thumb hovered over the button. He closed his hand tight instead. "When Mylo came back for her a couple of weeks later, I was glad. Keeping her alive was someone else's burden. I got on with my final papers and never thought about that night again. You might think the last woman I ever slept with would stick in my head, but it honestly wasn't worth remembering. The sex, I mean." He looked pleadingly at Lacey. "How bad is this? If they have my text?"

"It gives you a credible motive," she said with what seemed like deliberate brutality, "for bashing her over the head in a fit of anger. And you know your way around Jake's place because of all the parties we've been to up there. If Bart won't give you an alibi, you might have to choose: out him and let the chips fall for him with Orrin, or face a trial for murder."

CHAPTER NINETEEN

The drive north was the least comfortable Lacey had ever felt around Bart or Andy. She drove while they sat in the back seat, far apart and staring out opposite windows at the trees flickering by. The trail of dust spread out behind the vehicle, and gravel rattled under the tires, but otherwise there was nothing distracting her from wondering whether this was related in any way to Orrin's disappearance. The only reason Bart might have for making Orrin disappear would be if Orrin had found out and threatened to disinherit. Wouldn't he have blown up around the rest of the family, though? Thrown Bart off the ranch like he had Ben? But he hadn't. The very day he'd vanished, Bart and Andy had been at the ranch teaching Michael Matheson to climb.

If not that, then what had triggered the sabotage of Orrin's Rover? The last time the whole family had gathered was the previous weekend, for Tyrone's birthday. Cheryl, the only family intimate who wasn't actually a relative, would have heard about any arguments, but would she be too loyal to Sloane to repeat them?

When the ranch's first no-trespassing sign appeared, Lacey turned off Highway 40 and took the couple in by the south gate to avoid any media out front. She dropped them at their cabin and drove on to the garage. As she pulled in, a mechanic came to take over.

While he backed the vehicle out to the gas pump in the staff parking lot, the other mechanic said, "Driving okay? Any issues?"

"The air conditioning didn't cool as much as I expected. Don't know if that was the outside temperature or the coolant getting low."

"I'll take a look."

She nodded to him and hauled her kit bag from home up to the office. She should run down and change that lock on the workout room door right away, since Wayne had obligingly left a replacement lock at Dee's that afternoon on his way to Jake's. What she'd really like to do was have a shower and a cool drink, followed by a light supper. But she couldn't walk into Andy's cabin as if none of the afternoon's revelations had changed anything. She'd eat in the main kitchen for the first time and then occupy herself until bedtime. Meanwhile, here she was, back in her stuffy office, squinting at a monitor as she scrolled through the archived images from the weekend before the sabotage, trying to spot any heated discussions among family members. Earl's wife and daughters were all slim and invariably wearing ball caps or sunhats, so she never did figure out which was which as they came and went from his cabin. She guessed the older girls would be the same pair who briefly appeared on the stable camera one evening, but otherwise everyone appeared on good behaviour, even when Orrin jabbed his finger at their faces.

During a real-time camera sweep, she spotted Cheryl in an upper hallway, taking a tray downstairs. Lacey immediately headed to the main house, hoping to intercept and question the woman about events not caught on camera that weekend. As she hurried down the hallway with all the portraits, Earl's voice came from Orrin's study.

"I've told you everywhere I remember. Do you honestly think I'd hold back when my father's life is at stake?"

There was a crash, as if something had fallen off the big walnut desk. She turned. The back of a twin was stomping out the door she'd come in by. Probably Bart, unless Earl had finally given Ben a fob. Although Ben was more likely to have swept something off the desk in a rage. Whichever it was, they were still hunting down any place Orrin might have taken Tyrone for a test of manhood. Good on them. Now, which door led to the kitchen?

Cheryl was slumped in an alcove where house staff ate their meals, gazing blankly out at the trees. Sliding into a chair opposite her, Lacey asked, "Mind if I join you? I'm Lacey, the security company's rep."

Cheryl's brown eyes focused. "Is there something I should know about the search? Something you want me to pass on to Sloane?"

"Nothing to report, sorry. I'll check with the SAR base after I eat, to get the latest. How's Mrs. Caine doing today?"

"She's asleep, finally." Cheryl sighed. "I hope she stays that way until we have news of some kind. She's always lived on her nerves, and this is about the last ragged edge."

"I'm sorry. It must be awful for her."

"Yeah, it is. I'm trying to convince her to come to the city with me tomorrow, just for a few hours, to get her unstuck. She's afraid if she leaves here, she'll miss some crucial message."

"If it will help, I can take your phone number and immediately relay anything that comes in." Lacey waited a beat. "I'm curious, though, about why Mr. Caine would suddenly take off with Tyrone like that, not telling anyone where he was going or when he expected to return. Is that usual?" She knew the answer, at least according to Ben and Bart. But with everything she'd learned about their secrets in the past twenty-four hours, she could no longer afford to accept their versions at face value.

"Orrin's never been much for reporting his movements, even though he tracks everyone else's." Cheryl looked back at the trees. "There's two things that might be relevant that I can think of. And I might be completely off the mark on one of them."

"Bounce it off me, as an outsider, and see if it still seems likely."

"Okay. It might sound strange, but you'd have to know Orrin to see how it's possible."

"Consider me warned." Would this be a first-hand account of a family uproar that gave someone a motive?

"Michael Matheson," said Cheryl.

Lacey blinked. "What about him?"

"Um, you've met him, right? At that supper I heard so much about?"

Lacey nodded.

"Well, if you didn't notice, he and Tyrone look a lot alike. Sloane came home from Jake's place seriously freaked out about the resemblance. Even though it didn't seem like Orrin had ever met Kitrin Matheson before, she's afraid ... well, that Orrin is Michael's father. That he had an affair while she was pregnant with Ty." Cheryl looked across the table with an expression only half hopeful. "Would you know if Michael's adopted?"

"Um, no. Michael is not adopted, and I'm reasonably sure his mother never met Orrin before last Thursday." Unless there'd been a drunken hook-up right in that same window twelve years ago, and Kitrin didn't remember? Rob had said she was lonely and desperate for reassurance, and she'd had a thing for older men. But a third possible father for Michael was just too improbable. "No," she said again. "Kitrin is definitely Michael's mother, and she was nowhere near an oilfield when she conceived. Not even in Alberta."

"Oh. Well, she's dead now, I hear, so we can't ask her, anyway." Cheryl pressed the bridge of her nose between two fingers. "I'll pass that along to Sloane if she brings it up again."

"She didn't ask Orrin already?"

"God, no. He would torment her forever if he thought she cared."

A truly charming man. *Ugh.* "You said there was a second thing?"

"Yeah. Orrin has an obsession about boys becoming men at age twelve. We thought Sloane had talked him out of doing any of the stupid, dangerous things from the old days, but maybe we were wrong." Cheryl gave a rundown similar to what Lacey had heard from the twins: how Orrin would dump his sons on an off-roading trail or cutline and make them find their own way home. "This was all before my time, you realize. I've only been here since Ty was born."

"Orrin didn't try anything like this with his granddaughters?"

Cheryl laughed mirthlessly. "The only thing he did with them was make nasty comments about their makeup and clothes. They spent their time here avoiding him. Mostly they snuck down the bluff to smoke and drink with the cowboys. None of those guys would dare set a finger out of line, but it gave the girls something to occupy themselves with."

"I saw they'd damaged a few cameras so they could come and go without their grandfather finding out."

Cheryl nodded. "Orrin and his cameras are a pain in the ass. He put tracking on everybody's phones and vehicles, too. Except his own, of course."

"But not Tyrone's?"

"Oh, for sure Ty's. But the first thing he would do, if he was set on some crazy rite of passage, is take the phone away so Ty couldn't look up his location or call for help." She looked around the kitchen. The only other people in the big room were on the far side, chopping vegetables. She leaned forward. "Sloane thinks one of the family fucked up the Rover on purpose. Orrin's the only one allowed to drive it, you know."

Lacey stretched closer. "Any particular person?"

"If we had to guess? Earl. He hates her, and Ty, too. Orrin spent the whole birthday weekend claiming he'd change his will to leave Ty everything. Rubbing Earl's nose in how subservient he is — well, he said it less politely. Humiliating him in front of his daughters. He's always needling the older sons about all the ways they don't measure up, but this was the first time he straight-up said he'd move Ty to the front of the line."

"I heard him say something similar at Jake's."

There was a lull in the cooks' activity. Cheryl called over, "Can you throw me together a salad with some ham? Mrs. Caine is only having a smoothie when she wakes up." She looked at Lacey. "Did you want supper while we talk?"

"Sure. Same as you, I guess."

"Garlic bread?" Lacey nodded. Cheryl called out the additional items and got a wave back.

"So you and the staff are pretty informal?"

"Oh yeah. We've been together for ages, mostly in town. We don't winter out here unless Orrin takes it into his head to have an old-fashioned ranch Christmas. Which he does sometimes, when the weather's good or he wants to make everyone dance to his fiddle."

"So the house staff comes from his place in the city?"

"Yup. This house is kept just above freezing in winter, and Ike checks on it daily when it's not being used. He's here year round, with the stock and the hands."

"He's a tough man, I can tell," said Lacey. "I wouldn't want to winter out here. Can you tell me who all was here for Tyrone's birthday? Family and guests."

"Let me see ... all three of Orrin's wives, Earl, his wife, his girls, Bart, and Andy. I think that's everyone who was here for the cake and presents on Saturday."

"Not Ben?"

Cheryl shook her head. "He's *persona non grata*. Not that it stops him. The hands won't run him off. They just don't bring it to Orrin's attention if he's been around filling up his truck or working out in the gym or visiting Bart. I've seen him around myself, sneaking in at dusk, and kept my mouth shut to avoid another blowout."

"Sloane doesn't think the twins are a risk to Tyrone's inheritance?"

Cheryl checked that the cooks were still occupied far away. "Neither Bart nor Ben want to run the company. If Orrin left them nothing, they'd be okay. They'd need jobs of some sort, but they wouldn't starve. Their mother was pretty shrewd, for a pothead hippie type. Frankly, apart from Sloane, she's the woman I have the most respect for. She knew what she wanted out of Orrin, she got it, and she left."

"But she was back that last weekend of August?"

"Yeah, her first visit in years. I wondered if she came because Bart and Andy were going to announce they're finally pregnant, but if they did tell Cass, they didn't tell anybody else."

"And what about the first Mrs. Caine? Giselle, is it?"

Cheryl curled her lip. "She's here every summer when her granddaughters are. Way back, it was good to have extra hands with all those young kids, but I don't know why she still comes. Her daughter-in-law was never good enough for her precious son, and she makes sure Susie knows it. The girls don't like her much, either. But it's a tradition that Earl and Susie have weekends away in Banff during the August gathering — except for Ty's birthday, of course — and Granny always comes to stay with her precious darlings, even though they're old enough not to need her. She just likes to keep a foothold here, like that empress woman in *I, Claudius*."

A cook brought two generous plates of salad greens topped with spiralized carrots, radish roses, cucumbers sliced so thin they were almost see-through, and shaved ham only a fingernail thicker. The garlic bread wafted warm, buttery flavours over the table, and suddenly Lacey was ravenous. She was about to stab her fork in when the second cook came over with a pitcher of lemonade and a caddy filled with oils and vinegars for dressings.

"When did everyone leave?" she asked while she drizzled lime-infused olive oil onto her greens. "Was any of the family still around on Monday?"

"Andy and Bart went back to town on Sunday night to put his mom on her plane." Cheryl picked an oil with Provençal herbs. "I think Earl took his wife out for a last night in a hotel on Sunday, or was that Monday night?" She speared some salad and chewed. "No, I remember now. He took his wife and daughters to the plane on Monday and stayed over at the house in town that night." She gave another sour laugh. "Or maybe he slipped off to the nearest whorehouse. Who really knows?"

Lacey laughed along with her while taking mental notes about who was where last Monday night. "I'm curious why Sloane stays. Orrin can't be the easiest husband in the world."

"That's an understatement. If he was still trying for more sons, she'd be gone. But he got sterilized by prostate treatments years ago and doesn't bother her any more."

"So Tyrone's his last child? He didn't freeze any sperm?" Lacey forked up some salad.

Cheryl's lip curled. "And reveal to his HR department's benefits clerk that the mighty Orrin Caine was infertile? The only people who knew he even had prostate treatment were those clerks, and they'd never dare mention it."

This was turning out to be a most revealing conversation. "So life's good enough for Sloane for now?"

"Except now he's paranoid that she's making up for his deficiencies with the ranch hands or any other convenient males." Cheryl stabbed a cherry tomato. "Hence the cameras pointing at her suite. As if any woman would be that obvious."

"Sounds grim." That too was an understatement. After only a few months of coping with Dan's accusations of infidelity, Lacey had been a wreck. How had Sloane survived years of it? Probably having a close confidante in Cheryl helped. If Lacey'd had her current female friends back then, she might have been more resilient then, too. But every woman had her limit. Was Sloane behind the Rover sabotage? "So she wouldn't be too distraught if he crashed his Rover?"

"Nobody around here would be broken up if he'd driven himself off a cliff. But Ty ..." For the first time, Cheryl's voice trembled. She looked up at Lacey with haunted eyes. "If something's happened to Ty because somebody wanted Orrin gone, I will kill that person myself."

Leaving Cheryl to pick at a slice of cold cherry pie, Lacey stepped out the kitchen door past a smoker in a lawn chair and rounded the corner to the terrace, automatically looking up to check that the staircase camera still pointed where it should. She wasn't ready to lock herself away in the stuffy security office, and even less willing to intrude on Andy and Bart at their cabin. Instead, she found a bench in the thin wedge of shade by the house's north wing and sat down. Her feet ached. She'd been wearing these workboots since nine this morning, but her running shoes and sandals were both down in her room at Andy's. She'd have to suffer a bit longer, but at least she could do some of it out here while watching the sun creep behind a peak, shimmering redly through the heat haze. There ought to be a thunderstorm after a day like this, but no clouds boiled up behind those mountains.

Reviewing the day, she realized she hadn't had a chance to hear Jan's results from the garage video. She pulled out her phone, checked on Dan's last recorded location, and dialled.

Jan picked up on the second ring. "Lacey? I'm so glad you called. What an afternoon. I can't get my head around all of it."

Lacey leaned back, propping one foot on a nearby planter. "I'm guessing Rob's not with you just now?"

"Nope. He's gone for a bike ride to think about all this."

"You sure called it last week, about him being involved with a married man." Lacey stretched out her other leg, wondering if she dared remove her boots. The sweaty stench would probably kill the nearby flowers. She decided to leave them on.

"I'm wishing I was wrong. I was wrong about other things without trying."

"Such as?"

"I looked up Kitrin's life in Hollywood," said Jan. "In every single photo — which are always on Mylo's arm at some black-tie event, like she didn't exist without him — she looks so sad and fragile. I don't think I ever realized how awful her life was."

"Are you wishing you'd kept in touch?"

"Yeah, a bit. Or at least made more effort to see her once I knew she was here. We had maybe ten minutes after supper, and not two days later she was gone." Jan sighed. "But you'll be wanting to know about my video analysis. I could be out by a couple of centimetres on height, more if the person was wearing thick-soled shoes. There's only so much detail I could lift from that camera angle and that much shadow."

"I can send you more video if you think that will help, like of the mechanics when they're near that vehicle in daylight. I have that whole external hard drive filled with the archived images from the past month." Lacey flexed her feet again. Ten minutes with her toes in a cool tub would be heaven. "I've got a list now of people who left on Sunday or Monday, but many of them could have sneaked back in through one of the gates without cameras. The only people I can completely eliminate would be the ones who flew away before the video was made. Even those, I'll have to get Wayne to verify that they ended up where they said they were going."

"There was that much bad feeling around?"

"You met Orrin. He was awfully tough on Earl and Bart in front of strangers. Multiply that by ten for how nasty he was when it was just family."

"Ugh," said Jan. "If it weren't for Tyrone, I wouldn't give Orrin's fate a second thought."

"That seems to be the general sentiment," said Lacey. "I hear someone coming. I'd better quit shooting off my mouth. Are you going to be okay there tonight? Dee would sleep over if you asked her."

"Nah. She's rented rooms to two women security guards Wayne hired and won't want to leave strangers in full possession."

"Oh, is that whose stuff was stacked in the mud room?" Lacey said. "I meant to text her, but there was so much drama this afternoon."

"No shit. Anyway, Rob will stay over again. He needs the company, and we're used to each other."

"Okay. Any messages for Terry if I take a run down to the SAR base?" Now that the words were out, Lacey was struck by the brilliant simplicity of the idea: get out of this fraught atmosphere for half an hour and still feel like she was on the job.

"Tell him I miss him and to be careful out there."

Lacey hung up just as Ben's head appeared on the bluff staircase. He trotted over to her. As usual, he wasn't even out of breath.

"Hey, Lacey. Did I hear you say you're heading down to the SAR base? Mind if I come along?" No excuse came readily to Lacey's lips, and soon they climbed into Wayne's truck. "South gate's best. You remember the way there?"

Lacey reversed out of her parking spot and headed for the nearest road down into the valley. As they passed slowly along the row of buildings, she checked the angles of the various cameras. They all seemed to be pointing in the right directions at last. Did Ben realize he'd be recorded in at least two places the next time he sneaked into the workout room to meet Andy?

As if reading her thoughts, Ben brought up Andy. "I heard what happened in town today. Andy's pretty upset."

"Yeah, I guess she is." There wasn't much else Lacey could say. Was she about to be told to move her stuff out to the bunkhouse?

"I hope you'll talk to her before you go to bed," Ben went on. "She'll stay up all night worrying if you don't." He rubbed his forehead, just like Bart did when stressed. "You didn't see her at her best today, and she's kind of ashamed of all the screaming."

"She told you that?" Had she told him about Bart having a male lover? Or did he know that already, and that was why he didn't seem bothered about sex with Andy?

"Of course. We three, we don't keep secrets from each other. It's our chief survival technique."

"No secrets at all?" Lacey was a teeny bit ashamed of her suggestive tone. She pulled over to let a half-ton go past in the other direction. "Do you know what she was screaming about?"

"You mean about Bart meeting his lover, or there being paparazzi outside? Because of the two, she was much more upset about that guy with the camera than the guy with his pants off." After a pause he said, "She told me you know Rob?"

"He's my neighbour's best friend."

"Is he a good guy? Keeps his word and all that?"

"He's a good person. Hasn't been involved with any other man since I've known him."

Ben relaxed. "So you already knew he was gay, just not who he was seeing?"

"Uh-huh. Did they tell you why he needed to see Bart today?"

Ben nodded. "Last Saturday morning. If we knew for sure that Orrin's not coming back, I'd tell Bart to go to the police with the whole truth. As it is, we can't quite risk that. You used to be a cop. Would you buy it if they said they were just out mountain biking on Saturday morning?"

"I likely would have, if that was the first thing offered. But not after Rob stonewalled for three days about where he was and who he was with. At this point, he's better off to come completely clean than tell them a partial truth and leave them suspicious enough to keep digging."

"Well, fuck." They were coming up to the south gate, and Lacey slowed. Ben leaned out the window and said to the ranch hand, "All good here?"

"Yes, sir."

Ben said, "What's your beer? I'll send some out for you when I get back."

The ranch hand grinned as he opened the gate.

Lacey smirked. "So that's the secret to your popularity? You get them beer?"

"I'm not that popular."

"That's not what I heard. They don't rat you out to Orrin when you're sneaking in to fill your truck from his gas tank."

Ben laughed. "Yeah, there's that. They still let me go riding and stuff, too, as long as Orrin's not around. Now, the best road to the SAR base is straight back to Highway 40 and south, but we can take this back trail to cut off the corner."

Lacey followed his directions. Sooner than she thought possible, she saw searchers' vehicles near the airstrip. She parked beyond the last one.

Ben said, "Mind if I take one of these security caps? It won't keep me completely anonymous, but at least I can ask a few questions before I get mobbed by any reporters."

Lacey locked the truck and strolled along the gravel road, her feet protesting every step. Ben matched her pace. They moved through clusters of tired searchers grabbing food or sorting gear, crawling into tents for sleep or vehicles for the trek back home. Someone was loading horses into a trailer. They came face to face with the old woman whose truck Lacey had pushed out of the ditch. Was that only two days ago?

The woman nodded curtly to her. "You searchin' now?"

Lacey shook her head. "I'm stationed up at the ranch, keeping reporters out."

"Send 'em to my place," growled the old woman. "I'll tell 'em all about Orrin Caine. Things you won't see on his company website." She glared at Ben. "And about his liar sons." She stomped away.

"Whoa. What was that about?" Lacy asked.

Ben watched the old woman. "Remember I told you about the land Orrin bought across Highway 40? That he promised never to drill and then did?" She nodded. "Well, he bought it from Susan Norris, mainly because I convinced her he'd keep his word and put it straight into a nature conservancy like she was doing with the rest. If she never forgives me for that, I can't blame her."

Another person with a grudge against Orrin. Could the old woman possibly be tech-savvy enough to evade all the security cameras, find the one unsecured door, and get all the way up to the garage without being seen? Not to mention she'd have to know where the control panel was for the motion-sensor lights inside the garage. It didn't seem plausible.

Lacey scanned the searchers plodding around. When she spotted Terry, she hurried over, waving.

He waved back. "Lacey! How's it going up there?"

Mindful of Ben at her back, she said neutrally, "About what you'd expect. Can I introduce you to Ben Caine? He's twins with Bart, who we met last week at Jake's. What can you tell us about today's search?"

He led them to the map shelter and pointed out the quadrants that search teams had covered thoroughly.

Ben asked why they'd started with those and listened carefully to the answers. Then he said, "What about the drone that can pick up phone signals?"

Terry said, "The operator's followed all the roads away from the ranch, looking for Orrin's signal. If it was in range, the phone was either turned off or smashed. It could be running out of power by now, too."

Ben frowned. "Did they search for Ty's phone at the same time, or is each number a separate search?"

It was Terry's turn to frown. "There's a second phone with the vehicle?"

"Yeah, if they're still together. And Ty's is newer. It should hold a charge longer, right?"

Terry beckoned them as he hurried to the search manager's command RV. "Garry," he called, "did anybody give us the boy's phone number?"

A man hunched over a laptop shook his head. "Only one for the old man."

"Well, there should be a second one." Ben pulled out his phone to call up his little brother's contact information. On his lock screen was a photo of two nearly identical boys. Him and Bart as youngsters, or Tyrone and Michael last week? After he'd given Ty's number to the search coordinator, Lacey asked about the photo. Ben scrolled back to it. "This one? Yeah, Andy sent it to me on

Friday when Michael was at the ranch. They look so much alike, it's almost impossible to believe they're not related."

"That's what she said the first time we saw them together." Lacey thought back to Jake's and the dessert buffet on the terrace. Not even a week ago, but it seemed like a different lifetime. "Maybe a trick of genetics or a distant connection. It was obvious from Orrin's probing questions that he'd never met Michael's mother before. She was really uncomfortable with him."

"Orrin has that effect. Anything else you have to do here?"

A nearby searcher called Ben's name. She came running over, short, fit, tanned, and filthy from a long, sweaty day out in the bush. She threw herself at him, wrapping her arms and legs around him in a full-body hug. He hugged her back and then set her on her feet, laughing. "Lacey, meet Julie. We worked together on the Ghost Wilderness Land-Use Survey. Julie, meet Lacey."

The woman eyed Lacey from her dirty-blond hair to her dusty workboots. The message was clear: *Are you competition?* Lacey shook her head and turned away to talk to Terry.

The sun was well down behind the mountains when Lacey parked once more in the ranch's staff lot. She logged the kilometres in the book and climbed out into the green twilight, wincing as her booted feet landed on the gravel.

Ben, coming around the vehicle, winced in sympathy. "Sore feet?"

"Yeah, I've been in these boots since breakfast."

"Sure it's not from climbing yesterday? You use a lot of tiny muscles keeping your edge on those footholds."

"Huh. I forgot all about that."

Ben grinned. "Forgot the pain, time to climb again. Coming back to the cabin now?"

She shook her head. "I've got to do my nightly camera check and write my day's report for my boss. Please tell Andy I'll be happy to chat with her if she's still up in an hour." Truthfully, she wasn't that happy. She wanted no more emotional drama, just a shower and a soak for her aching feet, and then bed. But she was a guest in Andy's cabin, and if a chat tonight would smooth their relationship for the rest of her stay, she'd do it.

Ben said, "Six-thirty in the gym tomorrow? I'll make you my famous eggs again afterward."

"How can I resist?" After the day's revelation about Bart, she need not shun Ben on the grounds that he was an unethical jerk. She didn't know how or when his affair with Andy had started, but Ben as much as Bart was Andy's physical type, and it seemed she wasn't getting sex from her husband. Five years without would incline any hot-blooded woman to stray.

While she'd been thinking this through, she'd been strolling with Ben toward the nearest garage entrance. As she raised her fob he said, "Have fun. I'm going to grab a nap before I go back on the gate. See you in the morning."

She nodded good night as he headed off along the driveway, and she paused with her hand on the door.

The air was cooling at last. The fir trees were releasing their spicy scents to the dew. It was a terrible time to shut herself in the office again. After the report was sent, she'd stretch out on the main terrace for a bit before she went home, or even suggest to Andy that they have their chat outside. As if to encourage her, an owl hooted somewhere nearby. The breeze sounded like the flutter of wings. Reluctantly, she pulled the door shut behind her and climbed the stairs to the second floor.

Ike's apartment was quiet, but the sound of TV came from the kitchen staff's dorm. Someone's phone rang as she passed. She paused with one foot raised. Why hadn't SAR been given Tyrone's phone number from the first? Was it oversight, or obstruction? Did they have the correct number for Orrin for sure? Yanking her phone out, she texted Terry Brenner. *Double-check that SAR has Orrin's correct current cell #.* Then she trudged along the upper hall, her boots scuffing the brown all-purpose carpeting.

The building's metal joists pinged as they cooled. The storerooms rustled and creaked, overheated plastics and fabrics driving out the earlier aroma of dew-kissed pines. Would it hurt to open her office window and maybe prop the door open to get a breeze moving through? It wasn't environmentally friendly, but fresh air might keep her more alert.

The security office door didn't want to accept its alarm code. Maybe the heat had got to it, too, or there'd been a power surge while she was down at the airstrip. The error code was showing, as if the sequence had been entered incorrectly. She cleared it and tried again, but got the flashing -*ERR*- that signalled too many wrong entries. Muttering, she keyed in the master override and reset the alarm code, texting the change to Wayne for his records.

The office dust coated her nostrils immediately. She pulled up the blind, admiring the moon that was creeping over the roof while she opened the window wide, and wedged the door open with a coat hanger in the hinge. Then she settled down at the desk, ignoring the canned laughter from the cooks' TV. Dropping her phone into the desk dock, she plugged in names of artists Andy had listened to on the drive into Calgary. Those lazy guitars would ease the summer night, even if the lyrics focused a bit too much on lost loves, about which she had no sentimental feelings at all.

After she'd been typing awhile, the wind freshened. The sudden chill raised goosebumps on her arms. The door behind her shifted. She looked, but it was only swinging against the hanger that held it open. The hallway beyond was silent. The cooks must have gone to bed. She turned her music down a bit lest it disturb them and added another section to her report, a list of last week's visitors whose plane times or whereabouts for Monday night needed to be checked.

The door whined as another gust came in. A cloud raced over the moon's face, casting the rooftop and skylights into shadow. A new, harder-driving song came on, and she tapped her feet to the beat as she plugged in the last few names on her report. She hit Send, exited out of the program, and heard a thump that didn't match the music. The door again?

As she turned to reach for it, a black shape stepped through.

She started to her feet, but not fast enough. The figure leaped behind her chair, pinning her at the desk. An arm went around her throat. She grabbed the black sleeve with both hands. A gloved hand yanked her left wrist away. She pushed off with her feet, slamming the chair across the small office, crushing her assailant against the wall. A grunt came above her, but the arm tightened around her throat.

Nightmare images of Dan's assaults flooded her mind. Would she die here, now, when he was a whole province away? Panic choked her, as completely as the arm dragging her upward by her neck. Black spots spread in her eyes. She shoved her right hand into the elbow gap and made a fist, forcing the arm to loosen a fraction. Meanwhile, she untangled herself from the chair and kicked the base backward with all the power in her legs. It crashed and bounced back to buckle her knees. The arm at her neck yanked her up again. When she kicked the next time, the chair tipped. She shoved it backward hard and heard a muffled gasp before it was pushed aside.

Fully upright at last, pulled tight to a muscular body, she yanked her left wrist free and elbowed her attacker. The grip at her throat eased fractionally. As she caught a breath, the other gloved fist recaptured her left wrist. They jerked across the floor in a crazy polonaise.

Without warning, the attacker dropped her wrist and punched her in the ribs. Her old scar tissue screamed. She braced her free hand on the desk to keep from falling and kicked backward with all her might.

Her boot connected with a shin. Hot breath gasped in her ear. She'd hurt them. Good.

As she kicked again, the assailant loosed her throat, but only to grab her neck from behind. Her head slammed onto the desk. Stars danced behind her eyelids. Blood stung her mouth. Heavy shoulders fell across her back, pinning her down. She snatched where hair should be and got only a handful of black wool. A gloved hand grabbed her index finger and bent it back until she had to let go. Something scraped across the desk. She wrapped her loose arm over her head and braced for another blow.

It didn't come.

The weight lifted off her. There was a rush of footsteps.

Raising her head with difficulty, she saw she was alone.

Struggling to her feet, she staggered out to the hallway. The near stairs were empty. Leaning against the wall, she peered around the corner. The long hallway was deserted, too. Her attacker could be behind any of those half-open storeroom doors, waiting to strike again, or working their way toward the far stairs. Either way, she was alone, injured, exposed. She groped her way back to the office and slammed the door, locking it.

As she reached for the fallen chair, an empty space on the desk caught her still-flaring eye. She froze. The external drive, the one that held the entire last month's archived camera images, was gone. The cable it had been connected to dangled from the desk beside a blood smear from her rapidly swelling mouth.

CHAPTER TWENTY

Lacey slumped into the spare chair and concentrated on her breathing. Her heart was a hammer, smashing her battered rib with every stroke. The old nightmare images of Dan roiled up. She pushed them back, compartmentalized them, reminded herself of the calming ritual she'd found on the internet:

One: a thing she could see: her phone

Two: things she could hear: wind rattling the blinds, Frank Turner singing

Three: things she could smell: the disturbed dust, her own sweat, the pines on the bluff outside

Four: things she could touch: the plastic chair arm, the thigh of her work jeans, the spongy mouse pad, the keys on her keyboard

Five: things she could …

Which sense was she missing? Taste. She looked around. Except for the water bottle with its tepid liquid from hours ago, there was nothing to taste unless she licked the walls and furnishings. The image of herself with her tongue stuck to the window frame, like a kid in a frozen playground, made her giggle, then cough as her ribs clenched.

Shivering as the pain eased, she took stock. Ribs? A deeper breath said they weren't cracked again, just bruised. She wiggled her jaw, wincing as the lip split pulled. She'd have a hell of a mark on that cheek tomorrow. She dabbed the blood off her lip with a tissue and a splash from her water bottle. The song changed, and she tapped the phone to kill the music. If the attacker returned, she wanted to hear them coming.

Two immediate questions: who was the assailant, and were they recorded on any of the cameras or fob logs? Actually, a third thing: did they want anything besides the external drive? Fourth, how did they know to take it, and fifth, why now?

Before diving into any of that, she obeyed her old cop instinct to report in. She checked her watch and dialled Wayne's number.

He picked up on the fourth ring, sounding sleepy. "Problem, McCrae?"

"You were right about a family member being behind it, boss. Someone here just beat me up and stole the external hard drive with the archived garage images."

"Are you hurt?"

"Bruised."

"Do you need medical attention?"

"No. Ice pack will do."

"Do you want to be replaced?"

"Hell, no. I won't be taken off guard again." She didn't bring up the panic she'd felt about being strangled.

That was between her and a therapist, if she ever got one.

"They must not know you've already uploaded the archive to my office server."

"And sent the important images to Jan for analysis." She rinsed her mouth with the plastic-tasting water, washing away the acid leftovers of adrenalin and blood. "I should have realized something was up when I returned from the airstrip tonight and found the door had been tried enough times to reset that keypad. I'll check as many alibis as I can, using today's images. But you'd do me a big favour by finding out where the people on my list were last Monday night. I mean, it has to be the same person, right? We can't be dealing with two different perpetrators on this isolated ranch."

"We can't assume that, but you're probably right. Nobody in that family trusts each other enough to collude."

"Except the twins," said Lacey. "I'll check their whereabouts as soon as I hang up. And I'll fix that lock on the gym door first thing in the morning. It's the only place anyone can enter this building without leaving a fob trail."

"Good plan." Wayne paused. "You're sure you don't want backup?"

Lacey crossed her fingers. "I'm sure. This just guarantees I'm on the right track."

"I want twice-daily phone reports from now on. Stay safe out there."

As she gingerly bent again to set the tipped chair on its wheels, something sticky met her palm. She opened that hand to the light. A smear of blood. On the bracket that held the nearest wheel was another smear, with a small divot of skin stuck to it. She'd marked the bastard. Good.

Wiping off the bloody residue onto a tissue, she tossed it into the trash. Much as she'd like to believe it would identify her attacker, no police force on earth would DNA-test over a minor beat-down with robbery. Even if they did, the results would take months, if not years to be processed — far too long to be any use at all in the present circumstances. She set the chair upright, settled into it, and wheeled up to the desk to see if she could isolate her attacker's approach or departure through any of the working cameras.

The silence was complete beyond Lacey's door, but she found herself listening constantly, anyway. Could anyone come up on the roof and get through the window? If they tried, the returned moonlight would let her see them. She sped backward through the evening's logs to suppertime and started forward again, watching the mechanics pack up for the day and Bart drive a load of food from the kitchen entrance out the front gate. More for the searchers, presumably. She and Ben had missed him at the SAR base. She checked time-stamps and found his vehicle returning through the main gate just before hers left by the south gate. Then she traced his movements: into the garage with the vehicle, out of the garage on foot through the elevator lobby, crossing in front of the bluff staircase camera, entering his cabin in the woods. Later in the archive, she watched Cheryl and Sloane walk out to the terrace. Sloane moved in a slow shuffle, her shoulders rounded like those of a much older woman. They sat on chairs for a few minutes, watching the sunset, and then slowly went back to the house. In the moment that Sloane faced the camera, the shadow wasn't deep enough to hide the glistening tracks on her cheeks. How many tears had she wept since finding her son gone?

Earl appeared on the terrace soon after the women left, heading down to the machine shed. The kitchen staff approached the garage after the meal cleanup. She watched them into the elevator lobby, checked for them in the garage, and realized there was no coverage of the garage stairs or her office door. Not that she really suspected them, but someone could have been hovering near the door, beneath the camera, and come in with them. If so, the attacker had hung around in the building for a good hour before attacking her, trying the office keypad unsuccessfully and then hiding when she arrived.

Ben was the last option. Had he really gone home to nap when he left her? Or had he waited around the corner until she stepped inside and then darted back before the door closed behind her? She hadn't exactly hung around downstairs to make sure it locked. Scrolling back again, she tracked him past the garage, across the terrace, and picked him up entering the cabin barely five minutes after he left her at the garage. He didn't come out.

Lacey sat back and propped her aching feet, still in their workboots, up on the desk. One of these Caines must have been in this building tonight. Who was left?

Andy. She hadn't seen Andy on a single camera. Could Andy have climbed straight down the bluff below her cabin — avoiding the repaired terrace camera — and cut through the aspen copse to the road below? Was she strong enough to smash Lacey's head to the desk and hold her down? How would Lacey tell?

Her bruised ribs gave a twinge. Bruises, of course. Whoever was behind the chair would have not only missing skin on their ankle or shin, but bruises, too, possibly on their thighs from the chair-back as well as on their shins from being kicked. As soon as she could bring herself to unlock that door and head for the cabin, she could clear Andy, and maybe Bart and Ben, as well. At worst, all she had to do was wait for Andy to go work out in the morning. She'd be wearing shorts. Any damage would be visible. Same went for Bart and Ben. For sure, she would go climbing with Ben in the morning. His tight climbing shorts would reveal any marks on his legs. How she'd deal with the attacker once they were identified, she wasn't sure. If they'd only been after the archives, they wouldn't attack again, no matter how much her PTSD feared they would.

Something bumped beyond the office door. She angled her head and listened. Was that only another creak of the cooling building, or a footfall on the stairs? Were Cheryl or Ike coming back to their apartment for the night?

The creak occurred again. Someone was definitely coming up those stairs. She eased out of the chair, moved over to the door, and waited to see if they'd try the keypad. The footsteps came right up to the door and stopped.

Andy's voice called, "Lacey, are you still in there? I saw the light as I came across the terrace." She tapped. "Lacey? Can we talk? Please?"

"Are you alone?"

"Yep."

"Come on in." Lacey turned the handle, releasing the electronic lock. Andy stepped into the room, her posture relaxed and unthreatening. She was still in shorts, and her long, tanned legs were unmarred. "Take a chair."

"Ben said you'd be back in an hour, but you weren't." Andy looked at the scattering of papers that Lacey hadn't yet picked up, the smear of blood under the desk lamp. Then she looked at Lacey. "Oh my fucking God. What happened to you?"

Clearly, Lacey hadn't done a thorough job of cleaning up her face. "I tripped and face-planted on the desk."

"You poor thing. Come on home, and I'll get you some ice for that cheek. You're gonna be sore."

"Yeah. Like I've been in the wars." Lacey reflexively pushed her tongue against her swollen lip. She wasn't ready to leave this cloistered room and walk through the shadowy woods. Not even with Andy for escort. "Did you want to talk to me about anything in particular? Because if so, this place has no recording devices in it. For sure."

Andy looked around the small room again. "All this equipment, and no recording devices in here?"

"That's what I said. I think only Orrin ever came in here apart from Wayne's monthly maintenance checks, and he was busy recording what everyone else was doing."

Andy perched on the far corner of the desk. With one foot, she pushed the door shut. "I just wanted to apologize to you for freaking out this afternoon. I don't usually scream at people and throw shit." She nibbled her lower lip. "My only excuse is that I'm ovulating and trying to get pregnant. A little nervy from hormones. And stress."

"There's enough stress to go around, that's for sure." Lacey rinsed the metallic taste out of her mouth again with her last sip of water.

"I wish I could tell you everything," said Andy sadly. "If I knew Orrin wasn't coming back, I would. But it's not just me who'd be in the shit. I want us to be friends, Lacey. I want us to trust each other. Can you trust me enough that if Orrin isn't back in two weeks, I'll tell you the whole truth?"

The whole truth about what, exactly? Lacey parked her shoulders against the wall while she tried to dissect what Andy meant. She didn't want to get anybody in shit with Orrin? That was a given. As for being friends, did she mean that as sincerely as it sounded, or was she trying to get on Lacey's softer side? This was where all those years around male coworkers had messed up Lacey's instincts. The women she hung with now-adays — Dee, Jan, Marie — were all straight talkers. If they had something on their minds, they put it right out there. But she'd seen enough women who weren't like them to know there was a real possibility she was entirely misreading Andy's level of sincerity. All she could do was play along and see where the conversation led.

"I really want us to be friends, too," she said, "and I'm trying not to be intrusive as your house guest, because heaven knows you've had enough intrusions living around Orrin. Will you trust me enough to answer my questions now, and I'll tell you in two weeks what I'm really doing this week?"

Andy put her hand on her head. "I think that sentence broke my brain. What I think I heard is you're not telling me the whole truth about why you're here now, and you know I'm not telling you the whole truth, either, but we're going to trust neither of us is doing anything to hurt the other, and we'll spill our guts in two weeks. Is that right?"

"If Orrin isn't back by then, we can," said Lacey, trying not to predict how fast Andy's friendliness would evaporate once she knew Lacey was spying all along. "If he is back, well, we'll deal with how much we can each safely tell when it comes to it. Okay?"

"O-kay!" Andy lunged over and hugged Lacey around the shoulders, carefully avoiding her bruised cheek.

Feeling like a massive hypocrite, Lacey turned her face away and patted Andy gingerly on the shoulder.

When released, she said, "Now, since we're friends, and you're going to trust me that I have a reason that you'll know about eventually, can you tell me where you were all evening from when we got back from this afternoon?"

Andy's smile drooped. "Arguing with Bart in the cabin, mostly. He thinks we should tell you everything. Ben thinks we can trust you, too. I think we can, but

I'm paranoid about Orrin. Plus, I've been kind of on an emotional tornado ride today, and I don't think I'm capable of making a really good decision tonight." One of her tanned hands rested on her stomach. "I might be pregnant already and not know it. If what I say now ends up messing up my child's life, I'd never forgive myself."

Lacey stared at her. Trying to get pregnant. Ovulating this week. Screwing Ben in the workout room while Bart carried on his affair with Rob. "Holy shit!"

"What?"

Lacey reached past Andy and closed the office window. If her guess was correct, this was dynamite that Earl would use to blow both the twins out of the inheritance race. She leaned close to Andy.

"You're trying to get pregnant by Ben so the baby will pass for Bart's."

CHAPTER TWENTY-ONE

Dawn brought a text from Jan and one from Wayne. Lacey rolled over in bed and picked up her phone. Jan's message said *Insomnia, and almost sure now that you're looking for a woman who walked beside that Porsche Macan, wearing a balaclava.* Wayne's read *I will have that replacement drive for you by noon. Can you meet me midafternoon in Cochrane to collect it?* After texting them both back, she climbed into her shorts and T-shirt and headed downstairs to find the coffee ready.

Ben stood by the machine with two mugs. He looked her over carefully. "You don't look as bad as I expected."

"Andy told you about my face plant?"

"Yeah. You didn't damage anything except your cheek, did you? Are you fit to climb?"

"Sure. I've been much worse off than this." She hoped he wasn't going to ask for details. Between her RCMP decade and her past year's crime-solving, she had quite a collection of old injuries. "Ribs are a bit bruised, but hopefully that won't ground me."

He filled her mug and handed it across the counter. "We don't have to climb if it hurts. We could go for a run instead. Or a walk."

"I can run anywhere. This is the first time I've ever had a climbing gym and an instructor at my disposal."

"Cheers, then." He came around the island and sat his neon-covered butt on a stool to watch her take her first, appreciative sip of coffee. She watched his shins over the rim, saw no bruises there, and examined his muscular thighs up to the edge of his tight climbing shorts. There was no damage on his legs at all. Relief swept through her, stronger than she had expected. Ben was not her attacker any more than Andy was. Two of the people she liked most here were cleared.

That left Bart. She looked up as the other twin sauntered in wearing lightweight, full-length pyjama pants. He reached for a mug.

"I thought I heard voices. Glad you're back, Ben. I was in the office yesterday and heard some things we should talk about. Got a minute now?"

"Should I leave?" Lacey asked, hoping they'd let her stay. She hadn't heard anything from Wayne about a possible business motive for Orrin to disappear, and in all yesterday's drama she hadn't followed up on Bart's morning at work.

He shook his head. "We're not keeping secrets from you any longer."

"You'd find them out by Friday, anyway," Ben added. "I hate to discuss company shit on an empty stomach — or at all — but today I'll make an exception. What's on your mind, bro?"

Bart pulled up a stool. "First, Lacey, nobody was going to admit to me if they're happy Orrin's not around. Anyway, there aren't any big deals hanging that will be materially affected by him being out of contact. Lots of drilling, but it's all handled by the usual people. So whatever you were thinking, it's probably nothing to do with work."

Ben eyed her over his mug. "You thought somebody at the office wanted to bump off the old man? Nah. His top people have been with him for decades. They're all getting filthy rich on his coattails."

Lacey lowered her eyes. So much for keeping her suspicions on the down-low. "If we're going to be another few minutes, can I have my coffee topped up, please?"

Bart poured for everyone. "It won't take long. Just wanted Ben to know a couple of things. One: Earl was in there on Monday, trying to get Orrin's assistant to let him access the laptop and files. She told him to come back when he had a legal right. Two: I ran into Orrin's personal lawyer, who was dropping off some paperwork. He asked about the search effort, and then I asked him what we talked about the other night, about how things stand if neither Ty nor Orrin come back."

"And?"

"It's what we thought. Despite all that yelling at Sloane's birthday last spring, Orrin hasn't changed his will since right after Ty was born. The company's a six-way share split: twenty percent each for us four boys and ten each for Sloane and Debbie. That's our half sister," he explained to Lacey. "The Mount Royal house and the ranch go to Sloane for her lifetime if she's still married to him, and to Ty otherwise. The Coachella place and the one on Antigua stay in the family trust for all our use. Here's the kicker, though. Earl gets to vote Ty's shares, as well as Debbie's and Sloane's, to keep them from being subject to outside influence. No surprise Orrin doesn't trust mere women to put the company first."

"So I never was disinherited?" Ben rubbed his neck. "That's news, anyway. But if Ty's gone, do his shares get split to the rest of us or go to his mother?"

"Neither." Bart put down his mug. "Whether Ty's dead or alive, until the date of his twenty-first birthday Earl controls his shares. Only then do they go to Sloane."

"Well, fuck," said Ben.

Bart nodded gloomily. "Even though we don't want to run the company, we don't want Earl to have complete control, either."

"He'll drill this whole ranch in Year One," Ben told Lacey. "And everywhere else he can get a permit."

"This place is great the way it is," she said. "Why would he ruin it?"

"He spent too much time in the U.S. operations," said Bart. "Down there, cattle come second after oil, and the environment doesn't even get on the list. Anyway, I'd better get to my email. If I don't keep my finger on the office grapevine, Earl could bully some secretary into letting him into Orrin's private files." He pushed back his stool and took his mug to the sink. "Have a good climb, Lacey. Going to try the living rock this time?"

"No," said Ben. "She's not ready. Tomorrow, maybe."

Lacey watched Bart leave the room, hoping to spot whether there was any hitch in his gait. If only he'd been wearing shorts, she'd have been absolutely certain he wasn't her attacker, either. For now she could only go with her gut.

As she looked up, Ben gave a wry smile. "If you're finished checking out my brother's assets, can we talk about Andy?"

"You obviously spoke to her after I went to bed."

"Yep. She said you guessed our three-way secret." He looked at her with new suspicion. "You're some detective, aren't you? What else are you detecting around here?"

Yikes! Time to distract him from that line of questioning. "I fluked into that secret," she told him, eyes fixed on his to radiate absolute honestly. "She'd said at our first meeting that she wanted to get pregnant, and your father gave Bart a hard time about not having any children yet. When I found out Bart had a male lover, I assumed he was bi." She paused, but Ben didn't comment. "Then I was messing with the cameras and caught a glimpse of her in a clinch with you in the workout room. I thought you were Bart until I ran into him two minutes later. When she told me last night that she's ovulating this week, my first thought was that she was risking a lot by fooling around with you. And then it hit me. No detecting required."

"Jeez," he said, staring at her. "If you could put all that together so fast, who else might have guessed?"

"Probably nobody who didn't realize you had shifted the camera in the workout room and rigged that door so it wouldn't lock."

He shrugged. "Yeah, that was me. I originally did it for Earl's girls so they could sneak out to drink with the hands. I wish I'd realized sooner that you changed the camera angle, though. Pretty sneaky."

"It's my job to get those things done without disturbing the residents," she said. "Honestly, what you three do is your business. If there is a child, it will be Orrin's grandchild just as much as if Bart fathered it. But won't a DNA test give it away? I mean, your father is about as paranoid as they come, going by all the spying he does around here. He wouldn't pay without certification."

"Identical twins, it's a lot more specialized testing to determine paternity. Search it online if you don't believe me." He grinned ruefully. "We'd never have chanced it at the ranch normally, but with Orrin and Ty missing, we couldn't exactly stay in the city, and it would be too noticeable if both Andy and I kept finding reasons to leave at the same time. So it was either skip this ovulation cycle entirely or improvise. As long as Orrin has no suspicion, he'll get the basic test and be happy, and the baby will get a trust fund that will free it to pursue its own dreams."

"Sounds like you believe your father will be back."

"He's indestructible." He set down his mug and leaned toward her, his eyes hard. "But if you're here as Orrin's spy, and you screw this up for Andy and her child, it's only fair to warn you that both Bart and I will become your worst enemies."

Coming on top of last night's attack, the threat should have triggered Lacey to an insane degree, but her pulse gave only a slight flutter. Her subconscious had apparently slotted Ben into the category of not-Dan men, those who didn't attack women. Slightly dizzy from the realization that her guard could drop so far, so fast, she yanked it back up. Her subconscious was biased as shit. Just last year she'd almost gotten Dee killed by trusting the wrong person and not trusting someone who wasn't a threat at all.

She met Ben's eyes with her old calm police face firmly fixed.

"Andy's baby has nothing to fear from me." *But you might.*

"Call me Davey, darling," the art director reminded Jan gently as he paused her video again. "'Mister' makes me feel terribly old. Now, this second bedroom. Which way does that window face? Is there a usable view, or would we have to sleeve that, too?"

Jan oriented herself on her sketch-map of the Harder house's layout. "Um, northeast, approximately. There's a paved parking area and a utility pole just outside the gate. Some screening trees, but sound-wise you'd be at the mercy of intermittent cars going along the road. The hill across the way sends all the noise back to the house."

"Nothing irks dear Mylo quite like reshoots due to traffic noise." Davey's theatrical sigh wafted from Jan's computer speakers. "I'm afraid we're back on the hunt, darling. If Location sends you another couple of houses next week, can you cope?"

Next week meant she had several days to rest up. "Sure. With the previous caveat about stairs. Mylo knew my limits when he suggested the job, but ..."

Davey finished the sentence for her. "But what that means in practical terms didn't register with our cherished director. Oh, yes, dearie, you can count on me to remind them." The video box vanished, and his sharp-angled face appeared on her monitor again. "If you don't mind me asking, how did you get dragged into this infernal operation?"

"Over supper. I'm an old friend of Kitrin's and was invited up to where they're staying. Were staying. Mylo's still there but … well …"

"Sweet little Kitrin." Davey dabbed at the corner of his eye. "She was a humanizing influence, poor child. Is it true, this whisper that she was conked on the head, or simply a diversion from the even more awful truth that her anorexia and Mylo's neglect killed her at last?"

"Did everyone know how fragile she was?"

"Dear me, yes." Davey shook his head sadly. "She and the boy prince trailed after Mylo year after year, shoot after shoot, and still he managed to ignore them both for his new flavour of the month. He only took them along this time because he wanted young Georgie."

"Everyone knows about that, too? Poor Kitrin."

"Hollywood, darling. Under California law, she could have taken him for half any day she chose. But Mylo's lawyers would surely bring up the old scandal about the boy prince and —"

"What old scandal?"

Davey drew back physically from his end of the connection. "I shouldn't have said. It was such a long time ago and not at all the boy's fault."

All Jan's defender instincts flared up. "What wasn't Michael's fault?"

"If you will have it," Davey said sternly, "on your head be it. The boy couldn't have been more than five, and you know how they blurt things out."

"What did he blurt?"

"Well, dearie, we were shooting on a back lot in Sacramento, and they were visiting. It was one of those overdone costume dramas where an heir's parentage is in question. We'd just cut from a scene in which the vile accusation is hurled — with an inkwell, if I'm recalling correctly; yes, a fabulous repro Victorian affair, hideous to behold — and young Michael, as soon as the sound light went off, chirped up in his clear young voice, 'Why doesn't he spit in the cup like Daddy wants me to do?' Kitrin near fainted on her feet, and Mylo smashed a repro oil painting, and oh, dearie, the language! We had to clear the set, calm the leads, and start over the next day. Minus Mylo's beloved family."

Jan could imagine the scene all too well: Kitrin utterly humiliated, trying to protect her son from what a DNA test would actually mean while simultaneously pacifying her furious egomaniac husband. Worse were the implications for Michael's parentage now, and Kitrin's death, as well. Mylo surely knew about Kitrin's own father pressing that test, and how desperately hurt she had been, yet he'd been beating her down with the same accusation. Had Mylo taken one look at Rob that first day they met at the museum and decided he'd found the real father? Could he have managed to have his wife killed while he had an unshakable alibi?

"So did they ever get Michael's DNA tested?"

"Now that I'm not so sure of, dearie. They never spoke of it in public again." Davey glanced away from the monitor. "I've another call, dearie. If you really want to know, you could ask Tootsie Williams. She was about the only friend Kitrin had on any set."

A chance to clear Rob or to place him squarely in the picture? "How would I find Tootsie?"

"She'll find you if she's willing to spill. I'll tell her you're an old friend of Kitrin's and pass along your contact info. Chat to you next week, dearie. And lovely job on that video. I'd never know it was your first."

Jan disconnected with her head buzzing. Kitrin's preferred man was always the same type: dark haired, not too tall, and apt to take over her life and troubles. That description fit Mylo and Rob and ... Chad. Was this the motive for Chad's obsession with Michael? Had he too slept with Kitrin during that fertile week all those years ago? Something else she needed to talk over with Lacey, and probably with Rob, although knowing he had not one but two rivals for Father of the Year might be more than he could cope with right now. She'd wait until she heard from this Tootsie. Maybe the test had been done long since and shown Mylo to be the father, and all this hair-tearing over paternity was moot.

She set the laptop over on the coffee table, wiggled down the cushions until she was lying flat, and pulled her blindfold over her eyes. Time to set all this aside and rest up for the afternoon's job.

Three hours later, Jan looked around the hallway. Did she have everything? Shoes, bag, cameras, phone, keys, water bottle. She checked her watch. Two hours until her next pill. Not perfect timing, since she'd have to eat with it. Snacks? She rummaged in her bag. Yes, the pill was there, and the snack to take with it. She'd be good. As long as she could survive daytime Calgary traffic. If only Rob could come with them, she'd feel much more confident taking Michael along. But he shouldn't take another afternoon away from the office, not after being gone yesterday.

She was about to stand up and load up for the walk out to the van when her phone chimed. A text from Rob read: *Do you remember Kitrin's mother well? I only met her that one time, but someone who looked like my memory of her is in the museum now. If I can unobtrusively snap her, can you identify her?*

Jan frowned. She wouldn't be likely to recognize her friend's mother after ten years of that woman's daily wine consumption and her own intermittent brain impairments. She phoned Rob instead of texting back.

He answered at once. "Would you know her?"

"I have no idea. Is she there alone?"

"I think so. She's been hanging around the atrium, mostly, looking out the front doors like she's waiting for someone." His voice shifted as he walked. "No, she's gone now, on foot toward the bridge. Oh well, I might've been imagining."

Maybe. He was under a lot of stress and, considering yesterday's revelation — about which he still hadn't discussed his feelings — understandably protective of Michael.

"How are you doing today?" she asked. "Have you heard from Bart yet? Will he clear you?"

"Nothing yet."

She pictured him running his fingers through his hair, as he so often did when frustrated. He was probably not much good on the job today with all this hanging over him, but there was no way she could help except encourage him to vent whatever he was feeling, which he'd never spill while at work.

"I'm sorry," she said, "but I have to head out now. I'm picking Michael up and we're going to Calgary to look at more pictures. Orrin Caine's house, if you can believe it. I thought that would be off the table when he went missing, but his housekeeper, or whatever she is, called me yesterday and said they would be there between about two and five today if I want to come and look over what they've got."

"You're taking Michael to Tyrone's house? Have you told him yet that his friend is lost, maybe not coming back?"

"Not yet. I guess I have to, in case the housekeeper mentions it."

"No shit. I don't envy you that job. Are you sure you're up for both driving and childcare in the same afternoon?"

"Not sure at all. But it's got to be done if I'm going to be a good auntie to Michael plus keep on top of this work stuff. You know I can't afford to let tasks pile up. I have to pace them out and check them off every day that I'm strong enough to do anything."

He sighed. "If you're really determined to do both, stop here on your way out. Unless something urgent is going on, I'll take the rest of the afternoon off and drive you. I can call it scoping out Orrin's collection for later loan potential."

Relief made Jan's hands shaky. "Gosh, would you really?"

"I know you want to prove yourself on this job, and Terry will never let you accept another if you have a big crash from it. And, well, I want to spend time with Michael while he's here, even if I never get a clear answer about …" His voice trailed off. Not the time or place for letting those emotions run free. And absolutely not the time to tell him what she'd learned from Davey.

"I'll collect Michael from Jake's," she said, "and be down at the museum in half an hour or so. And thanks. You're my best friend for many good reasons."

Jan hauled her stuff out to the van in better spirits. With Rob to drive her, she could afford the extra energy to really enjoy the outing instead of gritting her teeth to get through it. She drove up to Jake's, stopped at the gates, and waited for the gate guard.

"Hi, Travis. How are you doing today? Chased off any reporters yet?"

Travis shook his head. "One helicopter buzzed us yesterday to film the pool area from above, but Mr. Wyman's pilot told them off for infringing on his airspace or something. They cleared out fast, anyway.

The RCMP does all the media briefings down at their Calgary headquarters, and Mr. Matheson went there this morning to make a public statement." He glowered. "It was on the noon news. He slipped in a plug for his movie. Can you believe that? His wife's dead four days and he's all business. Hell, I'd be more broken up if my ex died, and we've been split five years. 'Course, I'm not humping the nanny three times a day to distract myself."

"Does the whole place know about that?"

"No secret now." He poked up the brim of his blue ball cap. "I'm supposed to ask what your business is here."

"Picking up Michael for some art education. Do you know if he's waiting at the house?"

Travis shook his head. "Haven't seen him outside today. It's really too bad, his mother drowning in the big pool. That was his favourite place."

"Okay then, I'll find him myself."

Michael wasn't waiting on the front steps as arranged. She checked her watch. Ten minutes early, despite the chat with Rob. She went indoors and settled into her wheeled armchair, stuffing down the memory of the last time she'd driven this chair around, looking for Kitrin. Michael wouldn't be at the pool, so that was thankfully out. Would he be doing lessons with his nanny in the suite? Nobody answered her knock there. The library, games room, terrace, and workout area were empty, too. The house steward, tracked down in the laundry room off the kitchen, said Michael had mentioned the stables over lunch, and would Jan like him to phone over there or let her out the delivery entrance so she could cruise there in her chair?

She drove over there, pushing the wing-chair at full speed on the driveway, rocking a bit in the breeze. No Michael. The groom said he hadn't been there since yesterday. She checked the helicopter pad, but the pilot, doing a preflight check, said he hadn't been that way. She rolled on to the staff quarters and asked the cleaner, then followed the perimeter path past the tennis court and back to the big swimming pool's gate. She paused there, trying to tell herself the waterfall didn't sound menacing. It wasn't a reminder of her desperate struggle to save Kitrin. It was just a waterfall. Some day she would be able to be here without that churning sense of failure and grief. But today was not that day.

Today was about getting Michael away from his even worse memories of this place. She cruised around the pool into the house and tapped on the security office door. A woman she didn't recognize, wearing one of Wayne's blue T-shirts, opened the door.

Jan introduced herself. "I'm here to pick up Michael Matheson, and I can't find him anywhere. Can you use the cameras to pinpoint his location for me?"

"Yes, ma'am. Come on in." The woman turned to her monitors and began a systematic survey of all the cameras on the estate. Only the staff was visible around the grounds, going about the usual chores. On the house cameras, nobody showed at first. Then Georgie appeared in a one-piece bathing suit, stepping out of the guest suite on the second-level terrace. Behind her was Mylo. No question what they'd been up to. The bastard was still tucking in his polo shirt.

Jan punched in the house phone for the suite, but although she saw Mylo hesitate, he didn't turn back to answer it, just charged up the steps to the pool. What a nuisance. She'd have to try to catch him. She backed out of the small room and turned toward the pool doors, but he was hurrying past before she got them open and ignored her yell. By the time she got outside, the garage gate was swinging shut behind him. So much for that. Trying to avoid seeing the waterfall even from the corner of her eye, she spun a tight 360 to return to the security office.

"Where's Georgie gone?" she asked from the doorway.

The security woman pointed to a monitor. Georgie was by the swimming machine on the lower level, coiling her mass of curls into a messy bun. It seemed she couldn't face the upper pool, either.

Jan took the elevator down. As she entered the swim area, the machine started up. She yelled over the motor. "Georgie, where's Michael? We're supposed to be leaving for our afternoon outing."

Georgie stopped with both hands atop her head. "He's not with you? I thought he left half an hour ago."

"And you didn't check?" Jan didn't bother to hide her anger. Georgie was supposedly being paid to look out for Michael, not to fall on her back for Mylo. "He's not visible on the cameras, either. Where might he go if he wanted to be alone?"

"Tennis court?"

Jan shook her head.

"Stable?" Georgie tried again.

"No. I've been all over the grounds, and he's not here. Get your clothes on and get looking for him."

"Oh, fuck. Mylo will kill me." Georgie ran up the outside stairs, whether to change her clothes or dash around like a demented poodle, Jan had no idea. She backed into the elevator, pushing buttons, and reached the security office again without seeing anyone else.

She told the woman, "Michael's missing. Can you radio all the patrolling guards to hunt for him? And we have to go back through the camera images to see when and where he was last recorded." She might not have thought of that if she hadn't been looking at Lacey's archived images from the ranch for the past two days. "And track down Mylo Matheson. He should be told."

As the last word left her lips, the unmistakable thunder of helicopter blades passed the house.

The security guard picked up her radio, and said, "Base to pilot. Do you have Michael Matheson with you?"

The radio crackled as the pilot replied. "No. Only Matheson senior."

The woman looked at Jan. "Do I pull them back? How serious is this?"

Jan winced. She could screw up Mylo's schedule for what was nothing more than Michael sitting in a corner somewhere, grieving quietly. Against that was the possibility that his grandmother was in the neighbourhood and had found a way to lure Michael away. But surely they'd never let her onto the grounds without informing Mylo his mother-in-law had arrived?

"Have any visitors been checked in today?"

The woman shook her head. "You're the first."

Well, that settled it. "Let Mr. Matheson go. If we don't find Michael in the next few minutes, you'll have to call him back."

Soon the woman had every security guard on the estate searching and co-opted the outdoor staff, as well. She set the house steward checking all the rooms. Then she told Jan, "You watch this monitor, I'll watch that one, and we'll reverse through the last hour. He must be around here somewhere."

But he wasn't. Jan stared at her monitor, watching him walk backward through the back gate. She got the guard to start the images forward and watched him head out again, down the hillside trail. With Chad. Was Chad kidnapping him for Kitrin's mother, or from suspicion about his parentage? Either way, he mustn't get away with it. She got Travis on the radio.

"Chad took Michael off the grounds by the trail gate. Does he have a vehicle parked anywhere around here?"

"We drove out together," said Travis. "The keys are in my pocket. We'll bring the boy back right away. I'll send a groom out on the long loop, and I'll go downhill."

Jan wasn't convinced it would be that easy to find them if Chad didn't want them found. She phoned Dee. "Hi. Sorry to bother you, but I saw your car at home earlier. Just wondered if you heard the dogs bark at anyone on the trail behind your place."

Dee said, "Yeah, actually I did, about five minutes ago. I was surprised because school is back in now, and usually the trails are quiet during the daytime."

"But you didn't see anybody?"

"Nope."

"Do me a favour? Go up to your bedroom and see if you can spot a man and boy walking on the highway or the bridge?"

"Sure. Hang on." Rustling and thumping came through as Dee climbed the stairs. "There's a man on the trail now, by himself. Out the other way, I see a man and a child across the bridge, quite a ways away. Almost to the grocery store, looks like."

Jan thanked Dee and hung up. Then she got Travis back on the radio and filled him in.

He said, "I'm at the bottom of the hill, and I don't see them along the road. Is there a candy store or somewhere they might be headed?"

Jan thought back to her conversation with Michael yesterday afternoon. She'd told him about the art trip and promised him ice cream. She had even mentioned that famous old ice cream cabin down in the village and learned he'd been there once with Georgie. Hopefully he'd gone back there with Chad, and this wasn't a conspiracy between Chad and Kitrin's mother.

"They could've cut through toward the ice cream cabin. I'll pick you up."

After telling the security guard to stand down the search, Jan cruised her chair outside and climbed into the van. Three minutes later, she caught up to Travis, who was already across the bridge. Soon they were heading down White Avenue toward the ice cream shack.

And there were the missing, sitting on a plank bench in the shade, eating ice cream cones. With them, hidden under a droopy hat and huge sunglasses, was a lean older woman sipping from a water bottle. She was the same approximate height as Kitrin's mother, and her chin seemed vaguely familiar, but the inevitable brain fog from the stressful hunt was playing hell with Jan's ability to focus. How on earth would she get through the afternoon's photography session?

One thing at a time. Get Michael away from Chad and the woman. She climbed out of the van and approached cautiously. Not by a gesture or harsh word would she let Michael know how scared she had been, how sick the hunt had made her, or how furious she was at Chad.

"Hi guys," she said, smiling. "Michael, I've been looking for you. We were supposed to leave for Calgary twenty minutes ago."

"Oh." Michael lowered his gigantic waffle cone. "It took longer to get here than we thought."

"You shouldn't have left the grounds without asking Georgie."

"She was busy with Daddy." He licked a trail of melting ice cream.

Travis said, "Chad, can I have a word with you? Over here."

That woman said to Michael, "You enjoy your ice cream. See you around." She gave Jan a cursory smile and strolled away.

The voice was familiar, and so was the walk, but who was she? Someone recently met, or the tightly wound wine-guzzler last seen a dozen years ago?

"Who was that woman, Michael? Not your grand-mother from Regina?"

"Granny has yellow hair, not red." He shrugged. "She was walking here, too, so she came with us. She bought me a double cone. Can I take it in the van, or do I have to finish it first?"

Exhausted by the emotional cliffs she'd scaled in the past half hour, Jan sank down on the bench beside him. "You can finish it here while I rest up. There's something I have to tell you before we go."

By lunchtime, Lacey had installed and tested the new electronic lock on the workout room, searched the entire storeroom area for signs that someone had sneaked through there last night, and identified three places where the attacker could have collected a dark balaclava: in the machine shed's cloakroom, in the mechanics' miscellaneous bin beneath the stairs, and in the middle storeroom where several snowmobile suits and their accessories occupied a rack. There were plenty of gloves around, too. Anyone on the ranch could have used any of them at any time. Forensic testing would be as useless here as getting DNA from that blood on the office chair.

With Jan's suggestion in mind that a female had sabotaged the Rover, she hovered near the front drive while Cheryl moved Sloane's Porsche SUV toward the front door for their drive into the city. Those were the only two women whose legs weren't accounted for. But she was thwarted by Cheryl's loose khakis and Sloane's long, flowing summer dress. No visible shins.

Over a late lunch in the kitchen — bacon-wrapped scallops on a bed of greens, drizzled with warm maple-whisky sauce — Lacey chatted with the kitchen staff, trying to learn without leading questions about anyone running past their dorm last night. They variously said the wind had been banging things around and they'd had to turn up the TV because an owl was hunting over the climbing gym's roof. Nobody spontaneously mentioned running feet or letting someone into the building.

Ike, returning with the emptied lunch kits he'd driven round to the gates, said a change in the weather was coming. Wind and rain tomorrow, he predicted. That would complicate the search. Lacey hoped he was wrong, or exaggerating, but he didn't seem the type for either. Back to the cabin she went, to rinse off the dust before meeting Wayne for the new external drive. She'd suggested he leave it at Dee's, but he'd refused. He wanted to examine her injuries for himself to make sure she didn't need either a doctor or a Workers' Comp claim form.

Her phone pinged as she headed for the garage. Jan's message read *I told Michael his friend is lost, and you are up at the ranch helping to look for him. Any new news I can share, besides what Terry told me when he got home last night?*

If only …

Tell him there's a special drone hunting for Tyrone's cellphone signal now and there's a good chance we'll have news from that. Between you and me, I hope he's found before the weather changes. Ike (ranch foreman) says we could see rain tomorrow, and he should know.

The same reporters were parked near the front gate as she drove out. She nodded to the hands on guard duty and watched them firmly close the gate behind her. They turned their backs on the reporters who approached, like they'd been doing for three days already. No media vehicle followed her. They probably guessed from the security sign on the truck door that she wouldn't talk to them, anyway. She passed the airstrip, wondering if the drone had now searched all the relevant phone numbers.

Four nights Orrin and Tyrone had been missing. Would they have been found already if the search coordinator had received Tyrone's phone number from the first moment? Would they survive another night out in the wild if the weather turned wet and cold? The uncertainty bugged her so much that she did a three-point turn and headed back to the SAR base.

Before she'd gotten ten paces from the truck, she felt a new buzz around the camp. Search teams were walking faster, talking with greater animation than on her last visit. Had some promising trail been found?

Constable Markov, as usual on liaison duty, filled her in. "We've got three numbers up with the drone now," he said. "Not only the boy's phone, but apparently Orrin Caine had two phones with him, one personal and one business. We only had the personal number."

"Why wasn't that other phone reported up front?"

He shrugged. "Miscommunication between home and office. Each one thought the other had reported it. Today's good news, though: we can narrow the search area at last. A fellow from Water Valley, who was up north fishing over the weekend, heard the local news on his way home late last night and called in that he saw Orrin's vehicle last Saturday afternoon as he was heading out. It was definitely northeast of the ranch at that time, eastbound on 579 toward Water Valley."

"He's sure it was Orrin?"

"Yup. He's gone hunting with Orrin in that very Rover."

That explained the vibe around the base. Lacey wished him luck and got back into her truck. The airstrip vanished behind her, and she was alone with her thoughts as the gravel road spooled out between the unending trees. Cloistered at the ranch, with everyone from family to staff to ranch hands talking as if it was only a matter of time before Tyrone overcame a challenge set by his overbearing — abusive! — father, it was easy to go along with optimism instead of looking at the reality. Even with the new information, the already exhausted search teams faced hundreds of square kilometres of hostile terrain, not only heavily treed and crisscrossed by cutlines and OHV trails, but split by deep, rocky ravines filled with thick brush and rushing streams. Canyons like those were easy to climb down or fall down and sometimes impossible to get out of without a rescue tech dropping down hundreds of metres beneath a helicopter. She'd never say so to the searchers, and not to Tyrone's family, but this was a time when she really wished she didn't know the odds against finding the boy alive.

With an effort, she wrenched her thoughts back to something she could hope to achieve: discovering the identity of the person who had tampered with the

Range Rover. She must have gotten close enough that the individual tried to cover their tracks by stealing the camera archive. So who was it? Jan said it was likely a woman on that recording, but if she discounted the one who showed up Mondays to clean floors, there were only three women close enough to Orrin to be viable suspects: Andy, Sloane, and Cheryl. All were similar in height and build. She considered them one by one.

Andy: ruled out of attacking Lacey based on the lack of bruises today and because she was thought to be away from the ranch when the Range Rover was sabotaged. In unbiased eyes, though, she was a prime suspect. She must have known the workout room door was unlock-able, for one thing. She was paranoid about cameras and knew how to avoid them. Most male investigators would assume her affair with Ben meant she was capable of murder to cover it up. Going ahead with trying to get pregnant this week, though, indicated to Lacey that a) Andy really wanted a child, and b) she and the twins thought Orrin would be found alive and they needed to keep the secret about Ben's involvement.

After reassuring Andy that she wouldn't tell, Lacey had asked first whether Bart couldn't make himself do the deed for her sake. Andy confessed they'd tried that for a year and both been miserable. As for why they didn't go to a fertility clinic and get Bart's sperm implanted that way, well, between Orrin's obsession with snooping and the fact that all their health bills were paid by the company's benefit plan, going to any clinic was risky. Even if she and Bart paid privately, their bank statements would track the expense or their health-care ID might turn up in a database somewhere that the company's bean counters had access to. Questions would lead to an investigation, and Orrin would never let Bart live down a visit to a fertility clinic. He'd probably tell the child every day of its life, too. Ben was the only one they trusted to help them out, and his loyalty to Bart trumped even his eternal urge to piss off Orrin.

The online search of paternity testing protocols lurked on Lacey's phone. She hadn't wanted to leave a trace on the ranch's computers to give anyone else the idea. But it was just as Ben had told her: the standard DNA test for paternity would show the baby as almost inevitably sired by Bart. Only the much more advanced test could cast doubt about which twin was the sperm donor, and all three involved were determined that there would never be a reason for doubt. Would they bother to keep up the charade if any of them believed Orrin wasn't coming home?

As for the other two women, Sloane probably had the best motive for wanting Orrin gone, although why she'd wait twelve years to act was an open question. Also, why act before Orrin changed his will to leave everything to her son? She'd been at the ranch on that Monday night and could have tampered with the Rover. She hadn't been near the workout room all week, though. Was she physically strong enough to tackle Lacey and win?

Cheryl, now … She was tougher in all ways than Sloane, and she'd been on the workout room camera at least half an hour every day, working her muscles against the machines. She might have mixed martial arts training in her past, for all Lacey knew, or some other combat skill that would let her confidently tackle an ex-cop to wrest away the external drive containing the surveillance archive. By her own admission, she too had been at the ranch on the Monday night in question. Except ... she'd been the only person to mention that someone might have tampered with the Rover. Why raise that at all if she'd been party to it?

Come to that, how could she know about the archive drive? Who *did* know? While Lacey was discussing the archive footage with Jan, Ben had been on the bluff staircase. He could have heard the conversation, but equally Cheryl or anyone else could have eavesdropped through an open window.

Wayne hadn't bothered with a dossier on Cheryl because she was staff, not family. It probably hadn't dawned on him that, as a close friend of Sloane's from before the marriage, Cheryl wasn't simply working for a wage. She had been an integral part of Sloane's life for more than a dozen years, as close as any family member. Wayne's internet snooper must dig up Cheryl's background. If she was responsible for this throbbing bruise on Lacey's cheek, it would be a personal pleasure to take her down.

As she pulled over for a truck speeding north, Lacey considered the possibility that Jan might be wrong. It still could be one of the brothers on that video. Ben knew how to get there without being caught on camera, and maybe he'd learned Orrin was about to officially disinherit him. Bart, too, had motives she hadn't considered before: not only was he conniving to, in effect, defraud Orrin of whatever trust fund was set aside for a son, but he had been hiding his homosexuality all his life. If someone was threatening to tell Orrin, then Bart's inheritance too might vanish like a stone into the ocean.

Trees and forest: which were the clues, and which were irrelevant issues that only obscured them?

The towering trees on her left gave way to a broad meadow irregularly bounded by forest. A horse loped out of a gap at the far side. Its rider slowed and waved a hat at her, seeming to beckon her closer. She squinted. Something seemed off about the person's silhouette. Was that a second face below the first, and extra legs dangling? Likely someone's horse had got away from them. She checked her watch. If a searcher needed a ride back to base, she could do it without being terribly late to meet Wayne.

Something about that head and shoulders reminded her of old Susan Norris, who Ben had said owned land east of the road. She slowed further and pulled into the meadow. The horse sped up.

Susan Norris came up at a quick trot, the sun glinting off her horse's bridle. Now it was clearer: the old woman clutched before her an upright body, its legs and arms dangling and its head flopping sideways with every step the horse took.

"About bloody time someone showed up," Susan shouted as Lacey leaped from the truck. "I been yellin' for half an hour."

CHAPTER TWENTY-TWO

The Calgary traffic was thickening around the van when Jan pushed up her blindfold and opened her eyes. She wasn't quite recovered, but the lie-down in the back seat had done her good. Michael and Rob were chatting away in the front seats. After his first shock at his friend being lost in the wilderness, the boy had talked it over extensively with Rob. That was surely a good sign, both of their bond and of Michael's ability to cope with a second potential loss.

She waited for a pause in the conversation and then asked, "How much farther?"

"Ten minutes or so, I think," said Rob. "Do you have to take a pill or eat or anything before we get there?"

Jan pulled out her phone and looked at her reminders: *3:30 pill and snack*. It was only 3:15, but close enough. She sat slowly up and reached for her bag. "Sorry I sagged out on you there."

Rob met her eyes in the rear-view mirror. "Better you should rest now than crash out in the middle of taking your pictures."

Michael craned his head around as far as the seat belt would allow and watched her swallow her pill with a good guzzle from her water bottle. She split the wrapper on her coconut bar and offered him the spare.

"No, thank you," he said. "I'm still full from my ice cream."

They came to the gated driveway of the Caine house in Mount Royal. It wasn't as extravagant as she had expected. It was older, for one thing. Forty years maybe; not an exceptional era in Calgary architecture. This one was a basic brick box with lower wings — garage on one end and a slit-windowed extension on the other that was probably a single large room where parties were held. It seemed incongruent with arrogant Orrin and sophisticated Sloane. Maybe he'd kept it because the land was worth a mint, intending to eventually build a mansion to outshine its newer, larger neighbours.

Rob explained to whoever answered the gate buzzer what their business was. Then he drove them to the front door and unloaded Jan's wheelchair from the back.

Michael said, "You could walk before. How come you can't walk now?"

"I'm like a cellphone battery that's stuck on trickle charge. I can only go so many steps before I have to be charged up again. That's why Rob's driving us today. So I can recharge."

A dark-haired woman opened the door to them. She introduced herself as Cheryl and greeted Michael by name. Of course, they must have met when Michael went to the ranch.

He said, "Do you know where Tyrone is?"

Cheryl's eyes flicked to Jan and back before she shook her head. "Not yet. But I'm sure it won't be long now." She stepped aside for Jan's wheelchair. "If you'll tell me which era of pictures in particular you're interested in, I'll take you directly to them, or bring them to you if they're in an area of the house you can't get to."

"Thank you," said Jan. "Orrin — Mr. Caine — said he had Rocky Mountain art but he didn't know titles or artists. I need early twentieth-century and late nineteenth-century mountain landscapes."

"Come this way." Cheryl led them to the back of the house, into a low room that matched the exterior for 1980s blandness. The sofas were newer, mostly leather, and the off-white walls were hung with framed mountain art at eye level, if Jan stood up. Rob parked her by the patio doors, where the light was good. Cheryl pointed out pictures on the walls and left the room while Rob carried them over one at a time. As the medication kicked in and the food fuelled her brain, Jan found she was able to coherently explain to Michael that this was a Gissing, and a bit too late technically, but it might work, while that one over there that looked even more mountainous was clearly a 1960s version done in acrylic paints. "Acrylics were still pretty new then. That surface would shine oddly under film lighting."

Michael took it all in. He had a surprisingly good eye for composition, which Jan attributed to years of watching his father dissect film stills. When she commented on his grasp of light and shadow, he shrugged. "I had art tutors when Daddy was shooting in Italy."

Cheryl came back with three more pictures. "These are from the upstairs hall. There's one more in Mrs. Caine's bedroom, but she's resting in there, and I don't want to disturb her. If she's not awake by the time you leave, I can take a picture later and send it to you." Since Jan was at that moment showing Michael the back of a canvas, explaining to him what the stamps and other markings meant, she added, "Oh, I'll take a picture of the back, too."

Jan assessed eight paintings quickly, four of them good prospects that Rob arranged in the light from the patio doors. She set up her camera and let Michael take the actual photos. He didn't mention Tyrone again, and she was just congratulating herself on a successful diversion when a woman screamed from the doorway.

"Ty! Baby, you're home!"

Michael turned, looking eagerly for his friend. Sloane Caine stared back at him, her face whitening, and sank down where she stood.

After a few minutes, Cheryl coaxed her up to the nearest sofa. Sloane recovered enough to apologize to the guests and dredged up enough parental instinct to reassure Michael that she was all right now. She even told him she was sure Tyrone would be home soon and would be very happy to have him over to play. By the time she got that speech out, her voice was shaking. Michael leaned against Jan, trembling in the face of the woman's overwhelming emotion.

She hugged him over the arm of her wheelchair and whispered in his ear, "Ty's mom really wants to believe Ty will be fine, and we're going to help her, okay?"

He nodded. After a moment he straightened up and said, "Can I leave him a message for when he gets back?"

Sloane gave a tremulous smile. "You sure can. There are markers and crayons and things in his room. Cheryl, will you show him?"

Cheryl took Michael away. Sloane, her heartbreaking smile erased, excused herself and groped her way out of the room. Jan finished photographing the last painting and Rob began to rehang pictures. He'd just finished the third when Michael yelled from upstairs.

"Jan, Jan! They have a painting of my mom!"

"Oh, no!" she said softly to Rob. "He's imagining a resemblance because he misses her so much. Go get him away from whatever it is."

He left but came back a moment later, carrying another painting. "Jan, you really have to see this."

Michael was behind him, vibrating with excitement. "It's her! Just like when we went to England for BAFTA!" He had his phone out and was scrolling through photos before Rob had fully turned the portrait. "See? A different dress, but it's her!"

Jan stared. She'd never seen Kitrin with her hair piled up, but in the bright light of the patio doors, there was no mistaking the resemblance. That delicate face with the pointed chin, the wistful expression ... both were classic Kitrin. Only the clothing didn't fit. She couldn't ever recall seeing Kitrin in a wide-lapel jacket with a wasp waist.

Michael thrust his phone at her. "See?"

She looked from painting to phone. On the BAFTA awards red carpet, Kitrin wore a slim-line gown inspired by Second World War fashions, with a high-fronted hairstyle that might have been seen on any Women's Army Corps volunteer.

Cheryl came from the kitchen with a pitcher of lemonade and several glasses. "I thought everyone could use a cool drink before you face the heat again," she said. "Oh, that painting's far out of your period. It's a copy done from a much older photograph, of Mr. Caine's mother as a young woman."

"The resemblance to Michael's mother," said Rob, "is remarkable."

"It's her," Michael insisted, his lip trembling.

Jan suggested the first alternative that came to her. "Maybe Mr. Caine's mother and your granny were sisters. That would make you and Tyrone, um, second cousins or something."

He wasn't convinced, but the meltdown potential receded. "I'm going to call my granny when I get home and ask her."

"You do that," said Jan. "And if they are sisters, we'll come back and take a proper picture of this picture for you to send to your granny."

Cheryl's phone and Sloane's shrilled simultaneously. They both scrambled to check their messages. Sloane gave out a wordless shriek. Cheryl dropped her phone onto the tray, scattering the glasses.

CHAPTER TWENTY-THREE

Lacey ran to meet the old woman.

"You got a phone that will reach the airstrip?" Susan yelled, slowing her horse with practised coordination between her knees and the one hand holding the reins. "Call for a chopper quick. Boy's et somethin'."

Lacey took in Tyrone's flaccid limbs, the vivid red rash around his mouth, and streaks of greenish bile drying on his shirt front. His head lolled. His breathing was louder than the horse's. She hit her phone with one hand and steadied the boy with the other.

"SAR base, McCrae here," she said, praising the gods for all the oil millionaires who had ranches way out here and liked their cellphone service. "We have Tyrone Caine. Repeat. We have Tyrone." She ran her hand up his leg, noted that it seemed undamaged but his jeans were filthy. His tanned arms, dirt streaked and scratched, hung limp. His chest strained to pull in air. A tell-tale blue tinge to his lips, beneath the rash, was a sure sign he wasn't getting enough oxygen. "He's in medical distress," she reported. "His breathing is laboured. Looks cyanotic. Send EMTs and air transport. We are approximately eight kilometres south of the airstrip, in a field on the east side of Highway 40."

When she hung up, Susan lifted Ty's left leg over the saddle and slid him into her arms. She lowered him to the ground and parted his lips. Green foam bubbled in his throat. His tongue had swelled to almost fill his mouth. His larynx was probably swelling, too. How much longer could air reach his lungs? If this were a movie, she'd know how to do a penknife tracheotomy in the field, but it wasn't in her first aid training beyond the single curt instruction: don't ever attempt it. All she could do was put him into the recovery position, using the technique drilled into her long ago at Depot: left arm out, right arm bent to support his left cheek, right leg bent and then gently tilted to the left, bringing his limp body over onto its left side. She adjusted his head to open his airway farther and was rewarded by a slightly deeper breath.

"Can't you do that resuscitation breathing?" Susan demanded, having dismounted. She dropped her horse's reins, and it stayed, lowering its head to nose the dusty grasses.

"His throat's swelling shut," Lacey explained. "If he stops breathing completely, all we can do is chest compressions to keep what oxygen is in his blood moving around." She checked his pulse. Rapid, but what did that mean? "Do you know what he ate?"

Susan pulled a green stalk from her breast pocket. "Had this in his hand when I got there."

"Great! The medics will soon tell if that's what he ate, and if he's poisoned or having an allergic reaction."

Lacey laid her fingers against Tyrone's neck. His pulse was still rapid, and she thought his breathing was getting wheezier again. The blue tinge in his lips deepened, an ever-greater contrast to the paleness of his cheek. She shifted his head to open his airway farther and strained her ears for the thrashing of helicopter blades in the baked summer sky.

CHAPTER TWENTY-FOUR

As she watched Sloane and Cheryl hug each other, tears streaming down their faces, Jan's phone rang. She fished it out of her pocket. "Hello?"

Lacey's voice said, "You're going to hear it soon, but I wanted to tell you so you can break it to Michael if he's still with you. We've found Ty. He's in a bad way from something he ate out in the forest and being airlifted to Children's Hospital right now." Her voice trembled. "Jan, he might not survive."

"Thanks for telling me. Are you okay?"

"I don't know. Look, I've got to go. The search teams are arriving to try to follow his trail back to Orrin."

"You stay safe," Jan told her. She disconnected and said briskly, "Time for us to get out of the way. Rob, take this gear out to the van. Michael, can you push my chair, please?" She stopped by the weeping women. "You'll want to be heading to the hospital right away. My thoughts are with you."

Soon they were all three in the van. This time, too keyed up to lie down, Jan took the front seat. She settled her dark glasses over her eyes to limit the sensory overload from traffic whizzing past. Should she tell Michael his friend had been found or keep quiet until they knew whether he'd survive or not? What was the right decision for this child she hardly knew? She scanned rapidly through her mental contacts list and found not a single friend or acquaintance who worked with children and might offer guidance.

As the van waited at a stoplight, Michael asked, "Did they get bad news?"

Moment of decision. The truth had to win. "I think it's good news, but shocking. Tyrone has been found but ... well, he ate something that wasn't good for him, and he's being taken to the hospital."

"Oh." Michael was silent for half a block. "He'll be okay. I ate some berries in a park when I was little, and they took me to the hospital. The nurse gave me stuff to make me puke. It was so gross."

"But you were okay again soon?" Rob asked.

"Uh-huh." Michael grinned. "Daddy said it's not every day he sees purple puke. I wish he'd took a picture."

Jan breathed a sigh of relief. The truth was out, and Michael was putting it into context with his own experiences. While Tyrone might not be so lucky, he was in good hands now. They'd just have to wait for news.

"Terry may be called out again," she told Rob. "You want to keep staying at my place?"

"Sure." He turned on the radio, and they listened in silence to the rush-hour traffic reports. The hourly news came on, but without mention of Tyrone being found. Jan glanced at the dashboard clock. Only fifteen minutes since Lacey's call. Somehow the SAR base had managed to stave off an immediate media announcement, but it couldn't be long now. As soon as they cleared the city limits and didn't need the road report, she tuned to an all-music station and let that fill the silence for the rest of the drive.

They dropped Michael off at Jake's, seeing him right into his father's presence. They'd barely got out the gates when Jan's phone rang. She yanked it out. "Lacey?"

"Um, no," said a strange voice. "I'm looking for Jan Brenner?"

"That's me."

"Hi. Davey gave me your name. You are a friend of Kitrin Matheson?"

Ten minutes later, with the van idling in her own drive, Jan thanked Tootsie Williams and hung up. "Well, that's that. Poor Kitrin had virtually no friends down in L.A., and only Tootsie is going to Regina for her funeral."

Rob steered the van into the garage and stopped. "And the rest?"

"I guess you couldn't help overhearing."

"Enough to know you were talking about Michael's DNA." Rob silenced the motor and stared straight ahead. "Did Mylo have him tested?"

Truth was best, whatever the emotional fallout. "Yes. He's Mylo's son."

CHAPTER TWENTY-FIVE

Lacey's last sight of Tyrone, as he was loaded onto the helicopter, was as a thin body under a blanket, his face mostly covered with an oxygen mask. Her first sight had been only fifteen minutes ago. She watched the helicopter vanish over the trees and hoped he would still be alive when it landed at Children's Hospital.

Gradually, the noise faded and the smaller sounds around her came into focus once more. Three trucks filled with search teams had arrived. They were preparing to follow old Susan back to the distant cutline where she'd found the boy. Constable Markov was taking Susan's statement while the old woman leaned calmly on a fence post. Lacey headed toward them, knowing she'd be next and wanting to hear Susan's story for herself. They hadn't talked beyond Susan's curt orders on getting the unconscious boy off the horse and Lacey's equally short answers on the first aid options.

Markov asked, "And he was conscious when you found him?"

"Yup. Asked 'im what he et, and he showed me his hand. But he's a good little rider from way back and got up into the saddle okay, with a boost from me. Didn't pass out until we were halfway here."

"Why did you come this way? Was this the closest route back to the airstrip?"

"There's other roads, but they don't lead nowhere near the search camp. I come across the creek where I showed you, followed the cutline and come out when missy over there was driving by. Not more'n twenty minutes. My old Rebel is a good goer." Susan glared at the constable. "I yelled for help all the way. What's the point of having searchers traipsing over my land if none of them comes when I yell?"

When it was Lacey's turn, she described seeing the rider waving at her. "I turned off the road, thinking it was someone who needed a ride back to the SAR base. I recognized Susan from halfway across this meadow and saw she had someone up in front of her. I didn't know if he was unconscious or dead." That word cost her a moment's deep breathing before she kicked her brain back into report mode. "When she came closer, I saw it was Tyrone. We got him onto the ground, and I did a quick first aid check. He was wheezing. He had a rash around his mouth. There wasn't much I could do for him except put him into the recovery position, monitor his breathing and pulse, and hope like hell that help got here fast."

Her helpless feelings she didn't tell him, or how she'd counted the seconds sitting on the hot, dusty field, listening for each breath, watching Ty's hand whiten in hers, seeing his lips turn bluer than a day-old bruise.

"You didn't try to do CPR?"

"With his airway swollen shut, breathing for him would do nothing. I was prepared to do chest compressions until the paramedics got here. Of course I was hoping it wouldn't come to that. It would have been devastating to find him alive and then watch him ..." She couldn't bring herself to say the word.

Susan said, "Buck up now, missy," and handed her a leather-wrapped flask from a saddlebag.

Lacey didn't know what to expect, but she took a slug, anyway. It was lukewarm tea, stronger than tar and sweeter than pancake syrup. She took a second swallow. Susan had probably made it that way in case she found Ty and Orrin in shock. The sugar was just as welcome to Lacey at this moment, although she might have to sand-blast the tea off her teeth later. As she handed it back, she saw noticed that Susan's patient old horse was loaded down with a Western saddle, a rifle in its scabbard, a pack, and a bedroll tied on behind.

"You were camping out?"

Susan sniffed. "Waste of daylight going home and back every day."

"So you've been searching your land the whole time?"

Susan held out her hand for the flask. "Gotta get back to it. Still old Orrin to find. Not that he's any loss."

Markov held up the map. "You're sure this is the area you found the boy in?"

Susan gave him a look that should have shrivelled him where he stood. "My land. You think I don't know where I was?"

"Right." Markov backed away. "I'll show the search teams so they can mark off a new grid."

Susan took a slug from the flask and passed it back to Lacey. "Want some grub? Gotta trail mix in here somewhere."

"No, thank you. I had lunch just before I left." Lacey didn't mention that her bacon-wrapped scallops might be coming back up any minute. That green barf of Ty's had been smelly and frothy and altogether disgusting.

Susan looked away to the east at the cutline she'd come out of. "Thing is, that boy was not more'n a mile from where I found his big brother that time."

"You found one of the boys after Orrin dropped him off?"

"Yep. Young Earl, near the same age as Tyrone is now. 'Course, he'd only been out one night. Going in the wrong direction he was, when I found him, hungry and scared spitless. I took him up yonder, but he wouldn't let me bring him in his gate. Said his old man would beat him if he knew Earl needed help."

"He would have, too," Lacey said. "By all I've heard he was an abusive old bastard."

"Was? You think he ain't coming back?"

"I don't know. Ben and Bart have gone over all the places they can remember being dumped by him and come up empty. They've asked Earl everything he can remember, too. But I bet he didn't tell them you brought him home that time he was lost overnight."

"Your money's safe there." Susan's eyes narrowed. "Young Earl never told me where he started from. How far you figure a boy that age can walk in a day?"

"In the forest? I'd be surprised if he could cover five kilometres. Maybe more if he stuck to the cutlines and off-road vehicle trails."

"That's what I reckoned, too. Four days at four miles is only a sixteen-mile range. Less, considering young Tyrone likely wandered around some. Earl, now, he was only gone a day or thereabouts."

"Thirty hours." Lacey gazed northward toward the undulating lands that would some day belong to Bart and Ben. Where Orrin had been last seen. "Are you thinking Orrin might have dropped Ty off at the same spot as Earl? And then something happened to Orrin before he made it back to the main road?"

"You ain't stupid, I'll give you that." Susan crammed her hat back over her grey hair. "Earl only coulda walked maybe ten miles from where he started. If I can figure that out, I can find the crazy old man." She went back to her patient horse and swung into the saddle. "I'd be obliged if you'd leave a message at my gate when you find out how the young lad's doing."

She swung the horse's head around. Soon she had vanished along the cutline.

Markov came running. "Where's she going?"

"She thinks she can backtrack Ty's wandering to his father."

Markov blotted his forehead on his sleeve. "I hope she gave us the right coordinates, because we can't follow her trail that fast. Off-road vehicles are coming to take the search teams in. They'll fan out across the creek."

Lacey nodded. "I'm supposed to be meeting my boss in Cochrane. Do you need anything else from me right now?"

He shook his head. "Thanks, McCrae. You did good."

"All the credit goes to old Susan. Imagine, at her age, sleeping on the ground in a forest where cougars and grizzlies prowl, rather than waste an hour of search time going home and back. She hates Orrin, but she's going to go find him, anyway."

CHAPTER TWENTY-SIX

Jan struggled upward through the weight of sleep, her thoughts tumbling over each other like rocks in a grinder. She'd kept it together through the drive home, turning Michael over to his father, telling Jake Tyrone had been found, but not Orrin. Then Rob had brought her home, dragged her into the house, and sent her to bed. Now she lay in her darkened room, her aching eyes protected by her sleep mask and her whole body immobilized by the blankets like a truckload of gravel had been dumped on her bed. Her skin hurt. Her hair hurt. Her limbs wouldn't respond to her mental commands. She was paralyzed, and even the pulse of blood in her veins rasped on her over-wired senses. Somewhere nearby, a cement mixer was running. She drifted through the fragments in her head, wondering why the house wasn't finished yet, or were they building an extension and she had just forgotten?

After an age, the noise stopped. Her mouth was dry as the Drumheller Badlands, and she had to pee. She wiggled her right arm out from under the gravity-enhanced covers. Her left arm came slowly up after it.

As her long nerves began at last to wake up, she experimentally wiggled her toes. From there to rolling over on her side was another eternity. Her joints grated like C-3PO's when he had come through a sandstorm. She managed to push up her sleep mask, and the thin lines of light around the curtains told her the sun had moved west. How late was it? The sound of the distant cement mixer came again, and this time she recognized it: the blender in the kitchen. There was no smell of cooking, no sound of music, just a quiet house with the intermittent thunder of a distant appliance. After more self-coaxing, she managed to get herself out of bed and eventually groped her way along the walls to the living room.

Rob appeared in the kitchen doorway. "Oh good, you're up. Go straight to the couch, and I'll bring your meds. You're about an hour overdue, as near as I can figure."

An hour? That explained why her limbs wouldn't move easily. Without the new medication, every cell in her body was struggling to draw nutrients from her bloodstream. Limited fluids, sugars, and oxygen meant every muscle was stuck in a brownout. She'd be better physically in a few minutes, if not mentally. She settled into her pillows on the couch, accepted the water glass from Rob, and turned her head so her weak throat muscles could get the pill down. Then she lay back and closed her eyes again, covering them with her hands to hide from the primrose glow of sunset. Soon ...

As the drugs worked through her system, she wiggled her toes more freely and squished her shoulders back amid the pillows until her neck and head were more comfortable. Sounds ceased to hurt her ears, but the light still stung her eyes.

Rob came back. "Phase two: carrot ginger smoothie with that medicinal food powder in it."

"Oh, gross. I hate that chalky taste. You would, too, if you'd had to live on it for three years."

"Not the way I do it." He handed her the glass of bright orange goop. "You know when you're this crashed, your stomach doesn't have the energy to digest real food. So get that down you and see how you feel."

Just lifting the glass was a workout, but as the smoothie flooded her starving cells with nutrients, she experimentally flexed each muscle group. She winced. "Photographing those few pictures was too much for my arms on top of the bits of driving I did before you met us."

"The emotional wallop was probably the worst part," he said. "Having to hunt for Michael used up most of your energy too early, and you were running on fumes from that point on. But you got through, you did your job, and you didn't let Michael know how destroyed you were."

"I was afraid he'd think me as frail as his mother and start worrying I would die on him, too."

"He's more resilient than you might think." Rob took the empty glass from her. "If Tyrone pulls through, it will help a lot."

"Is there any word from anyone?"

"I heard your phone ping, but I didn't look."

Jan groped on the coffee table and checked her messages. One from Terry: *not home tonight.* A second from

Lacey: *Ty is responding to treatment. He can't speak yet but he's out of the woods, pardon the pun.*

Tears washed the remaining grit from Jan's eyes.

"Bad news?" asked Rob.

"No." She repeated the message. "I'll let Michael know. What a relief! Now all I have to do is get my head back in the video analysis game. Every time I look at those videos I feel like Sisyphus, rolling the boulder up a hill, knowing it's going to come rolling back down with absolutely nothing to show for all my efforts."

"Then leave it," said Rob. "There's nothing you need to do until morning."

She lay back for another while, marking time by Rob's puttering around as he cleaned up the kitchen. When he returned with tea for them both, she said, "I could be looking at that picture from Jake's garage-cam again. There's something about the shape of the head that keeps bugging me. Like I've seen it elsewhere." She dictated a text to her phone: *Lacey, have you got more stills or video footage of that person from Jake's garage? I'll look at them as soon as I'm fit for duty again. If you can round up staff head shots, or the backs of their heads from any other cameras, that would help me make comparisons.* It wasn't much, but it felt good to have a next step planned.

She was lying there in a half doze, her brain skipping from thought to image to half-formed plan, when feet thumped on the deck. Hammering started on the patio door.

Rob came running through the room. He opened the door and said, "Shut the fuck up, man. Jan's resting."

He went outside, closing the door after him. Murmurs came through the kitchen window farther along the deck. Okay, nothing to do with her.

She was drifting off again when a man's voice said loudly, "I have to see her. I have to explain about this afternoon."

Oh, crap. Chad. *Please don't let Rob let him in.*

Rob said, "She's had enough of your fucking drama for one day."

After a bit he returned. Jan opened her eyes. "Was that Chad?"

"Yup. I told him —"

"I heard. Fierce."

"Did you want to talk to him tonight? Because I told him to come back tomorrow."

"Oh." Jan yawned. "That's fine. I suppose I'll have to tell him he's not —" Almost too late, she thought better of mentioning Michael's paternity. "Not ever to take Michael off the grounds again. Do you know, I briefly wondered if he was in league with Kitrin's mother? She knew him almost as well as we did, and if she thought she could use him to get her grandson … it would be ugly, is all."

"No shit." The front doorbell rang. Rob stalked toward the foyer. "If that's him back, I swear I'll get violent."

When he returned, though, Lacey was behind him. Jan struggled to sit up. "What are you doing here? Not bad news?"

Lacey slid to the carpet and propped her back against an armchair. "Everything's okay, as far as I know.

Wayne gave me the night off. He's going to stay at the ranch instead."

Rob looked her over with a critical eye. "You've been through the wars all right. Tea, or something cold?"

"Beer?"

He nodded and went out. Jan stretched out and pulled her afghan up to her chin. With Lacey there was no need to pretend she was anything but flattened. "I'm glad you weren't hurt last night and thrilled that Ty is safe in hospital. So Wayne gave you the night off to recuperate?"

Lacey nodded. "Or he's been adding up how much he has to pay me for being there twenty-four-seven." Her hand went to her throat, as it often did when she was stressed. "Good news: he offered to put me on staff as of September first. He was going to wait until I pass my private investigations exam, but he'll take my word for it that I can do it by Christmas and is making me staff now so I can get benefits. I haven't had benefits since I left the RCMP."

That was something Jan had never considered about her single neighbour's existence: no spouse with a generous benefits package. In Alberta, with the country's highest rates for dental and massage and a whole lot of other services, that was a significant handicap. "Great news! What are you going to do first?"

"Get my teeth cleaned. They feel disgusting." Lacey rubbed her throat again. "And maybe find a therapist who deals with PTSD."

Jan nodded sympathetically. Years of witnessing traumatic events on the job could leave someone with

PTSD, all right. Plus there was Lacey's ex-husband, whom Dee had warned her never to ask about. Then Lacey had almost been killed last summer at the museum, right on top of finding her best friend near death in a ditch. Just yesterday she'd been beaten up, and today she had snatched a child from the very brink of death. If anyone needed therapy, she did, and yet she still got up every day and helped people to the best of her ability. The RCMP had lost a valuable asset when she quit.

Rob came back with a beer for Lacey and a whisky for himself. He said, "I'll be outside if you need anything," and went to the deck, closing the patio doors behind him.

Jan watched Lacey take a first appreciative swig. "Did you get my message about video from Jake's? That picture you sent me doesn't match anybody I know on the staff. I enhanced the colour and contrast and blew it up big to look for a birthmark or something unique to help with identification. If I had more footage I might be able to measure the ear cartilage or hazard a height estimate from the person's stride."

"You can gauge the stride from a few seconds of video showing part of a head?"

"Sure. The head moves up and down with the movement of the feet. In my life-drawing classes, we had to pay attention to how all the body parts were positioned during a step."

"I never would've thought of that." Lacey's admiring look was balm to Jan's steamrolled self-image. "I can go up to Jake's tonight and send you as much video as you can stand. Also staff photos from the files. You know,

I'm starting to think that person must have a hell of a reason for not coming forward already."

"Like they might have been the one who killed Kitrin?"

Lacey shrugged. "There's not a shred of motive that I can see for anyone who works there to murder her. And there are no hallmarks of a stranger murder. For one thing, a stranger would be noticed, and for another, impulse killers almost always leave clues. This was a surgical strike by someone who knew the pool camera was down."

"God, I didn't think of that." Jan frowned. "Who all knew about that camera?"

"Everyone who was at the supper that night, probably. I told Jake about it on the terrace." Lacey thumped her forehead gently with her open palm. "I know better than to reveal security information in public. But it's a bit confusing, being both a social guest and a worker around the same people. I've got that problem up at the ranch, too. Now that I'm in on Andy's secrets, she and the twins treat me like an old pal. But I'm no closer to figuring out who tampered with the Rover."

"I'll get on it first tomorrow." Jan glanced toward the patio doors. "Can you see Rob?"

"Yep." Lacey leaned sideways for a better look. "He's got what we used to call a thousand-yard stare. What happened to him today?"

"Um … apart from getting no answer from lover-boy about his alibi, he learned for sure he's not Michael's father. I guess now he's facing the fact that he'll probably never be anyone's dad." Jan bit her lip.

"Especially hard while he's involved with a married man whose wife is trying to get pregnant. Bart surely wouldn't leave her after they've gone to all that trouble to have a child."

Lacey settled back against her chair. "There's no sign they'll break up even if she doesn't get pregnant. But you know it's still possible Bart beat me up over that external drive. That's not exactly a five-star recommendation."

"You don't really suspect him, do you?" A beam from the setting sun invaded the living room. Jan put up a hand to shield her tired eyes. "Someone up there must have attacked you, but I thought you said everyone who could have rigged the Rover that Monday was accounted for last night."

"Almost everyone," Lacey corrected. "Bart isn't cleared for last night yet, even though Andy and Ben are. It's like one of those logic puzzles: Andy and Bart are X'd off for the Monday — Wayne found a neighbour who saw them on their deck until about ten o'clock, too late to be on a ranch camera at eleven. Well, unless they used Orrin's helicopter, and there's no sign it left the ranch that night. Besides, Andy could be giving Bart a fake alibi for last night. I won't know that until I see if his legs are bruised from the fight. Ben is cleared for last night, but he has no alibi for the Monday. Plus he knew which cameras were misaligned, and he was the one who rigged the workout room's outside door. Equally, he and Bart could have hatched a plan to get rid of Orrin before he could change his will to cut Ben out. Being identical twins, it might have been Ben with Andy on her deck while Bart snuck out to the ranch on the Monday."

"My head is starting to hurt," Jan complained. "But it really does look like a woman in the garage video. Could either of the twins shrink those muscular upper bodies to look like a woman's on camera?"

"Silhouettes can mislead," said Lacey. "As for women, there's still Sloane and Cheryl, who were both at the ranch on the Monday and last night. They could easily know Earl's daughters messed with the cameras. Cheryl at least has been in the workout room regularly and could have discovered that damaged door any time. The only thing I can't figure out is how they'd have left the house without being caught by any of the cameras around there."

"And why," said Jan thoughtfully, "they wouldn't have moved heaven and earth to keep Tyrone out of his father's Rover until the sabotage had done its job."

"That, too. I wondered if Sloane hadn't tampered with the vehicle originally and then, after Tyrone went missing with Orrin, she confessed to Cheryl, who came after the external drive last night to keep her from being identified."

Jan shook her head against the pillow. "I'm sure Sloane wouldn't risk her son." What hell she must have lived all week as things stood. It would be exponentially worse if she'd accidentally let her son vanish with her husband in the vehicle she'd sabotaged. "So, tomorrow, when you go to the hospital to see how Tyrone's doing, ask both women to show you their legs. Then you'll know."

"And how will I convince them to show me their bare legs?"

"Easy. It's either show you or show the RCMP after you report being assaulted on their property."

Lacey pressed the bottle against her bruised cheek. "Then they, and everyone else on the ranch, will know I've been investigating the Rover."

"Well, you have to come out with that soon, anyway. Isn't Wayne going to the RCMP with the garage footage?"

"That's what he said. I honestly can't see those two women risking Tyrone for an instant. But of course when they left that day, he was safely occupied with Michael. Orrin was off with Mylo. Nobody could have predicted how fast the situation would change. Then there's Earl. According to Wayne, he was at a Ranchman's Club dinner that Monday evening, in full sight of forty industry leaders. And he has no obvious accomplice. His wife and kids went back to Denver the day before."

"Earl and Cheryl?" Jan suggested.

"Unlikely. Cheryl outright told me Sloane believed someone sabotaged the Rover, and her pick is Earl. If Cheryl was in it with him, she'd hardly have suggested the vehicle was sabotaged or pointed a finger at him for it."

"Like rocks rolling uphill." Jan rubbed her eyes and yawned. "Sorry I'm being no help. My brain's garbage tonight."

"You've already helped by reminding me I can simply ask anyone I think is innocent to show me their legs. No bruises, no conspiracy."

"So you'll go to the hospital in the morning and let me know how Tyrone is doing, too?"

Lacey nodded. "Last I heard from Andy — she and Bart headed in right away — he still can't talk due to throat damage, so can't tell anyone where he and his father got separated. But he knew his mother and Cheryl right away."

"Wonderful. Take a picture of him and send it to me for Michael." Jan shifted on her pillows. "Chad's coming down tomorrow. I'll have to tell him that Michael isn't his son, either, and he has to stop this nonsense. I could have happily run him over this afternoon. What an ass."

"You're just saying that because he cost you a lot of energy you need for other things."

"Yeah, so?" Jan yawned again. "I'm going to fade out on you any second now. Tell me quick, what are your plans for tomorrow?"

"Hospital, early, then I'll corral Bart, Ben, and Earl with a map and make them show me everywhere Orrin ever took them in the Rover, whether he dropped them off or not. They've done a bit of that already, but as an outsider I can keep them on task, instead of them ripping each other's throats out after five minutes."

"No brotherly love there, huh?"

Lacey unfolded from the carpet. "Let's put it this way: I'm surprised they all reached adulthood alive."

A good romp with the dogs and a night's sleep in her own bed restored Lacey considerably. When she woke up Thursday morning, she felt ready to face the day's challenges, the chief one being to figure out who among the Caine clan were allies and which were enemies. After breakfast and packing up the clothes she'd washed over-night, she climbed back into Wayne's truck and headed for Calgary. Half an hour later, she saw the colourful Children's Hospital, stacked up on its hill like a build-ing made of toy blocks. She followed the signs uphill to visitor parking, got directions from the information desk, and got stopped by a nurse outside the ICU, who asked for her visitor code.

"I don't have one," said Lacey. "Can you ask if Sloane Caine or Cheryl Marr can come out here for a minute?"

The woman smiled. "Young Tyrone. One tough kid. He's just been moved to a private room."

Lacey followed her directions to Unit One and wove past a breakfast cart to peer into the room. Ty was propped up slightly in bed, asleep. The rash around his mouth had faded to dull blotches, and the green stains were gone. His skin was its normal healthy tan again on both face and hands. A small, hard knot in her chest released. He truly would recover.

Sloane slouched in a chair by the bed, her long legs folded under her. The hem of her wrinkled shorts was high enough up her thighs for Lacey to be sure there was no bruising or scraping where a chair-back or boot would have connected. Count out another suspect in the secu-rity office attack. She squinted at Lacey, then uncurled from the chair and beckoned her out to the hallway.

"Hi," she said. "Is something else wrong?"

"Not that I'm aware of," Lacey said. "I wanted to see for myself how your son is doing."

Sloane rubbed the heel of one hand into each of her eyes, careless of the mascara already smudged around them. "Pretty well, all things considered. They think he ate something he's allergic to. They had to put a tube down his throat so he could breathe. But they took it out last night when the swelling went down."

"I'm so happy to hear that. When I first saw him in that field, I was very worried."

Sloane tightened her lopsided ponytail. She looked emptied out from within, as if all the tears she'd shed had drained her. Hard to believe this was the same woman who had flirted with Mylo Matheson barely a week ago.

"He hasn't said anything about where he left his father?"

"He hasn't been able to talk yet. He scribbled *hut* on a piece of paper an hour ago but otherwise he hasn't been awake long enough to answer questions."

"Hut, hmm?" A solid lead at last. Someone among the searchers, the family, or the neighbours would know where there was a hut. Whether they'd reach it to find Orrin alive or dead — or there at all, if it was only the place he'd dropped off Tyrone before heading back — was far from certain. "I'll stop by the airstrip to ask the searchers if they know of any. Is Cheryl at the ranch?"

Sloane shook her head. "She went home to grab some sleep and a change of clothes. I expect her back soon."

"I hope you'll get some rest, too. You've had a really hard week."

"'Hard' doesn't begin to describe how exhausted I am." Sloane yawned as she said it. "But I'll wake up in a hell of a hurry if Earl shows his face here. He's not getting inside that door."

So she still thought Earl was behind the vehicle sabotage? Choosing her words carefully, Lacey asked, "Why in particular do you not want him here?"

"He hates my son." Sloane's tired face tightened. "He always has. When Ty wasn't even in preschool yet, Earl dropped a rock on him from the climbing wall and broke his arm. He mocked Ty for having allergies and went out of his way to make him seem weak in front of their father. He laughed when Ty tripped on the bluff stairs and fell down a whole flight and almost broke his neck. I wouldn't put anything past Earl. I'm sure he's furious Ty's been found."

That was a nasty catalogue of bad behaviour from an adult to a child, but not surprising in Orrin's oldest son, who had been raised in the same brutal manner by their father. But it didn't rise to the same level as deliberate sabotage of a vehicle.

"You're okay with the rest of the family visiting?"

"Oh, yes. Andy and Bart were in last night." Sloane closed her eyes as fresh tears seeped under her lashes. Her palms smeared the mascara further. "They brought my boy's favourite things from his room so he'll have them when he wakes up. Everybody loves Ty. Except Earl and his damned mother. I could kill that woman."

"What did she do?"

"Spent the whole of Ty's birthday weekend reminding Orrin that her son at that age had survived a night alone in the bush and found his own way home. She was needling us, saying Ty hasn't proved himself yet, that he isn't as tough as Orrin wants to believe. I'm sure that's why he took Ty out with him as soon as my back was turned. I'll never forgive her for that."

Who knew better than an ex-wife how to get under a man's skin? "The twins' mother was at the birthday, too, wasn't she? Did she join in the needling?" Not that Lacey thought Cassandra Landry, who had protected her own sons from Orrin, would encourage him to abuse the youngest one. But there wasn't confirmation from Wayne yet whether that Mrs. Caine had flown away before the sabotage occurred.

"Oh, yeah, she was there." Sloane groped in a pocket for a rumpled tissue and blew her nose. "You'd have to know Cass. She's too mellow to snipe at anybody. I think she's stoned half the time. She always reeks of pot. I kind of envied her, being able to detach. If she'd stayed another day, I'd have been down at the cabin smoking with her."

Lacey had a brief struggle with her habit of keeping secrets from civilians and lost. "If it makes you feel any better, Earl didn't find his own way home that time he was lost overnight. He'd been going the wrong way entirely. Old Susan Norris found him. She let him off outside the gate and never took the credit because he was afraid Orrin would beat him for needing help."

Sloane's raccoon-ringed eyes focused on hers. "Are you serious? Earl's great adventure was bullshit all along? I bet Giselle knew it, too. She set my son up to fail a test that her son cheated at. Fucking witch."

Cheryl stepped into the hallway from the elevator lobby. Her short linen skirt showed bare, unmarred legs.

Another suspect cleared. That left only Bart and Earl. Lacey made a silent wish that it would be Earl she'd have the pleasure of taking down. Then she remembered she was a civilian and could only report him to the RCMP … assuming she found evidence to back up an accusation of assault, much less attempted murder. If she found the hut, she'd probably find the Rover, too, but that wouldn't help convict Earl, since he hadn't been the saboteur. That co-conspirator's fingerprints wouldn't be there if Jan was right about them wearing gloves, but maybe a stray hair? How could she convince a crime scene team to go over every inch of the motor with a microscope?

She dragged her head from her inner calculations and greeted Cheryl with a smile that still felt lopsided from the bruising. Cheryl hugged Sloane, peeked into the room to check on Ty, and stared at Lacey's face.

"Did you run into a door or something?"

"Occupational hazard of working around ladders," Lacey lied. "Straightening all those deranged cameras. I've been meaning to ask if you knew the workout room's exterior door wouldn't lock." She was safe asking that now that Cheryl wasn't implicated in beating her down for the archive drive.

"Another legacy of Earl's daughters." Cheryl grinned. "Can't blame them for treating Orrin's property like crap. They all know he has no use for girls, especially girls who won't marry for his business advantage like their parents did."

"That's utterly feudal," said Lacey. "Good on them for standing up to him. Anyway, I fixed the door yesterday, so you'll need your fob to use it. Is there anything else you can think of around the place — security related — that I should get out of the way today?"

Cheryl gave Sloane a sideways glance. "If you could accidentally disconnect all the cameras pointing at Sloane's suite, we'd both appreciate that. But I suppose you'd better wait until Orrin comes home. Or doesn't." Sloane returned the look but didn't bother pretending she cared whether Orrin returned. Honestly, if these two women weren't both cleared of the attack in the security office, they'd be prime suspects in engineering Orrin's "accident."

Despite their lack of interest, Lacey volunteered to let them know if there was news at the SAR base and took herself out into the sunshine. Clouds were piling up over the mountain peaks, reminding her of Ike's weather prediction. Rainstorms would make the searchers' task infinitely more challenging.

Even by the shortest route — north to Highway 1A and straight out past Cochrane — Lacey's drive still took more than an hour. As the grasslands gave way to rolling hills and then to the evergreen forest, she contemplated her mental logic puzzle, adding and subtracting suspects, making and breaking accomplice combinations. The natural pairings were strong: Bart/Ben, Bart/Andy, Andy/Ben, Cheryl/Sloane. In each pair, one partner was already eliminated from either the Rover sabotage or the security room attack. Earl was everybody's favourite suspect, but was that for real, or because he was an ass-hole and a bully? Was he hers just because he evoked Dan so strongly that she could hardly bear to look at him and yet would never willingly turn her back on him? Reflexively she pulled her cell and checked the Dan-locator. Still where he should be, near the West Coast.

Regardless, Bart's and Earl's legs must be seen to be eliminated. Bart's would likely be on camera in workout shorts somewhere today, but Earl's every appearance beyond his bedroom door had been in long pants and polo shirt. It wasn't likely he'd change his habits now and hand her any evidence against him. Maybe she could spill hot coffee on his pant-leg to force him to strip down fast.

As she passed the meadow where the helicopter had picked up Tyrone yesterday, she slowed. No sign today of searchers beyond the mess of tire tracks that had crushed the dry grasses. Sending out a grateful thought to the universe for Orrin's helicopter and the SAR medics being so close at hand when needed, she cruised up to the airstrip and parked. When she stepped out onto the road, a cool breeze twined around her ankles. A cloud momentarily blocked the sun. The most distant peaks were shrouded in mist. The searchers would be lucky if they found that hut, and hopefully Orrin alive inside it, before the clouds tumbled off those hidden peaks and smothered the Ghost Wilderness in much-needed rain.

Markov was with the search coordinator when she reached the map tent. She reported the word *hut* from Tyrone and left them poring over each team's notes for any mention of one.

Finding Terry on a bench outside the Red Cross tent, eyeing the western sky with a frown on his grimy face, she sat down. "Hey, dude. How come you're not out searching?"

He lifted his left leg. Right up the inside of his calf was a long, oozing scrape embedded with bits of bark.

"What'd you do?"

"Fell off a log," he grumbled. "Search fatigue. We all got a boost from Tyrone's rescue, but there was nothing to show where he'd come from, and the odds are decreasing again that we'll find his back trail. They'll be even worse if it rains. Volunteers from the Stoney Nakoda Nation are combing the forest on their land. If he was ever that far east, they'll find his tracks."

"They have land up here too? I thought theirs ended below the Ghost River."

"It used to all be theirs," Terry said, waving his arm. "There's still a large block east of Susan Norris's. The hunters know how every plant and rock should look at this time of year. If one's been recently turned over, they'll spot it." He stretched his neck to one side, then the other. "Man, sleeping on a cot after a hard day's hiking gets old fast. I don't know how that old Susan does it. She's putting us to shame, spending her days in the saddle and sleeping on the cold ground night after night. She only went home today to check on a mare in foal. I left her a radio so she can call in if she goes out again."

"She's one tough bird," Lacey agreed. "Say, when you went out yesterday, did you see any huts or hunting shacks over east of her place, where Tyrone was wandering? That's the only word he's let out so far, and I hope that's where he parted from Orrin."

"I didn't see one. I'll double-check with the others on my team. Jan said to tell you she'll get on those videos by tonight. She was pretty crashed this morning still."

"I bet. Yesterday was rough for a lot of people." Lacey turned away and turned back. "If Susan does call in, ask her if she knows of any huts. She's been out here something like forty years. She'll know, if anyone does."

There were five sets of reporters crowded around Orrin's main gate, but the guys on duty opened up promptly and waved her in past a staccato chorus of clicking cameras and shouted questions. Well inside, she stopped and called one of the men over. "Nobody's tried to breach the defences?"

"Nope." He shrugged. "A guy offered me a hundred bucks for an on-air quote."

"Did you take it?"

"Hell, no." He spat off to the side. "My job's worth a lot more than that. Your boss is up in the office, keeping an eye on the cameras."

"Thanks." She put the truck in the staff parking and headed indoors to check in with Wayne.

The first thing he did after she'd shut the door behind her was point to a new iPad in a bracket by the light switch. "See that? No more surprises." The small screen showed the top half of the staircase and the hall-way immediately outside the office door.

"Cool. What else has changed around here in the past eighteen hours?"

"More reporters, and one slipped over the fence near the south gate in the dark. The guys there didn't take a shot or even a swing at him. They followed protocol and called me down. Ike told me afterward that you gave them all a barn-burner of a speech about holding their fire. Looks like it stuck." He walked her through the list of people and vehicles checked in and out. "Doors closing after the horse is gone. Same problem at the Wyman place. We didn't know anyone was going to be murdered there, or we'd have tightened up security sooner."

"I assume the RCMP has raked Chad over a hot grill about turning off those cameras," Lacey said. "But did they also ask him if he noticed anyone unusual while he was dodging around doing errands for his ex-girlfriend?"

"Be a rookie mistake if they didn't," he said. "Now, the last alibi to come in for the Monday night is Cassandra Landry Caine's. She took a plane out of Calgary when she was supposed to and landed at Victoria airport, but she didn't turn up at her home in Cumberland. Neighbour says it's not unusual for her to wander off on a whim, but if she jumped in a vehicle and drove straight back here to get rid of Orrin before he could formally disinherit her son, we might never be able to prove that."

Lacey quickly reshuffled her logic box to add a new pairing: Bart and his mother, conspiring to keep Ben in the money? She'd seen no trace of a strange woman on the ranch all week, so likely Cassandra — if it was her on the garage video — hadn't hung around after that one night. But Bart's legs were back in the picture, and that disappointed her. She liked him too much to willingly believe him capable of attacking her, much less of conspiring to kill his father.

"Has Bart Caine headed down for his morning workout yet?"

"Not that I noticed." Wayne flicked on the archive monitor and scrolled backward through the last hour's images. "Nope. Hasn't left his house, unless he climbed down the bluff."

"Okay. I'm going to risk a direct approach." Lacey pulled out her phone and called Andy. She set it on speaker. "Say," she said after the usual greetings. "Remember that two-weeks deal we had?"

"Sure," said Andy, sounding sleepy.

"Well, I'd like a photo of both Bart and Ben's bare legs, from their shorts down. Will you trust me to tell you why later?"

"Really?" Andy yawned. "Okay, whatever."

They heard some rustling around, and Andy's voice calling the twins' names, and then footsteps. Ben's voice said "What for?" and Andy replied, "Maybe she's just into legs." A moment later the text came: a photo clearly taken in Andy's white kitchen with the morning sunlight filtering in through the surrounding evergreens. Bart's sweatpants were pooled around his ankles, and the bottoms of Ben's denim cut-offs were just visible at the top. She could tell Ben's legs because of their deeper tan and the bulge of his calves. Funny what a person noticed in daily climbing and running sessions. But neither set of limbs had any two-day-old bruises or scrapes.

"How's that?" Andy asked.

"Perfect, thanks." Lacey hung up and told Wayne, "The only way to be sure they couldn't jerk me around by sending the same undamaged legs twice was to get them both in the same frame in real time."

"Sharp," he said. "Too bad you didn't ask them where their mother is."

"I can do that while we're going over the map, looking for a hut. Can you hang here and watch the gates for another hour or two?"

Wayne nodded. "You're earning your overtime on this one, McCrae."

With a laminated map of Orrin's entire holdings rolled under her arm, Lacey skirted the main house and took the path to Bart's cabin. All three inhabitants were clustered around the kitchen island, snacking on grapes. Andy offered coffee and a muffin, as well. Lacey accepted the coffee and laid out the map with a sugar bowl at one corner, the grapes at another, and twins' hands at the rest. She set a grape on the approximate spot where Susan had found Tyrone.

"I need your input. The search didn't find traces yet, but if either of you were ever dropped off in that area, now's the time to remember."

Ben shook his head. "Orrin didn't own anything across the road back then."

"That's right," said Bart. "It all belonged to Susan Norris. As well as her home quarter out here, which she already owned, she'd inherited a huge parcel of land in what's now Huntingdon Hills."

Ben took up the story. "As I recall from all Orrin's swearing about it, she swapped that land to the province for a parcel four times the size out here, right up Highway 40 to 579. Orrin wanted it, but his best pal in the legislature got on the wrong side of the premier, and he lost out to Susan. She intended to put it all in a nature conservancy and resisted every deal Orrin offered her. He would never have turned us loose on her land while he was trying to convince her to part with it."

"Which she didn't until we were teenagers," said Bart, "and she bonded with Ben over a lost calf that he brought home for her. He convinced her that —"

Ben said sharply, "Yeah, whatever. Orrin lied to us, and I repeated that lie to her, and she's never going to forgive any of us."

Bart dashed into the living room and came back with a much-creased Ghost Wilderness map marked with several red X's. "See, that down there is all Susan's original land, and here's all the drop-off locations we came up with between us and Earl."

"As many as Earl would admit to," said Ben.

"If you hadn't chucked a paperweight at him," Andy said, "he might have remembered more."

Lacey leaned over their map, transferring marks to the laminated copy. None were east of Highway 40. Could Tyrone have been dropped off west of the airstrip and crossed the main road in the dark without realizing? It seemed unlikely. A road was a lifeline to anyone lost, and Tyrone had been over that road many times this summer alone. He'd have easily gotten oriented if he'd hit the gravel anywhere down there.

"Any hunting shacks or huts near any of these marks?" Just saying the word *hut* made it more real. She could almost see it in her mind's eye, hidden among trees, a shabby little building made of poles with their bark still attached, with Orrin cursing inside and a green Rover nose-first into a nearby gully. *Please let the motor not be too damaged for evidence purposes.*

Bart shook his head. "No huts that I ever saw. We had a couple of one- or two-person portable camouflage blinds we took along on hunting trips. Just big enough for a stool and a rifle. When we stayed out overnight, we slept in the back of the Rover until we didn't all fit anymore, and after that we took tents."

"Maybe Earl knows of a hut?"

Andy rolled her eyes. "Good luck asking him. I don't think he cares if Orrin ever comes back. Except it's really inconvenient for him that he has no keys and no passwords. It interferes with his attempt to take complete control."

Bart frowned. "Last night he talked about drilling the locks on Orrin's file cabinets. I had to convince him the remaining board members might vote against him for chair if he acts precipitously."

Ben sneered. "He'll want Orrin declared dead by this time next week."

So Earl wasn't willing to wait any longer to seize the reins? And just when the odds of finding Orrin were finally looking up. Interesting. Lacey swallowed the last of her coffee. "We still have to ask. I'll come with you to keep the peace. No throwing things."

"I'll try," said Ben. "He just pisses me off, even on a good day."

They tracked Earl down in Orrin's study. As they walked in, he dropped the lid of Orrin's laptop, but not before Lacey had seen, in the mirror above the fireplace, a log-in screen with its line of red lettering that usually meant *Incorrect Password*. He pretended to be staring at his own laptop until they were all four lined up across the desk from him and then snarled, "What do you want?"

Lacey laid out the laminated map. "Tyrone's woken up once, long enough to mention a hut. He wasn't specific that it's where he parted from your father, but it's the best lead we've had all week. There must be hunting shacks or deer blinds or something on all this land that could be called a hut."

Earl didn't give the map a second glance. "There's nothing like that on our land. I should know. I've been on it for forty-five years. Decades longer than these two." His lip curled. "They were off being surfer boys and smoking pot with their hippie mother."

Ben's fist lifted. "Leave my mother out of it, or I'll give you some hard truths about yours."

Andy put her hand on Ben's arm. "Let it go. Come on, Earl, we have to try everything. Surely you see that?"

Lacey took over. "I want you to mark on the map any place you remember Orrin dropping you off to walk home when you were a boy. I realize you already told the twins a bunch of that, but I'm an outside observer and might see a pattern that's eluding all of you."

Earl glowered at the map and added a couple of markings well to the west of the ranch buildings.

"Anything farther north?" Lacey prompted. "Up near the river, perhaps?" He glared but added one more. She measured by eyeball. "You must have covered twelve or fifteen kilometres some days. Good going!"

He shrugged. "It was a challenge; I mastered it. Once you find a cutline or OHV trail running in the right direction, you can cover a lot of ground. My dad used to trick me by driving a really long way around to get there, but I caught on after the first time I tried to follow the same route home. After that, I navigated by the peaks and the angle of the sun."

Ben made a disgusted sound.

Lacey frowned at him, "It was very brave of you, as a young boy. Your father was a hard man to live up to."

"He was just toughening us up. He didn't want to leave this business to someone who would wimp out on a good opportunity."

"Did he ever take you east on 579 and drop you beyond Waiparous Creek?" This was the crucial question. Orrin must have because — like Tyrone this week — if Earl had come to a main road at twelve years old, he would have stayed on it rather than strike off through the bush again. Would Earl tell the truth?

Earl shook his head. "I never was. We didn't own any land over there then."

A flat lie. Interesting. Was he only hiding his embarrassment at needing rescue? Lacey could call his bluff right now, but not in front of his brothers. She picked up the map, covertly signalling to the others that they should leave. "We should take this map down to the airstrip and compare it to theirs. Bart, Ben, can you go get a truck, please?"

Earl held up one hand. "I'm not wasting my day hovering around the SAR base, getting in the way of the professionals."

"You don't need to come, if you're sure you've marked everything on this map." Nobody had moved yet. She caught Andy's eye and jerked her chin at the door. Andy raised her eyebrows and then left, taking Bart and Ben with her. When Lacey saw them splitting up on the terrace, she spread the map on the desk again and leaned on it with both hands, pushing into Earl's personal space. "Now you can tell me the truth."

His eyebrows snapped together. "I don't know what you're talking about."

"Susan Norris found you east and south of her ranch house, not much more than a mile from where she found Tyrone yesterday. Where were you dropped off that time, Earl?"

"Are you accusing me of lying?"

"Not exactly." Now that she'd got his undivided attention, she straightened up, giving him space. "I'm saying that I can see why a scared, exhausted boy lied to a father who would never have let him live down a failure. I didn't blow your cover story in front of your brothers." She'd already blown it to Sloane, but he wouldn't find that out until long after she'd got what she needed from him. "Talk to me. Tell me the truth."

Earl's hands balled into fists. He stood up, leaning forward until his summer-weight dress pants brushed the desk. Was there bruising under those dress pants? A line of lost skin? If she kicked him in the shins, would his face show pain? Any such action could expose him as her attacker, and she didn't have backup or the right to slap handcuffs on him. Or a set of handcuffs on her belt. She met his heated gaze with her old police calm. Beneath the mask, as long as she was eyeball to eyeball with a lifelong bully who looked and sounded way too much like Dan, she stayed supremely alert for signs he would attack again.

Recalling her main objective here, she tapped the map approximately where Tyrone been found. "You couldn't have walked more than ten or twelve kilometres to reach that spot in the thirty hours you were missing. So where were you dropped off? You might as well tell me, because there are search teams crawling all over that ground now."

Sulkily, he put his index finger on the map, two finger-widths farther east. "Orrin tricked me," he said bitterly. "He told me I had to get across all of Susan Norris's land without being spotted by her."

Another lie. Susan hadn't owned all that land then, only her home quarter, which was farther north and right by the highway. If there were a hut in that vicinity, Susan or someone would know. Meanwhile, let him think he was believed, even while her old RCMP senses were tingling. He'd lied about this, and probably a lot more than this, in the past week.

She said, "I'll talk it over with the SAR people and see if they've been that far east. I don't suppose you know what road he took to get there?"

Earl shrugged. "I wasn't driving yet. I didn't pay much attention. Just that we went a long way south and then east and back north."

Such a vivid memory from thirty-plus years ago? Liars often added too much detail in an effort to seem convincing. She tapped the land well east of Waiparous Creek. "Through Stoney 142b? The Nakoda land block?"

"I guess."

"Well, it's somewhere to start. Thanks." She rolled up the map and left the house, texting to Wayne, *Almost sure now it was Earl who attacked me. Still couldn't have sabotaged the Rover. Not enough to lay charges either way.* Then she texted Ben about where to meet. An answer came back promptly: *On our way up, front of house.*

While she waited in the lee of the house, shivering and wishing she'd thought to put on a sweatshirt earlier, she texted Terry Brenner. *I'm bringing down a map with a bunch of places the older Caine sons have marked off as possibles. Can you round up Corporal Markov and meet me at the map tent?*

Ben drove up in the neon green monster machine she'd been in before, with Bart beside him. She climbed up behind Bart and strapped in. As they pulled away she said, "Would your mother maybe know where there was a hut or hunting shack?"

"She might," Bart said. "I'll give her a call." He rolled up his window, cutting out the damp breeze, and pulled out his phone. Lacey leaned forward between the seats to hear as much as possible. Bart put his phone in the dashboard slot, adjusted the volume, and said, "Hey, Ma, how's island life?"

"Just fine, honey-boy," came a languorous drawl through the truck's speakers, along with some guitar music in the background. "Just fine."

"Hey, Ma," Ben called. "You baked already? It's not even lunchtime."

"I'm down in Sooke, baby. You remember Fred?"

"Pothead Fred?" Bart stuck his tongue out the side of his mouth and crossed his eyes. "Why there?"

"House concert with some pals from Oregon, and I haven't left yet. How's it all at the ranch?"

"Have you even watched the news since you've been there?" Bart asked.

"No, baby. No TV, no Wi-Fi, no electricity. Remember?"

"Ma," said Ben sharply. "You didn't know Orrin and Ty have been missing all week? They found Ty yesterday, but no sign of the old bastard."

"Oh." The voice lost its drawl. "Hush up there, Fred. This is important. Now, boys, tell me what's been going on."

"The most important thing," said Bart, "is that Orrin and Ty were at some hut on the east side of Highway 40 last Saturday. Old Susan Norris found Ty on her land yesterday, but he's pretty sick. And nobody knows where this hut might be, so they can't hunt for Orrin there."

"Do you really want to find him?" his mother asked.

Meeting Lacey's gaze in the rear-view mirror, Ben rolled his eyes. "No, but if he might be still alive, we have to try."

"Oh, I s'pose you do. Let me think on it." The guitar started up softly in the background. They hadn't gotten far when her voice came through again. "Do you know which way they headed from the ranch?"

"North," Ben said. "Then they went east on 579, toward Water Valley."

"Seems to me," Cass said, "that Orrin took me to some hunting shack around there for a sexy weekend before we were married. Kinda like Fred's place, or I might not have remembered."

In the back seat, Lacey unrolled the map and traced her finger east along 579, looking for side roads or bush trails.

"Do you remember how you got there?" Bart asked.

"Not really. I was young and in love. I do recall it was some Crown land he wanted bad. As we were bouncing along this horrible bush track, he kept saying he could almost smell the oil under it. He had some backroom deal going on to get a lease, if not a buy."

Bart and Ben looked at each other. Bart said, "Would that be the land he bought off Susan Norris and promised to put into a nature conservancy?"

"Honey-boy, you are so smart. I bet that's just where it was. I see a truck coming up this road. Might be my ride up-Island. You tell young Ty he can come visit me when he's better. I'll teach him to surf. Love you boys!" The guitar music cut off.

Ben parked in the closest empty space to the airstrip. "Well, fuck."

"Yeah," said his twin. "Why didn't we call her first thing?"

Lacey wondered that, but even more she wondered why Earl, who had already been an adult and working in his father's business when that land was drilled, had not mentioned anything about a road or a hunting shack that must be very close, relatively speaking, to the Range Rover's last known location.

In the map tent, Lacey found Terry and Markov waiting with the search manager. She laid the ranch map beside theirs. "I have reason to think we're looking for a hut in an approximately square area bordered north to south by range road 579 and the top of the Norris land, and west to east from Highway 40 to approximately the longitude where Tyrone was found. It'll most likely be accessible from 579. Can anyone tell me what roads and tracks have already been cleared up there?"

CHAPTER TWENTY-SEVEN

The pounding on the patio door came again. Jan reluctantly lifted her eye mask, wincing at the afternoon light. Her movement had evidently been seen, for the pounding changed to a light tapping. She sat up, every joint and muscle in her body protesting, and looked over the back of the couch. Chad waved.

"Oh, shit," she muttered. Of course, Rob had told him to come back today. He obviously hadn't said "call first," much less "wait for an invitation." The last thing she needed in her current crashed state was to be polite to this doofus who had cost her so much squandered energy yesterday.

"Jan?"

He clearly wouldn't leave unless she told him to. She rose unsteadily to her feet, holding onto the couch back until her head stopped whirling. Then she staggered to the patio door. "Say what you have to say and then please go away."

"Sorry to wake you," Chad said, "but I have someone in the car who really needs to see you."

Chad had a car? Yesterday he had no vehicle.

He disappeared around the corner of the deck. After a moment, while she still stood clutching the patio door, the front doorbell rang. Aching at every step, she groped her way to the foyer. Opening the door wasn't as bad as she had feared. Clouds had piled up over the mountains, casting their grey shadows over the river valley, a relief for her overtired eyes.

"Hello?" The woman who spoke was almost invisible beneath a long-sleeved cotton overshirt and a wide-brimmed sunhat, her face half hidden by large sunglasses. Her chin, though, was Kitrin's. She removed the glasses, exposing tired hazel eyes heavily painted with brown eyeliner. "Jan, I don't know if you remember me? Barbara Davenport?"

Kitrin's mother. Surprised that her foggy brain had remembered Kitrin's real surname, Jan said, "Come in," not because she wanted them in but because she had to sit down very soon, and shutting the door in their faces would likely cause more problems later. She led them into the kitchen, because it was easier, and because she remembered her pills were in there, and water to take them with, and food.

With the pill inside her, soon to be restoring nutrients to her starving cells, Jan offered each of them a glass of iced tea and hunted through a cupboard for Terry's secret stash of cookies to put before them. Women of Mrs. D's generation had standards. Chad alone wouldn't have rated any refreshments at all. He took his glass of tea and leaned on the wall, saying nothing. Mrs. D took a chair at the table and looked around, making a few meaningless comments about the lovely view. Jan sat down opposite.

"I'm so sorry about your daughter. I understood she's going to be sent home to Regina for burial. What brought you here?"

"I'm hoping to be allowed to say goodbye to my grandson. Once he's back in California, I might never get to see him again."

"Surely Mylo won't keep him from you forever."

"I don't know." Mrs. D looked at her glass, not at Jan. "He isn't there right now, and they won't let me in the gate. Chad says he can't sneak me in either because of something that happened yesterday." She looked up then. "Is my grandson in danger?"

"Why would he be? From whom?"

"I don't know," Mrs. D repeated. She fiddled with the arm of her gigantic sunglasses. "Maybe from someone they met here? Kitrin called me, you know, the day after you had supper with her. She said you had passed on greetings to me and that you were very kind to Michael."

Considering Jan had only said about five words to Michael that night, "very kind" was an exaggeration. "He's a good kid."

"She said a man there was very curious about me," said Mrs. D. "Orrin Caine."

A spark kindled in Jan's brain. "What did she say about Orrin?"

"That he was nosy. She wanted to know if I'd met him when he used to go to Saskatchewan on business."

Given all that Rob had revealed about Kitrin's paternity, Orrin's obsessive interest in her and Michael — which Jan had completely forgotten about in the chaos over her death and his disappearance — took on a whole new relevance.

"You knew him, didn't you? Back in Saskatchewan."

Mrs. D turned the sunglasses upside down, folded the arms and unfolded them, and then, finally, staring at her reflection in the outsized lenses, whispered, "Yes."

"Obviously there was something between you. I've seen pictures of …" Jan looked up at Chad. "Do you want to talk about this in front of Chad?"

"He's already asked me about it. My daughter told him about our family problems years ago." Kitrin's mother fixed her weary eyes on Jan's. "What do you mean, you've seen pictures?"

"I recently saw a photo and oil painting of Orrin Caine's mother. She strikingly resembles your daughter."

Mrs. D dropped the sunglasses. "Then I don't have to spell it out for you."

She didn't seem able to stop herself, though. "I don't have any excuses. We lived in Estevan, when my husband was working his way up the oil company ranks before he went into politics. He was away a lot, and I was bored. You have to understand, in those days Estevan had no nightlife beyond that one bar, and I couldn't go there without my husband or the whole town would've been talking. Orrin was in town with a government-sponsored investment tour, and as an oil company wife I was invited to a cocktail party and supper. They all went for drinks at the bar afterward, but I invited Orrin for a drink at my house. He came by every night that week. It wasn't the first time I'd entertained someone when my husband was away. But his business trip went long that time, and before he got back I'd already suspected I was pregnant. He suspected, too. It clouded Kitrin's whole life."

"Did you ever tell Orrin?"

"What would be the point? I knew he was married. I only slept with married men so there wouldn't be complications." She lifted her reddened eyes. "Why would he care after all these years?"

Jan sipped her tea, gathering her words. "You couldn't possibly know this, but Orrin was disappointed with two of his three older sons, and he had no grandsons." She thought back to the table conversation. "I think he suspected from the moment he saw Kitrin, because of the resemblance to his mother. And everyone there saw how much alike his youngest son and Michael were. He really wanted fresh blood in his family line, and I think he also wanted a tie to the big-shot Hollywood director. Eventually he might have claimed both Kitrin and Michael."

"That would be the last straw for my marriage." Mrs. D was back to fiddling with her shades. "He hasn't said anything else, or been around since she ... died?"

"Orrin and his youngest son went missing in the wilderness last week. The same day that your daughter was ..." Jan couldn't bring herself to say the word *murdered*. She didn't want to remember the chill water dragging at her long skirt or her desperation to pull Kitrin clear of the waterfall.

"I am so sorry you were the one who found her," said Mrs. D. "But I'm grateful she was with a friend at the end."

Chad slid a box of tissues onto the table. Jan and Mrs. D both sniffed and blew their noses. Chad sat down.

"I'm sorry about yesterday, Jan. Michael was alone so much without Kitrin, I just wanted to give him one good memory."

"Why sneak him out the back gate?"

"My brother had already warned me off. I never told him there was a chance Michael was my son."

Jan barely suppressed her second "oh, shit." She had completely forgotten she'd have to tell Chad. "Whatever you might have wondered, Michael isn't yours. Mylo had DNA testing done years ago."

Chad traced a drop down his glass. "To be honest, I thought he was Rob's. They kind of look alike."

"You knew Kitrin slept with Rob, too?"

Chad nodded. "She told me years ago. I used to work security around Vancouver movie sets, and we hung out a bit when Mylo was filming there. But I'd never seen Michael in person until last week. I didn't know when his birthday was until then, either." He looked at his hands. "I'm even more sorry for him now. Mylo ignores him a lot."

Conversation lagged after that. Jan wasn't going to ask where Mrs. D was staying in case the woman expected her to offer a guest room. Soon Mrs. D stood up.

"We'd better go. I have a suite reserved at a B&B across the river. I'm really hoping Mylo will see me tonight and let me spend some time with Michael."

"I wish you all possible joy with that. He's a wonderful kid."

It wasn't until after the visitors were gone and Jan was back on the couch with her blackout mask that she thought about the coincidence of Orrin recognizing his daughter two days before she was killed and he went missing. Could there possibly be a connection?

CHAPTER TWENTY-EIGHT

In the map tent, while the others compared the Caine brothers' markings to the search grids, Lacey beckoned Markov away.

"Can you tell me where the drone operators got Orrin Caine's phone number for their first sweep?"

He flipped backward through the search manager's binder and pointed to a line. "Earl Caine."

Lacey added that to the tally of Earl's lies and omissions. She was debating whether to share those suspicions with Markov right now, or wait until she discussed it with Wayne, when a text came in from Jan. *I just learned the connection between Kitrin and Orrin. Is it possible her death and his disappearance are connected?*

She texted back immediately. *What's the connection?*

She's his daughter. Looks like his mother. Her mother just confirmed & is worried about Orrin making it public.

Lacey bit her lip. Then she texted Wayne. *Is the thing Orrin asked you to look into an unknown daughter from an affair in Saskatchewan thirty-three years ago?*

While she waited for Wayne's response, she told Markov, "Earl not only withheld two relevant phone numbers from the search, today he outright lied to me about a hut Orrin dumped him at when he was Tyrone's age. He got lost. Susan Norris found him that time, not far from where she found Ty yesterday."

Markov frowned. "Are you suggesting Earl Caine is implicated in his father's disappearance?"

"So far, only that it's very convenient for him to drag out the search until his father is presumed dead."

Her phone vibrated again. Wayne: *Where did you get that? He told me in confidence.* She texted back: *From my video expert. She's good with faces.* Next she texted back to Jan: *Good going. You may have blown this case wide open.*

Now to find that hut. It would be someplace Earl didn't want them looking.

Susan Norris rode into the camp on old Rebel. As she dismounted, Lacey called her over. "I think Orrin is at a hut on land that you either still own or used to own. Any idea where that would be?"

Susan gave a curt nod.

"Come and show me on the map." Lacey crowded aside people to make room for Susan.

The old woman put her finger on a spot northeast of the airfield. "Hunting cabin up on a bluff. You get there off 579. Past all them oil wells Orrin drilled."

Lacey looked around the table. "Surely the roads leading off 579 were checked?"

The search manager flipped a page in her binder. "First day. Three OHV trails petered out, one cutline likewise, one road led to a locked gate. The team reported no sign of a vehicle near the gate, so they assumed Orrin had not gone that way. You can see them all on the satellite blow-ups of the area."

As Lacey bent over the images, Ben spoke up. "That's Orrin's land. He had a key. Didn't anybody tell you that?"

Markov, his face grim, said, "I'll go check it out right now."

Bart said, "You'll have to cut the lock off. I'll come along and take responsibility for that."

Ben asked Susan, "Is there a way up through your land? That might be faster."

The old woman glared at him. "Now you're asking permission?"

"For that old bastard, yes," he said. "As much as I hate him, he is my father."

Susan eyed him from under lowered brows. "You'll have to do some climbin'."

Ben looked at his twin. "Back to the ranch for gear, then we split up."

"I'll go with Ben," Lacey said, rather than let him confront Earl without witnesses. "Markov, you take Bart. It's a long way around by the road, and you'll drive faster. Susan, will you come with us to show us the way?"

The old woman nodded. "Meet me at my yard. You'll need that big truck that tears up the earth."

"Thank you," said Ben. "I'll try not to rip it up any more than absolutely necessary."

The party split up, with Markov talking on his phone while Bart followed him toward the RCMP truck. Ben and Lacey jogged to the green machine, pushed along by a gusty wind that spun dust devils across the dry ground. As soon as she was buckled in, Lacey called Wayne.

"Locate Earl, please. He'll be wanted for a police interview ASAP."

On reaching the ranch, Ben headed straight for the machine shed. Finding Ike out front, he called, "We've got a lead on Orrin. Can you give a hand to load up some climbing gear?"

Ike followed them into the gym. "That'll be where Mr. Earl raced off to?"

Lacey looked back. "He's not here?"

"Left ten minutes ago in the other Jeep, with a chain-saw for bush-whacking."

Shit. If he got up that road ahead of Bart and Markov, he could drop trees across it and stall them while he made sure of his father's death. He might know of a back way out from the hut, one that wouldn't appear viable on satellite but that the Jeep could handle. It was either catch him in the act or lose him entirely due to lack of evidence.

She grabbed the coils of climbing rope Ben pointed out, slung one over each shoulder, and trudged back to the green Jeep. When she hurried in again, Ike was holding a tub as Ben filled it with chocks, cams, equalizers, carabiners, and every other piece of gear she'd ever heard of.

He threw climbing clothes at her. "Get changed. You'll need layers with this wind, and bring your climbing shoes." Two harnesses landed in the bin. "I wish I'd tried you on living rock before today, but we'll have to train you as we go."

Lacey hurried into the workout room's washroom, donned neon-pink climbing shorts and a long-sleeved T-shirt, then pulled her jeans back on. Still chilled from the damp wind, she yanked open the drawer labelled *Andy* and found a sweatshirt, also pink and splashed with huge purple flowers. Not her style at all, but that didn't matter today. She pulled it on as she hurried to the gym, and passed the chalk bags and gloves at Ben's command. There seemed to be far more gear than they'd ever need.

"How high is this cliff, anyway?"

Ben grabbed two pairs of safety goggles. "We won't know until we get there. Better to have too much than be missing something vital. Get those helmets, would you? I think that's everything. I'll change clothes and meet you at the truck."

"Meet me up top," said Lacey. "I need to report to Wayne."

In the security office, Wayne was flicking rapidly through camera images, speaking quick and sharp into his phone. When he disconnected, he said, "Clock's ticking again. The boy woke up enough to communicate that his father was alive but badly injured when he left the hut three mornings back. Say sixty hours."

"Shit. Did Earl get that message, too? He left in an off-road vehicle nearly twenty minutes ago. If he knows Orrin's possibly alive, he'll beat us to the hut to finish the job." She caught him up on the search situation and ended with Jan's bombshell. "It's too much of a coincidence that Orrin's rediscovered daughter died the same day Orrin himself vanished. Find out where Earl was on Saturday morning. He was present last Thursday when I told Jake Wyman the pool camera was down." As she turned away, she added, "I hope I'm right that Markov already called this in. We'd split up before I knew Earl was on the move."

Wayne picked up his phone again. "I'm on it. Good hunting."

As Lacey reached the driveway, Andy ran from the main house with insulated food sacks. "You might need these," she said. "Stay safe, and if the rain starts, get off the wall fast."

"I borrowed your sweatshirt," Lacey said. "I hope that's okay."

The green machine rumbled up the hill, its outsized tires gouging the gravel. Ben jumped down, hugged Andy, and kissed her forehead. Andy hugged Lacey, too, and stood waving as they roared toward the main gate.

"She's treating this like a major expedition," Lacey said, "not a short scramble."

"She cares about us. And the rock around here is loose and often unstable, so there's a bit of risk involved. In the rain I'd never take you up an unknown route, but time is short."

He didn't know how short, and Lacey wasn't going to enlighten him in case it made him take risks to beat Earl to the hut.

"If we're lucky," he went on, "the bluff will be hardly more than a scramble, but if it's higher, well, that's trickier. The main differences between living rock and the climbing wall are two: we have to test every hand- and foothold before we commit to it; and we might have to belay more than one pitch. Plus we're placing gear as we go, which will slow us even more. Any questions so far?"

"No." Not that Lacey would share with him. But what if she couldn't face a cliff with the same glee she'd felt on the climbing wall? What if the mere sight of a rock wall sent her spiralling back to that grey, rainy afternoon at Capilano Gorge, and she froze? *And if you don't freeze, you'll have to tackle Ear at the top. So yank up those neon-pink shorts and deal.* "Wait. What's a pitch?"

"One stage of roping, when the second climber joins the first partway up. Could be fifty metres or twice that, depending where the best place to anchor and switch the belay is. I'll know it when I see it. Now, you'll want to follow as close to my route as you can. I'll know by the sound what's a solid grip, and I'll chalk where I put my weight so you can use the same holds as much as possible. The comms are the same indoors or out. I'll say 'climbing' and you say —?"

"'Climb on.' If you say 'take,' I tighten up any slack in the rope, and if you say 'slack,' I let some out."

"Right. And if we need to start a second pitch, I'll build an anchor partway up. You'll join me there. But you don't start climbing until I say 'on belay' and you've answered …?"

"'Climbing,' I guess."

"You got it." He glanced sideways. "If I yell 'rock,' it means one is falling toward you. Do not look up! Tuck your hands as tight as you can against the wall and tip your head down so your helmet takes any damage, not your face." He sent a brief grin her way. "I promise not to purposely drop anything on you. All good?"

Lacey breathed out slowly, mentally rehearsing the calls and answers. "All good."

Ben wheeled into Susan's yard on a wave of thunder that shivered the air. The old woman hurried from a simple wooden house with firewood stacked high under the wide eaves and scrambled into the back seat.

"Straight on past the barn," she said. "A mile in, take the cutline on your right."

Ben drove conservatively, for him, but even so, the tree branches whipped against Lacey's window and her teeth rattled in her head. The cutline, when they reached it, was straight as any road, although overgrown with grass and small shrubs. They crossed a meadow, then back into trees.

Susan leaned forward. "You ain't climbin' in them jeans and boots."

"No. I just put them on to stay warm."

"Near there now, so git 'em off."

"You'll have a minute for that while I sort the gear," said Ben and steered slowly into the rock-walled ravine Susan was pointing to. Eventually he could go no farther. He shut off the truck and opened his door. "Now you can strip."

While Lacey eased her jeans down over her shorts, she eyed the narrowing cleft, its bottom strewn with boulders through which a small stream twisted. Not such high walls yet; she could manage a climb here. The sky might pose a different problem. What little showed between the pine-topped cliffs was a mass of grey clouds tumbling over themselves. Rain coming for sure, and maybe lightning, too. She grabbed the lunch bags from the front and joined the others at the tailgate.

Ben handed the keys to the old woman. "You'll wait in case the hut's empty?"

"Two hours. If you ain't back by then, I'll send help."

Adding the lunches to the two backpacks, Lacey loaded her pack onto her shoulders and followed Ben deeper into the ravine. No turning back now. Either they'd find the hut and Orrin, hopefully still alive, or they'd be stranded in the wilderness in a thunderstorm, and Earl would be free to kill without consequences.

As her foot splashed into the rocky stream, she hoped this ravine wasn't like a desert arroyo that would fill rapidly with racing water, scooping up everything loose in its path and churning it all downhill. What had Ben said about the lost pair when they'd first met? Something like, "If they're in one of those canyons, we won't find them until they wash out in the spring." It wasn't spring, and surely the rain wouldn't come hard enough or long enough to flood this ravine. But the walls were rising higher, and for the first time she felt the tremors of her old claustrophobia. She shrugged the pack higher and trudged on. Somewhere overhead, thunder rumbled again.

CHAPTER TWENTY-NINE

The farther they walked into the ravine, the cooler and heavier the air grew. The song of the stream became a living thing. From time to time, Ben checked his position on a satellite photo. When Lacey asked, "Did you lift that photo from the SAR base?" her voice whispered back from the rocky walls.

Ben half turned, holding out the laminated sheet. "We're about here. From the shadows, the bluff is lower farther along. We'll get to the top faster there."

"I appreciate that. This part must be four times as high as your climbing wall." Lacey looked up — and up — at the wall towering over them, and the lanky pines crowding the rim. Pines, not towering cedars. This was not Capilano Gorge. "You're sure we won't miss that hut?"

Ben tapped the page. "We should come up just ahead of that clearing."

They trudged on through a mossy twilight world. In the rocky depths, the air tasted of water; that might be moisture from the stream or a sign of rain in the west. Lacey checked the time on her phone. Earl might already have reached the hut. They'd been twenty minutes behind at the ranch, and now another twenty, plus whatever time it took to climb. The hush of the forest was screwing with her ability to calculate time or distance. There was no internet signal, either. Why hadn't she snagged a radio from the SAR base? It wouldn't work down here, either, but it could catch a signal once they reached the top.

Ben stopped and slung his pack onto a boulder. "This is it. Still a two-pitch climb, but we have to reach the top before the rain hits."

Lacey shivered as she stepped into her harness. She kept the windbreaker and sweatshirt on. Ben was clipping carabiners and other equipment to his harness, and he hooked a handful to hers, too.

"I'll set gear as we go," he said, "and you clean it as you follow. If you can't get it out easily, leave it. If you get into trouble or just need a rest, clip in wherever you are. Now we'll do a buddy check: your harness, your knot, your GriGri." As he said each one, he tugged at her connections. "Now you do mine." After that he slung his pack back on and clipped it across his chest. "All set?"

What else was there to say but yes? Lacey's heart thudded like the steepest stage of a treadmill run. Her palms dampened. She wiped them on her thighs. Then she closed the GriGri over the rope and fed out the first slack as Ben put his hand on the rock face.

"Climbing," he said.

"Climb on."

He seemed to flow upward in a series of yoga poses. She tried to mark each place he put a hand, and where his foot shifted sideways rather than up, and made mental notes every time he gave a verbal command. She'd never remember it all. Even with the chalk trail he was leaving, following him up there would be a slow and clumsy scramble.

He reached a wide ledge and hooked on securely. "First pitch. I'll build an anchor here." When he was ready, he gave her a thumbs-up. "Belay on."

Her turn. Resisting the impulse to check the time again, for surely it couldn't be nearly as long as it felt, she answered, "Climbing," and put her right hand on the first chalk-marked rock.

She was nose first into a vertical twice her height when she lost focus. Somewhere up there, Earl would be reaching the cabin soon. If Orrin hadn't died of his injuries, he'd be killed. Suddenly in a hurry, she grabbed a round cobble above her head and pulled herself upward with her right foot groping for its next hold. The cobble fell away beneath her hand. It rattled past her leg and ricocheted from boulder to boulder across the ravine.

The sound clattered back between the walls like the chittering of monsters in a horror movie. She clung by one foot and one hand, belly to the wall.

Ben had taken up the slack the instant the rock loosened, holding her there, but it took some concentrated breathing on Lacey's part to calm her heart rate. Her left arm tingled and wouldn't obey the order to stretch to another handhold. She left it for the moment and nudged her loose foot onto a tiny protuberance. Then she stretched again for the tiny ledge Ben had marked and followed his verbal directions for every move after that.

She came up level with him and stepped thankfully onto a shelf twice as deep as her feet, clipping immediately into the anchor. He nudged her shoulder.

"Good job."

He didn't sound sarcastic, the way Dan would have. She grinned weakly. "Now what?"

"We switch the ropes over, and you belay me up the next pitch just like if you were standing on the ground. It isn't as vertical so will be easier. Like before, watch my marks and try to use those holds only, because they're already tested against my weight." He switched the strap that held the draped belay rope from his harness to hers. "Make sure you turn that GriGri so the rope doesn't cross itself."

That done, she got her hands back into position. A stray gust of wind sent grit over the ravine's rim. The glasses protected her eyes, and she didn't bother to raise a hand to wipe the rest of her face. It was just dirt. Her hand on that rope was a lifeline, for Orrin as well as for Ben.

Ben's first upward surge took his feet past her head. Watching, she recalled the first time she'd seen him, halfway up that immense sandstone wall above the Ghost River. If he could climb that, this one was a walk in the park. For him. She concentrated on feeding out the rope's slack as he called for it, grateful that the basic communications were the same whether in a safe, plastic, prebolted gym or when clipped onto a natural rock wall way out in the wild, with the threat of rain and the distant thunder and, somewhere up there, a would-be murderer. Maybe Orrin was already dead and this race was for nothing? She shook her head, refocusing on Ben's every movement. He seemed to be aiming for a ledge that sloped gently up to the right, almost a natural path that would be easy to scramble up even without a rope. She'd need easy by then.

As she gazed upward, trying to gauge how far they still had to climb, something moved among the trees. At first she thought it was the wind rustling the branches, but then her brain translated the moving thing to green camo fabric. A head in a dark balaclava leaned out between two trunks. She called, "Hey, who's up there?" but the new knot in her gut already had the answer.

Ben was splayed spiderlike across an almost sheer stretch of rock. He looked down at her voice, and then up as something tumbled off the ravine's rim.

"Rock!" he yelled and tucked tight to the cliff.

As his voice echoed, she flattened against the wall, clutching the belay rope. A fist-sized stone ricocheted past her. Ben yelled "Rock!" again, and more words she couldn't make out. The belay writhed like a snake in her hands. Pebbles and dirt stung her exposed skin and skidded off her helmet. Was he falling?

When the stinging shower passed, she risked a glance upward. Ben hung from the wall by one hand and one foot. She leaned out and adjusted her grip on the braking rope, making as secure an anchor as she could. He didn't move on, just hung there exposed to the next missile from above.

"Ben? Are you okay?"

"The bastard got my shoulder." Ben's voice sounded strange. "You'll have to take more weight for a bit."

"Was it Earl?"

"Likely. If he throws anything else, yell. Climbing." The rope jerked in her hands as he began a three-point crawl sideways and up.

Another rock came crashing over the edge, easily as big as her head. She yelled, "Rock!" and slammed her body against the wall again. When the sand, grit, and crashing passed, she dared to look up. Ben was still on the rock face, crabbing sideways faster than she would've dreamed possible. He went under the ledge she'd seen earlier, instead of up on top.

Earl hefted another rock at his brother. It bounced off the ledge and shot across the ravine. When Lacey lifted her head again, he had vanished into the trees. The belay rope had stopped moving. An empty loop drooped from the ledge. Her climbing partner was gone.

"Ben?"

There was no answer. Fearful, she leaned sideways and looked down, the impossibly long way down, to the tumbled boulders of the creek. The broken body she feared to see existed only in her imagination. Then where was he?

As she stared up again, Ben's head appeared above her, one finger at his mouth.

"Shh," he half whispered. "You're tied on to a tree now, since my arm's useless. Come up slow, take in your slack, and you'll be fine."

Behind him, something moved.

"Earl," she yelled.

Ben dodged as a heavy body tackled him from the side. The two rolled out of her sight. Crashing brush and yells racketed down. She heard her name and something about the ledge, but thunder crashed almost overhead, and she lost the rest of Ben's instructions. Then the noise faded, leaving her alone on the cliff with no belayer and absolutely no faith in her ability to follow Ben's path to the top without direction. The stream's song rose in the sudden silence. For a moment longer, she clung to the security of the anchorage, steadying her breathing. Then she tested the belay rope, unclipped from the anchor, and began to climb.

CHAPTER THIRTY

Against all her instincts, Lacey forced herself to move just one limb at a time, to test each hand- or foothold, to press into the rock instead of pulling out. Each new handhold was a victory. Each foothold took her closer to the fratricidal struggle above. The growing noise assured her Ben was holding his own: blows and grunts from both men, the crunch and snap of forest debris beneath their thrashing bodies. She pushed the final loop of trailing rope up over her shoulder and reached the sloping ledge. If she moved her left hand over here, and then her left foot, the right hand should be able to reach that tree root sticking through the crumbly soil at the top …

Just in time, she stopped herself grabbing the tree root. It might be dry, rotten, not attached to any living tree. Her hand moved on, crimped onto a tiny crack in a much larger rock. One foot nested into a gap. Her other hand found a hold, and she rose waist high above the ledge, a metre-wide path of mingled rock and dirt. She tested all her hand and footholds and then lifted the lowest leg up, and farther up, until her knee brushed her chest and her foot settled firmly on the flat surface.

The relief sent tremors down her arms. She suppressed them, took a few deeper breaths, and dragged the last foot up. Then she cautiously stood up. Thunder cracked. Damp wind slammed into her, shoved her stumbling up the slope. She fetched up against the tree her rope was tied to. Unclipping, she followed the trail of broken bushes along the lip of the ravine. Rain spattered down, releasing the dusty pines' aroma, turning the rocky gorge more like that distant Vancouver afternoon with every step.

By the time she reached the brothers, Ben was down, his face buried in dead leaves and his legs over the ravine's rim. One arm lay limp at his side, the other was crooked around an exposed tree root almost as thick as his wrist. Earl, bareheaded now, with blood streaming from a gash above his eye, alternately kicked him in the ribs and stomped the tree root. If he broke it free of the sandy soil, Ben would fall. With every breath haunted by visions of Capilano Gorge, Lacey crept forward. With every yank of Earl's arm, more dirt crumbled away. With each kick at Ben's ribs, his torso slid farther off the rim. How could she stop Earl without sending them all over the edge?

Lacey spotted the dead branch just before she stepped on it. One end was jagged, as if it had been stepped on or rolled over during the struggle. She crouched and wrapped her cramped fingers around it. Lifting it silently, she rose as Earl shifted his weight to kick again. Branch raised, she loped toward him.

Earl stared. Then he swung himself around a tree, away from the ravine, and crashed away through the undergrowth. Ben groaned. The hand clutching the tree root was white beneath the blood and dirt. The other dangled, half over the edge.

Lacey knelt beside his head. "Hold on while I get you up." She grabbed his backpack strap and tugged. When his hips were within reach, she got a hand through his climbing harness and, with a lot of help from his legs, hoisted his lower body fully onto the lip. He rolled away from the edge, panting, unable to even raise a hand to wipe the twigs and needles off his battered face.

"Lie still. I'll be back."

Picking up her branch, she ran after Earl, who could still faintly be heard crashing through the trees. Wind-driven rain pelted her exposed skin. Every rock and stick stabbed into her thin soles. She came out on a patch of gravel and skidded around the Jeep parked sideways across it. Huddled amid the pines was a weathered wood cabin with a roof so moss covered, it was almost indistinguishable from the branches above. No wonder it hadn't been spotted from the air.

Avoiding the sagging front step, she peered in the tiny window. In the pale green light from a rear window, she made out a table and stool, a small iron stove next to a loose pile of branches, and a set of rough bunks against an end wall. One lower bunk was occupied. Earl bent over it with his balled-up camouflage jacket in his hands. About to smother his father?

No time to wait for Markov. Lacey crashed through the half-open door.

Earl flung the jacket down and charged at her. She sidestepped. His fist caught her shoulder. Bending with the blow, she grabbed his wrist and pulled. Momentum carried him into the wall. He hit with such force that dust fell from the rafters. As he rebounded, she swung her branch hard against his back. It broke with a further explosion of dust. Coughing, she backed away. Earl straightened up and tackled her again.

Ducking his clutching arms, she punched him square in the gut. As he gasped, she veered aside and twisted his arm up his back. He spun out of it. She saw his fist coming barely in time to duck away. His hand smacked the window frame. The pane shivered and fell outside. If it broke on landing, the sound was lost amid the rain on the roof.

Earl came at her again, arms flailing. She snatched his wrist again, pivoting. He went sprawling over the rickety wooden table, sending empty cans flying. The table tipped, spilling him sideways. He rolled and sprang up. She grabbed the room's only stool and used it as a battering ram until he wrenched it from her hands. As he swung it wildly at her, she jumped backward. His discarded jacket caught her heel. She staggered, half falling against the bunk support. Earl kicked her feet out from under her and fell on top of her, grappling for her throat.

Shades of Dan! Fighting the panic, she gouged at his eyes with one hand. Her other hand groped toward the stove. Splinters dug into her palm as she tugged a branch from the pile. Once, twice, she smashed at Earl. At last, as her vision was blacking around the edges, he loosed one hand to grab the log. As his weight shifted, she rolled with it, dumping him to the floor.

Grunting, he reached for her, but not fast enough. She rammed a knee into his back. He rolled away, groaning. Gasping, she flipped him over and sat on him, yanking his forearm up between his shoulder blades. She pinned his trailing arm with her knee. He cursed, his words slurred against the rough wooden floor. When he bucked, trying to throw her off, her knee ground his wrist into the dusty planks. He screamed.

CHAPTER THIRTY-ONE

As she caught her breath, Lacey twisted Earl's arm a little higher up his back. Now what? No handcuffs, no backup, and all that long, lovely rope was tied to a tree at the cliff-top. Earl was limp for the moment but no doubt analyzing his chances of escape. Of course, he didn't know Markov was on his way. All Lacey had to do was keep him subdued until the constable arrived. With her free hand, she fumbled through the gear Ben had clipped to her belt. One piece was a loop of strapping sewn at intervals into pockets. She unclipped it and slipped one loop over Earl's wrist. Then, before he could react to that, she yanked his other arm up beside it and scooped that into a different loop. She wound the rest of the strap around and between those two loops and secured the whole thing to his belt with a carabiner. It was the best she could do for now.

Breathing heavily, she got to her feet and approached the bunk. Orrin Caine lay on his side, covered to the neck by a torn blue tarp. His face was purple with fading bruises, and blood matted the filthy white hair. Now that she had time to notice it, he reeked of blood, sweat, and urine. Sniffing hard to acclimatize her nose to the stench, she felt for a pulse at his neck. His lips moved, but no sound came. Still, he was alive. All else could be dealt with.

"You'll be okay, Mr. Caine," she said as she'd said so often at accident scenes during her RCMP years, whether the victim could hear her or not. "Help is coming."

She checked Earl's bonds, added a chain of carabiners around his ankles and hooked them to one foot of the heavy little stove and then retraced her steps to Ben.

He lay where she had left him, cradling his damaged arm. "Earl?"

"Tied up at the cabin." She helped him to sit up. "Your dad's alive, barely." Folding her windbreaker into a rude sling across his chest, she got him to his feet and slung his good arm over her shoulder. They were limping across the gravel to the cabin when an RCMP vehicle roared into the clearing. Bart and Markov jumped out. Surrendering Ben to his brother, she told Markov, "Orrin's inside. Alive but will need Medevac."

As Markov entered the cabin, Earl lifted his head. "Officer! Arrest that woman. She assaulted me and tied me up."

Lacey gaped. "You were about to smother your father with that jacket."

Earl said, "I was putting it under his head to make him more comfortable. Officer, I was trying to save my father from Ben."

"I'll take your statement in a moment," said Markov. Orrin groaned. Markov went to check him out. Then, leaving Earl tied up, he returned to his truck and radioed his dispatcher.

Lacey followed. "You're not buying Earl's story, are you?"

Markov frowned. "I can't arrest him for attempted murder on your word alone. The Crown would chuck the charges before the ink was dry."

Frustrated, Lacey glared around the clearing. After misdirecting the searchers for most of a week, hoping his father would die what appeared to be a natural death, Earl had raced up here to finish the job. It should be obvious.

"Then arrest him for assaulting me last Tuesday evening in his father's security office. If you check his legs, you'll find older bruises and at least one healing scrape from my office chair."

"Still your word alone. He could claim he got those anywhere. Did you file a report about that assault?"

"Not yet." She should have, if she was going to use it now. "I did, however, report it to Wayne right away. You can still see the older bruise on my cheek from where he mashed it into the desk. He was wearing a balaclava that night, very like the one he wore when he chucked rocks down a cliff at us a few minutes ago. Ben might want to press charges against him for that, too."

CHAPTER THIRTY-TWO

After sixty hours of nausea, brain fog, and alternating sweats and chills, Jan sat in the shower, revelling as warm water streamed down her limbs. Nothing hurt much, just a residual ache from the last lactic acid clearing out of the muscles. Eventually, she huddled into her terrycloth bathrobe and stretched out on her bed to recuperate. A text from Lacey waited on her phone: *Are you up for company?* She immediately texted back: *You bet. Dying to hear how it all went down.*

When she walked to the front door, Jan marvelled at the strength her legs had already regained. What that woman from the online support group had told her was bang on. *Once you've burned your mitochondrial reserves,* she'd typed, *you're stuck on trickle charge. Small exertion = two days. Big exertion = five days. Simple.* The formula was easy to remember and gave her hope when the bad days seemed endless. She let Lacey in along with a fug of sultry air. No storms like yesterday, but the sky remained grey and brooding. She hugged until Lacey squeaked.

"Sorry. I forgot you might be hurting. Is it bad?"

"Scrapes and bruises."

"You could've been bare-knuckle boxing. I was so terrified when Terry said you'd gone off into the wild after a possible killer. Come in, tell me all about it. Do you want tea?"

"No, thanks." Lacey followed her to the living room and settled on the floor. Jan crawled back on the couch and pulled her afghan over her legs.

"So all I know is that you and Ben climbed up a cliff in a storm, and he was hurt, so you tackled Earl on your own."

Lacey rested her arms on her bent knees. "Basically, that's the whole story. The bastard threw rocks down on us, trying to knock us off the cliff. One broke Ben's collarbone. He climbed the last stretch one handed. Earl tackled him at the top, wearing a balaclava at first like when he attacked me in the security office. Ben ripped it off him during the struggle." She shifted position, grimacing. "Markov found it eventually and decided it showed premeditation. If Earl really hoped to save his father from his evil twin brothers, he wouldn't cover his face. But I guess it was the best story he could think of while he was lying there tied up. The arrogance of the rich white male. He was totally pissed that Markov didn't automatically believe him and untie him."

"What gall." Jan could too easily picture it. To a man raised to believe he was untouchable by anyone except his tycoon father, it was unthinkable that a law-man wouldn't take his word over that of a mere woman. "And then the helicopter came, and more Mounties?"

WHY THE ROCK FALLS

Lacey shook her head. "The thunderstorm crashed over us before the helicopter could get there. It was really ferocious up on that bluff. The trees were bending so far, I thought they'd come through the roof. That old hut would have been smashed to splinters, and us with it." She shuddered. "So picture this: Earl handcuffed and Orrin unconscious, Ben with a useless shoulder, and me oozing blood from various scrapes because we'd used up all the Band-Aids in Markov's first aid kit. Rain blasting in the broken window. And did I mention there was only one stool? Nobody wanted to sit in the bunks near Orrin, because he frankly stank to high heaven. So we all sat on the floor. Bart made us tea he found in a tin box, and we split up Andy's food. Then we just waited until the storm rolled on to beat up the next hilltop.

"After that, we — me and Bart and Markov — had to go out and move the vehicles around, shine the head-lights on the gravel space, because it was getting dark by then and the chopper still had to drop the rescue tech and basket. Did I mention the road down was blocked by the windstorm? They were working on getting it clear, but I sure as hell didn't want to be stuck up there all night with Earl tied up and Orrin maybe dying on us. Another quarter hour and it would have been too dangerous for the helicopter to hover near those treetops, so there we were."

Jan clutched her afghan closer. "I'd never have survived it. But at least Earl's under arrest, right?"

"Not for attempted murder. He stuck to the claim that he was protecting his father. If Markov hadn't stopped to check out Orrin's wrecked Rover farther down the hill, he'd have arrived while Earl was trying to kill us. But he didn't."

Jan scrunched sideways. "How is it possible that he got away with it? He knew exactly where to find his father, and he didn't go there for five days, lied to the search manager about phone numbers and claimed he didn't know where the hut was. When he did finally go there, he beat up the people who were coming to rescue Orrin."

"Well, he's not totally in the clear. They've got him on assault charges for the first attack on me and reckless endangerment for the rock-throwing, which might yet get upgraded to aggravated assault or even attempted murder. He had to go to the RCMP post for processing, have his old and new bruises photographed and measured, get his fingerprints taken. He'll hold a grudge for that humiliation, you can bet. His lawyer talked a good game, though, and they let him go on his own recognizance."

"Not even a night in jail? That's ludicrous."

"It's far from over." Lacey looked at her battered hands. "I spent this morning with the RCMP, giving them a statement about all the ways he obstructed the search. And I met the search manager as I was leaving. She gave a statement about him suppressing two of the three phone numbers, never saying that his father owned that land off 579 or that Orrin had a hunting hut up there. Of course they should've checked who owned it and gotten permission to search, but when you're looking for a vehicle and you come to a locked gate, you're more likely to assume the vehicle didn't go that way than that the person you're searching for is the owner and has a key."

"I don't understand how he knew which hut as soon as you asked him."

"He hasn't admitted it, but Susan Norris figures that's where Orrin dumped him all those years ago. There's a way down into the ravine behind the cabin, a lot easier than the route we went up. Orrin probably sent him down that way. At the mouth of the ravine there are cutlines that intersect, and he got tangled up following them to where Susan found him. Same route Ty took, most likely."

"So he's going to get off with a slap on the wrist?"

"I doubt it. Now that he's on the RCMP's radar, they'll go into his phone records and finances, discover every place and person he's recently been near."

Jan stared at the ceiling. "But he didn't tamper with the vehicle."

Lacey sighed. "Nope. He had an accomplice. We have to figure out the identity on that garage video. Are you up for it today?"

"I will be, as soon as I get some food into me. Stay for lunch?"

"Sure. Maybe now that you've brightened up the video, I'll spot something useful simply because I know the ground and the people."

Over a light lunch of salad greens with cold salmon, Jan reported in more detail on her meeting with Kitrin's mother. "I really hope Mylo gets over his snit and that she doesn't try to take Michael away again. That poor kid needs some stability. I've neglected him while I was recovering. I glanced through Jake's staff's pictures this morning, but none of them twigged. Maybe when I see their back views. I'll get Chad down later and make him look, too."

"Are you a hundred percent sure Chad didn't do it himself? I mean, he was running around up there with the cameras off during that half hour."

Jan shook her head. "I didn't know it until yesterday, but he had cleared up a few things with Kitrin over the years. She'd even told him about Rob. And he seems genuinely concerned about Michael. Speaking of him, any news on Tyrone today? I know he's not in the same hospital as his father. Is Sloane going back and forth between the two?"

"Nope. Orrin is so sedated, he'll never know if she's there or not. Once he's awake, they'll have private nurses at his bedside twenty-four-seven. Cheryl said Ty will be released later today. Tough kid. Although I understand he was in the hut with Orrin and a bit of food for all but one of the nights. So not as bad off as he could have been."

"I'm glad one of them is recovering." Jan pushed her plate away. "Are you ready to tackle these videos?"

Two hours of playing videos on Terry's big monitors got them no further. They looked at dozens of samples of Jake's staff walking past security cameras, and each person was too tall, or too broad, or too hairy down the neck, or something else disqualifying. Although Lacey, like Jan, was teased by a faint sense of familiarity about the staffer at the pool gate, the context didn't fit anything in her recent memory. Eventually, they viewed the enhanced video from the ranch garage, but that too was a dead end. There were plenty of details visible now, but the person in the balaclava was too narrow-shouldered to be Earl, and Lacey still swore it was none of the women she'd seen around the ranch.

Midway through the afternoon, as they were shifting to the living room so Jan could lie down, Lacey got a text from Wayne. It read: *Earl was with his mother all Saturday morning.* She frowned. "I don't understand. Earl would want Kitrin out of the way fast, before Orrin could change his will to include her or Michael. He clearly didn't know Orrin had already ordered Wayne to investigate."

Jan shook her head. "More arrogance of the rich white male. He won't ask questions and doesn't listen, so he misses out on vital information."

"Cynical much?"

"If that ape got my friend killed just to inherit the whole pile of bananas," said Jan, "I want him put in prison with a lot of big, mean bikers to show him his place in their jungle. But how would he know there wouldn't be more sons, anyway? Sloane's young enough, and Orrin wouldn't have revealed his infertility. Virility is key to his alpha-male status."

"I wondered about that, too," Lacey admitted. "I only found out about it from Cheryl, and probably only because she was so exhausted and stressed, her filters were down. When I checked the dossier again, I realized

Earl was VP of Human Resources and oversaw the company benefits plan for many years. He could have kept tabs on his father's health all along." She frowned. "The other thing that worries me is what Earl will do now. Orrin's still alive. He might cut Earl off like he did Ben, and he could still make Michael one of his heirs."

"Are you suggesting Michael might be in danger?"

"Not from Earl. The RCMP will keep him on a short leash until they've figured out what other charges to file."

"Then we have to find out who sabotaged the Rover for him. He could send them after Michael."

"And after Ty," Lacey added. "With both of them gone, and neither twin interested in the company, he'd rule it all."

"God, you're really scaring me now." Jan stretched the knots out of her neck. "If only we could put those boys under guard, somewhere Earl can't easily reach them."

"That eliminates any place Orrin owns." Lacey sighed. "I can try to convince the RCMP that the boys are in danger, but they won't believe me without evidence. It's exactly that situation that led to the disaster at Capilano Gorge and me leaving the Force. Sometimes your gut just knows, but as a cop you can't act on it in the absence of evidence."

Jan closed her eyes, trying to visualize a safe place, but all that came to mind was Jake's swimming machine, where Kitrin had nearly drowned on her first full day in Bragg Creek. "Hey, wait. Jake's place. He's got security to the eyebrows now, right?"

"Sure. I can tell them all to take special care of Michael. But Ty's still exposed."

"Maybe not. Watch and learn." Jan snagged her phone off the coffee table and called Jake's cell. "Hi," she said. "How's it going up there today? How's Michael? ... Yeah, I'd be bored in his shoes, too. Listen, did you know Tyrone Caine is getting out of the hospital today? What do you think about inviting him to recover at your place? The boys can distract each other better than any adults would. Of course you'd have to have Sloane, too. She won't want to let Ty out of her sight so soon."

After a few more exchanges, she hung up. "There. If Sloane distrusts Earl as much as you say, she'll leap at the offer. Jake will invite some of his pet hockey players up, too, for ball hockey if Ty's fit enough, and video games if he's not. He wants me to do art activities with them, and he invited Michael's granny to stay. He thinks Mylo's being unreasonable to keep them apart right now."

"You are a master," Lacey told her, unfolding from the floor. "Manipulator, that is. I'll go up and brief security about not letting Earl or anyone connected to him onto the property unsupervised. They can't throw him out without Jake's say-so, but they can track him on camera and put a team with the boys while he's there."

"I'll have to nap soon, but I'll tackle the videos again when I wake up. Before I fade out, you didn't say what Earl's alibi was for Kitrin's death. His own little sister."

"He was with his mommy all morning," said Lacey. "Even if he wasn't, what mother would turn in her son on a murder rap?"

She left and Jan pulled her blindfold down. As she retreated into darkness, the mothers in the case drifted across her mental movie screen: Kitrin and her mother both threatened by paternity tests; Andy sleeping with her husband's twin to get pregnant; Sloane staying with a man she despised for the sake of her son; Cass, whose lucky double pregnancy gave her the financial where-withal to leave; and Earl's mother, an unknown quantity who might lie to help her son inherit all Orrin's wealth. Would she also kill for him?

Dusk was creeping into the room when Jan woke from a nightmare about a balaclava-wearing figure skulking through Jake's hilltop mansion. She lay there listening to the house's silence. Terry wasn't home yet. It seemed odd not to have Rob around, either, but between waiting for Bart to clear him of Kitrin's murder and finding out Michael wasn't his son, he'd had a lot to process. She crawled off the couch, made some tea, took her pill, had a few bites of leftover salmon, and contemplated her empty evening. Since she was wide awake and jittery, she might as well be working.

Accordingly, she called up the ranch's garage video and Jake's pool gate video, one on each monitor. For a few seconds, the two figures walking across each screen were side by side, moving away from the camera. She stared. She stopped each video and backed it up. She started them again. Then she picked up her phone and texted Lacey. *Jake's pool-gate person and Orrin's garage person might be the same woman. That's why she looked familiar to both of us. We'd each been staring at the opposite images.*

The phone rang thirty seconds later.

"You're telling me the person who went into Jake's pool area last Saturday morning was a woman? Jake has no female staff except the cleaner from the village, and she doesn't wear the staff polo shirt. The female security guards didn't start until days later."

"There's more I can do, to be sure — measuring the head/neck ratio and so on — but yeah, it looks like the same woman. No wonder the RCMP couldn't match it to a staffer."

Lacey sucked in a breath. "You know what this means, right?"

"Not really."

"If it's the same woman in both places, that's Earl's accomplice. You're looking at the person who murdered Kitrin."

"Holy shit," said Jan.

CHAPTER THIRTY-THREE

At a plastic-covered table in Jake's gigantic games room, Tyrone worked a gobbet of blue air-dry clay between his fingers. "It's like I told Michael already, miss," he said to Jan, his voice still raw from the breathing tube. "After the truck crashed, Pops said Earl would find us in a couple of hours. Pops' phones were both smashed, and mine had no signal." He gave a scratchy cough. "We got up the road to the hut — Pops was way slow and needed my help — and spent the night there, but asshole Earl never showed. Sorry, miss. I'm not supposed to say 'asshole' in front of ladies."

"That's okay, this one time." Mindful of Sloane's earlier instruction that the boy be encouraged to talk freely about his experience, Jan said, "And then what happened?"

"The next day, we ate some canned beans and things that were in the tin box he keeps there, and still nobody came. Pops just lay there and gave me orders about food and stuff." Ty focused hard on his clay. His voice trembled. "When I woke up the next day, he couldn't hardly talk. He had a big purple bulge on his stomach and he … puked. I had to go rinse out the bucket in the creek after."

"Gross, bro," said Michael.

The house steward appeared with a flat box.

Jan looked up. "Yes?"

"A courier brought these, Mrs. Brenner."

"Oh?" Jan took the box from him. The card tucked under the ribbon read *Treats for the brave boys, from Andy and Bart.* She handed it to Tyrone.

"Chocolate? Rad." Yanking off the lid, he bit into one, only to spit it back into his hand. "Strawberry? Andy knows I only eat nuts and caramels." He bit into several more, but they were all soft inside. Dumping the mangled rejects onto a paper towel, he pushed the box toward Michael. "You want these?"

Michael was fitting a coil of red clay onto the front of a robot. "In a minute."

Tyrone went back to his blue clay. The steward collected the paper towel and quietly departed.

Jan flattened the base of her three-point white antler onto her brown deer's head. "You were telling me about your dad being sick?"

The boy nodded. "After the second night, I thought I should find help. There's a path down the ravine that was supposed to lead us home after he was rested up. So I went down that, but at the bottom I couldn't tell where I was anymore. The cutline went the wrong way, and I couldn't see which other way to go before it started to get dark."

"He spent the night in a tree," said Michael with great enthusiasm.

Jan smiled. "It probably wasn't that cool when it was happening."

"My mom hates that part." Tyrone squeezed another blob of clay between his fingers. "Hearing it makes her scared all over again."

"Well, then, it's a good thing she's having a rest right now," said Jan.

"And Granny, too." Michael rolled red clay into a long tube. "She needs a lot more naps than she used to."

The first crack of thunder sent Jan's heart leaping. The boys looked over their shoulders and then went back to their builds while she eyed the roiling clouds through the glass wall. Her phone vibrated. A text from Lacey read: *Can you talk? Important.*

"I'll be right back, boys," she said. "Try not to destroy the place."

Winding her armchair past the workout machines, she opened the French door and rolled out under the overhanging balcony. Fat raindrops bounced and sizzled on paving stones still hot from the earlier sunlight. She called Lacey. "Okay, what?"

Lacey's voice was low. "Everything all right up there?"

"Fine. We're doing clay art in the games room. Why?"

"I'd ask if you're sitting down, but you almost always are."

"Bad news?" The goosebumps on Jan's arms weren't all from the damp breeze.

"Could've been worse, but yeah, it's bad enough." Lacey breathed deep and then came out with it. "Orrin nearly died this morning."

"I thought he was out of danger?"

"Someone doubled his morphine levels. If he hadn't been hooked up to a respiratory monitor, he'd have stopped breathing completely before the nurses noticed anything was wrong."

Jan shivered. "Someone tried to kill him in the ICU? Was it Earl?"

"No. As usual, Earl had a rock-solid alibi. That alone is suspicious in my book."

"How solid?"

"The best. He was at Cochrane detachment, trying to convince the RCMP that his obstruction during the search was all done from the purest of motives." Lacey's breath hissed. "He'd been at the hospital earlier. A supervised visit, under the circumstances. He wasn't left alone for an instant. And Orrin wasn't in respiratory distress until hours later."

"Then it's his accomplice again? I suppose nobody got a photo of this person's face?"

"Not fully. Nursing-station cameras showed someone dressed in nurse's scrubs, bending over Orrin's bed like they were checking vitals, and then shoving what looked like an eyedropper into his mouth. They figure it held sublingual morphine. On top of the drugs already in him, and how weak he was, it could easily have killed him."

"But they don't just let strangers walk into an ICU."

"Nope. They either came in with another nurse, or someone gave them the code."

Jan rubbed a sudden ache in her eyebrow. "And then what? They waited around to be sure it worked?"

"Apparently sublingual morphine peaks in the body around half an hour later. The fake nurse was long gone by then."

"God." Was someone coming after the boys next? "It has to be the same woman. Do they at least have a hair colour to watch for now?"

"Sorry. She was wearing one of those hospital caps. Probably short haired, but that's all I can give you."

"Whoever this woman is, she seems to be a genius at getting into places she's not supposed to be. Can I call one of the security guards down here?"

"Yes. And I'll be there in five minutes."

"Sooner if you can." Jan disconnected and stared in through the window at Michael and Tyrone lining up all their robots, oblivious to possible danger. A strange woman knocking someone over the head was an obvious threat. Less obvious was a drug that acted after the person administering it was well out of the way. Or … having it delivered? She called Lacey back. "You have Andrea Caine's number? Can you ask her right now if she sent candy to Tyrone and Michael?"

"I already know she didn't. She and Bart are planning to visit this evening, and she's going shopping for treats this afternoon."

"Shit!" Jan shoved the patio door open with her foot and whirled her chair around. She smacked into the door frame and had to take another run at it. Then she was inside, zooming around the treadmill and elliptical, brushing under a pull-bar as she cut a corner past the weight machine. "Michael," she yelled as the boy's hand lifted to his mouth. "Don't eat that!"

CHAPTER THIRTY-FOUR

Under the sink light on the game room's snack bar, Lacey turned over a strawberry cream chocolate. The hole in the bottom was obvious. She showed it to Chad and Jan. After Chad had taken a photo for evidence purposes, she laid the chocolate on a paper towel and sliced the bottom away. Amid the pink strawberry filling was a hard white object. Chad took another photo. She fished out the object with the knife's point and wiped it on the paper towel. Pink lines of fondant stayed behind, showing the number 54. Chad photographed that.

Lacey put a hand to her neck. "I'm not sure what those numbers mean, but nobody puts pills into candy with good intentions. Did anyone else touch these? Sloane, or Michael's grandmother?"

"They're both napping in their rooms."

"The nanny?"

"Out. She borrowed a staff car for the afternoon. Jake's holed up in his study. He might be napping, too, but he wouldn't announce it." Janet glanced back at the boys. They were absorbed in their robots, unconcerned about the future of chocolates they weren't allowed to eat. "It must have been Earl or his accomplice. Chad, did you see who brought these?"

Chad, lining up another angle on the little white pill, said, "A woman in a dark-blue ball cap and a grey windbreaker. She wasn't in a courier vehicle, but I thought she must be a local contractor. Lots of smaller towns don't have regular UPS or FedEx delivery. I signed for the box and brought it to the kitchen entrance."

Lacey turned over more chocolates. Five had gaps in the bottom. "And nothing was unusual about that delivery?"

"Well, she said she was supposed to bring it to the house herself. I told her I had orders to keep everyone out, and she just handed it to me and left."

"Her vehicle will be on the gate camera." Lacey pointed to the chocolate box. "Take shots of the box before I turn more over."

Chad did so and then texted the pictures to her. She skimmed through them before forwarding them to Wayne, Sergeant Drummond, and Constable Markov. Her accompanying text was straightforward: *Someone just tried to drug/kill Tyrone Caine and/or Michael Matheson. I am preserving the evidence at Jake Wyman's. Please advise.*

She went back to the boys' table. "I'm not going to be angry, but I need to know if either of you ate those chocolates. Even licked one of them."

Michael looked up. "Were they rotten? My friend found a worm in a chocolate bar once."

Lacey shook her head. "No worms, but they were contaminated with stuff a lot of people would react badly to."

Tyrone said, "I didn't think I was allergic to plants, but whatever that plant I ate was, they said I was allergic to it, and I might be allergic to other plants in the all-ee-um family now. Is it that? Because I bit a couple. But I spat them out right away. They were gross."

Lacey forced a grin. "You should be safe enough. Alliums are things like garlic, onions, leeks, and asparagus. Can you imagine chocolate filled with garlic?" Predictably, both boys gagged. She went back to Jan and Chad. "You two stay here with them. I'll track down those chocolates the steward took away and then go over the camera archive for this woman's face."

Jan backed and turned her armchair. "My laptop is in my pack. We can compare her with the garage ones, too. Both garages."

"Good." Odds were that the same woman would be identifiable at Orrin's ICU bed this morning. After all, how many accomplices could Earl take into his confidence?

Upstairs, Lacey dug the paper towel filled with bisected chocolates out of the kitchen garbage and carefully examined them. Two contained little white pills. Others were too mangled to tell if the bottoms had been breached. Ty had better be telling the truth about swallowing nothing.

Her phone pinged. A text from Sergeant Drummond read: *Instant-release morphine sulphate 30 mg. Any ingested?*

No, she typed back, and asked the steward, "Is there a naloxone kit in the house?"

He looked scandalized. "Of course not."

She added *Bring naloxone in case* and sent it, only to receive another text saying *Delayed. Semi overturned on Hwy 1 overpass.* She was on her own. She bagged the chocolates — box and all contents, whether mangled or not — in a paper grocery sack and got the steward to lock it in the household safe. Smoothing masking tape over the door's edges, she wrote her initials over the makeshift seal.

"Nobody disturb this until the police get here."

Shocked and silent, the steward and cook nodded.

In the security office, the woman on camera duty cued up the point where Chad had accepted the box. The delivery woman kept her head down, leaving the dark-blue brim of her ball cap toward the camera. The only part of her vehicle that showed was one brown front corner, obviously older. The RCMP would have the challenge of matching that to a make, model, and year. Lacey asked the duty guard to copy out the full clip and send it to Wayne's Calgary office.

As the footage uploaded, the woman said, "Wait. What's this?"

Lacey looked over her shoulder. The gate hadn't been entirely closed when the woman left. She'd walked away when Chad was watching, but as soon as he went toward the house, she ran back and squeezed through the closing gate. She raced toward the stables, her messenger bag flying out behind her.

Lacey grabbed the guard's radio. "All security personnel, attention. Intruder alert. A woman approximately my height, wearing a dark-blue baseball cap and a grey windbreaker, entered the grounds twenty-four minutes ago. She was heading for the stables. She may have changed to staff clothing there, so watch for any women and stop everyone you don't personally recognize. Coordinate a perimeter sweep and buildings check with Travis." She told the guard, "Scan forward from that point on. If she's changed clothes, or if there's a facial shot, I want to know ASAP."

She left the office, locked the pool doors, locked the door into the garage, and then phoned the steward on her way back downstairs. "Please lock every outer door and window in the house immediately. No exceptions. If Mr. Wyman complains, I'll take full responsibility." She hurried into the games room. "Slight change of plans, guys. We're going to move your art project into the guest suite for now."

As Jan helped the boys pack up the robot army and other supplies, Lacey took Chad aside. "I realize this might bring back some stress for you because of Capilano Gorge, but you have to protect these boys. Stay in the suite with them, windows and doors locked, curtains drawn, until I or the RCMP gives you the all-clear. The woman who delivered these chocolates, she's inside the grounds."

Chad paled under his tan. "I won't fail again."

Lacey slapped him on the shoulder. "I'm sure you won't." But she wasn't sure at all. His errors had compromised security here at every stage. At least this way, she knew where he was. Out in the grounds, he'd be on his own and potentially even more of a liability.

She escorted the group into the suite, checked each room, and then double-checked that the French doors were locked, drawing the curtains across.

"All of you stay here until I come back."

She was only three paces down the dim hallway when her phone dinged. A photo text showed a woman with short auburn hair grabbing at a blue ball cap beside the stable wall. Where had she seen that face before? Turning back to the suite, she held the phone out to Chad.

"Is this the woman who brought the chocolate?"

Chad nodded.

Jan came to look, too. "That's Mrs. Harder."

Tyrone looked up from his robot warriors. "Earl's mom? What's she doing here?"

Lacey stared at the photo. Giselle Harder, formerly Caine. She'd been the climber in the helicopter with Lacey and Jake, catching a lift down from the Ghost River cliff. Which day was that remote well-site trip? Tuesday, said her phone calendar. The morning after Orrin's Range Rover was sabotaged. Giselle had been at the ranch for the birthday weekend and not left until Tuesday. Except for that midnight visit to the garage, she'd stayed off the security cameras during the birthday weekend, not much of a challenge when her granddaughters had damaged the ones covering the main terrace, bluff staircase, and gym exit. Earl could easily have obliterated her name on the fob list. For all Orrin's paranoia, security locks, and surveillance cameras, he'd been taken down at last by an overlooked ex-wife from a thirty-year-old divorce.

Where was Giselle?

CHAPTER THIRTY-FIVE

Jan gaped at Tyrone. "Earl's mother is Mrs. Harder? The one who lives on West Bragg Road?"

Tyrone shrugged. "Somewhere around here."

"Oh well, interesting." Jan tried to smile as she backed her chair away from the boys' table. Lacey and Chad followed her to the far side of the room. In a near-whisper she said, "Mrs. Harder had a whole basket of her dead husband's cancer drugs. I accidentally photographed them in her spare room. They might be expired, but you can bet she learned how to use them while nursing him."

Lacey said, equally low voiced, "She's been here at least once. We brought her before all this started. She's seen the layout from the air, too."

"She's been here a lot more than once," Jan said. "Jake told me she's been trying to make him her third husband."

Chad's head jerked between her and Lacey. "One woman by herself? I can take her if she comes in here."

Lacey said, "Someone who looks weaker can dull your reflexes, slow you down. Don't be fooled."

Cold rage vibrated every cell in Jan's body. "If you need motivation," she told Chad, keeping her voice low by sheer willpower, "that woman killed Kitrin."

Chad gawked. "Are you sure?"

"I bet if you saw her in one of Jake's polo shirts, you'd remember seeing her that morning." She pulled her laptop from her backpack. "I meant to show you this picture, anyway. It's just the back of her head, but you might have seen her near the pool and assumed she was staff." As she scrolled back through the collection of photos, Jan remembered speeding past the security office that morning and clipping the garage door onto the heels of someone in a staff polo shirt and hat. Two minutes earlier and she might have saved Kitrin's life.

Lacey's phone rang. When she'd answered it, she told them, "The generator building's on fire. I have to go. You two stay here, and keep the doors locked!"

She hadn't been gone two minutes when a particularly loud crash of thunder started the lights flickering. Jan and Chad looked at each other, and at the boys. Chad turned on his phone flashlight as the lights flickered again and then died.

CHAPTER THIRTY-SIX

The rain slashed at Lacey's face as she crossed the terrace outside the guest suite. Six more windows and two more doors to check here. All were locked. She headed down to the third terrace, battling a gale determined to push her up. The drop-off beyond the railing, hundreds of metres down to the flailing spruces along the river, took her right back to Capilano Gorge. It had rained that afternoon, too. She and Chad between them had saved the child but lost the woman and carried their own scars ever since. Today, she was determined everybody would stay alive. No new scars.

Lightning cracked almost on top of her. The hillside shook with its thunder. Lights deep in the games room flickered. A moment later, they vanished. The backup generator should be starting automatically, but not today. The timing of that fire was not coincidental; the generator house was a double-duty distraction, drawing away all available staffers and ensuring there would be no backup power. She tried the first set of doors into the workout area. Locked. Wiping the rain from her face, she went under the overhang and found the next door unlocked.

Had there been time for Giselle to get down here and
into the house? Surely not. They'd all been in there, with
a clear view of the lower terrace, until ten minutes ago.
She reached through, turned the lock, and shut the door.

As she headed back up the steps, the wind alternately lifted her and tried to flatten her. Yet for all its
force, the storm was ebbing. A wedge of blue sky widened between two mountain peaks. In the lee of the
upper pool's high walls, she double-checked the glass
doors near the security office and carried on to the gate
beside the garage. There she paused, one hand on the
wrought-iron crossbar. Right here, the murderer of
Kitrin Devine had passed. Today she'd returned, hoping
to kill Kitrin's son. She could not succeed.

Hurrying along to the front door's portico, Lacey
phoned the security office. "Anything?"

"Not since the stables. She may have slipped out the
back gate during the worst lightning."

"Keep checking that terrace camera outside the
guest suite. Anybody goes near it, yell."

The rain eased as Lacey worked her way around the
outer pool walls. Everywhere, trees dripped and leaves
rustled. The waterfall's plash greeted her at the farther
pool gate, but the area remained empty. She replaced a
striped chaise cushion and headed for the upper terrace,
casting a longing glance at the bridge far below. No flickering lights yet. Surely the RCMP would be here soon.
They could bring in dogs, track Giselle to wherever she
was lurking or back to her vehicle. Giselle wouldn't yet
know she'd been identified. She might go home and try
to brazen it out. Then they'd have her.

Across the upper terrace Lacey went, testing windows and doors to Jake's private suite. All locked. The double doors to the great room were locked. She peered in, but nothing moved in the gloom. Next came an alcove with two matching chaises. Above them were identical windows that glowed with yellow light from candles or lanterns. Jake's study. Had anybody told him what was going on? She was the senior security person; it was up to her. If he was awake, not napping on his couch.

The left window was wound slightly open. She stepped onto the nearest chaise to peer in but had barely got her fingers on the sill when a woman said, "Of course I'm relieved Orrin's been found."

Lacey cautiously raised her head. Giselle Harder sat in a leather armchair, vivid in a bright pink blouse. A pink and orange paisley scarf hid her short auburn hair. From the messenger bag at her feet protruded the sleeve of a grey windbreaker. While the whole security team was hunting her, Giselle was holed up in the one room no staff member ever entered without an invitation.

Giselle's eyes met Lacey's with a look of mild irritation. "Why is someone peering in your window?"

Jake's grizzled head turned. "Lacey?"

Lacey's mind raced. Did she blurt out that he was harbouring a murderer? It suddenly struck her that Giselle didn't know who she was, much less that she knew about the earlier attacks. Finally, an advantage! The woman would sit right there, unsuspecting, until Lacey got indoors to subdue her.

"Sorry to disturb you, sir. I'm doing a perimeter check after the storm. This is the only window left open."

He nodded. "Thanks."

She scrambled down to the wet paving stones and hurried around to let herself in by the pool doors. In the security room she said to the duty guard, "She's inside, with Jake. Call everyone up to cover the house exits. I want Travis outside the study windows. I'm going to flush her out."

But when she opened the study door, Giselle was gone. "Where is she?"

Jake looked up. "She went down to say hi to Tyrone. Are they still in the games room?"

Lacey didn't bother explaining. She ran.

CHAPTER THIRTY-SEVEN

Jan carried a second lamp to the boys' table, mainly to disguise her nervous pacing. The constant motion would drain her energy reserves, but then she'd already burned a lot in her simmering rage at Earl's mother. Chad kept checking the windows and doors through the curtains. They should have gone upstairs, straight to Jake. They'd be safe with him. Down here, they couldn't see anything but the terrace or hear anything but the pelting rain. What was Lacey doing out there? Had she found Giselle yet?

Michael said, "It's not dark outside. We wouldn't need another lamp if you opened the curtains."

"Not right now," said Jan firmly. "I … I'm scared of the lightning. When it's over we can open them."

A tap came on the hallway door. She froze. Chad whipped across the room on silent feet. "Who's there?"

"Ty? It's Mommy. Can I come in?"

Tyrone glanced up. "Sure."

"The door's locked. Come and open it."

Tyrone was coiling red clay onto a robot and didn't answer. Jan listened hard. She'd only heard a few words from Sloane at the dinner last week.

She leaned over. "Are you sure that's your mother? Does she really sound that high pitched?"

Tyrone shrugged.

The woman outside said, "Ty, honey?"

Chad beckoned Jan over. "You open the door when I say," he whispered, "and if it's that Harder woman, I'll grab her the instant she steps inside."

"Are you sure? What if she's got a gun?"

"She doesn't know we're on to her."

"Let me call Lacey first."

"Ty? Baby, you're scaring me. Open the door."

Both boys were staring at Jan, waiting for her to open that door. Should she tell them there was danger, or try to bluff it out? Grabbing an amethyst carving of a mother and child off the nearest end table — the closest thing to a weapon she could see — she put her hand on the knob. "Ready?"

CHAPTER THIRTY-EIGHT

When she heard the scream, Lacey was halfway down the main stairs. She leaped the last five steps and skidded across the parquet floor, bounced off the library entrance, and raced down the dim hall. The guest suite's door was open, spilling lamplight and shadows. She burst in.

Sloane Caine, gripping a chair-back, yelled at Chad. "What were you thinking? You scared me half to death!"

Jan said, "Sorry. So sorry. Calm down, please. You're scaring the boys."

Lacey yelled over the noise. "What happened?"

All the faces turned toward her. Chad said, "I grabbed her. I thought she was —"

Sloane stared past Lacey. "Giselle?"

The red-headed woman stood in the doorway, her eyes fixed on the two boys. "Tyrone," she said in a soft voice. "Are you feeling okay?"

"No thanks to you," Jan screeched and hurled the statue. As the crystal cracked on the wall beside her, Giselle ran.

"Lock that door!" Lacey yelled as she followed.

The older woman darted into the library. She snatched an afghan off a chair and flung it. Lacey batted it aside, only to trip over a coffee table. As she staggered, Giselle sprinted out to the drenched terrace. She was out of sight in seconds.

Lacey limped outside. The terrace stairs were ringing. She followed the sound up, her boots skidding on the wet treads. Giselle scurried across the pool terrace, her feet slipping in the puddles. As Lacey closed the gap, she upended a chaise. Lacey leaped over it, but it cost her precious seconds.

Travis appeared at the perimeter gate. Giselle veered toward the waterfall. Rushing over the little bridge, she started down the far side of the pool. As Lacey followed her, another security guard appeared at the garage gate. Giselle reversed course, saw Lacey cutting her off, and leaped straight at the rock wall.

She went up the slick stones like a lizard: hand, foot, hand, foot. Lacey jumped, snatching at her arm, and caught her trailing scarf instead. Giselle jerked free, abandoning the paisley, and scrambled higher. She plucked a loose stone from the waterfall and heaved it at Lacey. Dodging, Lacey grabbed her ankle, boots skittering on the wet bridge.

Giselle's hand slipped. For a moment she hung one handed, and then she twisted, catlike, to leap at Lacey. They landed in the pool with a huge splash.

Lacey surfaced, shaking the water from her eyes, to see Giselle floundering toward the house. She dove and took the woman's feet out from under her. Then, as Giselle flailed, Lacey took her in a headlock. She walked backward through the water, towing her prisoner with cold satisfaction, dodging the clawing hands as the older woman struggled. Earl had dragged her by her neck in the security office. Now it was her turn.

After a vicious swipe of Giselle's nails over her bruised cheek, Lacey shook the woman hard. "Do that again and you'll be breathing underwater."

By the time the stairs hit the back of her boots, Travis was beside her. He grabbed one of Giselle's arms, and together they yanked her up the steps. They plunked her down on a chaise. The duty guard loomed up on the other side. Above their heads, golden sunlight flooded through a break in the clouds. Up from the valley came the welcome sound of sirens. It was over.

EPILOGUE

Lacey propped her bare feet up on Jan's deck rail and surveyed the mountain peaks, their shadows stark against the primrose and pink sunset. The valley below and all the treed wilderness as far as the eye could see seemed to be relaxing with the advent of autumn. She said to Dee and Jan, lounging nearby, "We won't be able to sit outside without jackets much longer. Hard to believe two weeks ago we were baking, and it was still full daylight at this hour."

"Yell if you need a jacket," said Jan, "or want to borrow a pair of socks."

Dee stretched. "I can't believe I missed the whole thing. You guys were totally rocking the investigation stuff, and I had my head down shuffling real estate paper." Rob bustled out with a tray that he plunked down beside the barbecue and fluttered around the table, rearranging napkins. As he hurried back indoors, she added, "He's a little nervous tonight."

Jan said, "You would be too if your boyfriend and his wife were coming for supper."

Dee smiled lazily. "Never happen. I avoid the

slightest potential for melodrama. I'm glad they'll get to meet again under better circumstances, though."

"I think they'll get along fine," said Lacey. "Andy's really sweet when you get to know her, and everyone adores Rob."

"Clash of the adorbs," said Dee. "Is the hot, single mountain climber coming, too? Gotta keep those options open."

Lacey wiggled her toes. "He's not an option as long as he's sleeping with his brother's wife."

"But you can still climb with him," said Jan. "You don't want to give that up."

"When nobody's trying to kill me, sure." Lacey grinned. "Right now, I'm still into the joy of having totally clean teeth."

"And yet you're about to stain them with red wine," said Dee, "only four hours after you finally got them cleaned."

A car door slammed. Jan turned her head, and the dogs sat up to look hopefully toward the drive. "That'll be the Caine gang now."

Instead, a lone man rounded the corner. His hair was short, almost military. He wore jeans and a blue sweatshirt with a heavy metal logo.

Terry looked up. "Ray, good to see you, man. Come and meet my wife." The newcomer shook Jan's hand. "And Lacey of course you know."

Lacey squinted. Ray seemed familiar, but the context was wrong.

He grinned at her. "Hi, McCrae."

The voice gave it away. "Markov?"

"Yep." He accepted a glass of red wine from Rob.

Lacey said, "Your given name is Ray? With a last name like yours, I expected it to be Vladimir or something else Eastern European."

"It's really Rayko, but don't tell the guys at work."

While Lacey adjusted to Ray in his civilian disguise, Dee told him, "I'm so happy to see you again, and in warmer weather than when you drove my car last winter."

"I'm happy to see your leg has recovered," said Ray.

Dee waved that aside. "It would be tactless to bring up all the criminal matters once the Caine twins get here, but I'm dying to know about the case against Earl and his mother. Whatever you can tell me, that is."

Ray glanced at Lacey. "You haven't told them everything?"

"I don't know everything. Not on the Force, remember?" She thought she'd figured most of it out, but Ray might have something she'd missed. She looked at Dee. "What do you want to know most?"

"Everything! Start with why Earl was finally charged with conspiracy to commit murder after Ray wouldn't arrest him on your word."

Ray shrugged. "Finding that external hard drive in his Jeep sealed it. He probably intended to drop it and the balaclava down a gully far, far from the ranch as soon as he'd taken care of Orrin. If Lacey and Ben hadn't arrived when they did, from a direction he wasn't expecting, he'd have succeeded."

"Let's see if I've got this right," said Lacey. "Not only did that external drive implicate Earl in the attack on me, it also got you a warrant for his phone and text records."

"Not me personally."

Lacey gave him a look. "You know I meant the Major Crimes Unit. Those led you, er, them, straight to his mother, which rendered her alibi for him suspect, and earned a warrant for her phone, too, leading to the conspiracy charge."

Ray nodded. "The GPS on his phone put him up this road when Kitrin died, and the one on Orrin's vehicle placed that right outside Jake's."

Jan pressed her thumb into the crease between her eyebrows. "So when I saw his vehicle that morning on my way in, he was waiting for his mother while she was killing Kitrin?"

"Exactly," said Ray. "Twenty minutes, right over the time Kitrin Devine was killed. Travis, the guard, identified both Earl's vehicle and Giselle Harder, whom he'd admitted to the grounds because she was driving a convertible belonging to Mr. Wyman. Not that Earl's admitted to any knowledge of his mother's actions."

Jan groaned. "I wasted so much time hunting for Kitrin in the house. If I'd thought to go straight to the pool, I could have stopped her."

Dee patted her arm. "They'd have found another way. Still, it was a huge risk for Giselle Harder to take. A staff member could have walked in at any time."

"She's been visiting Jake for years," said Jan. "Once in the garage, via the automatic opener that's always in his vehicles, all she had to do was grab a staff polo shirt and hat off the shelf. It's only a few steps around the corner to the pool."

Lacey filled in more gaps. "Giselle must have been inside the garage when Travis and I came across the lawn. She could've heard me tell him we couldn't fix the pool camera while Kitrin was there. God, I never realized. I'm the one who told her where to find Kitrin and confirmed that she wouldn't be caught on camera doing it."

"Don't blame yourself," said Ray. "The part you don't know is that Giselle Harder was paying Mylo's nanny to spy on his wife. When Georgie was confronted with the evidence of her own texts to Mrs. Harder, she told us how she'd met the woman their first day at the estate and then was approached by her the next morning while out on a walk. Mrs. Harder told her Kitrin Devine was angling to be the next Mrs. Wyman, and that she only wanted to find out if there was already something between them."

Jan's lip curled. "And since Georgie wanted Mylo to herself, she was only too eager to spy on Kitrin."

Ray nodded. "Saturday morning, she informed Mrs. Harder that Kitrin was in the pool and that the staff had orders not to disturb her. Then she left the grounds. Nothing suggests she had foreknowledge, though, and why would they trust her with that? The actual killing looks premeditated to me, but whether a jury will agree ..." He shrugged.

Lacey swirled her wine. "In the dossier it said Giselle Harder did theatre studies at university. Probably just enough to know how a slight change of appearance and a confident walk will get you almost anywhere."

Dee stared from one to the other. "But Earl was in it from the start?"

Ray nodded. "He was on the phone to his mother before he ever left the Wyman place that first evening, probably telling her about Orrin's odd reaction to Kitrin, and Michael's resemblance to Tyrone."

"Giselle must have known Orrin cheated while they were married," Lacey added. "Maybe she suspected other children existed, too. But that wasn't her motive. She'd already rigged the Rover and primed Orrin to take Ty out to the wilderness. I wonder if she told Earl about the sabotage afterward, or if it was his idea and she just carried it out."

"She's drunk deep of the patriarchal Kool-Aid," said Jan. "Orrin was a philanderer and a major asshole, and he threw her over after nearly twenty years —"

"With as little alimony as he could get away with," Lacey added, "to the point where she had to get a job to survive."

"Huh," said Jan. "Orrin likely put all the assets in the company name and took only a minuscule salary. A lot of guys in the oil patch do that. Anyway, it sounds like her second husband chose her mainly to look after his elderly mother, and then after him. He left most of his assets to his kids from his first marriage and very little to her. But instead of waking up and smelling the rotten bill of goods she'd been sold, Giselle doubled down on making sure Earl was rich enough to support her in her old age. It didn't matter to her how many people died. She even tried setting up Andy and Bart to take the fall for the doped chocolates, cutting out one more of the heirs. Patriarchy or not, I don't feel sorry for her at all."

"Me, either." Ray swallowed some wine. "So, to answer your initial question, Dee, there's enough to charge Earl with conspiracy, but since he didn't actually kill anyone — didn't even succeed at killing his father — he'll probably get a shorter sentence. His mother, who did most of the dirty work whether with his collusion or not, is looking at multiple sentences, possibly consecutive."

"Rich white male arrogance wins again," said Jan. The dogs at her feet sat up. "Oh, someone's coming."

A moment later, Andy, Bart, and Ben trekked around the corner of the house, carrying bags from the wine store down in Bragg Creek.

"Are we late?" Andy cried.

"Not at all." Lacey took the bags.

As Rob and Terry came out of the house, Andy walked up to Rob and held out her hand. "I owe you an apology. I yelled and swore and was altogether very rude when you were in my house. I hope you will visit often and not fear a repeat performance."

Rob's lips compressed. After a moment, he took her hand in both of his. "Thank you for that. I hope we can get to know each other and that the worst is behind you as a family."

Bart, beaming, threw his arms around both their shoulders and kissed each of their cheeks. "My two favourite people in the world."

Ben said, "What am I, chopped avocado?"

Bart punched his shoulder. "You're one of Andy's favourite people. Don't be greedy."

As Rob sorted out drinks and everyone settled around the table, Dee murmured to Lacey, "Gotta say I like that woman's style. Relationship repair is her jam."

Terry fired up the barbecue. "We've got Black Angus steaks, bison sausages, venison burgers, and plenty of each, so think about which you'll want to start. Meatless burgers for Ben, but the sauce and smoke from the rest will give them some flavour. How's your father doing this week?"

Ben shrugged. "Technically, he's recovering, but it's like he's aged twenty years. Mind as well as body."

Bart nodded. "We make a show of consulting him, but honestly, most decisions are beyond him now. The company must move on without his direction." He glanced at his brother. "Ben's coming back, or, I should say, coming into the fold at last. We're officially going to set up an alternative energy division of Caine International. His first job is to sound out all the existing staff and management to see which ones would like to make a lateral jump. It's probably a lot more of them than Orrin would expect, given how many closet greenies work in the oil patch."

Lacey raised one eyebrow. "Ben's going corporate? For real?"

He grinned at her. "I refuse to wear a suit and tie, but I might stretch to clean pants and a polo shirt."

Andy laughed. "Get a haircut, hippie."

"And be mistaken for my much more dapper and presidential brother?"

Dee said, "Ben, thanks for teaching Lacey to climb. She really loves it." She ignored Lacey's side-eye and carried on, "I hope you won't mind taking her out again sometime, now that nobody's going to throw rocks at you on the cliff."

As the dusk deepened and the air cooled, and the level in the wine bottles dropped, Lacey noticed two things: one, Andy was sticking to sparkling water, and two, her own bare feet under the table were still warm. She mentioned the feet first.

Terry grinned. "Somebody noticed! I put in a solar heat collector. It's a panel hanging off the deck below the railing, and it pumps heat into a black block under the table all day, which radiates it out again at night. Totally green."

Ben's eyes lit up. "Mind if I look?"

While all the men and Dee were peering under the tablecloth, shining their phone flashlights over the setup, Lacey leaned over to Andy. "No wine in your glass? Does that mean …?"

Andy shook her head. "Just that I'm the designated driver. Now that Orrin isn't around to harass us, we're all taking a step back. The year is going to be interesting enough without adding a child to the mix. Beyond Ty and Michael, that is." She sighed. "We wanted to go to Kitrin's funeral, since she was in fact Bart and Ben's half-sister, but Barbara asked us not to. She doesn't want to have to explain us just yet, needs space to sort out her grieving and her marriage. Meanwhile, Michael will be with us during the movie's filming, and afterward he can spend holidays with us, too."

"So the boys won't be completely separated?" said Jan, who had seen all the solar-collector fittings often enough.

"Not if we can help it," said Andy. "We'll invite Barbara to visit whenever Michael's there, as a friend of the family. Mylo doesn't seem to care about them being together now."

"Or," Jan suggested, "since you're honouring Orrin's agreement about filming, he won't jeopardize a good movie set merely to prevent Mrs. D taking off with Michael. All business is Mylo."

"Cynical much?" Lacey asked.

"Rich white men rule the world," said Jan. She pushed back her chair and gathered up plates.

Andy nodded. "They do. For the first week, it looked like Earl might wiggle out of the most serious charges. I wouldn't sleep a wink if he and his mother were free to go after the boys again." After Jan left with a load of dishes, she looked at Lacey. "So … it's been two weeks, but you already guessed every secret I ever had. Will you tell me now why you really came to the ranch?"

Lacey had almost forgotten their pact, or her worry even then that Andy would be furious with her for investigating. "I'd hate for you to hate me over this."

Andy bit her lip. "So you really were hired by Orrin to spy on me and Bart?"

"Never! Is that what you thought?" Lacey squeezed Andy's hand where it lay on the tablecloth. "Orrin told my boss, Wayne, to investigate Kitrin's parentage. When he vanished, Wayne feared someone in the family had gotten rid of him before he could claim her publicly. I was sent to find evidence for or against that theory. I had no idea you and Bart had any secrets at all." She let go Andy's hand. "And if you thought I was Orrin's spy, why didn't you make me sleep in the bunkhouse and share a bathroom with all those guys?"

"Friends close, enemies closer." Andy leaned over and hugged her. "I'm so glad you weren't there to spy on us. I mean, you were, but not the way we were most afraid of." As the rest of the group crawled back into their chairs, she said, "Everybody pick up your glasses. I want to make a toast. To Kitrin Devine, taken too soon from the family she didn't even know she had. All she wanted was to be seen, and loved, just as she was. In respect for her, I vow in front of all of you that I will do my best to make sure her son is seen and loved just as he is. Whoever he turns out to be. And I want you all to help me."

Rob's voice was the first and loudest. "Hear, hear!"

ACKNOWLEDGEMENTS

Although there exists an enduring impression that novels are produced alone in secluded rooms filled with books and possibly cats, my author reality includes many individuals who contribute time, feedback, and expertise about people and professions in the Alberta foothills. Despite best efforts, I sometimes get things wrong in their subject areas, either accidentally or because my fictional reality demands to diverge fractionally from objective reality. All errors are on me.

For this book, thanks are due to:

Matt Lunny, former owner of Stronghold, the Calgary Climbing Centre, whose patient explanations of climbing gear, terminology, technique, and the differences between wall-climbing and rock climbing were invaluable in teaching Lacey enough to get up that cliff when she had to; Fiona Pinnell and Liz Jepson, who illuminated how it feels to follow a vastly more experienced climber up an untried route; Lynn (Radar) Goddard, whose decades of experience as a rural firefighter and Calgary paramedic helped get my lost boy into and out of his life-threatening peril; ICU nurse Kathy Zimmerman, who guided his theoretical recovery at Alberta Children's Hospital; Andrea Rayburn, who talked me through Search and Rescue (SAR) camp organization and shared experiences of being a SAR medic.

My respects to Andy Genereux, whose lifetime of pioneering climbs in the Ghost Wilderness and his resulting book, *Ghost Rock*, informed the experiences of the Caine brothers; to author Lisa Christiansen, whose inspiring book, *Hiker's Guide to Art of the Rocky Mountains*, informs Jan's local art knowledge and brings the beauty of those peaks, valleys, and hidden lakes to whole new audiences; to Kevin Van Tighem and Stephen Legault, fellow writers whose lifelong commitment to environmental defence has vastly extended my understanding of the fight to preserve wild habitat atop the Eastern Slopes of the Rockies while there's so much drillable oil and gas beneath.

My thanks to all the women in the Myalgic encephalomyelitis/chronic fatigue syndrome (ME/CFS) online community who share their experiences of illness and wellness to help me plot Jan's necessarily erratic progress from housebound and helpless back toward the career she loves. Her life-destroying illness, ME/CFS, is shared by nearly 600,000 Canadians, up to 3 million Americans, and an estimated 20–60 million people (mostly women) around the world. It drives 75 percent of sufferers out of the workforce — half of them forever — and permanently traps 25 percent inside their homes or darkened bedrooms. Thankfully, new research is taking place all the time. If you're suffering or know someone who is, you're not alone. You'll find help and support in patient groups on Facebook and other internet forums, as well as current research and self-management options on the following Resources page.

As ever, thanks to Kevin for feeding, housing, comforting, encouraging me … and for listening (or pretending to) while I obsess about characters and their relationships for a year or more, but never in enough detail that he can actually follow the plot until he reads the finished book.

ME/CFS RESOURCES

For information about management, treatment, and supporting a loved one with ME/CFS, check out any or all of the following sites.

A mid-2019 summary of current knowledge about ME/CFS from Dr. A. Komaroff: Advances in Understanding the Pathophysiology of Chronic Fatigue Syndrome:
   jamanetwork.com/journals/jama/article-abstract/2737854

The Open Medicine Foundation resource page pulls together current ME/CFS research from Stanford & Harvard in the USA and Uppsala in Sweden:
   omf.ngo/resource-center/

The International Association for CFS-ME has a resource page:
   iacfsme.org/educational-services-and-clinical-management

#MEACTION's MEpedia pages contain a continually updated overview organized by symptom area:
    me-pedia.org/wiki/Welcome_to_MEpedia

ME-FM Action:
    mefmaction.com

The Bateman Horne Center, a leader in biochemical research and life-management skills for patients:
    batemanhornecenter.org/medical-provider-library/

Action For ME covers severe patients' experience:
    actionforme.org.uk

ABOUT THE AUTHOR

 J.E. Barnard is the Calgary-based author of the award-winning women's wilderness series The Falls Mysteries. Her YA Steampunk novel, *Maddie Hatter and the Gilded Gauge*, was a 2018 Alberta Book of the Year. She has claimed the CWC Award for Best Unpublished First Crime Novel, the Bony Pete, and the Saskatchewan Writers Guild Award, and has been shortlisted for the Prix Aurora, the UK Debut Dagger, and the Book Publishing in Alberta Award. In addition to her involvement with Crime Writers of Canada, Calgary Crime Writers, and the Women Fiction Writers Association, she's a determined advocate for better research and treatment for the 580,000 Canadians living with ME/CFS.